आ नो भद्राः क्रतवो यन्तु विश्वतः ।

ā no bhadrāḥ kratavo yantu viśvataḥ

Let noble thoughts come to us from every side

- Rig Veda I - 89-i

BHAVAN'S BOOK UNIVERSITY

THE VEDAS

Pujyasri Chandrasekharendra Saraswati

BHAVAN'S BOOK UNIVERSITY

THE VEDAS

Pujyasri Chandrasekharendra Saraswati

Paramacharya of Kanchi Kamakoti Peetham

2025

BHARATIYA VIDYA BHAVAN

Mumbai - 400007

Sudakshina Trust, Mumbai.

First Edition	-	1988
Second Edition	-	1991
Third Edition	-	1993
Fourth Edition	-	1998
Fifth Edition	-	2000
Sixth Edition	-	2005
Seventh Edition	-	2006
Eight Edition	-	2009
Ninth Edition	-	2011
Tenth Edition	-	2013
Eleventh Edition	-	2014
Twelveth Edition	-	2016
Thirteenth Edition	-	2018
Fourteenth Edition	-	2022
Fifteenth Edition	-	2025

Price ₹ 375 /-

Printed in India by **Sri Amirtha Associates,** Chennai - 600064.
and Published by **P.V.Sankarankutty,** Director
for **BHARATIYA VIDYA BHAVAN,** Kulapati Munshi Marg, Mumbai - 400007.
E-mail: bhavan@bhavans.info / publications@bhavans.info
Website: http://www.bhavans.info

The Vedas

The Vedas are without a beginning. This might militate against commonsense. Our modern scientific mind always looks for a source, a cause and a date for any historical event. And the compilation of a work like Vedas must definitely have had a beginning. Concepts like eternity, beginninglessness, limitlessness are simply taboo for any scientific study, as these do not permit of the application of mathematics for their further development and study. However, the fact remains that the Universe, both the Phenomenal and the Noumenal, extends far beyond 'Space' and 'Time', the two basic devices and tools used by us to measure any phenomenon. Only some modes of this Universe fall within space and time and are apprehended as physical universe by our conditioned and limited consciousness. We (like the proverbial fish in water) do not and cannot see the limitless ocean, but can see only the waves, wave-fronts and froth in it. If the Universe is the manifestation of the Reality, the Dharma or the cosmic order is Its Will or design and Satya and Rita ('Spoken Truth and 'Truth as it is') are its very nature.

When it is said that the Vedas are the emanations of the breath of Brahma (the creator), it is to be understood that the Vedas constitute both essential and sustaining knowledge, as vital as the breath for life.

The four Vedas, Rig, Yajur, Sama and Atharva, which are believed to be vibrations in space and synthesised 5,000 years ago at the beginning of this Kali Yuga, by Bhagwan Veda Vyasa, consisted of 1,131 sakhas (recensions), 21 in Rik, 101 in Yajus, 1000 in Sama and 9 in Atharva. They were preserved in the Parampara (line) of Rishis (seers), viz., Paila, Vaishampayana, Jaimini and Sumanthu, by oral tradition, from father to son and guru (teacher) to sishya (disciple). Of late, the notion that education other than Vedic studies alone would ensure a livelihood, has led to many in the line taking to secular studies, resulting in many Vedic sakhas not being available today. In some, those who can chant from memory could be counted on one's fingers.

At present, only 10 recensions are available, and His Holiness is keen on preserving and propagating atleast these.

अनन्ता वै वेदाः।
Infinite are the Vedas

– **Veda**

प्रमाणं वेदाश्च।
The Vedas are the proof of all Dharma

– **Apasthamba**

वेदैश्च सर्वै अहमेव वेद्यो।
I am known through all the Vedas

– **Gita**

वेदो नित्यं अधीयतां।
तद् उदितं कर्म स्वनुष्ठीयतां।।
Practice the Vedas daily
Practise well their prescriptions

– **Adi Sankara**

यस्य निश्वसितं वेदाः।
He whose breath are the Vedas

– **Vidyaranya**

वेदोखिलो धर्ममूलं स्मृतिशीले च तद्विदाम्।
आचारश्चैव साधूनामात्मनस्तुष्टिरेव च।।
The entire corpus of the Veda, Smriti or the secondary remembered texts and the virtuous acts of the knowers of the Veda, the actions of holy men and what produces contentment to oneself are all rooted in dharma.

– **Manusmriti**

व्यासाय विष्णुरूपाय व्यासरूपाय विष्णवे।
नमो वै ब्रह्मनिधये वासिष्ठाय नमो नमः।।

I hail Thee, Vyasa, again and again,
Thou, God in human frame,
Thou, scion of Vasistha's ancient race,
It is from Thee that all knowledge springs.

श्रुति स्मृति पुराणानाम्
आलयं करुणालयम्
नमामि भगवत्पादम्
शंकरं लोकशंकरम्

"I salute the sacred feet of Sri Shankara, the abode of Srutis, Smritis, Puranas and of compasion, and who ever accomplishes the good of the world.

PREFACE TO THE FIRST EDITION

His Holiness Jagadguru Shri Chandrasekharendra Saraswati, the 68th Pontiff of the Kanchi Kamakoti Peetham, is well known as the Paramacharya or 'Periyaval'. He assumed the Pontificate in 1907 when he was 13. After nearly half a century, he voluntarily gave up the administrative duties of the Pontificate in order to devote his time to penance for the welfare of mankind. Those who are lucky to have his *darshan* realise that they are in the presence of a divine personage with abounding grace.

Shri Thirunavukkarasu of Vanathi Pathippakam (Vanathi Publishing House) has published several volumes in Tamil, compiled and edited by Shri R. Ganapathi, containing the discourses given by His Holiness at various places. Shri R.V. Raghavan of Sudakshina Trust took a keen interest in this publication. His Holiness deals with a wide range of subjects but mostly they relate to the Vedas, the Vedic religion and philosophy:

Paramacharya's thoughts are conveyed to us through his discourses. No verbatim record has apparently been kept of all the discourses. Although Shri Ganapathi's compilation in Tamil makes absorbing reading, one can never know how much the original has suffered in recapitulation and print. It is, indeed difficult to recapture in print the flavour of the original spoken word; the listener is in a more advantageous position, as he can follow the modulations of the Paramacharya's voice and feel the fervour of his appeal. There is a second aspect: translation from one language into another. Syntactical differences and idiomatic usages pose problems for the translator.

This book contains selected discourses of the Paramacharya rendered into English from Tamil by the late Shri N.S.S. Rajan. As we go through the pages, we are amazed by the wealth of knowledge that our ancients have bequeathed to mankind. The Paramacharya's knowledge is vast and deep. Readers of the book will never cease to wonder 'how this small head could carry all that he knew'. He has spoken from what he had experienced. Could there be a better teacher to take us through the labyrinth of esoteric knowledge and its subtleties? The Paramacharya truly lives up to the definition of a Guru – the one who removes the darkness of ignorance.

The distinguishing feature of the book is that, of the 14 *'Vidyas'*, the Paramacharya deals more elaborately with the six *Vedangas* and the four *Upangas* than the four *Vedas* themselves. There are few books which give succinctly and in such depth all about *Vedangas – Siksha, Vyaakarana, Chhandas, Niruktam, Jyotisha* and *Kalpa*.

Even those who are allergic to grammar will find something fascinating in the way the Paramacharya deals with *Vyaakarana*. Linking the origin of grammar with the Dance of Siva, the Paramacharya explains the concepts of 'Sabdam Brahma' and 'Nadam Brahma'.

The message the Paramacharya lucidly conveys through these discourses is that the Vedas form the bedrock of culture and that once we transcend the scientific concepts of time and space. we can realise the Ultimate Truth. that is *Brahman.* The Vedas are the very breath of *Brahman.* 'I am the person who is to be known by all the Vedas'. says the Lord in the *Bhagavad Gita* - 'Vedaicha sarvai-r-ahameva vedyah'.

A revival of interest in Vedic knowledge is vital for many reasons. Firstly. unless activated. disuse may lead to decay. India. nay the world. will be so much the poorer if the rich heritage of the Vedas is not preserved and nurtured. The Vedic message has no barriers of race. creed. clime or religion. It is universal and eternal.

The greatest assets of the Bhavan are the grace of God and the benedictions of the Godly. The Paramacharya blessed the Bhavan with the following benediction in 1962 on the occasion of Bhavan's Silver Jubilee:

"The Bharatiya Vidya Bhavan has made the intellectuals of Bharata Varsha evince interest in the various aspects of our culture and progress.

May we pray: Give fresh vigour to the Bhavan. a unique institution. in directing its attention more and more with greater fulfilment to the dissemination of moral principles and devotion."

The offering of the first edition of this book to the Paramacharya was made on his 95th birthday in 1988. This second edition is being brought out in commemoration of the 98th year of Pilgrimage on Earth of the Paramacharya. May the Paramacharya ever continue to be the spiritual beacon-light to humanity.

C. Subramaniam
Governor of Maharashtra and Presidenf of
Bharatiya Vidya Bhavan

20th September, '91

PREFACE TO THE FOURTH EDITION

This is the fourth edition of "The Vedas", being the discourses (rendered into English from the Tamil) of His Holiness Chandrasekharendra Saraswati, the 68th Pontiff of the Kanchi Kamakoti Peetham, well-known as the Paramacharya or "Periyavaal". We once again look upon this as our humble offering at the lotus feet of His Holiness.

The first edition was published on the Paramacharya's 95th birthday in 1988, and the second edition on his 98th. The third edition came out in 1994, the centenary year.

A Hindi edition is under consideration.

The Vedas form the foundation of our religion. The Paramacharya was keen that this foundation should remain strong forever. In other words, it is our bounden duty to preserve and protect the Vedas by promoting their study.

When, in 1986, Shri R.V. Raghavan, Executive Trustee of Sudakshina Trust, approached the Bhavan with a proposal for a joint publication, we had little hesitation in accepting the proposal.

The Paramacharya's thoughts are conveyed to us through his discourses, and, as we go through the pages, we are amazed at the wealth of knowledge that our ancients have bequeathed to mankind. The Paramacharya's knowledge was vast and deep. His 'Upadesa' (teaching) is a product of his 'anubhava' (spiritual experience).

The distinguishing feature of the book is that, of the 14 'Vidyas', the Paramacharya deals more elaborately with the six Vedangas and the four Upangas than the four Vedas themselves. There are few books which give succinctly and in such depth all about Vedangas - Siksha, Vyaakarana, Chhandas, Niruktam, Jyotisha and Kalpa.

Even those who are allergic to grammar will find something fascinating in the way the Paramacharya deals with

Vyaakarana. Linking the origin of grammar with the Dance of Siva, the Paramacharya explains the concepts of "Sabda Brahman" and "Nada Brahman".

While the Sudakshina Trust came into existence in 1974 at the benign command of the Paramacharya, the Bhavan has received in ample measure the Paramacharya's blessings. In his benediction in 1962 on the occasion of Bhavan's Silver Jubilee, the Paramacharya said : "The Bharatiya Vidya Bhavan has made the intellectuals of Bharata Varsha evince interest in the various aspects of our culture and progress."

Mumbai,
December 10, 1998.

PUBLISHERS

Acknowledgement

Words are poor vehicles of expression when our deep feelings are involved. How can one adequately express one's indebtedness to the late Shir N.S.S. Rajan for having accomplished the marathon task of translating into English Periawaal's discourses in Tamil on the Vedas and allied subjects !

On his retirement from the Defence Ministry, Delhi, Shri Rajan had settled down in Madras and, in between his daily recitation of the Ramayana and the Bhagavata, he spent many hours on this translation.

Till the end came in the form of terminal cancer, Shri Rajan, like King Parikshit, found solace in Srimad Bhagavatam and the translation work he had taken on hand.

One's thoughts, therefore, go to Shri Rajan, when his work is seeing the light of day.

Another person to whom an acknowledgement is due is Shri Thirunavukkarasu of Vanathi Pathippakam (Vanathi Publishing House), Madras, whose publications provided the basis for the translation. A great devotee of the Sage of Kanchi, Shri Thirunavukkarasu readily gave permission when approached.

There is one more good soul, to whom we owe a debt of gratitude. He is Shri N. Anantharama Iyer, Retired Commissioner of Income Tax, Bombay. An ardent devotee of the Sage of Kanchi and a sound scholar in our ancient lore, he devoted much time and energy to the final editing of the manuscript.

Grateful thanks are also due to Shri K. N. Iengar of Bangalore for providing the excellent chart attached at the end of this book.

Note for pronunciation

The vowel sounds in the transliteration of Indian words and names in this book are not on the international scheme with diacritical marks. The scheme followed here is, it is hoped, easy to follow, being in consonance with English spelling and pronunciation. The main difficulty in correctly reading romanised Sanskrit is the short and long vowel. It is hoped that the scheme followed in this book, the single 'a' for the short अ and double 'aa' for the long आ tides over much of this difficulty.

अ	a
आ	aa as in 'war', 'call'
इ	i
ई	ee as in 'sheep', 'seen'
उ	u
ऊ	oo as in 'moon', 'cool', 'loop'
ए	e as in 'say', 'way', 'made'
ऐ	ai
ओ	o as in 'code', 'roll'
औ	au

CONTENTS

1

AUTHORITATIVE TEXT ON VEDIC RELIGION

There are many books available today on a variety of subjects. There are several books on each of the religions. However, the pride of place is given in each religion to a particular book. Each religion has a founder and his writings and preachings are given pride of place in that religion. It is believed that the founder's book is the most authentic and authoritative. In some cases, the book is worshipped and enshrined in a temple. For example, the Sikhs do so. They reverently refer to their holy book as the"Granth Sahib". Similarly, every religion has adopted a particular text as showing the path to self-betterment and salvation. Although a book may be named after its founder, it is believed to contain the Lord's own words- His commandments coming through the founder or Savant or Prophet as the case may be. They are, therefore, called 'Revealed Texts'. We Hindus call the Vedas, our Sacred texts, as *Apourusheyam* - meaning not authored by purusha or man, man being merely an instrument of God to spread His words.

What is the authoritative book on which one's religion is based? People of other religions can unhesitatingly reply to this question. The Christians call it the 'Bible'; the Mohemmedans call it the 'Koran'; to the Buddhists it is 'Dhammapada'; and to the Parsees, the 'Zend Avesta'. But for us Hindus, there is no similar ready answer because it is not a single book; nor is the authorship attributed to any human being.

Some will consider the Ramayana to be our sacred text - some others, the Bhagavad Gita; yet others will say that the Vedantic texts are the books to be followed. This was not always so. The confusion and divergence in view points have arisen because, whereas in other religions there is a basic religious education provided through a basic text book, in Hinduism, we have no such preliminary religious education being insisted upon. Hence nowadays we find that we ourselves criticise and denigrate our holy books while the followers of other religions safeguard their own texts and sometimes even vilify other religious doctrines.

If we learn the essential texts of our religion even in our childhood as other religionists are doing, we will not be doubting about our religious texts, nor will we have the present-day ignorance about them.

We have to know what our religion is and this can be learnt only through our sacred texts. Before that, we must know why we should have a religion. Religion does not mean mere ritual. It means *Dharma*. What is *Dharma?* That which, if we follow, will make us contented and happy. To know *Dharma* and the principles of *Dharma,* we must refer to certain specific texts or books. Such books are referred to as *'Dharmapramana'.* *"Pramana"* means that which establishes the truth. So *"Dharmapramana"*means that which gives one the true knowledge of *Dharma.* Which are the sacred texts that speak about true *Dharma*?

Angaani Vedaaschatwaro meemaamsa nyaaya vistarah
Puraanam Dharmasaastramcha vidyaahyetaah chaturdasa.

अंगानि वेदाश्चत्वारो मीमांसा न्याय विस्तरः
पुराणं धर्मशास्त्रंच विद्या ह्येता श्चतुर्दश ।

These are fourteen and they are : The four Vedas (Rig, Yajur, Sama and Atharva); the six Vedaangas or auxilliaries to the Vedas, viz., *'Siksha'* which is euphony and pronunciation; *'Vyaakarna'* which is grammar; *'Chandas'* or metre; *'Niruktha'* or etymology; *'Jyotisha'* or astronomy; *'Kalpa'* or procedure, *'Meemaamsa'* or interpretation of Vedic texts; *'Nyaaya'* or logic; *'Puraana'* or mythology and *'Dharma Saastraas'* which contain the codes of conduct.

Knowledge and wisdom are enshrined in these. Hence these fourteen are known as the *'Vidyaasthaanas'.* (विद्यास्थान)

To these fourteen may be added four more which are called *'Upaangas'* or appendices to the Vedaangas. They are : (1) Ayurveda or the science of life; (2) Arthasaastra, the science of wealth or economics; (3) Dhanur Veda, the science relating to weaponry, missiles and warfare and (4) Gaandharva Veda or the treatises on the fine arts like music, dance, drama, etc.

The four Vedas form the core of our religion. They are the supreme authority – *Pramaana*. The Vedas form the basic structure from which have been derived the six Vedaangas and the four Upaangas, in order to supplement the understanding of the Vedas. The Vedas are meant to be studied with the other ten of its constituents.

No beginning – no authorship

The Vedas are called *Anaadi* – (अनादि) – (i.e.) without a beginning in terms of time. That is to say, anything previous to it or older than it does not exist. This means it has existed at all times. How can this be accepted? A book has necessarily to have an author; at least one, if not more. The Old Testament is a collection of the sayings of many prophets. The Koran contains what Mohammed, the prophet, propagated. These people existed at some point of time. Before their time, their teachings were not available. Likewise, logically, the Vedas should also have had one or more authors who must have lived at some time or the other. Before their times, their teachings should not have been available. May be, this was a long time ago; long long time ago; millions of years ago. Even then, it would be wrong, according to some, to call the Vedas as 'without a beginning'. Such doubts naturally arise if one assumes that the Vedas were written by men. Then, how else would a book come to be written? Authorship is a pre-requisite of any book and the author must have existed at some time. Ordinary logic does not seem to support the claim that a book could have no author.

A theory has, therefore, been put forward that evolved persons called 'Rishis' or sages wrote the Vedas. It is stated that the Vedas contain many 'Suktas' or words of wisdom, wise sayings, attributed to several sages.

Before reciting the Veda mantras, it is customary to mention the name of the Rishi or sage concerned with that particular portion, the *'chandas'* or metre in which the mantra appears or is composed and the *Devata* or the presiding deity of that mantra. Since the Veda mantras refer to a number of rishis, this has led to the belief that there should be many authors. In most cases, the geneology of the rishi is also mentioned to avoid confusion with two rishis having the same name. For example *"Agastyo Maitra-Varuni"* that is, Agastya, the son of Mitra and Varuna. So, if a mantra is in his name, does it not mean that Agastya is its author? Then does it not prove that, before his time, the Veda mantra was non-existent? Then how can we call it *"anaadi"?* i.e. without beginning? But the real fact is that this, or that Rishi or for that matter any other rishi, did not compose the mantras. That is why the Rishis cannot be called the authors.

By definition, the Vedas are *"Apourusheya"*(अपौरुषेय) or of non-human origin. *"Pourusheya"* is the work of man. Since it is not the work of man the rishis who were human beings could not have written them. If they had written them, they (the rishis) would have been called *Mantra Kartas* (मंत्र कर्ता) or the composers of the mantras. But in actual fact, they are called only *Mantra Drishtas* (मंत्र द्रष्ट) or the seers of the mantras. This means that the rishis "found" or discovered the Vedas and did not compose them or create them.

What does it mean when one says that Columbus discovered America? Did he create America? No. He helped to bring America which was already in existence to the notice of the world. Newton, Einstein and other famous scientists did not create the laws for which they are honoured. Does an object fall due to the gravitational pull not existent earlier to Newton? These scientists understood the laws already in operation but made them known to the world for the first time. Likewise, the rishis cognised the mantras already in existence and made them known to the world. The mantras had existed always. Since the rishis discoverd them, their names are associated with the mantras. Therefore credit is due to the rishis for having brought the already existing but till then unknown Vedamantras to the knowledge of men. We therefore bow to their memory by touching our head when mentioning their name. This is the gesture in recognition of their great service. We acknowledge it by mentioning their name before the recital of the mantra. Well, if the rishis discovered the mantras, where were they existing before discovery? If they are called *'anaadi'* does it mean that they were there always? Where did they exist? In space?

If we suppose that the Veda mantras appeared along with the first creation, it would imply that the great Lord created them along with the world. Did God write the Vedas and keep them in storage so that the rishis may subsequently discover them in parts? In any case, if the Vedas came into being with the first creation, they cannot be said to be without beginning. The present creation by Brahma is calculable in terms of time. The four *Yugas (Krita Yuga, Treta Yuga, Dwaapara Yuga and Kali Yuga)* have each a specified duration of time. A thousand four-yuga cycle is reckoned as a day for Brahma as distinct from night. Another thousand four-yuga cycle constitutes his night. On this basis, it is believed that today Brahma is just over fifty years of age. His span of life is one hundred years, calculated on this basis. Before that, this Brahma was not there; another Brahma was in existence. Therefore, the present Brahma and creation are not *'anaadi'*. Then what is *'anaadi'?* The Paramaatma must have existed before Brahma, before any Brahma. Brahmam, or the impersonal God, existed at all times. He is the time continuum, from which the universe and all matter appear and disappear from time to time. The Paramaatma does His creation through Brahma, maintains the creation through Vishnu and annhilates through Rudra (Siva). Eventually, Brahma, Vishnu and Siva also cease to exist as such. That is why Brahma's age is calculable. After completion of his term of one hundred *'Brahma Varsha'*, he merges with the *Paramaatma*. Then another Brahma takes over.

Getting back to the Vedas, did the *Paramaatma* or the Supreme Being create the Vedas before any of the Brahmas, before creation itself?

It is known from the Saastras that the Vedas existed prior to creation because Brahma himself is said to have undertaken creation with the aid of the Veda mantras which merely existed as sound in space. This is borne out by one of the Puraanas, Srimad Bhagavata, which, amongst other things, describes how Brahma created the worlds.

Then, is it correct to infer that both God (Paramaatma) and Vedas are *anaadi*? On reflection, it would appear that even this assumption is not correct. If it is understood that God created the Vedas before he created the world, then it would imply that there was a time (before their creation) when they did not exist. This would imply that, although created prior to the Universe and Life, the Vedas were created only after God created the'time concept'. This would also discredit the epithet of *"anaadi"*.

God could not have created the Vedas if both He and they were *anaadi*. If he created them, they would have a beginning. All things have emanated from *Iswara*. Since there is nothing apart from Him, both *Iswara* and Veda must have existed side by side without a beginning. But this does not seem to be right. Uncreated by *Iswara*, not having an existence independent of him but still being *anaadi* (wihout a beginning) - well, how is this posssible?

This confusion is cleared by Veda itself. *Brihadharanyaka* Upanishad (2.4.10) says that the Veda in the Rig, Yajur, Sama and Atharva forms are *Iswara's* breath *'Nishwasitam'* (निश्वसितं) is the word used denoting exhalation of breath.

Can we exist without breathing? Likewise, the Vedas are the life breath, as it were, of the Paramaatma or the supreme self. If the Paramaatma who has no beginning in time exists forever (without any end in time), then the Vedas as his life breath, are naturally *anaadi*, as they coexist with Him or it.

The point to note here is that even God is not said to have brought the Vedas into existence. It would be incorrect to say that we created our own breath. It exists from the time we started existing. So are *Iswara* and the Vedas. Even He cannot be said to have created them. They have always existed together.

Vidyaranya who wrote the Veda Bhaashya (commentary on the Vedas) regarded his guru (teacher) as *Iswara* or God himself, and whilst singing his praise says "whose *'niswasitam'* are the Vedas." In addition to giving us an idea of how deeply his guru was immersed in the Vedas, Vidyaranya's commentary stresses the fact that the Vedas are not even the creation of Iswara.

Lord Krishna says in the Gita "I am the person who is to be known by all the Vedas - (वेदैश्च सर्वैरहमेव वेद्यः) *(Vedaischa Sarvairahamev vedyah.)* Further, instead of calling himself as the one who made the Vedas, he calls himself as the one who is the subject of all Vedanta - *Vedantakirt.* - not as *Vedakrit.* He calls himself as the one who knows all the Vedas - Vedavit. In his absolute and conceptual state as described in the Vedanta, before He made himself the end-product of human evolution, even before creation, *Iswara* and the Vedas have co-existed.

As in the Gita, the Bhagavata Purana also does not talk of God having made the Vedas. The Vedas are said to have manifested from his heart. The word used is *'Sputa'* which means sudden manifestation of something already existing. It does not refer to a situation where something not already in existence has been brought into being. Brahma, the first born was the first rishi who came to know all the Veda mantras. He is made aware of these by *Iswara.* How? Did he recite them to be learnt by Brahma? No, He gave them through his heart. The opening verse of Bhagavata Purana refers to it as *'Tenay Brahma hirdaya adikavaye'* (तेने ब्रह्महृदाय आदिकवये). It is clear, therefore, that the Vedas always existed within Him as his breath. Brahma became aware of them as soon as *Iswara* willed it. Brahma began his creation with the guidance he got from the vibrations received from the Lord's heart. Is this possible? Can vibrations amount to much?

the Brahman manifests itself as the various objects of phenomenal existence. Whether it appears to exist or otherwise, it has to be conceded that the same Primal Force appears differently as the inanimate world and the animate beings. Even if called illusion *(Maaya)*, it has to subsist on a base *(Maayin)* which is none other than *Iswara*. Therefore, even *Maaya*, in its various forms, is manifest as vibrations in the *Para Brahman*, (परब्रह्म) Notwithstanding such vibrations which are manifest, the *Para Brahman* is not in a state of vibration and deep inside it stays in a state of quiescence. Nevertheless, to our sense-perception, the vibrations are manifest. These cannot be chaotic. From the orbiting of the myriad solar systems down to the creation of a small blade of grass or mosquito, there is an orderly behavioural pattern, a governing law.

The well-being of the world is possible only by the operation of this good law of governance. The natural forces have been harnessed by the Paramaatma for the creation and goverance of the world. But it would sometimes appear that God looks on when orderly existence gets slightly out of hand or awry.

Thus, we sometimes see the forces of nature stepping out of bounds. The rains do not come in season. Or, there are floods or some other natural calamity.

In the matter of departure from the normal, nothing can go as far wrong as the human mind. The lure of the flesh is great. Although by and large, there exist in nature very definite rules of conduct, order and discipline, the mind discards all the bonds of discipline and restraint and strays far and wide like a mad creature.

The question arises whether it is possible to correct the forces of nature when they act counter to the well-being of men. Similarly, is there any method to control the mind when it runs amuck?

If the origin of phenomenal existence is traceable to vibrations and sound, then it stands to reason that the same vibrations and sound can correct the erring forces of nature and cleanse the mind of improper thoughts. The Vedas are merely such vibrations and sounds.

It is possible for controlled breathing through Yoga to establish rapport with the Cosmic Breath and perform beneficial acts for general, as well as individual well being. The vibrations of the pulses and nerve centres are not audible to the human ear. This view is now being accepted by many.

Thinking on these lines, science is no enemy to the true concept of religion. On the other hand, it can go a long way to help the impact of religion on society. A century ago, before the advent of the telephone and radio, we would have found it difficult to satisfy the doubts of those lacking in faith as to the credibility of the sonic effects of the Vedas and breathing. Now, these discoveries lend us full support.

The capability of the insentient radio receiver can well be acquired by sentient beings. Nay, we can do even better. *Tapas* or penance is what gives such ability.

Tapas is to focus the mind and mind force constantly on an objective, discarding the comforts of hearth and home, heedless to the demands of hunger and thirst, sleep and rest. In all this exercise, it is necessary to eschew the awareness that 'I am taking all this trouble and making all the effort and, therefore, I am bound to arrive at the Truth.' Humility should permeate through all the effort in the belief that, notwithstanding all human endeavour, the grace of God is a vital ingredient to the success of any mission. The Rishis did such penance and reached the summit of yogic capabilities.

The Rishis became aware of all the vibrations that resulted in the creation of the world, that is to say, of the cosmic breathing, as it were. Not only that. Just as electromagnetic waves are converted into sonic sound waves, cosmic vibrations became audible to their ears. These they gave to the world as Veda mantras.

One thing strikes me. The Vedas are called 'Sruti' or that which is heard. The ear is called *Srotra* (श्रोत्र) in Sanskrit. Without being committed to writing ancient history from material taken from Vedic texts and, in the process, introduced the till then unheard of concept of Aryans and Dravidians, which created mutual hatred. Their conclusions were based on what they called 'rationalisation', according to which anything outside the ken of the sense organs can only be regarded as allegorical. This would permit them to regard the ancient Rishis as primitive men inferior to the moderns. Their analysis of our religious texts was motivated by the desire to show Christianity as a better religion. All the while they kept up the facade of impartial research and, in the process, denigrated our religion.

Noting the points of similarity between Sanskrit and their language, many studied our texts purely in the interests of comparative philology.

We can admire them for their tenacious research, and the publicity they gave to the greatness of the Vedas. But they missed the essential purpose of the Vedas which is to ensure the well-being of the universe at large by spreading the sound of Vedic chant and ensuring the performance of Vedic rites. Setting aside these two essentials, the Vedas, which are beyond its reach, have been sought to be analysed by the brain. What should subsist as a living force in word and deed of the common man has been entombed in voluminous books adorning the shelves of libraries, like keeping fauna in museums which house skeletons and archaic objects.

Research on the age of the Vedas incorrect

Why I brought in the foreign scholars here is to project their point of view when talking of Vedas as *"anaadi"* or having no beginning. Their mind does not accept the fact that the Vedas are without beginning. Notwithstanding the impartiality which scientific research demanded, some of them could not tolerate the excellence of our sacred texts. Some others, who were perhaps not so motivated, found themselves unable to rise above the constraints imposed by common sense and syllogism. Unable to accept the theory of 'without a beginning', even 'educated' Hindus have found it necessary to undertake 'deep' research.

According to such research, the determination of the time factor has two aspects. One is through the evidence of astronomy. The other is through the style of the language used. Have they come to any irrefutable conclusion by such process in determining the age of the Vedas? No, they have not. Each researcher has a different opinion. Tilak says that the Vedas came into being around 6000 B.C. Others fix 3000 B.C. as the date. Some others have come to more recent times, as near as 1500 B.C.

There are no such differences of opinion on other religious texts. Opinion is undivided that the *Thripitaka* of the Buddhists was written during the time of Emperor Asoka but the teachings of Buddha which it contains date back to centuries before Asoka, roughly 2500 years ago, when Buddha lived. There is also unanimity on the date of the New Testament of the Bible which is some 2000 years ago. All agree that the Koran was composed about 1200 years ago. Only in the case of our Vedas, there is lack of conclusive evidence as to its age.

Let me elaborate as to what I meant by two kinds of approaches in determining the age of the Vedas.

At certain places, the Vedas mention the planetary position of stars. Based on the astrological conjunction of planets, the astronomical calculations of some fix the age of the Vedas at 6000 B.C. or some other period as per such calculations.

But, how can it be said that such a planetary conjunction can happen in 6000 B.C. only and at no other period in time? Similar positioning of planets could have happened in the hoary past, let alone reckoning from the time which the current Universe was created. The same disposition of stars could have occurred long ago, not once but many times. How to determine which one does the Vedas refer to? Such calculations do not therefore fit in with the Vedas which were given to us by the Rishis who could see beyond the confines of time. The astronomical references which are regarded as the internal evidence contained in the Vedas, do not, in reality, clarify the position.

Another approach to fixing the age of the Vedas is through the language used. The chief constituents of language are style and script. All the scripts which are today in evidence in India owe their origin to the Braahmi script.

Today, it looks on a superficial comparison that there could be no connection between, say, the Tamil script and the Devanagari script. But calligraphists have prepared a chart showing the changes that have taken place in the original Braahmi script every hundred years. This reveals that changes have taken place in various regions at various times and, although, today, it looks as though there is no common link at all, the scripts of the various languages appear to have originated from a common script. I used to think, in a lighter vein, that the modern scripts look like the original with moustaches. If you looked at the chart yourself, you would appreciate what I say better. The letters 'u' and 'oo' (उ, ऊ) in Devanagari would convincingly illustrate this. Similarly, the Tamil script looks as though the original script has sprouted horns. It is possible to understand the changes which have occurred from time to time from an examination of edicts and proclamations of ancient kings carved in stone and engraved on metal. Thus, the script is helpful in determining the age of an edict.

But, in-so-far as the Vedas are concerned, these were nowhere engraved in stone. The question of the script determining the time does not therefore arise. The only other method left is the examination of the style.

Here again, the image created by words and the impact of sound on understanding have also changed from time to time. Many Tamil words current at the golden age of Tamil literature are today unrecognisable. So is the case with other languages. Some sounds have not only become eroded with age but the meaning has also changed.

Vedas are not as easily understandable as the later day literature. Such shift is noticed in all languages. For example, the Anglo-Saxon language - old English - which is under 1000 years old - cannot be easily understood by the modern generation of Englishmen. In America, English has changed its form within the last 300 years to such an extent that, today, it goes under the changed name of American English.

Researchers have calculated the rate at which erosion takes place in the sound of words as a result of usage. It has not been possible to determine, with equal accuracy, the time it takes for the meaning of words to change.

Therefore, the age of the Vedas has been determined by these researchers solely on the evidence offered by the changes in the sound of words used in the Vedas. According to them it takes roughly about 200 years for a sound to change noticeably. Going back to the Vedas, from words not in use, it is possible according to them to arrive at the number of changes or mutations that must have taken place. Thus, if ten changes have taken place, then it means the word is 2000 years old. If a word in the Vedas had changed 30 times, the age of the Vedas can at best be 4000 B.C. That is, the Vedas could not have existed earlier than that and so on.

This theory is fundamentally incorrect. Words in daily usage undergo changes in sound (pronunciation) and also get corroded in meaning. Although the Vedas may be chanted every day, the beauty is that the purity of the original sound is kept intact unchanged without any erosion. Great care has been taken to safeguard the original form of every word in the Vedas. Therefore, the Vedic sounds did not suffer any mutations as words in everyday use did, as assumed by these researchers.

According to these scholars, amongst the Vedas, the Rig came first; then the Yajus, then the Saama and lastly the Atharva Veda and in every Veda, the *'Samhithas'* are the first part; the *Braahmanaas* next and the *Aaranyakaas* last. So arguing, the researchers calculate the age of the Vedas. They compare the mutations in words from the Vedas to Valmiki's Ramayana, then to Mahabharata and then to Kalidasa's works. However much they may examine evidences, none of these can be of any avail as they ignore the basic premises. Even assuming that Vedic words could change, in spite of rigid safeguards, such changes cannot happen in a short span of 200 years. It would take thousands of years for even a small change to take place. If it is conceded that the wear and tear of words in use in literature as well as in the spoken language does not apply to Vedic words, it will be understood that the calculation on the age of the Vedas is incorrect.

The establishment of a separate language called Hindi occurred only a few centuries ago. Even so, it has spread over a large area. It has also undergone many changes during its short life, because it has accepted within its fold words from many languages such as Sanskrit, Urdu, Persian, English and so on. Although Sanskrit had spread (even more than Hindi) all over the country it was not a spoken language and hence did not change. When that is the case with its literature, it would indeed be rare for any changes in Vedic words, whose purity was zealously guarded. Therefore, on the basis of the calculation of the researchers, changes that would take a thousand years to occur in the case of an ordinary language would perhaps take over a hundred thousand years in the case of the Vedas.

The reason why the Vedic sounds have been maintained in their pristine purity is because, only by the correct intonation of words, would the mantras attain their power. Lest any mistake should creep in, a separate dedicated section of the community had made it its business to hand it down safely from one generation to the next, unsullied and in its original form.

Research cannot find out what exactly happened, unless this basic fact is recognised. The various methods of chanting bear testimony to the success with which the purity of the sounds have been guarded.

4

ERROR-FREE METHODS OF CHANTING

Without resort to writing, our forefathers had devised many ways to prevent even a small error to creep into the Vedas. The fullest benefit from the Vedic mantras can result only if no word is changed; no unauthorised upward or downward drift in the note occurs in recitation. Hence the numerous safeguards.

How much time should it take to utter each word is indicated by resort to the notation by maatras - (the time it takes to pronounce a short vowel). How to regulate breathing so that the vibrations can occur at what part of the body to give birth to the pure word-sound is also laid down in the *Vedanga* called *Seeksha*. The *Taittareeye Upanishad*, for e.g., begins with *Seeksha* thus :

शीक्षां व्याख्यास्यामः। वर्णस्वरः। मात्राबलं। सामसन्तानः।

(Seeksham Vyakhyaa syaamah - Varna Swarah - Maatraa balam - Saama Santaanah)

Seeksha deals with Varna, Swara, Maatra, Strength, Saama and Santaanah.

A fool-proof method used is to chant each mantra in various patterns and combinations known as *Vaakya, Pada, Krama, Jata, Maala, Sikha, Rekha, Dhwaja, Danda, Ratha, Ghana,* etc.

Some learned pandits are called *"Ghanapaatis"*. This means that they are learned in the Vedas to the extent of chanting of Vedas in the pattern called *Ghanam.* When we listen to a *Ghanapaati* reciting Vedas in *Ghana* form, we note that he repeats the words in various ways back and forth and in different patterns. This would be pleasant to the ears and creates a sense of happiness within. It would seem that the natural grandeur of the Veda mantras is heightened, as it were. So would be the effect of recitation in the other prescribed patterns of *Kramam, Jata, Sikha, Maala,* etc. But the main object of reciting them is to make no mistake in the original meaning and sound pattern of the words.

Vaakya Paatha (वाक्य पाठ) or *Samhita Paatha* (संहित पाठ) is to recite the mantras in a sentence straight. When mantras come in sentences, some of the words therein have to be conjoined in chanting. To recite the Veda mantras, *pada* by *pada* or word by word, instead of joining the words and stringing them together, is *Pada Paatha.*

Pada Paatha occurs after *Samhita Paatha.* In *Pada Paatha* the sentence is broken down to 'words' or *pada.* This gives the student of the Vedas the knowledge of each word in a sentence. Next is *Krama Paatha* (क्रमपाठ). In this method, the first word of a mantra is added to the second, the second to the third, the third to the fourth and so on, until the whole sentence of the mantra is completed. This *paatha* or method of recitation helps the student understand not only the individual words but also how two words can be combined in recitation and what modification occurs in *swara* in such a combination.

In certain ancient edicts, notably gift deeds, at the end of the names of some illustrious persons, there would be a suffix *'Krama Vit'* (क्रमवित्). Like 'Vedavit', "Krama Vit" means that a person is well-versed in reciting the Vedas by the *Krama Paatha* method. There are many such edicts found in South India.

Next is *Jataa Paatha* (जटापाठ). In this, the first word and the second are first recited together and then the words are recited in a reverse order and then again in the original order. Whereas in the *Krama* type of recitation the order of words is 1-2; 2-3; 3-4; 4-5 and so on, in the *Jataa Paatha,* the order will be 1-2-2-1-1-2, 2-3-3-2-2-3, 3-4-4-3-3-4, 4-5-5-4-4-5 and so on. Just as two words are repeated forwards and backwards in the *Jataa Paatha,* the *Sikha Paatha* requires three words to be so linked.

The *Ghana Paatha* (घनपाठ) is more difficult than the above. There are five more types. They all are different ways of chanting by changing the order of words by various permutations and combinations*.

Just as in a laboratory, a life giving elixir is preserved with the utmost care, the Veda mantras, which are for universal benefit, have been preserved by the ancients, without suffering erosion or corrosion even a bit and without resort to writing by such methods of recitation. It must be remembered that, while chanting words backwards and forwards, the *swaras* of each have to be properly preserved and the student learns how the combination of words affects the *swaras*.

The *Samhita Paatha* and *Pada Paatha* are called *Prakriti* (or natural) *Paatha*, as the words of the mantra occur in normal sequence. The rest are called *Vikriti* (or artificial or not natural). In *Krama*, although the words do not occur in the natural order of one, two and three, since they do not revert like one after two and two after three, it cannot be called fully *Vikriti* or artificial. The *Vikritis* are eight in number:

जटा माला शिखा रेखा ध्वजो दण्डो रथो घनः
इत्यष्टा विकृतयः प्रोक्ताः क्रमपूर्वा महर्षिभिः

Jataa maalaa sikha rekha dhwajo dando Ratho ghanah
Ityashta vikrtayah proktah kramapoorvaa maharshibhih

The above system of complicated recitations was devised in very early times in order to preserve the purity of the word, sound, intonation, pronunciation, accent and sound combinations of the Vedas. By repeating the words in manifold ways, the correct tally of words also was kept which has naturally ensured its purity. To enable the scholars to take up the difficult methods of recitation, it was even laid down that the more difficult methods of chanting earned the chanter more punya or merit.

*The combination of words will be 1-2-2-1-1-2-3-3-2-1-1-2-3; 2-3-3-2-2- 3-4-4-3-2-2-4; and so on in the *Ghana* form.

Since the ancients had taken so much pains to keep the form of the Veda mantras safe and pure the method of the modern researchers to measure in terms of time the changes in the sound of Veda mantras is unrealistic and cannot help to understand the truth.

God's Words

It is not correct to dispute that the Vedas are a revelation. Not only in our country but those belonging to other religions also do believe that their sacred texts are but a revelation. Jesus said that his preachings were not his own, but those of God which he only propagated. Mohammedans say that Mohammed merely preached the instructions of Allah which were revealed to him.

Our theory of revelation is repeated by them too as "Revealed Texts". God's words have become available to us through saints. Thus in all religions, God's words have been revealed to great seers, prophets and Rishis who have made them available to mankind for its betterment.

A person who delves deep, with a single-minded purpose, into any field, is bound to discover the truth. This is called the flash of understanding or intuition. It is said that Einstein did not arrive at the theory of relativity by any thought process but that the equation flashed through his mind. If we can accept this as a fact certainly the fact that the Rishis with highly developed and disciplined minds and spiritually attuned became conscious of the mantras deep down in their hearts cannot be disputed and has to be accepted as correct.

5

VEDAS ARE WITHOUT END

If the whole of creation and all that is before and beyond creation is involved in the world of vibrations, it must indeed be colossal in magnitude. That being so, the question arises as to how all of the manifold universal activities are encompassed within the Veda mantras.

It has to be understood that the Vedas are vast and what has come to us as Vedas is limited in extent. What is stated in the Vedas is that they are verily endless - *"ananta vai Vedah"* (अनंता वै वेदाः). It cannot be said that the Vedas in their entirety got revealed to the Rishis. Only a portion — a small portion of the limitless Vedas — became revealed to them. The four Vedas and a thousand and odd Veda *saakhaas* (or branches) of the Vedas are only a portion of what was made known to them.

The breath of the Paramaatma, whose resonance inspired Brahma to undertake creation, still exists in space in spite of all destructive deluges which have happened from time to time even after many Brahmas. This has no decay or death. Every Brahma who comes after the Great Deluge or Pralaya undertakes creation with the help of these vibrations of the Veda mantras or primordial sound.

Their origin is vibratory movement. This movement was captured by Brahma as Vedas and, on chanting them, creation became manifest.

It is said that if certain sound vibrations are released near plants, these induce faster growth and higher yield. Similarly some vibrations retard growth. That sound vibrations are capable of creation, preservation and destruction, is thus clearly proved even in such ordinary matters as the growth of plants.

Brahma was able to create the whole Universe with the aid of Vedic sounds by his *Tapas* or power of meditation.

How does it happen that a saintly person is able to cure a disease by chanting only once the *Panchaakshara* mantra (five syllabled word) which we chant daily? Obviously because he has greater power of concentration and power of invoking the vibrations in the proper manner. In addition, the mantra should be chanted in its purity without any change of words or tone. Only then can result be obtained. Since Brahma manifested Himself from the Paramaatma solely for the purpose of creation, his mastery of the Vedas was total.

With the aid of electricity which gets released from the empty skies, a great many things are nowadays performed or achieved. Likewise all creation emanates from the attributeless Brahman which is all consciousness. During the deluges, the consciousness is quiescent. When a wrestler sleeps, his strength remains unfelt. It is only when he is wrestling or indulging in some such activity that his power is known. Similarly, during creation, the cosmic force performs a number of jobs. From out of the quiescent being, a force is released to do such jobs. Brahma came out of such a force. Since he was born in the form of *Tapas,* he was able to absorb all the Vedas with their full vigour. He created the universe with the help of Vedic resonances. The Vedas are limitless, as creation is also varied and manifold.

When Brahma took form, all the Vedic sounds were born in his heart — inner self. They showed him the path of creation. He felt the Vedic sounds all around and to him all the Vedas became known intuitively.

There is a story about the limitlessness of the Vedas. The great sage, Bharadwaaja, studied the Vedas through three spans of earthly life, specially granted to him for the purpose. Lord Parameswara appeared before him and said "I will give you a fourth span, What will you do with it"? Bharadwaaja replied that he would utilise the extra time also in the study of the Vedas. Since it was not possible to study all the Vedas even during countless spans of life, the Lord took pity on the Rishi's futile efforts and desired to correct him and give him an idea of the tremendous difficulty that he faced. He made three huge mountains to appear there and picking up a handful of earth said, "What you have so far studied is equal to this handful of earth. What you have yet to learn is of the order of these mountains". The episode of Bharadwaaja Rishi is found in *Kaathaka* (काठक) portion of the Vedas.

Thus, we see the limitlessness of the Vedas. The codification into four Vedas and the thousand and odd *saakhas* is something that came much later.

Mantras are, therefore, revelations to the Rishis who performed deep *Tapas.* They are the Rishis to whom the mantras are said to belong. They have the divine ear to hear those mantras. *Yoga Saastra* says that, if the spatial expanse in the skies and the space which exists in a microform in the mind are unified, all the suspended sounds in space will become audible to us. Those who feel in unison with all objects in creation can alone feel the sound. Thus, the Rishis brought forth the mantras for the benefit of the world and did not create them. Even so, they have rendered a great service to mankind by bringing to its ken what was already in existence but not known. We make obeisance to a person who brings us the Ganga water. Did he produce the Ganga water? He only brought it to us. Nevertheless, we thank him for bringing it to us from a long distance. Similarly no praise is too high for the Rishis who have vouchsafed to us the mantras which were beyond our grasp.

Yoga Mantra and Mantra Siddhi

All the fourteen worlds are a kingdom. This kingdom is ruled by an emperor. All the created beings are His subjects. The emperor and the subjects have no beginning in time. If there is a kingdom and there is an emperor, there must be a set of laws. Since all the three are without beginning, the laws are also without a beginning.

This law without a beginning is the Veda. Although the kingdom is without a beginning, from time to time, it has a temporary end after which it reappears in creation. But the Paramaatma, who is the emperor, and the Veda which is the law are truly without a beginning and without an end.

The phenomenal world that we know of is created; it grows and then is lost in the deluge after a few million years. Again it is created. Thus, it goes on. However, the emperor and the law remain stable. At the start of each creation, the emperor creates authorities-in-charge. He infuses them with the necessary powers so that they could perform their assignment.

As I said earlier, the *Yoga Saastra* says that there is a link between one's ear and the spatial expanse of the universe. If this is established, one obtains 'divine ears', so to say. With the aid of these divine ears, those in authority were able to cognise the sound waves which are diffused in the sky from time immemorial, by the grace of the Paramaatma. They thus became the first to know the Vedas. They are the *maharishis* to whom mantras belong.

We hear as well as utter different sounds. By the vibration of each nerve centre, a certain emotion is created in the mind. Some create passions, some laziness, and some others unhappiness. Putting it differently, when one is in a passion, a certain nerve vibration occurs and similarly when one is in anger.

Thus, with every kind of emotion, a different set of vibrations are caused to the nerve centres. These are evident from our actual experience. Mental peace produces a certain calmness which is reflected in the face. This is because certain *naadis* get cool and composed. Similarly passion and anger get reflected in the face. The pulse beat alone produces these signs. Thus, if certain emotions caused by the mind result in changes in one's pulse beat, by controlling the pulse beats we can exercise control over passion or anger. Thus, *Raajayoga*, which is one of the paths leading to realisation uses breath control *(Praanaayaama)* as the chief instrument in the control of the mind.

Similarly, *Mantra Yoga* is another path, When we utter a word, the life breath is allowed to pass though the gaps in the throat, tongue, lips - upper or lower - mouth, etc. Only then the sound of the word emanates and becomes audible. Vibrations are caused to the nerve centres situated in these areas through which breath passes to produce the sound of the word. Veda mantras properly recited with the proper discipline produce the necessary emotions in the mind which ensure well-being to the person reciting as well as to the world. Other baser emotions are also kept out in the process.

By definition, mantra means that by repeatedly meditating upon which one is saved. (मननात् त्रायते इति मन्त्रः) It is the duty of a brahmin to chant the mantras repeatedly so that the necessary vibrations are created again and again, resulting in his own well-being and, through the power so created, cause the general well-being of the world.

If one is to succeed with the mantras and get the fullest benefit from them, there is a prescribed method for chanting it. Learned people consider six methods of recitation, as not correct and advise that they be avoided.

गीतीशीघ्री शिरःकंपी तथालिखितपाठकः।
अनर्थज्ञः अल्पकण्ठश्च षडैते पाठकाधमाः।।

Geetee seeghree sirah kampee thathaa likhita pathakah
Anarthajnah alpakantascha shadaitaypathakaadhamaah

Geetee (गीती) is one who chants in a sing-song fashion. This is not correct. Though Samaveda is musically recited, it can be recited only in the approved musical way and not as one pleases. Further, since the sound and its variations have potency, recitation other than in the proper *swara* is not only not proper but harmful. It should be recited only in the prescribed mode. *Seeghree* (शीघ्री) is one who chants in a quick tempo and ends the recitation quickly. This is also wrong. The Vedic words should be intoned by closely adhering to the time limits prescribed for uttering each word-sound if full benefits are to result. *Shirahkampee* (शिरःकम्पी) is one who shakes and nods his head needlessly while chanting.

One should sit straight in concentration and allow the pulse vibrations to occur naturally by themselves. Nodding of the head like a musician disturbs the vibrations. *Likithapaathakah* (लिखितपाठकः) is one who reads from the written script. This is not right. As I said earlier, it should be learnt by the ear from oral chanting by a teacher and committed to memory in the proper manner. *Anarthajnah* (अनर्थज्ञः) means one who does not understand the meaning. It is necessary to know the meaning of the words of the mantras in order to have the full beneficial effect. *Alpakantha* (अल्पकण्ठ) is one who recites in a feeble voice. In order that the sound vibrations have good effect, the sounds should be properly audible and not mumbled.

The use of sound and material

Here, I must say something which occurs to me, in a lighter vein. If the suffix *'taram'*. (तरं) is added to a Sanskrit word, it denotes that a certain thing is better than another, comparatively speaking. *Veeryavat* (वीर्यवत्) means one with power. *Veeryavattaram* (वीर्यवत्तरं) means more power than the ordinary. It is stated in Chaandogya Upanishad (1.1.10) that better results *(Veeryavattaram)* accrues to those who meditate on the *omkara,* understanding what it connotes. It is obvious from the use of the suffix *"taram"* that those who meditate without understanding the significance obtain only lesser results. Adi Sankaracharya, in his commentary, however, says that, although not at par with those who understand the meaning, others also get sizeable benefits.

Whether one understands the meaning or not, a job done in the belief that the learned ones of the past had prescribed its performance, produces good results. More than in other acts, this should be stressed in the practice of Vedic Japa, because the vibrations created by correct intonation alone produces essential results. Here, the effect that sound produces is all-important. The effect of the meaning is secondary.

Thinking of this, in a lighter vein, sometimes I feel that knowing the meaning produces ordinary *(Veeryavath)* results; not knowing produces better *(Veeryavattaram)* results. How do I think that lack of understanding produces better results and not understanding?

There is a Collector.* A farmer engages a lawyer to write a petition for him addressed to the Collector. He himself submits this petition to the Collector. Although illiterate his submission ends with a prayer for favourable orders from the Collector. The Collector would naturally conclude that the poor man does not know much but has faith in his justice. And so he passes favourable orders. So, is the case with mantras. Their full import is only known to God. We should not, however, be mischievous in our approach. If there is a fault in the lawyer's argument, the Collector is naturally annoyed. He would be more annoyed if he thought that the farmer also was aware of the fault, whereas, if the Collector thought that the farmer was not responsible for the fault of the lawyer, he would be favourably disposed towards the farmer. Therefore, it is not correct to say, "I do not understand. So what is the use of chanting it?" As I said, recitation without understanding works even better, provided there is innocence. This was said for fun. In the present-day world, however, intellect has become sharp. When I find that the humility of the uneducated is undermined, I feel that it would perhaps be better to have faith devoid of intellect instead of intellect devoid of faith.

But, in truth, one must have intellect with humility. Although the meaning of mantras is only secondary to the sound of their correct intonation, since the mantras are our Dharmic laws, we can act accordingly only if their meaning is understood. Hence one must try to understand the import of the mantras also to lend greater strength to the chanting of the same.

Vedas must be chanted with grandeur, so that the sound can be properly heard. Vedic mantras not only produce beneficial vibrations in the pulse of the one who chants them properly but also similar vibrations in those who may hear them. Since it is spread in the atmosphere, it ensures well-being here and hereafter. Therefore, it must be audibly chanted so that it can spread far and

* Collector in India is a head of a revenue district of a State.

wide in the atmosphere.

The power of the Vedas

The main characteristics of the Vedas as mentioned already are: (1) They are without a beginning *(anaadi)*, (2) they have no human authorship *(apourusheya)*, and (3) they are at the root of all creation. But this is not all.

The sound while chanting them activates our nerve centres and also affects the atmosphere, resulting in individual as well as collective well-being of the world. Collective well-being does not refer only to humanity.

No other religious text emphasises the well-being of animals and plants as much as the Vedas. "Not only two-legged but four legged beings should prosper," says the Veda. (शं नो अस्तु द्विपदे शं चतुष्पदे) It goes even further and stresses the well-being of shrubs, trees, mountains and rivers — in fact all creation.

The Vedic texts contain a wealth of meaning. Besides its poetic grandeur they contain detailed injunctions for a well-ordered society and social life, great philosophical truth and even scientific laws.

It is not necessary for the Veda mantras, which are essentially vibrations of sound, to have a verbal meaning as we commonly understand it.

In every day life, we find the *Raga Aaalapana*, or the detailed delineation of musical notes or Ragas which contain no words but only a symbolic meaning nevertheless capable of producing emotions of joy and sorrow. Experiments have shown that the yield of vegetables has been increased by instrumental music. This shows that sound has a creative ability. That apart, the most important thing to note is that, since the sounds emanate from a musical instrument, there is no question of any words or meaning being essential for effectiveness. The very musical sound itself has an effect.

The outstanding feature of the Vedas, therefore, lies in the fact that the sound of the mantras by itself when chanted, has a meaning, apart from the words which are also full of meaning.

Thus, the greatness of the Vedas lies in the mantras having properties of sound and meaning. A pill may be bitter but may be good for health. A sweet may taste well but may cause harm. How nice it would be to have something that would not only taste well but also improve health like a sweet tonic? Veda mantras have this two-fold advantage.

Vedas contain injunctions for ensuring the well-being in this world and the world to come. It guides the actions of a person from the moment of birth to the moment he breathes his last and thereafter to ensure his salvation. It does not stop at individual salvation. How should society behave, what are the duties of the common man, how should a brạhmin conduct himself, how should the king govern the country, what should be the conduct of women — all these matters have been presented to us in a codified form in the Vedas.

6
YAJNA

Of the various merits of the Vedas, Yajna or performance of Vedic ritual is one important aspect of it.

Yajna involves the performance of the prescribed rituals with the aid of Fire or Agni to the accompaniment of Veda mantras. Yajna is derived from the root word 'Yaj', which means to worship - to sacrifice. To perform a rite or ritual whole-heartedly with a feeling of devotion to the Paramaatma or Supreme self and the devatas is "Yajna".

As already explained earlier, "mantra" means that which protects the chanter. To offer protection when chanted is the job of the mantra. "Manana" or meditative chant is to utter a word repeatedly with the mind also involved in it. Though ordinarily mantras have to be recited audibly, in some cases, it is not necessary to utter the word audibly. Even by silent utterance of the words, the necessary beneficial vibrations are created in the nerve centres. The same when chanted aloud, as Veda mantra, has a grandeur which has an exhilarating effect, even when its meaning is not known. That which exists in the mind and is uttered silently comes out in words when chanted aloud and is translated into action through a bodily act. To fulfil the Vedic injunctions, the requirement is for the unification of the functions of the mind, the speech and the body - *mano vaak kaayam* - representing total involvement. That is to say *manana,* or meditative utterance, comes out in sound through the mouth and gets expressed through the body as action as in the case with a Yajna. Therefore, Yajna is one of the most important of the Vedic injunctions.

Not available in other faiths

Ritualism as such is not found in other faiths. Since it is based on Vedas, our faith is called *"Vaideeka Matam"* (वैदीकमतम्) or Vedic faith. There is one big difference between this and the other faiths that are prevalent in the world today. Christianity, Islam and such faiths stress that there is only one God whom all should worship. The Vedas also say that what exists is a single God — who includes all souls.

But this concept of "one God" can only be experienced by introspection through knowledge. To reach such a stage of realisation calls for a high degree of mental discipline. When we are unified with the one God, the world ceases to exist as an object of our perception. We have to attain that stage where realisation results only through disciplining our lives which, willy-nilly, are involved with worldly matters. Living as now, we should follow the path of Dharma, do the rituals which lead to the cleansing of the mind and its maturity. At that stage, the worldly ties will be snapped. The Vedas have given us innumerable ways and means towards such an end. Of these, the most important karma is Yajna. Yajna is offering oblations to various divinities instead of to one God, but ultimately, surrendering the fruit of the action to one God. This Yajna is peculiar to our faith and is not found elsewhere.

Yajna requires many substances to be consigned to Agni (fire) attended by the chant of mantras. This kind offering is called "Homa". Although consigned to Agni, it does not mean that the offerings are all meant for Agni. What is specifically offered to Agni by name through mantras falls to Agni's share. And those offerings meant for other divinities, like Rudra, Vishnu, Indra, Varuna, Vaayu, Soma, etc., are, though accepted by Agni, despatched to their destination by Agni without keeping them for himself. The main difference between our Vedic faith and the other faiths is that, although affirming the existence of only one God, we offer oblations not only to Him but to other divinities through Agni.

We say that God is pleased if humanity is served. Social workers proclaim "service to man is service to God; service to society is service to God". Similarly, serving the divinities who are amongst God's creations by Yajna earns for us God's grace.

The Vedas proclaim emphatically that the one and only God has split itself into so many divinities. Whenever a particular divinity is mentioned, it is described as Paramaatma itself, which shows that the Vedas postulate monotheism only. The emphasis is on the distinction and difference between the divinities and the one God. Because many divinities are mentioned as God, it is incorrect to label the Vedas as postulating polytheism. It talks of one God manifested through many divinities. To regulate the management of the Universe, He has created many divinities. These divinities are meant to administer various functions. The divinities have been created in the same manner as ourselves. He has created us from out of Himself. According to Advaita, the Jeevaatma (the individual soul) and Paramaatma (the cosmic soul) are one and the same. Likewise, He (the Paramaatma) represents the divinities too. Even so, until we fully ripen to absorb the Advaitic faith, the Vedas postulate that we should assume ourselves to be separate entities from the divinities and perform the prescribed Yajnas and Poojas, for mutual benefit. The elements and other forces of nature are contained and regulated by the Devas (divinities) as ordained by the Paramaatma. Therefore, if we and the world around are to get the beneficial effects of natural forces, we have to please the respective Devas individually. The Veda says that Devas can be pleased by Yajnas (stipulated rituals). When spiritual awakening occurs, and when one has direct experiences of the Paramaatma, the need to propitiate the Devas separately ceases to exist. But, so long as we remain at the level where the subject and object are separately cognised *(Dvaita)*, we have to offer worship to individual Devas. This is what the Vedas ordain.

The threefold benefits of rituals

Yajna (ritual) has threefold advantages. One is to ensure well-being for ourselves and those around us through the grace of the Devas whilst living in this world. The second is to live happily after death in the world of the Devas. This life is in the world of the Devas or Devaloka, not for ever. We can live there only so long as our merits *(Punya)* last. The happiness available in Devaloka is in no way comparable to the total bliss *(Aananda)* of the *Bhakta* (highly devout) or the *Jnani* (spiritually evolved). Adi Sankaracharya, in his *'Maneesha Panchakam'*, has categorically affirmed that the happiness of Indra (the king of Devas) is not even a small fraction of the real *Aananda* of the realised soul. Nevertheless, life in *Swargaloka* (heaven) is paradise compared to the existence in this world. So, the performance of rituals with the desire to attain happiness is the second of the threefold benefits stated earlier.

The third is the most important. This is what is stated in the Gita : the performance of Yajna without desiring any results or reward. Well-being in this world and a happy life in *Devaloka* after death are results or rewards. Without wishing for these, if one should perform the Yajnas as one's duty for the well-being of the world and without any thought of gain for one's self and without attachment, it speedily leads to purification of the mind. This in turn takes us on the path of knowledge *(Jnaana maarga)*, whose destination is *Moksha* or release from the cycle of birth and death and the state of total bliss. In short, we merge with the Infinite.

Aadi Sankaracharya who preached the realisation of the self and true knowledge as the essence of Advaita has said, (वेदो नित्यमधीयतां तदुदितं कर्म स्वनुष्ठीयतां) - *"Vedo Nityam Adheeyataam Taduditam Karma Śwanushtheeyataam."* (Study the Vedas constantly; do well the rituals prescribed therein.) This obviously refers to the third benefit. He did not say this to enable us to live luxuriously in this world or in *Swarga* or heaven. His intention was that performance of the rituals without the expectation of personal reward would lead to clarity of vision and purity of the mind.

Mutual help between Devas and mankind

The performance of rituals is thus the most important aspect of Vedas. Lord Krishna has referred to this in the Gita.

When Brahma originally created the world, he also created the Yajnas for performance by men. "Continue to perform the Yajnas.

Live well as a result of the benefits that would follow. Regard this Yajna as *Kaamadhenu*," says the Bhagavad Gita.

The Veda mantras being the root cause of creation, the mere chanting of Veda mantras would by their vibrations, make the Devas appear in person. The chanting of mantras in a yajna is like writing the address on a postal envelope. Only if the oblations are made with the chanting, would Agni carry the message to the Devas.

Amongst animals, the cat, the dog, the horse, the elephant and the lion have progressively more power than the other in the order mentioned. Likewise in creation, there are beings who have more power than mortals. They are the Devas. They coexist in the five elements in this world but in *Devaloka* have an individual form. If full benefits are attained by correctly chanting the mantras, we can see them in their corporeal form in *Devaloka* in addition to their material favours here. Their appearance in the Paramaatma is as a result of the vibrations caused by the basic sounds of these mantras. Putting it differently, one can say that the mantras are the forms in sound *(Sabda Roopa)* of the Devas.

In Yajna, the chant of a mantra pertaining to a particular Deva calls forth that Deva. Those who are spiritually evolved can see them in person. Even if not visible to the naked eye, their presence will be subtly felt. Even so, directly offering oblation to them is not proper. Only oblations made in Agni (fire), along with the chant of the prescribed mantras, will make them assume the form in which they become acceptable to the Devas.

One must not wonder as to how the oblations can reach their destination when fire has consumed most of them and the rest has been eaten by the performer of the Yajna as *Prasad*. The Devas do not have bodies physically constituted like ours by the five elements (Earth, Water, Light, Air and Space). They do not need the type of material food that we consume. Even for us, the digestive organs convert the food into different forms before absorption by the body. In the same way, the sacrificial fire converts the oblation to a subtle state before carrying it to the Devas. This transformation is also due to the power of the mantras.

Let us take an ordinary everyday example. Even today, at a dinner according to the custom of Westerners, toasts are proposed for the health and well-being. One eats and the other gets the benefit, that is the belief. How can this happen? These are indications of goodwill. The idea is that, if done with sincerity and full force of conviction through thought-power transfer, such results are possible.

When the thought waves of the Paramaatma have come to us in the form of vibrations which are mantras, they must perforce be only beneficial forces. The oblation, offered strictly in accord with the stipulated mantras, increases the power or potency of the Devas. Although superior to ours, their power is also limited. They also have desires and needs.

The Yajnas alone can satisfy these. If they are to help us to improve our lives in this world here, we should also help to increase their power by doing Yajnas to satisfy their requirements. If we do these with a mind dedicated to their welfare, they also would respond by showering their favours on us.

Although the Devas depend on us, we should not forget that they are superior beings. We should show them proper respect. Other religions directly pay their homage to a single God, offering prayers to Him direct. There is no such method as pleasing diverse divine forces through rituals. In our religion, only *Sanyasins*, i.e. those who have renounced worldly riches and pleasures need not approach the Devas but pray to God directly. Others should please the Devas and seek well-being through their benevolence. In order to please the Devas, oblations, yajnas, etc., have to be done.

To illustrate this by a mundane example : All cannot have direct access to, say, the king of a country. People approach the officials of government for the redress of their various grievances. The officials do not act in their personal capacity but under the direction of the king or Government. People cannot directly approach the king or head of the state even though he is the one who indirectly attends to their needs.

So, many practices in our religion are similarly ordained. Parameswara is the emperor. The citizens are the entire mankind. Varuna, Agni and Vayu, etc. are the officials. We should get our benefits through them.

We perform Yajnas to give more power to the Devas. The oblations we give constitute the food for Devas. Only things that we offer renouncing our right in them reach the Devas. Things consigned to the fire should unequivocally be offered to the Devas. This is why when offering an oblation we say, *"na mama"* - "not for me". The path that the food for Devas takes is through Agni. Similarly, through Agni and Veda mantras we give offerings to the spirits of our departed ancestors.

The significance or the purpose of the Yajnas

In analysing the reason why in our religion alone the rituals exist, let us have a look at the behavioural pattern of sustenance. If a particular region produces a certain commodity in plenty we send it over to another region where it is scarce and obtain from that other region what it could give in return and what we do not have. When craftsmen such as carpenters and masons work for us, we give them wages which are necessary for their livelihood. We feed the cow and it gives us milk in return. We pay taxes to the Government, which provides for our safety and for other amenities. Similarly, we have certain bilateral arrangements with the other worlds.

Engineers can only arrange for the proper flow of rain water through canals and for storage in reservoirs; they cannot make rain. If we are to get rains, we must send some commodities to the *Devaloka.* This mutual exchange agreement is what Gita refers to when it says :

सहयज्ञा प्रजासृष्टा पुरोवाच प्रजापतिंः। अनेनप्रसाविष्यध्वमेष वोऽस्त्विष्टकामधुक्।
देवान् भावयतानेन ते देवा भावयन्तुवः। परस्परं भावयंतः श्रेयस्परमवाप्स्यथ।।

"You please the Devas through Yajnas — let the Devas please you by rains and such other things. Thus, helping each other may you prosper."

Different routes but same destination

Briefly stated, Yajna means offering libation to each Deva through mantras. In a sense, the Saama Veda mantras constitute the form of the Devata. Like the substances offered in sacrifice, the words of these mantras become the food, as it were, for the Devatas and thus increase their power. Mantra, thus, has a manifold purpose. We pay different taxes which go to swell the government's revenue. Nevertheless, there are different places where the different types of taxes have to be paid, viz., income tax, sales tax, land tax, vehicle tax, etc. A different kind of receipt is issued for each by a different authority. Likewise, for each ritual, there is a separate mantra, Devata, sacrificial object, time, etc. Thus, although there is a different procedure for performing each, the ultimate goal is to please the Supreme Being. We know that although paid in different offices, all taxes are credited to the government's revenue. We should regard the various Yajnas done to various Devatas as reaching the Supreme Being, through these Devatas.

7

THE FOUR VEDAS

"Ananthavai Vedhaah" (अनन्तावै वेदा:) – Endless are the Vedas", but the Rishis have been able to capture for us only some mantras out of the vast limitless Vedas. These are sufficient for our happiness here and salvation hereinafter as well as for universal welfare. Although we refer to the Vedas as four in number, there are different versions and differing methods of recitation of these four. These are called *paataantharam* – (पाठान्तरं) or way of recitation.

Each school of recitation or recension is called a "saakha", meaning branch. Each of these is a branch of the Vedic tree. The Veda stands in majesty like a banyan tree with innumerable main and subsidiary branches. Even though it has innumerable branches, they have been classified and grouped as belonging to the main branches viz., the Rig, Yajus, Saama and Atharva which are called Rig Veda, Yajur Veda, etc., because of their importance as a group.

Although modern research assigns to Rig Veda a date earlier than Yajur Veda, according to our Saastras, and our beliefs, they are all without beginning in time. No credence can be placed on the findings of researchers that this (Veda) came first or that came later when we find that, at the beginning of creation, all the four Vedas were available in the universe.

Similarly "researchers" err in deciding the sequence in which the portions of Vedas such as *Samhita, Braahmana,* and *Aaranyaka* are to be placed. Calculations on the time factor in regard to the origin or sequence of the Vedas would become inappropriate, if it is seen that the Vedas were discovered and presented to us by the Rishis when they reached a stage which transcended time and from which they could see the past, present and future.

The extent of the discovery of the Veda mantras may have varied depending upon the period of transcendental state.

Rig Veda itself contains references to Yajus and Saama Veda in many places. *Purusha Sookta,* which appears in the tenth *mandala,* ninetieth hymn of Rig Veda, refers to the other Vedas as well. Does this not show that there can be no question of some Vedas being "earlier or later"?

In each *Saakha,* there are three portions called *Samhita, Braahmana* and *Aaranyaka.* This again is a classification. Generally when we speak of Veda *adhyayana,* we mean the recitation of the *Samhita* portion. This is because the *Samhitas* are the foundation or life breath, as it were, of a *saakha.*

Samhita means that which has been collected and arranged. It brings out the purport of a Veda in the shape of mantras, systematically arranged.

Rig Veda

The whole of the Rig Veda Samhita is in the form of verses. What in the later age came to be called *slokas* (stanzas) was earlier known as 'Rik', or a hymn in praise.

The whole of the Rig Veda Samhita is only in Rig or hymn form extolling different Devatas. Each Rik is a mantra. A number of Riks constitute a *"Sookta"* (सूक्त).

Rig Veda – that is the Samhita portion of it – contains more than ten thousand Riks (10,170 to be precise). The Samhitas of all the four contain 20,500 mantras. Rig Veda, which contains 1028 Sooktas or collection of hymns has been divided into two containing 10 *mandalas* and eight *ashtakas.* It begins with a sookta on Agni and also ends with it. Amongst the Vedas, the Rig Veda is wholly in the form of hymns in praise of Devatas. Since in the beginning *(Upakrama)* and end *(Upasamhaara)* it talks of Agni, some think that the purport of the Veda is fire-worship. It would be more correct if Agni is taken to mean the light of the soul's.

consciousness *(Aatma chaitanyam)* – the glow of the soul's awakening.

Although the last Sookta of the Rig Veda pertains to Agni, it contains verses of universal appeal : "Let all men meet and think as with one mind. Let all hearts unite in love. Let the goal be common. May all live in happiness with a common purpose," so ends the Rig Veda.

The pride of Rig Veda is that it contains hymns in praise of all Devatas. Wise men honour it, for it describes the ways of social living better than others. For example, the marriage rites have been created on the pattern of the marriage of Soorya's daughter, which it details. Dramatic situations like the dialogue between Purooravas and Urvasi also find a place in Rig Veda. In later years poets like Kalidasa have expatiated on these.

Discerning men (cognoscente) extol the portions in Rig Veda like those dealing with Ushas, the goddess of dawn, as masterpieces of poetic composition. There must be some reason indeed why Rig Veda has been assigned the first place amongst Vedas. The action which Yajur Veda predicates and the musical recitation which Saama Veda dictates emerge from the basic Riks in Rig Veda.

Yajur Veda

The word "yajus" is derived from the root "yaj", which means worship. The word yajna (sacrificial worship) is also derived from it.

Just as the word 'Rig' itself means a hymn in praise, so also the word 'Yajus' connotes spelling out the ritualistic procedure of the yajna. True to its name, the chief purpose of Yajur Veda is to give the mantras in Rig Veda appearing in the form of hymns a practical shape in the form of Yajna or worship. Yajur Veda also refers to many mantras in hymn form from the Rig Veda. In addition, it describes in prose the procedural details for the performance of different yajnas. Rig Veda helps in chanting the praise by hymn. Yajur Veda helps in the actual performance of yajnas using these hymns and mantras.

In addition to having many branches (saakhas), as in the other Vedas, Yajur Veda has two main branches with numerous recensions in each branch.

The main branches are called Sukla Yajur Veda and Krishna Yajur Veda. Sukla (शुक्ल) means white and Krishna (कृष्ण) black. The Sukla Yajur Veda Samhita is also known as *Vaajasaneyi Samhita. Vaajasani* is the Sun. As Rishi Yaajnavalkya is believed to have brought this Samhita to the knowledge of the world after learning it from the Sun God, it is called *Vaajasaneyi Samhita.*

There is an interesting story as to how Yaajnavalkya learnt the Vaajasaneyi Samhita from the sun. When the Vedas were classified by Veda Vyasa into four, Yajur Veda had only one version or branch. This was entrusted by Sage Vyasa to Sage Vaisampaayana for preservation and propagation through disciples. Yaajnavalkya learnt this from Vaisampaayana. Due to a misunderstanding between them, viz., Vaisampaayana and Yaajnavalkya, the teacher asked the pupil to return what he had taught him. Yaajnavalkya saw the justice of this demand and complied accordingly. He then prayed to the God Soorya (Sun) to accept him as a pupil. Soorya taught him the Yajur Veda in a different version.

Thus, it gained the name of *Vaajasaneyi* or Sukla Yajur Veda. Since this was called Sukla (or white), the earlier one taught by Vaisampaayana came to be called the Krishna Yajur Veda.

Krishna Yajur Veda is not wholly divided into Samhita and Braahmana portions. The Braahmana portions are at times conjoined with the Samhita mantras in their respective places.

The glory of Yajur Veda lies in its good presentations of Vedic Karma or rituals. Yajnas like *Darsa Poornamasa* (दर्शपूर्णमास), *Somayaga, Vaajapeya, Rajasooya, Asvamedha* and many others are made known to us in all their procedural detail by the *Taittareeya Samhita* in Krishna Yajur Veda. In addition, some mantras which are hymns of praise and which are not contained in Rig Veda are also found in the Yajur Veda. For example, the Sri Rudram, now in vogue, is from the Yajur Veda. Although five Sooktas called "Pancha Rudram", find a place in Rig Veda, today Sri Rudram refers only to that which is contained in Yajur Veda. That is why the great Siva Bhakta, Appayya Dikshita, is stated once to have felt sorry that he was not born in Yajur Veda as he could adequately worship Siva only through Yajur Veda. He was born in a family which traditionally followed the Sama Veda. Today, a vast majority follow the Yajur Veda. While Sukla Yajur Veda is the prevalent school in Northern India, the Krishna Yajur Veda is the prevalent school in South India. The *Purusha Sookta,* which appears in the Rig Veda, also appears with certain changes in Yajur Veda. But if *Purusha Sooktha* is mentioned by name, as such, it generally refers to the version which appears in Yajur Veda.

Yajur Veda is of special significance to Advaitins – those who understand and believe in the "non-dualism" school of philosophy. Any philosophical doctrine *(Siddhaanta),* according to the learned, should contain a *Sootra* or aphorism, *Bhaashya* or commentary and *Vaartika* or an explanatory note. Sootra is to enunciate the doctrine in a condensed or pithy form. Bhaashya is a detailed commentary thereon. Vaartika is a further elaborate elucidation of the Bhaashya. In Advaita Siddaanta, the word *Vaartikakaara* (one who has written the Vaartika) refers only to one person, viz., Sureswaracharya, a disciple of Adi Sankaracharya. To which Bhaashya did he write a Vaartika? If the Upanishads are regarded as Sootras, Adi Sankaracharya wrote Bhaashya thereon. He also wrote a Bhaashya on Brahmasutra, composed by Sage Baadarayana or Veda Vyasa.

The direct disciple of the Acharya, Sureswaracharya, wrote the Vaartika thereon, i.e., on the Upanishad Bhaashya. In doing so, he did not take up all the ten major Upanishads (for commentary); he took up only two. These are the *Taittareeya Upanishad* and the *Brahadaaranyaka Upanishad,* pertaining to the Krishna Yajur Veda and the Sukla Yajurveda respectively. Both the Upanishads are of the Yajur Veda. Thus, Yajur Veda is of great importance to the followers of Advaita philosophy.

Saama Veda

"Saama" means to bring *"shanti"* or peace to the minds. In other words, to make mind find happiness in peace. Of the four methods of tackling an enemy, viz., *saama, daana, bheda* and *danda,* the first is saama or conquering the enemy by love and conciliatory words. Many of the Riks or mantras in Rig Veda are set to music in melodious hymns in Saama Veda. The mantras are the same as in Rig Veda. But, instead of the *udaatta,* (upward swara) *anudhaatta,* (downward swara), etc., for chanting the Rig Veda Mantra, the Saama has set the mantras to music with lengthened notes. *Saama Gaana* can be said to be the basis and source of the seven Swaras or notes fundamental to Indian music systems. Saama Gaana or singing of hymns as per rules of Sama Veda propitiates all Devatas. In Yajnas, in addition to offering libations, there is a priest called *"udgaata"* who chants Saama Veda, in order to ensure the grace of the Gods.

Although basically they are mantras from Rig Veda, they are set to music which is greatly conducive to the spiritual evolution of the self and the grace of the Gods. This is the special virtue of Saama Veda and so, in the Bhagavad Gita, Lord Krishna Bhagavan declares: "Amongst Vedas, I am Saama Veda." In Lalita Sahasranaama, which gives a thousand extolling attributes of Goddess Lalita, the Divine Mother, one of the epithets mentioned is *"Saamagaanapriya"* - meaning one who is pleased by the recital of Saama Veda.

Atharva Veda

Atharva means a purohit. There was a Rishi by that name. The mantras in the Atharva Veda were brought to light by this Rishi, called Atharvan. This Veda contains many types of mantras designed to ward off evil and hardship and to destroy enemies. The Atharva mantras are in prose as well as in verse. In Atharva Veda are found mantras which pertain to Devatas not mentioned in the other Vedas.

Atharva Veda also contains many hymns dealing with creation.

The hymn which extols the wonder of creation called the "Prithvi Sooktam" appears in this Veda.

The pride of this Veda is that Brahma who supervises the conduct of yajnas is representative of Atharva Veda. Amongst the ten major Upanishads, the three viz., *Prasna, Mundaka* and *Maandukya* are part of this Veda.

There is a saying that, for a *Mumukshu* or seeker after truth, *Maandukya Upanishad* alone can ensure Moksha or liberation. The importance of Atharva Veda can be judged from this.

Gaayatri, which is regarded as the greatest of all mantras, is said to be the essence of the three Vedas, viz., Rig, Yajur and Saama. Obviously, Atharva Veda has a separate mantra. Therefore, before undertaking the study of Atharva Veda, it is said that a separate *Upanayanam* or sacred thread ceremony has to be performed and *Brahmopadesa* obtained before a study of Atharva Veda.

The Gaayatri to which boys are initiated during Upanayana is called *Tripaada Gaayatri,* i.e. three legged. It is so called since it has three limbs. Each *Paada* or limb, is the essence of one Veda. Atharva Veda, however, has a Gaayatri of its own. Hence the necessity to get initiated into Atharva Gaayatri and then learn Atharva Veda. On the other hand, a person belonging to one of the other three Vedas and who wishes to learn the other two among the three need not get a second Upanayana performed for himself. That is because there is a common Gaayatri for all the three Vedas, Rig, Yajus and Sama.

There are very few persons who are learned in the *sakhaa* of Atharva Veda in Northern India where it was once prevalent. In South India, there are no pure Atharva Vedins at all. Thus, the position of the recitation of the *Sakhaas* of this Veda at present is indeed pitiable. There are eighteen subsects amongst Brahmins in Orissa. One of them is called *"Atharvanika"*, which means those belonging to Atharva Veda. Even today Atharva Vedins can be found although in small numbers in Gujarat, Saurashtra and Nepal.

Although the four Vedas may appear different, in certain observances or precepts, in the mode of recitation, etc., all of them have a common goal, viz., to ensure the well-being of the universe and to help every one towards spiritual progress.

A distinguishing feature of the Vedas, is that no Veda says "this is the only way", "this is the only God." All of them say that any good path followed with faith and loyalty and any Devata worshipped in whatever way, will lead one to the true goal. Further, there is no other book of religion in this world which advocates the pursuit of diverse paths. Every religion says that its doctrine alone will lead to heaven. The Vedas alone have such a breadth of vision as to say that the same truth can be realised in many ways by those pursuing diverse routes. This is the greatness of the Vedas.

Braahmana and Aaranyaka

So far, we have been referring mostly to the Samhita portion of the Vedà, when we were talking about the Vedas. The main text of a Veda is its Samhita portion. In addition, each Veda has a part called *Braahmana* and another called *Aaranyaka.* The portion called Braahmana, lists what the Vedic Karmas are (rituals to be performed) and explains how they should be performed. When the mantras contained in a Veda Samhita are converted into action, called yajna, the Braahmanas serve the purpose of a guidebook or handy manual explaining how each word should be understood, or what construction should be placed on each word used, in other words the proper use of the mantra.

'Aaranyaka' (आरण्यक) is derived from the word *'Aranya'* (अरण्य) meaning "forest". However, neither the Samhita nor the Braahmana advocates that a person should leave the town or village and seek the solitude of the forest. Yajna and other rituals are prescribed only for those who live in homes and lead the life of house-holders. But it has to be understood that Vedic rituals are intended to confer not only material benefits but also mental purity by constant discipline. Having obtained mental purity *(Chiththa Shuddhi)*, one must seek the solitude of forests for further concentration and meditation. Chanting of Vedas,

performance of yajnas and rules of discipline are all meant as preliminaries for the ultimate meditation on the true nature of the self and true nature of reality.

The Aaranyaka portions of the Vedas are meant to explain the inner meaning, the doctrine or philosophy contained in the Samhitas as mantras and in the Braahmanas as Karmas. Aaranyakas enlighten us about the obscure and distant imagery which the Vedas contain. According to Aaranyakas, it is important to understand the reasons why yajnas are required to be done and not merely their actual performance. Modern research is of the view that Aaranyakas are the result of the meditation of sages who sought the solitude of the forests. The Brihadhaaranyaka Upanishad, which is a combination of Aaranyaka and Upanishad, begins with an explanation of the Aswamedha Yajna on such a note of analytical philosophy.

8
UPANISHADS

Upanishads come towards the end of the Aaranyakas. If the Samhita is likened to a tree, the Braahmanas are its flowers and the Aaranyakas are its fruit, in an unripened state, the Upanishads are the ripe fruits. The direct method of realising through the path of knowledge *(jnaana maarga)* the nonduality *(Abhedha)* of the Supreme Being and the soul are explained in the Upanishads. Although Upanishads contain reference to various disciplines of learning (Vidyas), Yajnas and worship of devatas, etc. essentlally, their main theme is a philosophical enquiry and dealing with that state of the mind with all shackles destroyed.

On this basis, the Vedas are generally considered to have two portions, viz., *Karma Kaanda* (portion dealing with action or rituals) and *Jnaana Kaanda* (portion dealing with knowledge). These are also referred to as *Poorva Mimaamsa* and *Uttara Mimaamsa*.

After analysing the Karma Kaanda, Maharshi Jaimini expressed the view that it was the end-product or fruit of Vedic philosophy. His treatise is called *Poorva Mimaamsa.* Similar analysis of the Jnana Kaanda by Sage Veda Vyasa led to the conclusion that it was the quintessence of the Vedas and these he stated in the form of aphorisms - *Brahma Sutra.* Compared to the Karma Kaanda, the Upanishad portion of Jnana Kaanda is very small in extent and is in a condensed form. Whereas Jaimini's Poorva Mimasa Sutras contain 1000 sections, the Brahma Sutra has only 192 sections. Just as a tree has a profusion of leaves but only a relatively small number of flowers and fruits, so also the tree of Veda has many leaves in the form of Karma Kaanda and the Upanishad portions are much fewer like the fruits of a tree. Foreign scholars and philosophers in their intellectual approaches have not delved deep enough to touch the fringe of *Satyam* or Transcendental Truth. Experimental verification of the conclusion which is reached by the intellect is necessary. The special characteristic of the Upanishads, which other philosophical systems do not share, is that they contain mantras which translate philosophical thought through the aid of vibrations of the mantras into actual experience.

Unlike other philosophies, which are in the nature of intellectual research, the Karma Kaanda of the Vedas prescribe a way of life which would make it possible for the realisation of its philosophy. If one lived according to its dictates, it would lead to purity of thought, when one could withdraw from worldly activities. If, at this stage, one studied the Upanishads assiduously, it would not be merely a mental exercise but a way of life, a part of one's experience of life, as it were.

It is at this summit of philosophical experience that the non-duality of the Soul and Supreme Being (Jiva and Brahma), becomes clearer. It is to reach this stage that a person, who has conditioned his mind by the performance of Karma, has to leave all activities and become a Sanyaasi. At this stage, one gets initiated into what are called, *Mahaavaakyas.* Each of the Vedas has many Mahavaakyas or great sayings. But four – one from each Veda – are very important, thought-provoking and powerful. These spell out the non-duality of Jiva and Brahma. If these are chanted and one meditates deeply, the non-duality will be actually experienced. These four Mahavakyas are contained in four Upanishads. Although there exist numerous rituals or karmas, varieties of worship and ways of life as propounded in the Samhita and Braahmana portions, when it comes to reaching the end of the journey and realising the ultimate objective, the Upanishads alone are of help.

There is a Mahaavaakya (great saying) in *Aitareya Upanishad* of the Rig Veda which says that exalted actual experience alone is Brahman. *"Prajnanam Brahma"* (प्रज्ञानं ब्रह्म.) (अहं ब्रह्मास्मि) "I am Brahman", is another Mahaavaakya from the Brihadhaaranyaka Upanishad of Sukla Yajur Veda. The fourth chapter of the Taittareeya Upanishad contains a slightly different Mahaavaakya – (अहमस्मि ब्रह्माहमस्मि) *"Ahamasmi Brahmahamasmi".* There is a

Mahaavaakya in Chaandogya Upanishad of the Sama Veda in the form of a Guru teaching his disciple to the effect that "that thou art". (तत्वमसि). The Atma (soul) is Brahma, (अयमात्मा ब्रह्म) *Aayamaatma Brahma* is the Mahaavaakya from Maandukya Upanishad of Atharva Veda.

Adi Sankaraacharya's terse and pithy advice to spiritual aspirants is contained in *"Sopaana Panchaka"*, a string of five verses which outlines the steps to be taken on the ladder of spiritual ascent. He starts by saying, "Study and recite the Vedas; perform the various rituals/acts prescribed therein," and concludes: "Be guided by the Mahaavaakyas, meditate on them constantly and reach the state of Brahman." Thus, it will be seen that the Uoanishads contain the ultimate message and purpose of the Vedas. They are, therefore, known as "Vedanta", the word *Anta* meaning "end". Upanishads are the end of the Vedas in two senses. When each (Veda) Saakha is taken, first comes the Samhita, then the Braahmana and then the Aaranyaka, at whose concluding portion comes the Upanishad. The second sense in which it is understood is this : The ultimate goal or aim of the Vedas is contained in the Upanishads. Thus, the Upanishads are the "end" of the Vedas both in the sense of textual presentation and realisation of the end-product.

A temple in a town, a Gopura for the temple, the summit of the Gopura are all in an ascending order of height. Likewise, the Upanishads are the summit and end of Vedas.

"Upa - ni - shada" means "to sit by the side". What was taught by making the disciple sit by the side of the teacher is the Upanishads. It can also be taken to mean "that which makes you reach the side of or near "Brahmam". Just as *Upanayana* (the sacred thread ceremony) can be taken to mean both ways, viz., "leading to the Guru" or "leading to the Paramaatma", the Upanishads also permit a dual interpretation. Instructing by keeping close to the disciple implies that the thing taught is in the nature of a secret personal advice. It is not for those who are not mentally conditioned to absorb the teaching. That is why the Upanishads, when propounding subtle truths, says pointedly :

"This is Upanishad. This is Upanishad." That which is latent in the Vedas is called *Rahasya* or secret. The Upanishads are such confidential personalised instructions to those fit to receive them.

9

BRAHMA SUTRA

I said earlier that every philosophical doctrine contains three adjuncts, viz., *Sutra, Bhaashya and Vaartika*. The various doctrines propounded by Sankara, Ramanuja, Madhva, Srikanta (Saiva Siddhaanta Acharya) and others in our country are called by the generic name of *Vedanta mata* (वेदान्तमत) or - Vedaantic religion. Each of these Acharyas adduces arguments to prove that only the doctrine he propounds alone is enunciated in the Upanishads. Bhaashyas or commentaries on the ten principal Upanishads have been written by them. Therefore, for the Vedaantic religion, the Upanishads play the role of Sutras.

It is only so in a manner of speaking. In actual fact, the Upanishads are not and are not like Sutras (Aphorisms).

How should a Sutra be? Sutras are aphorisms with minimal use of words to project a thought. That is why, according to this definition, Upanishads cannot be called Sutras. However, there exists in the form of aphorisms a basic text containing all that the Upanishads propound.

These are the Brahma Sutras composed by Sage Baadaraayana, also known as Sage Veda Vyasa. Baadaraayana was so called as he lived for some time under a Badari tree. There are several commentaries on the Brahma Sutras depending upon the school of philosophy followed by the commentator. What is *Jiva?* (Soul)? What is *Jagat* (Universe) in which it lives? What is the basic material *(Tatvam)* that is the root cause of all this? These are the three important matters which are dealt with in Brahma Sutras which is the book of reference in all matters pertaining to Vedantic doctrines.

But even this does not purport to give Vyasa's own interpretation. He wrote it on the basis of the knowledge of the Upanishads already existing. Since the Upanishads form the latter part of the

Vedas, they are called *Uttara Mimaamsa* and the Brahma Sutras also, therefore, form part of Uttara Mimaamsa.

There are about 500-odd (555) Sutras in the book which is divided into four chapters. Each chapter has four parts. Altogether, there are 192 adhikaranas or sections.

Since the Brahma Sutra deals conclusively with the goal of Sanyaasis, it is called *Bikshu Sutra* also. *(Bikshu* = an ascetic mendicant). Since it is an enquiry into the *Atma* (Soul) within the *Sareera* (body), it is also called (शारिरक मीमांस) *Sareerika Mimaamsa.*

The word Sutra means also a string. The *Mangala Sutra* (auspicious thread which a married lady wears on her neck) derives its name from the string used in it. Keeping the imagery in view, Adi Sankara, in his Bhaashya, says in some place :

"Vedaanta Vaakya Kusumagrathanatwaat"
(वेदान्त वाक्य कुसुमग्रथनत्वात्)

How can one wear the garland of loose Vedanthic flowers which the Vedic tree has shed, unless they are strung into a garland? Therefore, the Brahma Sutra is the string which holds them together, so says the Acharya. If today Brahma Sutra is the authority for all the traditions and doctrines attributed to what is known as the Hindu religion, then the authority behind the Brahma Sutra is the Upanishads.

That is why all denominations of Vedic religion have come to be called *Oupanishadic* religion, meaning religion of the Upanishad.

Since the Upanishads are the most important part of the Vedas they are also called *"Sruti Siras"* or the head of Vedas, since the head is the most important part of a body.

10

DO VEDA AND VEDANTA CLASH?

What is recommended for performance in the Karma Kaanda or ritualistic portion of the Vedas, is sought to be given up by the Upanishads which form the Jnana Kaanda. In the Karma Kaanda, the Veda ordains men to worship the Devatas or deities and also lays down procedural details for such worship. On the other hand, in the Upanishads, the same Veda denigrates the performer of sacrifices as a cow — as a witless person.

What appears at the beginning of the Veda is negated by it at the end. This appears strange indeed.

One side is all action, the other all *Jnana* (knowledge-wisdom) and totally different. So much so, in common usage, the term 'Vedas' have come to mean the *Karma Kaanda* and 'Vedanta' or the Upanishad as the *Jnana Kaanda*

Lord Krishna has preached only Vedanta in the Bhagavad Gita. It is commonly said that Gautama Buddha and Mahavira were the pioneers in condemning the Karma Kaanda of the Vedas. This is not true. Lord Krishna had already done so, long before these two. He says to Arjuna "Veda pertains to the three gunas, *Satva-Rajas-Tamas.* You must reach a stage which transcends the three gunas."

त्रैगुण्य विषयावेदा निस्त्रैगुण्यो भवार्जुन।

He says further, "Those who follow the words in the Veda in a limited and literal sense are motivated by the desire (Kaama) to dwell in Swarga (Heaven) which offers enjoyments. (II-44)" They (Vedic Karmas) will not lead to a steadfast state of mind which transcendental meditation *(Samadhi)* creates.

वेदवादरताः पार्थ नान्यदस्तीतिवादिन। II-42
कामात्मनः स्वर्गपरा जन्मकर्मफलप्रदाम्। II-43
व्यवसायात्मिका बुद्धिः समाधौ न विधीयते। II-44

Some may say that there is a contradiction here. Earlier, we have seen that the Vedas are at the root of all Dharma (righteous action). If carefully examined, it will be found that there is no real contradiction here. At the level at which we lead the normal worldly life, it will not be possible for us to comply with and put in practice the philosophy ot the Upanishads, i.e. in order to understand the state of absolutism of the Atma, one has to break the shackles imposed by the three gunas and meditate on the self with unwavering concentration. The karmas prescribed in the Vedas are designed to lead us by stages to that state. So long as we think that the world is 'Real', we have to worship the Devatas so that we may live well and in comfort. Since we think the world is real, we also bring well-being to it. We also think that the Devaloka or the world of Devatas is also real like this world and, by pleasing the Devatas, we get many benefits in return. As in this world, we also hope to enjoy life in Devaloka. But, if we stop here, it would mean that we have become oblivious to the main goal. The truth is that our aim is to become one with God for ever and ever. It would be folly to forget this and rest content with other material rewards which the performance of Vedic Karmas may bring.

At the level of worldly existence, we cannot honestly accept that the world is 'unreal'. The Vedas say, 'it is all right if you think so', and has accordingly given karmas which when performed will bring about Universal welfare. They have given us various Devatas for worship because, in our present state of mind, we cannot conceive of Paramaatma in a formless state or have the realisation of non-duality. *(Abedha).* But, whilst performing the karmas and worshipping the Devatas, we must clearly understand that the Vedas have prescribed these so that wc can get purity and clarity of mind and singleness of purpose to reach a stage at which the world as we know ceases to be real and all action will cease and the feeling that 'we' exist separately from the Paramaatma will vanish and we merge and feel one with Him.

It will be in the nature of a mundane business if we performed Yajnas as payment made in return for well-being granted by the Devatas. Even in Devaloka (in the world of the gods) there is no bliss equal to what the realised Atman experiences.

Furthermore, stay in Devaloka will come to an end as soon as the accumulated *'punya'* or credit for good deeds is exhausted and then one has to revert to the cycle of births and deaths and be born again according to the requirement of the Karma. Though, in order to make allowances for the present state of development of the Atma and to gradually prepare it for higher efforts, karmas and worship have been prescribed by the Vedas, it behoves us to look beyond and make efforts to progress further.

While it is not proper if one does not follow the injunctions of the Vedas regarding karma and worship *(karmanushtaanam)*, to say that one should never give them up is also wrong. There is now-a-days a tendency to bypass the karmas such as Yajnas or study of the Vedas in the traditional way (adhyayana) but to go straight to the study of the Upanishads. As a result, many people are becoming familiar with the contents of the Upanishads and are even able to discuss them at length at an intellectual level. However, this has not produced anyone who has peace of mind, is free from passions, or has in practice realised the Truth about the Self or Atman. Why is this so? The reason is that the preliminary preparation in the shape of complying with the Vedic injunctions regarding Yajnas and worship has been ignored and the mind and body have not been disciplined. Hence, to omit to study the Vedas and perform the Karmas and straightaway try to imbibe the truth in the Upanishads is as wrong as performing only the rituals, taking their meaning literally and not proceeding further to understand what the Upanishads say.

During the days when Lord Krishna lived and taught, a large majority were only at the stage of performing Vedic Karma. It is they whom He chastised. What may appear as His censure of the Vedas was, in reality, directed at those who did not fully comprehend the purport of the Vedas but stopped at the level of karma. It is, therefore, incorrect to say that He condemned the practice of karma. His incarnations were only to save and preserve the Vedas and those who adhered to the path of the Vedas. Lord Krishna took to task only those who followed the Karma path and stopped there. This was appropriate for His times. If He were to preach Bhagavad Gita now, He would surely rebuke those who ignore Vedic Karmas and study of the Vedas and try to go direct to the Upanishads. In fact, He may even use a stronger language than He did earlier, because the modern practice leads to a bigger mistake than the earlier one.

All this I have said to show that there is no conflict between Veda and Vedanta. Veda (Karma Kaanda) exists for the sole purpose of preparing one for Vedanta. If the Vedic injunctions are complied with and there is a clear awareness that it is a preparation for reaching the stage of transcending the three gunas at which the world is left behind and worship as also the object of worship do not appear separately, then one is automatically led to the Jnaana Kaanda and the path of knowledge. However another problem arises. If we were to become enlightened beings *(jnani)* by forsaking the world as illusory, the question arises as to who will look after the welfare of the world. Although the world may seem illusory to the enlightened it definitely appears real to common people like us. Since the welfare of the world is of importance to us, if the enlightened ones do not perform yajnas, how can they bring prosperity to the world? The answer is that, if we consider the exalted state which an enlightened one has reached, it is not necessary for him to do yajnas and other rituals to bring about welfare and prosperity. Whether he considers the world as totally non-existing or he considers it as the "sport" *(Leela)* of God, the grace of God always exudes through him. Why do crowds gather round the *jnaani?* Even if he runs away from the multitude, why do people fall at his (jnaani's) feet? To seek his blessings and grace, because, through him, flows the grace of God and, in his presence, people get solace.

The enlightened person, who has realised the great truth that he is one with Divinity is able to do more good than even the minor gods to propitiate whom various rituals are performed. Because he does not perform Yajnas, it cannot be said that he does not contribute to the welfare of the world.

Some people, especially those belonging to other religions, see a dichotomy between the Vedantic thought and the Vedic karmas and say that "the Hindus consider that individual salvation is more important and give no thought to the world at large or the commonweal and their meditation *(Yoga)* and *Samaadhi* (transcendental stage) are all centred around individual salvation." It is also said that, unlike Christianity, Islam and Buddhism, Hinduism does not develop social consciousness by preaching love, brotherhood, etc., directly. However, properly understood, it is not correct to separate Hindu religion into Vedic and Vedantic. The same person who in the earlier part of his life has contributed to the good of society by studying Vedas and performing Yajnas, becomes a seeker after truth by Vedantic enquiry and attains self-realisation later on. By the process of systematic purification through Veda Karmas, he attains a state where he can seek and tread the path of Vedanta which leads to 'Mukti'. Even after immersing himself in Vedanta and becoming a *jnaani,* he is able to contribute to worldly welfare without performing Vedic Karmas, by his very enlightened presence. If a man belonging to any religion does not become enlightened and reach the summit by practising its injunctions, then there is no use of that religion. Karmas and worship are means to reach that state of enlightenment. The many different disciplines laid down for persons born with different background and states of mind *(Varnaashrama)* and injunctions as to who could perform specified karmas, are all designed to lead to a state of mental exaltation, where finally no difference will be felt.

Therefore, first comes karma, that is, the performance of actions as Veda directs. But this should be done with the full realisation that this is only for reaching the stage where karmas disappear and self-experience or realisation *(Atmanubhooti)* manifests. Similarly, Devata worship is certainly necessary in the beginning to get material benefits. But it should be understood that this is only the first step towards the realisation that the Devata that is worshipped and the worshipper are not essentially different. In the beginning, the differences must be observed. If mundane business has to be done satisfactorily, we have to divide the work involved into various categories. Each one should adopt these methods and perform such duties as would help the furtherance of the various categories of work for realising the final objective. While doing the Karmas it should be kept in mind that the study of Vedas and performance of Vedic karmas lead to the great experience where there is no need for Vedas. There can be no fruit without flowers. The flowers may look very beautiful. But unless the flower disappears by development, we cannot have the fruit. Persons who go straight to Vedanta without performing any Vedic Karmas, do not take the natural course. Similarly, those who stop at karmas without aspiring for Vedantic wisdom are equally not doing the right thing as they do not reach for development. There should be a sense of perspective here.

When the Vedas are referred to as 'Sruti', the term refers not only to Samhitas but also to Braahmanas and Aaranyakas. The Bhagavad Gita is not 'Sruti' and is not part of the Vedas. It is regarded as belonging to the category of Smrti. The Smrti, which is Gita, says that the Vedic karmas and worship are of no use, unless they lead ultimately to jnaana or enlightenment. The Puraanas also which are next in importance to the Srutis at some places say that stopping at the stage of Vedic Karma is short-sightedness. The Saivite Puraanas describe how the Rishis in the Daaruka forest thought that the path of Karma was the ultimate goal to be reached and were taking pride in the performance of yajnas and how Lord Siva destroyed their pride. The Srimad Bhagavata also narrates a similar incident pertaining to the learned brahmins and their wives. It says that, though not well-versed, the wives realised that Lord Mahavishnu Himself had come before them as Balakrishna — the child Krishna. Their husbands who were steeped in Karma did not have that realisation and regretted it later.

It may be argued that Sruti contains both Karma and Jnaana Kaandas and since it is mostly the Upanishads which form part of the Jnaana Kaanda which extol the path of jnaana. They naturally deprecate karma. But the Karma Kaanda itself condemns the the view that Karma is all-important and it is the goal. A telling example is given in the *Taittareeya Kaataka Prasna* thus: "One who merely performs Yajnas without feeling the presence of God, is merely feeding the fire with firewood and raises only smoke. He is a fool. He will never realise the self." (Taittareeya Kaatakam — 1st Prasna — last Anuvakam — 4th mantra). If the fire is kindled, then the cooking pot should be placed on it for cooking rice. The person who merely performs Yajnas lights the fire in the oven but does not keep the cooking pot on it. (The word used here is *"pakvam"* — in Sanskrit - which means cooking well. The reference is to the hard grain of rice getting cooked in fire to become soft and edible.)

If the results of Vedic karmas are surrendered to God *(Iswaraarpanam)*, it will begin to untie the knot (of worldly bondage), instead of binding us to the world.

If Karmas are performed without expectation of results *(Nishkaamya)* and solely for the glorification of God, it gives mental purity and leads to a place beyond the reach of the three gunas.

The term "Yajna" signifies this alone. In English, it is called 'Sacrifice'. "Yaaga" means "Tyaaga", giving up — renouncing. The offering of oblation in fire saying "Na mama" (नमम) "not for me" — which shows the spirit of Selflessnes is the essence of the Yajna. What is thrown in the fire cannot be reclaimed. Within a second, its form has changed. Likewise the feeling of 'I' and 'Mine' should be reduced to ashes. When the performance of Yajna is meant to give lofty results, it is pathetic that transient and trivial gains are set as the goal by many.

Thus it would be seen that there is no contradiction between the Karma Kaanda and Jnaana Kaanda. Karma Kaanda itself accepts its limitations and holds Jnaana Kaanda high. They are complementary. "Purusha Sooktam" and "Tryambaka Mantra" which propound lofty truths, and are wisdom-oriented, appear only in the Samhita portion of the Veda and not in the Upanishad portion. Similarly Upanishads also describe some Karmas like "Nachiketaagni". Many of the mantras used in the performance of Vedic karmas are found in the Taittareeya Upanishad.

The authority for the statement appearing in Bhagavad Gita, which is a Smrti, that, for obtaining wisdom (Jnaana), one has to sacrifice the *karmaphala* to God is to be found in the Upanishads which are part of Sruti. The foremost of the ten Upanishads, "Isaavaasya", proclaims this at the beginning itself.

कुर्वन्नेह कर्माणि जिजीविषेच्छतः समाः एवत्वयिनान्यथेतोऽस्ति नकर्मलिप्यतेनरे (Isa 2)

"Perform the Vedic Karmas for a hundred years but do it with the thought that it is all meant as offering to God (not for personal gain). Then you will not be bound by the results of Karma," says the Upanishad. Therefore, to regard the Upanishad as a gospel of inaction, something at variance with Karma, is erroneous.

Karma should not be regarded as the end. One should not stop at the stage where mental purity and ensuing universal well-being are ensured by worshipping the Devatas. Wisdom should dawn, whereby a stage is reached when the feeling arises that there is no self other than the Paramaatma, and that there is no such thing as the world apart from the supreme self. If this stage is reached, even Vedas will cease to have any significance for the realised soul. What is Veda? It is the law of God. This should be strictly followed by all persons, as citizens follow the law of the land. But, if a person attains wisdom and is wholly submerged in the Highest Truth *(Paramaatma Satyam),* there is no need for him to perform karmas in accordance with these laws.

For a Jnaani who becomes one with the Paramaatma, even the many Devatas who have originated from the Paramaatma do not appear as different or separate. When he merges with the Infinite and becomes part of it, the Devatas also are contained within him. Even at the stage when he was worshipping the Devatas, although he did not experience it, he should have thought that 'the Devata whom I worship is different from me, even this is not separate from the Atma'.

Although, in everyday life, we perform various duties with a sense of differentiation, the feeling should persist that all the differences will shrink and ultimately all will merge in the Basic

Truth. On the other hand, one who worships the Devatas as wholly different from himself, does not understand the reality.

Although more evolved than mankind the devatas also have not realised the state of complete bliss. Their happiness is not even a small fraction of the happiness of a being who is born as man but reaches the stage of a Jnaani. The Taittareeya Upanishad (2.5) and the Brihadaaranyaka Upanishad (2.3.33) have described the bliss of the world of ours, that of Pithru Loka and then that of the Devaloka and, amongst Devatas, the quantum of happiness enjoyed by Indra, then Brahaspathi and then Prajaapati are all expressed as progressively increasing 100 times more at each level, which reads like a multiplication table.* The bliss of the Jnaani comes last and is called *Brahmaananda* - that enjoyed by Brahma.

Therefore, Devatas have their own limitations. Further, they do not strive to attain the Jnaana which makes up all shortages. Their expectations are confined to what humans can offer them through yajnas and other forms of worship. Thus according to many puranic stories they do not favour men who try to become Jnaanis. Brahadhaaranyaka Upanishad says so unequivocally. "The Devas do not like men to realise their self (Aatma)" (1.4.10). What is the reason? If he realises his self, then, he will not perform karmas and yajnas, which bring good to the devas.

If the Jnaanis are those whom the Devatas do not like, it follows that they like those who are not Jnaanis. This means that one who has not attained the state of true knowledge. That is why Vyakarana or Grammar texts have coined the phrase *Devaanaampriyah* - (देवनांप्रिय:) one dear to the Devas - as referring to a fool. This phrase derives its authority from the Upanishad.

Note : The various gradations of bliss as described are:(1) Manushyanaamaananda or the happiness of a healthy young man with reasoning and capacity to enjoy. Next the bliss of a Manushya Gandharva, Devagandharva, Chiralokaloka Pitru, Aajaanaja Deva, Karma Deva, Deva, Indra, Brahaspati, Prajapati and Brahma, each succeeding one a 100 times the bliss of the immediately preceding one. One can then have an idea of the Supreme Bliss as compared to one unit of full human happiness. At each stage the Upanishad says that the bliss can be enjoyed by a jnaani. The Brahmaananda is also attainable by the realised one who has n desires.

Vedanta teaches us how to reach the state of fullness where karmas and worship of Devatas are both abandoned and everything becomes 'self', as it were. It behoves us to see that at least these Upanishads are preserved and studied.

The Rishis could only capture for us a portion of the limitless Vedas and since, in Kaliyuga, the intellectual capacity of men is feeble as compared to those of the earlier Yugas, even these have been divided into 1180 saakhas (branches) - each saakha being meant for specialisation by one group of scholars. With the lapse of time even the study of one Saakha has become difficult of achievement and, to us of this generation, will perhaps go the credit or discredit of bringing Vedic studies to a state of total neglect. Let this rest here.

What I wished to convey was that, in each saakha, there is an Upanishad. But there are Upanishads belonging to the Veda Saakhas where the Samhitas, Braahmanas, etc., of the parent saakha are not being studied. Not only are they not being studied but many of the texts are not even available for study. Nevertheless, their Upanishads have come through the ages unscathed. For example, in Rig Veda, the Samhita portion of what is called the *"Sangaayana saakha"* is not found in use. We have lost it. But the Upanishad coming at the end of this Sakha called *"Kausheetaki"* Upanishad is very much alive. *"Baashkala Mantropanishad"* from Rig Veda itself is available. But nothing is known of the Samhita or Braahmana of the Baashkala Saakha of Rig Veda, to which this Upanishad belongs. *Kathopanishad* belongs to the Katha Saakha of the Krishna Yajur Veda.

I said that the Upanishad is the concluding portion of the Aaranyaka. But although the *Kathopanishad* is quite famous and is one of the ten important Upanishads, its relevant Aaranyaka is not available to us. Though the study of Atharva Veda is barely kept alive in Western India, in the South, Saakhas of Atharva Veda are no longer studied. The three Upanishads, namely, *Prasna, Mundaka* and *Maandukya,* out of the ten important Upanishads in use, belong to the Atharva Veda and fortunately these are still available for study and have not been lost.

In short, although the saakha or that portion of it which is important for performance of karmas has been allowed to languish, the essential philosophy contained in some of the Veda saakha has not been lost sight of. Thus, the Upanishads which are conducive to Jnaana have been especially nurtured and preserved. This is some consolation.

11
THE TEN UPANISHADS

Adi Sankaracharya selected ten of the Upanishads, called Dasopanishads and wrote Bhaashya or commentary on them. He highlighted the non-dualist (Advaita) doctrine propounded in them. Ramanuja and Madhva, who came later, also wrote Bhaashyas on these very ten Upanishads but each of them emphasised their respective doctrines, viz., Visishta-Advaita (qualified non-dualism) and Dvaita (Dualism).

The following sloka enumerates the ten upanishads :

Isa Kena Kathaa Prasna Munda Maandukya Taithari
Aitareyam cha Chaandogyam Brahadhaaranyakam Dasa

ई.ाकेनकथाप्रश्न मुण्ड माण्डूक्य तैत्तिरी।
ऐतरेयंच छान्दोग्यं ब्रह्दारण्यकंदश।।

Adi Sankara has written his commentary also in the above order of texts.

Eesaavaasya Upanishad (ईशावास्य)

Isa or Eesa is Eesaavaasya Upanishad. It appears at the end of Sukla Yajur Veda Samhita. It is so called because it begins with the words 'Eesa Vaasyam'. Isaavaasya begins by saying that Iswara or God pervades the whole world and we should reach the state of realising the 'Paramaatma Tatva', by offering the fruit of all actions to Him alone.

ईशावास्यमिदंसर्वं यत्किंच जगत्यां जगत्। तेनत्यक्तेन भुंजीथा मागृधःकस्य स्विध्दनम्।।

Kenopanishad

'Kena' is Kenopanishad. It is also called Talavakaara Upanishad because it appears in the Talavakaara Braahmana of the Jaimini

Saakha of Saama Veda. There is a saying "search for what is lost in Kena." This Upanishad describes how Ambika Herself, the Divine Mother, imparted divine wisdom to Indra, the king of the Devas when the Devatas in their pride could not find the Paramaatma who is without a beginning or end, although they searched high and low. The *Paraa Sakti* (Ambika) discloses that all our powers are derived from the *Mahaasakti* or Supreme Power. Adi Sankara, instead of being content with giving word by word interpretation of this Upanishad, as in the case of some of the other Upanishads, has written a separate Bhaasya, sentence by sentence. In other words, this Upanishad has the distinction of earning two Bhaasyas from Adi Sankara. Keeping this Upanishad mainly in view, Adi Sankara says, in the devotional composition on the Divine Mother, the "Soundarya Lahari" : "Please keep your feet also on my head, the sacred feet which you have kept on the head of Mother Veda." Like Vedanta, the Upanishads are also known as *Veda Siras* or *Sruti Siras*, i.e., head of the Vedas or head of the Sruti. The Upanishads alone are the concluding portion or end of the Vedas and, at the same time, are the most important (like the head) of all the parts. To say that the feet of the Divine Mother rest on the head of Veda Maata or Mother Veda is tantamount to saying that they rest on the Upanishads.

It is only in the Kenopanishad that the Divine Mother appears in the form of Mother Wisdom. Fittingly with the name of *Saama Gaana Priya*, which is one of her attributes mentioned in 'Lalita Sahasranaama", Her glory is especially manifest in this Upanishad from Saama Veda.

If we say, we see an object, duality is established - the object which is seen and the subject who sees it. We are able to perceive our body as an object (objectively). It becomes an object when we say 'my body is well or ill'. It follows that something calling itself "we" keeping itself as a separate entity as subject, sees an object. This (subject) which sees is the "Aatma". This "subject" cannot at all be understood or perceived. If it is, then that becomes the real "subject" instead. The real Aatma "we" can never become the object but can only remain as the 'subject'. Therefore, leaving aside objects such as body and such like this subject called 'we' can only exist separately by itself but cannot be made to know it. To know is to posit a separate object. In the case of Aatma this phenomenon is absurd and cannot be established.

If we are to know it, the knower should be different from the Aatma. What can there be in us that is different from the real self? What is there different from Aatma which can know? Nothing. Therefore, in the expressions 'knowledge of self', 'knowing the self', the act of knowing does not conform to the normal rule of one subject seeing an object. The act of "experiencing the self by the self" is referred to as knowing and knowledge. That is why the Kenopanishad says : "one who says he knows the Aatma, knows it not; one who stays at the level of not knowing it, knows it; one who sees it, sees it not; one who cannot see it, can see it."

Kathopanishad

The Upanishad 'Katha' (कठ) or Kathopanishad (कठोपनिषद) or Kathakopanishad (कथकोपनिषद) appears in the Kathaka Saakha of the Krishna Yajur Veda. It contains the dialogue between the God of Death (Yama) and Nachiketas, a brahmachari boy dealing with the question of what happens to the soul after death. Although it begins like a story, it expounds a great truth. In the Bhagavad Gita, Lord Krishna repeats the very words of this particular Upanishad. For e.g. :

नजायतेम्रियतेवाकदाचिन्नायं भूत्वा भविता वा न भूयः।
अजोनित्यः शाश्वतोऽयंपुराणो नहन्यते हन्यमाने शरिरे।। K-II-18

The grains of corn are stripped clean off the stalk in a sheaf. The thin skin is peeled off the coconut leaf to expose the single broom stick. Similarly, from the object which is the body, the Aatma which is the subject should be stripped smoothly but firmly and the Aatma should exist by itself. Passion, anger, hate, fear, these belong to the mind and do not belong to the Aatma. Hunger, thirst and such other wants pertain to the body and not to the Aatma. We should, thus, learn to practise to identify all objects and substances which are other than the Aatma. If we constantly practise this way of thinking, the deep-rooted feeling that 'we' comprise only the body and mind will start fading and will eventually ly vanish. We can be the pure Aatma without getting involved with the many impurities which assail the body and mind. We should regard our body clothed in flesh as a sheath situated close to the Aatma. We should train the mind to view the body as an external object.

When we live in this world and when we feel here and now that we exist in the body, we should start the practice of regarding the body as "not I" - "not mine". Then, it would not be necessary to think in terms of getting liberation after death. Moksha means liberation from all attachment. A liberated soul *(Jeevanmukta)* is thus one who in this world itself has lost the awareness of the body and finds happiness within himself subjectively (आत्माराम) without recourse to outside objects of enjoyment. The supreme purpose of the Vedas and Vedanta is to thus make a man into a liberated soul. Lord Krishna says this very thing in the Bhagavad Gita: "Before the life departs from the body *(Praak Sareera Vimokshanat)*, when living in this world itself, *("ihaiva")*, one who controls the forces of passion and anger and becomes steadfast in a state of Yoga (Unison with the Paramaatma) enjoys eternal bliss." That is, whilst living in this world itself, if a person realises the true nature of the Aatma, and has such an experience, it wound not matter even if the body perished, because he had regarded it as not himself or his even when alive. Thus, even before death claimed the body he had given up the body. The term body includes the mind as well. If it is not ours, then death does not matter, as it will not affect us.

Because he gets free from mortality *(mrithyu)* he becomes immortal *(amara)*. The act of remaining in this state is referred to in various mantras such as the Purusha Sookta, which appear in the Karma Kaanda. In the Upanishads, this theme is repeated again and again.

What causes misery to us is the body and through it the mind. The absence of misery and being always blissful is what is called 'Heaven' - Moksha - in all religions. All faiths, other than the Advaita doctrine, say that, to enjoy eternal bliss, one has to go to another world. Adi Sankara has proved that whilst living in this world itself by totally giving up bodily attachment and getting deeply rooted in Aatma, one can enjoy greater bliss than what is available in the other worlds. In Brahma Sootra Bhaashya (1.1.4) he says : "Tadetat asareeritvam mokshaakhyam" (तदेतत् अशरीरत्वं मोक्षाख्यं). What we commonly understand by Asareeri, is the voice from the skies (without a body). The word 'Asareeri' only means being without a body. The loss of awareness that 'I am the body' is Asareeratvam - the state of being without a body. The Acharya has defined Moksha thus : If desires are gradually reduced, and eventually made extinct, attachment to the body will totally disappear. The soul within will then shine forth. There is no need to go to other worlds for this. This is what the Vedas and Vedanta refer to as "Ihaiva-Ihaiva" - here itself.

The smriti that is Bhagavad Gita says that the two main enemies who stand in the way of our reaching this blissful state are desire and passion anger. The authority for this is in Chaandogya Upanishad which is a Sruti.

मधवन्मर्त्यं वाइदगुं शरीरमात्रं मृत्युना तदस्यामृतस्या शरीरस्यात्मनोऽधिष्ठानमात्तो वै सशरीरः प्रियाप्रियाभ्यां नवै सशरीरस्य सतः प्रियाप्रियथोरपहतिरस्यशरीरंवाव सन्तं नप्रियाप्रिये स्पृशतः (Chaandogyopanishad-Bhashya — 8-12-1)

The expressions are Priya and Apriya, meaning like and dislike. 'Like' is desire; dislike is passion. "Likes and dislikes do not touch a person without a body", says Chaandhogya. In other words, it says that, if you wish to get free from likes and dislikes, you should regard the body as not the "self".

It is customary to classify the feelings of the Jeevaatma (soul) arising from the sense of 'I' and 'mine' into three ways : *Gaunaatma, mithyaatma, mukhyaatma.* The elders have put it in the form of a sloka which Adi Sankara has quoted as an example in his Brahma Sootra Bhaashya :

गौणमिथ्यात्मनोऽसत्वेपुत्रदेहादिबाधनात्।
सद्ब्रह्मात्माहमित्येवबोधेकार्यं कथं भवेत्॥

Gaunamithyaatmano asatve putradehaadi baadhanaat
Sat brahmatmaham ityeva bodhe kaaryam katham bhavet

Brahma Sootra Bhaashya (1.1.4)

"We, our children and close friends are the same as ourselves; their joys and sorrows are ours too." This attachment is the characteristic of "Gaunaatma". Gauna means an attribute. Although it is known that we and the children and friends are all different from one another, the feeling of being one with them is strong. The attachment to the body which is closer and stronger than the attachment to one's friends and relatives is "mithyaatma". When one actually experiences that the pure Aatma has been isolated and "I am none else than a form of Brahman," the Brahman itself becomes the Aatma. This is "Mukhyaatma". If the first two, (gauna and mithya) are removed, the connection with children and friends, body and sense organs will snap. Then the knowledge dawns that "I am truly Brahma Swaroopa". The purport of the sloka is that there is nothing further beyond this stage.

The motto "Arise, Awake" which Vivekananda devised for the Ramakrishna Mutt has been taken only from the Kathopanishad. Many of the mottos which are in use today are taken from the Upanishads. For example : (1) The expression that the Aatma cannot be reached through learning or intellect (नायमात्माप्रवचनेनलभ्यो नमेधया नबहुनाश्रुतेन); (2) the mantra that states that the *Jeeva* (Aatma) is the owner of the chariot, the body is the chariot, intellect is the driver, the mind is the harness bit, the organs are the horses: आत्मानं रथिनं विद्धि शरिरं रथमेवतु। बुद्धिं तु सारथिं विद्धि मनः प्रग्रहमेवच (3) the fact that the Parama Purusha resides in the cave of the heart as light, the size of the thumb; (4) the mantra chanted during Deepa Aaradhana (burning camphor) : viz. in God's presence, the sun, moon, stars and fire all lose their glow, meaning that, since He is the source of their brightness, they cannot throw light on him; (5) since our feeble intellect has emanated from the super intellect, we cannot intellectually grasp Him; (6) the topsyturvy tree (ऊर्ध्वमूलमधःशाख) which Lord Krishna refers to in the Gita - the Aswatha tree of Samsaara or worldly existence; (7) the fact that, if all the desires springing from the heart are destroyed, man becomes immortal here and now and tastes the bliss of Brahman. All these which are oft-quoted today are from Kathopanishad.

Prasna, Mundaka and Maandukya

The three Upanishads, Prasna, Mundaka and Maandukya, coming after Kathopanishad, belong to the Atharva Veda. Prasna means a question. How did creation begin? Who are Devas? How does life get connected to the body? What is the truth about the states of awakening, sleep and dreaming? What is the benefit of worshipping Omkaara? What is the relationship between the Purusha and Jeeva? Since it answers these six questions, this Upanishad is named *Prasnopanishad.*

Mundaka means shaven-head — tonsure. Mudakopanishad is to be followed by persons like Sanyaasis, with mature minds and a disposition free from attachment. This Upanishad talks of *Akshara Brahmam,* which means that which is free from decay or dissolution. "Akshara" also means sound or syllable. We talk of *Panchaakshara* (five syllables) and *Ashtaakshara* (eight syllables). *Pranava* (Omkaara) is basic to the Aksharaas. To reach the target or aim, called *Akshara Brahmam,* the Akshara or the syllable 'Om' plays the chief role. This Upanishad says that the arrow of the Aatma should be shot from the bow of Omkaara at the target of Brahma without wavering so that they (arrow and target) are conjoined and become one.

प्रणवो धनुःशरो ह्यात्मा ब्रह्मतल्लक्ष्यमुच्यते। अप्रमत्तेन वेद्धव्यं शरवत्तन्मयोभवेत् (M.2.4).

It is in this Upanishad that the following imagery appears; Jeevaatma and Paramaatma are the two birds living in the peepul tree called the body (Sareera). The Jeevatma bird eats the fruit (of action) whilst the Paramaatma bird remains a mere witness *(saakshi).*

The motto of our country at present *(Satyamevajayate)* - Truth alone triumphs - is a mantra from the Mundaka Upanishad.

सत्यमेव जयते नानृतं
सत्येन पन्था विततो देवयानः (M.3.6)

There is also a mantra here regarding those Sanyaasis who are Jeevan-muktas (liberated souls) in this life and, when devoid of their bodies, (after death) stay liberated. When honouring sanyaasis with poorna kumbha (a pot full of water) this is one of the mantras chanted. This Upanishad says that, just as when various rivers with different names fall into the sea, they lose their separate identities and become the Sea itself, so also the *jnaanis* (wise men) lose their names and forms and become one with the Parama Purusha.

यथा नद्यः स्यन्दमानाः समुद्रे
स्वं गच्छन्ति नामरूपे विहाय
तथा विद्वान्नामरूपादि मुक्त
परापरं पुरुषमुपैति दिव्यम् (M.3.8)

Next is Maandukya Upanishad. Manduka (मन्डुक) means a frog. Why is it called the Frog Upanishad? One reason appears to be that the frog does not have to climb each stair. It can jump from the first to the fourth. This Upanishad shows the way to transcend the three stages of *Jaagrati* (wakefulness), *Swapna* (dream) and *Sushupti* (sleep) and reach the *Turiya* or the fourth stage. It says it is possible to reach the final stage in one leap by means of worshipping Omkaara. Is that why it is called the Frog Upanishad?

Some say this Upanishad belonged to those tribes who adopted the frog as a symbol (Maandukya). It is also said that the Rishi to whom this Upanishad was a revelation was Varuna in the form of a frog.

This is the smallest of all Upanishads. There are only twelve mantras. But, for fame and efficacy, this has a special place. This establishes the doctrine, by using the four parts of Pranava, that Jeevaatma and Paramaatma are the same. It is also famous for describing as "Sivam Advaitam" (beautiful and without a second) the fourth and final stage to which finally all creation shrinks.

(प्रपंचोपशमं शान्तं शिवमद्वैतं चतुर्थं मन्यन्ते स आत्मा स विज्ञेयः)

Adi Sankara's Guru's Guru called Gaudapaadaacharya has vividly explained this Upanishad in "Maandukya Upanishad Kaarika". Adi Sankara has written a Bhaashya on this Upanishad Kaarika.

Taittareeya Upanishad

More than any other Upanishad, this Upanishad is widely studied. The mantras used in most of the rituals (Karmaanushtaana) are taken from this. Seekshaavalli, Aanandavalli and Bhriguvalli are the three parts of this Upanishad.

Seekshavalli deals with the many aspects of imparting education. This part teaches the controls or restraints involved in celibacy (Brahmacharya) and its glory, the order in which Veda should be studied, the worship of Pranava, etc. The Aavahanti Homa, which the teacher performs with the invocation that the disciples should come without restraint and receive the Veda, is from this Upanishad.

Precepts such as "tell the truth", "follow the dharma" *(Satyam Vada, Dharmam Chara)* appear only in this. The study of Vedas and following of one's dharma should never be abandoned. To perpetuate these in the world, one should marry and beget children to pass on the torch of Dharma or as the Upanishad says without breaking the thread of continuity. Mother, father, teacher and guests should be treated like divinities. (मातृ देवो भव, पितृ देवो भव, आचार्य देवो भव) — these mantras are found only here. The virtues of charity (दान) and duty (धर्म) are extolled in the teachings of this Upanishad.

That part of this Upanishad which contains the ascending order of bliss culminating in Brahmaananda is Aanandavalli. *Annamaya kosa* (the sheath of food) is the body which thrives on nourishment; the *praanamaya kosa* (life) which breathes inside it; the *Manomaya kosa* (mind) which creates thoughts; and, inside it, the *Vigyaanamaya kosa* (knowledge), which distinguishes right and wrong, are the four kosas. Aanandamaya kosa is at the core of these. It is explained (in this part of the Upanishad) how the Aatma resides here in its natural element and in a state of bliss.

Each *kosa* has been 'personified' into a bird and the teachings allegorically describe the head, the left wing, the right wing, the body, and the tail of the bird etc. The oft-quoted *"yato vaacho nivartante"* and mantras such as "there is nothing to fear for one who has realised the blissful state of Brahman, without being able to reach which speech and mind return" appears in this Upanishad.

"यतो वाचो निवर्तन्ते अप्राप्य मनसा सह।
आनंदं ब्रह्मणो विद्वान् न बिभेति कदाचन॥

Bhriguvalli is what Varuna taught to his son, Bhrigu. Although the term taught (upadeṣa) is used, it does not mean that the teacher dictated all the lessons. The teacher, Varuna, encourages his son to personally conduct deep enquiry and actually experience the results. It is thus that Bhrigu himself does penance and first realises the Annamaya kosa or that the body to be ultimate truth, but continuing his penance he progressively ascends by each stage viz. *Praanamaya* (life), *Manomaya* (mind), *Vigyaanamaya* (knowledge) and reaches the state of bliss — *Aanandamaya* — the stage where by experience he comes to know that bliss is the ultimate truth.

This does not mean that the Upanishad thinks low of the common worldly life which stops at the level of the body - Annamaya. One must understand the highest Truth even whilst pursuing worldly objectives.

By leading a dharmic existence, this life should be treated as a means *(upaaya)* — a device, as it were, to reach higher stages. That is why after reaching the state of bliss - *Aanandamaya kosa* - the Upanishad proclaims "do not regard food with contempt; do not waste food; grow more food" and so on. The text ends thus: "The Jnaani thinks that he alone is the food, the one who eats it, the one who created a connection between the food and its consumer and that he sings in happiness in the thought that God and he are also the same."

Aitareya Upanishad

The next is the Aitareya Upanishad, which appears at the end of the Aitareya Aaranyaka. It is so called because it came into use through a Rishi called Itareya. This Upanishad deals with how a Jeeva (soul) enters the mother's womb from the father, then is born in the world, takes birth again and again in various worlds according to sin and merit (*paapa* and *punya*) and how liberation from birth and life is possible only through realising the nature of the Aatma. It talks of how a Rishi called Vaamadeva, came to know all about his various births whilst still in his mother's womb and how he scaled all the walls and flew towards liberation like a kite flying high in the sky. *Prajnaana* (प्रज्ञान) or actual mental experience of the Aatma is spoken of in high terms in this Upanishad. It is not correct to say that Brahman is realised by such a process of thought. "The thought (Prajnaana) itself is the Brahman" is the most important message of Rig Veda.

Chaandogya Upanishad

The last two of the ten upanishads, viz. Chaandogya and Brahadaaranyaka are very big in size. These two together are bigger than all the rest of the eight put together.

What appears in the Chaandogya Braahmana of Saama Veda is Chaandogya Upanishad. 'Chaandogya' is what Chaandogyam refers to. 'Chaandoga' means one who sings the Saama Gaana.

It is said that just as Kathopanishad is largely used in the Bhagavad Gita, the Chaandogya Upanishad mantras constitute the chief authority *(pramaana)* for the Brahma Sutra of Vyasa.

Chaandogya and Brahadhaaranyaka contain the combined messages of many Rishis.

In the beginning, Chaandogya names 'Omkaara' as Udgata, (उद्गाता) and details its study (upaasana). Many vidyas or disciplines, e.g., Akshi Vidya - Aakaasa Vidya, Madhu Vidya, Saandilya Vidya, Praana Vidya, Panchaagni Vidya, etc. are mentioned. These help understand the Paramaatma Tatva in various ways.

At the apex appears the Dahara Vidya. The Jeeva (soul) realising in the small space (aakaaṣa) within himself the limitless spatial expanse which is the Paramaatma is Dahara Vidya.

In this Upanishad, the truth is taught through the medium of many interesting stories. In Chaandogya Upanishad appears the story of Satyakaama, a youngster who did not know his ancestry but did not hide the fact. As a result, Gautama took him to be of good Brahmin birth and accepted him as his disciple. The earlier teacher of Satyakaama subjects him to many tests. Even his (Guru's) wife intercedes on behalf of Satyakaama. When all this is seen in the Upanishad, it looks as though the Upanishad brings the ancient Gurukula life into our vision like a motion picture. Just contrary to Satyakaama, the Brahmachari, Svetaketu, who was swelling with the pride of knowledge was first made to become humble by his father, Uddaalaka Aaruni, and was, at the end, taught the non-difference *(Abeda)* between Jeeva (soul) and Brahma, contained in the expression *"Tat Tvam Asi"* (that thou art). This is the point at which the Mahaavaakya or the supreme message of Saama Veda touches the high note. Unlike Svetaketu, Maharishi Narada was struggling in vain to understand the truth of the Aatma, although he had learnt all the Saastras faultlessly. It is in this Upanishad that he is taught the secret by Sage Sanatkumaara. As in Taittareeya, which develops the theme higher and higher starting from the Annamaya Kosa (body), Sanatkumaara also starts from purity of food *(Aahaara Suddhi)* and goes up to the purity of mind/soul, only at which stage the bonds will be snapped and Aatmaananda (bliss) will result.

Brahadaaranyaka

The Brahadaaranyaka Upanishad is the biggest of all Upanishads. 'Brihada' means big. Generally an Upanishad appears at the end of an Aaranyaka. As an exception to this, the Isavaasya Upanishad comes in the Sukla Yajus Samhita itself. What appears in the same Sukla Yajus, as a whole Aaranyaka, (the entire Aaranyaka instead of the latter protion), is the Brahadaaranyaka Upanishad.

There are two versions of this. One is in the Maadhyandina Saakha and the other is in the Kaanva Saakha. Adi Sankara has written the Bhaashya on the version in Kaanvasaakha only.

This contains six chapters or Adhyayas. The first two are called Madhu Kaanda; the next two are called Muni Kaanda, after Yaajnavalkya's name and the last two are called Khila Kanda.

Madhu can be taken to refer to the sweet juicy stage of bliss. If it is understood that everything is the manifestation of the Paramaatma, the Jeevas will feel the whole world to be sweet like honey. The Jeevas will also be sweet to the world. This is the subject dealt with in Madhu Kaanda.

It is in this Upanishad that the Aatma is described negatively as "not this, not this" - meaning that it cannot be described as this or that (4.4.22). It is not like anything known to us. This is called the 'Neti Neti' (नेति नेति) vaada or negative argument. By the grammatical rule of conjunction, *na + iti* (not this) becomes 'Neti', which means, 'that which cannot be described'. According to the Neti doctrine, first the world, body and mind have to be rejected and the Aatma realised as transcending classification or description through words. After such realisation, the Bhaava or feeling will be that the phenomenal world and all creatures are also made of Aanandarasa or the juice of Aananda.

The Brahadaaranyaka starts with the mantra '*Asato Ma Sat Gamaya*', which these days is repeated as a prayer. This means : "Lead me from the perishable to the imperishable".

The first canto (Kaanda) deals with how the Brahmin called Gargya received instructions from the Kshatriya King, Ajaata Satru. It is known from this Upanishad that kings like Ajaata Satru and Janaka were Brahma jnaanis or realised souls. Likewise, we learn, from the reference to one Gargi (a lady) who had participated in the discussions on equal footing with the Rishis in Janaka's Council of the learned (Vidwatsabha) that women were also Brahma Vadins - those able to discuss the nature of Brahman. This Upanishad describes how Yaajnavalkya had two wives, one of whom called Katyaayini was an ordinary woman of the world and the other, Maitreyi was a Brahmavaadin (Philosopher). The teachings of Yaajnavalkya to Maitreyi are repeated twice in this Upanishad as Madhu Kaanda and Munikaanda but with a small difference in each. This is a beautiful mixture of an anecdote and philosophy.

Yaajnavalkya decides to leave the house and to become a Sanyaasi and divides his property between the two wives. Katyaayini is satisfied with her share of the property. But Maitreyi asks : "You are going to take Sannyas only because it provides more happiness than all this property. What is the nature of that happiness? Why don't you tell me this?" Yaajnavalkya replies, "You have always been dear to me. By this question, you have become dearer to me," and thus begins teaching.

He elaborates on the concept of 'priya' (love) and attachment. "The love which the wife has for the husband, the love of the husband for the wife, likewise, the love towards children, love for wealth - all these kinds of love do not arise objectively from the husband, wife, children or riches but the act of loving brings satisfaction to oneself. One indulges in the feeling of love, because it brings happiness to the Aatma. Therefore, does it not mean that the nature of Aatma is love, happiness? In order to learn it in isolation, one has to leave all that has been near and dear so far and become a Sannyaasi. After learning its nature, it will become clear that nothing other than that exists. All will become equally dear. Earlier, when attachment existed towards some objects, dislike was also manifest towards other dissimilar objects. If now all these are left in the middle as it were and Aatma is realised, then the feeling of difference (high and low) will vanish. All will appear to be manifestations of the Aatma, and, instead of feeling dislike for some objects, hatred as such will yield place to love towards all." Thus goes the teaching.

Muni Kanda narrates how Yaajnavalkya, before becoming a Sannyaasi, had a philosophical discussion in King Janaka's Council with Kahola, Uddhaalaka Aaruni, Gargi and others and, later, how he imparted knowledge to King Janaka too. The authority for the doctrine of Antaryaami (subtle internal existence of the Paramaatma) which is the chief feature of Visishtaadvaita Philosophy (modified non-dualism of Ramanuja) is contained in the reply Yaajnavalkya made to Uddaalaka Aaruni. The essence of this doctrine is, unlike Advaita, which regards the whole phenomenal world as Maaya or illusion, if the world is regarded as the body (sareera) then, Paramaatma resides within it like life. Although Yaajnavalkya at some stage accepts this to a limited extent, mostly he talks of complete Advaita only. When concluding his teachings to Maitreyi, he is wholly advaitic.

"How can the 'thing' create the sensation of sight, hearing, taste, smell and thought, be seen, heard, tasted, smelt and thought of and through what medium"? - Thus he talks of the undivided, unitary feeling. To Janaka also he expounds Advaita.

The two chapters that appear last in this Upanishad consolidate many messages lying scattered at various places and that is why it is called 'Khila' Kaanda. (If something is scattered, it is said to have become 'Khila'. *Akhila* means not scattered at all but together.)

One of the anecdotes in Khila Kaanda deals with how, based on the relative quality of the aspirants *(saadhaka),* the same message can be interpreted in three different ways. The Devas, the humans and the asuras, solicit instructions from Prajaapati. He offers the single syllable; *Da* (द) as his teaching. Devas who lack self-control take it to mean "damayata" (दमयता) meaning control or restraint. The humans, whose nature is to accumulate property, take 'da' to represent *'Daana'* giving away in charity. The asuras whose nature is cruelty, take *'da'* to refer to "Dayatvam" as being kindness or having compassion.

A certain mantra appearing towards the end of Brahadhaaranyaka Upanishad used to fascinate me and act as a solace. What does this mantra say?

If a sick man suffers from fever, that can be taken as his big penance *(Tapas)*. If one thus understands disease and calamity, he will reach heaven after death, says this mantra (Br. Up. 5.11.1).

This does not seem to make sense. What is the point that is made here or the consolation offered? I will explain.

Conditioning the body with *Vrata* (self-imposed austerity), not only helps one to shed the inordinate love for the body, but atones for earlier sins. *Tapas* or the practice of severe austerity acts as an atonement for sins of earlier births. Sins committed earlier by the body have to be paid for by bodily discomfort alone.

That is why the Puraanas (mythological texts) mention even evolved souls as having practised austerities or *Tapas.*

Ambika, the Divine Mother Herself, did not pay heed to the advice of Parameswara and came to the yajna which Daksha was performing. She was humiliated and she gave up her body then and there. She manifested herself again as the daughter of Himavaan - Lord of Himalayas. She was convinced that, unless she atoned properly for her earlier sin of disregarding her husband's advice, she would not be able to regain the same husband. Kalidasa has described this beautifully and touchingly in "Kumara Sambhavam". How cold must be the Himalayan peaks during winter. She used to sit on ice slabs or stand in the freezing waters of the lakes and do her penance. In summer, in the scorching Sun, she used to kindle the fire on all the four sides around her, and sit in the middle for the same purpose. Since, in addition to the four fires around, the burning sun was above, this is called "Panchaagni (five fires) Tapas". Many great men have done similar penance.

We have neither the will nor the ability to perform a millionth part of their penance. Then how would our sins be washed off?

Typhoid, Pneumonia and such fevers with a temperature of 105, 106 °F ravage the body with intolerable heat. Thank goodness God has sent us the fever since we have not done the *Panchaagni Tapas*

- this should be our solace.

Thus any ailment or injury should be regarded as *Tapas* - not *Tapas* which we have voluntarily undertaken but imposed on us by God.

By practice, this mentality will begin to harden. Thus we will develop the capacity to bear illness or sickness with fortitude. We should not reject the opportunity that has come to us of its own volition to liquidate the effect of our past deeds of evil. We will have obtained the lofty stage of "Titeeksha" (तितीक्षा) where troubles appear to be no trouble at all.

All this, the mantra in the Upanishad says pithily. This mantra acts as a balm sent specially to us by God in lieu of penance when we feel "we have committed many big sins but are not doing any *vrata* or *tapas* to atone for them, we not only fail to perform them, but we are not capable of performing them."

In the last chapter of the Brahadaaranyaka, which is also the end of the ten Upanishads, as though to stress that Vedanta is not at all opposed to Karma Kaanda, it talks of the Panchaagni Vidya and the duties of householders who desire children - good children.

12

PURPOSE AND PURPORT OF THE VEDAS

There is another question. When the Vedas deal extensively with many subjects, how can we say that the main message of the Vedas is the realisation of the self (आत्म साक्षात्कार) as stated in the Upanishads?

The Vedas praise Agni-hotra, Soma Yaga, Satra Yaga and Ishtis (provision of welfare-works beneficial to the community, e.g., construction of shelters, digging of wells, etc.) Why can't these be regarded as the aim of the Vedas? There are many other matters mentioned in the Vedas such as conduct of marriage ceremonies, funeral rites, Sraadhas, etc., how a good government should be run, how one should conduct oneself in a learned assembly etc. Of these, which should be regarded as most important?

Apart from yajnas and methods of worship, the Vedas also mention many methods of meditation and prayer (upaasana), of Dhyaana or meditating in solitude, etc. Mention is also made of how the Aatma enters the body, what happens eventually to the body, how the Aatma enters another body again, etc.

Further, the Vedas also deal with various kinds of medical treatment to ensure bodily health, and *Shantis* or methods to pacify enemies and to avert the harm contemplated by them. When one looks at all of these the question arises as to what is the purpose or objective of the Veda?

The Upanishad says "all the Vedas together talk of a single Being". (Kato 2.15). What is that Being? Vedic consensus is that the Being is that which is represented symbolically by the sound *'AUM'* ॐ.

Some western scholars are of the view that ancient Indians were struck with wonder by the sun and moon and natural phenomena and since these were the days when science had not advanced much, each thinker expressed his view according to his appreciation of the natural phenomena, that not all were able to sing them as hymns and only some could and that these sayings or songs were gathered and labelled as mantras, which became "Vedas" on compilation.

Thus, although the Upanishads avow that all the Vedas talk of only one being, it appears that diverse objects are referred to and not merely one.

There is a sloka (stanza in verse) regarding Ramayana:

वेद वेद्ये परे पुंसि जाते दशरथात्मजे।
वेदः प्राचेतसादासीत्साक्षात् रामायणात्मना।।

Veda Vedyey parey pumsi jathay Dasarathatmajey
Vedahprachedasaadaaseet Sakshat Raamaayanaatmana.

Veda Vedyey is one who has to be known by the Vedas. Who is he? The Supreme Being, who had to be known through the Vedas took birth in this world. When he came in the form of Rama, Dasaratha's son, the Vedas took the form of Raamaayana - the child of Valmeeki.

This is the meaning of the above sloka. Even here, the Supreme Being - the Parama Purusha or the absolute truth called Omkaara is the common goal of the Vedas. Lord Krishna in Bhagavad Gita says : *"Vedaischa sarvaih ahameva vedyah'* (only I am to be known through all the Vedas).

When all these are considered, it is clear that, although many subjects are dealt with in the Vedas, all the Vedas talk with one voice on a central subject, viz., the one Supreme Being.

Then we might wonder why the Vedas have to talk of many things and beings to describe One?

It is only through the agency of the many beings, can that one Being be known. Yoga (body and mind control), Dhyaana (meditation), Tapas (practice of austerities), Yajna (sacrifice), Karmaanushthaana (observance of specified duties - marriage and other rites), affairs of state, social life - all these ultimately converge towards a Central Being which is the real essence of the Vedas. All other things are changeable, mutable, which become legends as time passes. The world appears to us in various ways and not as a unitary object. The Vedas deal with various themes so as to lead us through any one of these to a central figure.

If we are to know the one Infinite Being which the Vedas point to, we should practise certain mental disciplines so that the thought of that Being keeps coming to us. The performance of sacrifices, doing penance, giving in charity, renovating temples, digging wells for supply of water, social service, marriage rites and such duties are meant to lead to mental purity *(chitta suddhi)* and steadying the wavering mind *(Chitta Vrtti Nirodha).*

The objective of the various duties and acts enjoined is to help realise God through a disciplined path.

The word Veda means —to know. The Upanishad defines Aatma as that by knowing which all things will have become known. The goal of the Vedas is to make known that Aatma. Whether it is the Karma which comes in the beginning, or knowledge (jnaana) which comes at the end, i.e. at the start or the beginning and at the conclusion or the end, the central theme is Iswara - Brahman Aatma all of which ultimately mean the same.

Karma is divided into different types, and jnaana exists unitarily but the central subject matter in both is the same. The sense organs have been created in such a way that they cannot see the Aatma but can only see thing and reach outwardly.

When a person allows his attention to drift from the thing in hand to something outside, he is said to be looking elsewhere. Aatma alone is the real matter in hand. Not seeing it, but looking outward is looking elsewhere than where one should. The mind will not heed the advice not to see outside. Therefore, whilst doing things which point outward, one should develop the ability to see inward. Instead of letting the sense organs and mind drag one where they will, one should perform the prescribed Vedic rituals more and more. This alone will develop the capacity to see inwardly. Only after learning, analysing and weighing other outward things, the intellect which is capable of grasping everything can reach "That" by knowing which all things will have become known. Only for this purpose, the Vedas talk of so many disciplines, observances, karmas, arts and social duties. The attachment to the physical body should become progressively weak by the continued performance of karmas. The mind and intellect should get dissolved, as it were, by cognition, searching examination of truths and practice of self-discipline. Attachment to the body increases by impure acts. These lead to the unsteadiness of the mind. On the other hand, the performance of Vedic karmas and observance of Vedic injunctions, which are based on mantras and which are designed to bring universal well-being, bring about a certain relaxation in the tempo of the activities of the body and mind. In the end, it leads to maturity and ripeness to be able to see inwards. After so seeing, a person gets supreme bliss, *Moksha Aananda,* here itself. Moksha means "the state of being released" - 'freedom' from the worldly involvements. If the body and the mind can release themselves from the sense of ego, it also spells release from Samsaara.

The aim of the Vedas is to help one obtain Moksha whilst living in this world itself. That is its glory. If, as in other faiths, we were to get Moksha only in another world after death, one cannot conceive of its nature whilst living in this world. Those who obtained it will not come back to tell us their experience. As a result, doubt and disbelief may arise. But, whilst in this world one were to abnegate all desires and wants, and engage in self-analysis, Moksha will be achieved here itself. From such an avowal by the Vedas, it is clear that it talks of the irrefutable truth.

Other paths merely ensure temporary solace just as a dose of quinine may bring down the temperature in high malarial fever. If the non-recurrence of fever is to be ensured, the root cause should be found and destroyed. The Vedic faith goes to the very origin of the "Jeeva" (existence), to the very spot where it branches off from the Paramaatma and destroys the sense of separatism *(Bheda)* thus providing permanent release instead of a temporary cure.

The injunctions in the Karma Kaanda of the Vedas are also in the nature of temporary cures. But then it is not possible to convert one struggling desperately in "unrest" *(Asaanthi),* with a single stroke, as it were, into an *Aatmaaraama,* (आत्माराम), i.e., one who finds happiness within and one who can remain in a state of tranquillity. That is why the karmas which bring temporary benefits have been prescribed but, in the process they help develop purity of mind which is the basic prerequisite for lasting mental peace. Although *Yajna* (sacrifices), *Vrata* (self-imposed restraints) and *Poorta* (public service) are prescribed with great elaboration, it does not regard any of these as the end or goal. These (karmas) have been designed to reduce the attachment to the body. By diverting the mind towards them, concentration is developed and the mind is cleansed of impurities. Thus, although various subjects are dealt with at great length by the Vedas, their aim is to lead to philosophical enquiry, as contained in Vedanta.

When we see an article or speech delivered by someone in a newspaper, we naturally wish to know what is stated. The speech or article is long and there is no time to go through it from beginning to end. So we just read a little from the beginning and then quickly go to the last paragraph. This gives us an idea of the contents. The perusal of the beginning and end is sufficient to shrewdly guess at the entire contents. Likewise, at the beginning of the Vedas and at their end, the same *Iswara Tatva* is dealt with and that alone is the central subject matter of the Vedas, as I mentioned earlier.

The Government enacts many laws. But, quite often, there is doubt and difference of opinion as to the exact intention behind the laws. Then these laws are explained or elucidated according to the intention of the original enactment according to the rules of interpretation. In the same manner, to interpret the Eternal Law, viz., the Vedas, the Meemaamsa Saastra serves as the Rule of Interpretation, to clarify the intention, so to speak. Meemaamsa forms one of the fourteen disciplines (Vidyas) and I will tell you more about it later. Here I wish to confine myself to one aspect of it.

The *Meemaamsa* talks of six ways through which the purport of a Vedic Mantra can be ascertained. These six are : *Upakrama, Upasamhaara, Abhyaasa, Apoorvata, Phala, Arthavaada,* and *Upapatti.* Apart from the Vedas, these six can be applied to determine the exact scope of an article or speech.

Upakrama (उपक्रम) is the beginning. Upasamhaara (उपसम्हार) means the conclusion. The first method is to examine the beginning and the ending - this is the Upakrama and Upasamhaara method. If both talk of the same subject, then it can be taken that that is the subject matter. 'Abhyaasa' (अभ्यास) is to say a certain thing again and again repeatedly. For e.g., the physical exercises, pull-ups are done again and again, and they constitute *'Dehaabhyaasa'* (देहाभ्यास).

In an article or speech, if a theme is mentioned repeatedly, then it is clear that that is the gist which is being repeated for emphasis.

Apoorvata (अपूर्वता) means what has not been mentioned earlier. Then that would be an indication of what would constitute the gist.

"'Phala' is the consequence or result. "If so done then a certain result would follow", this is another way of saying. "Do this and such and such result will follow." That is, the objective is to lead us to a particular result. This method is called 'phala'.

In the *Arthavaada* method many things are dealt with and a story is narrated based on these and, as a result, some particular point is brought out. We should take it that the point brought out is the core of the matter. In the method called *upapatti,* a subject is postulated and then its origin, purpose, appropriateness, etc., are explained in order to make it clear that that is the point at issue.

According to a person who had scanned the beginning and end of the Vedas - "The main purport of the Vedas is fire worship or Agni Upaasana. In the *'upakrama',* i.e. the beginning, it starts with *'Agni meelay'.* At the end, i.e. at the *Upasamhaara* stage, it also ends with Agni. The beginning and end are both Agni. Therefore, the supreme message of the Vedas is Agni."

Though there is also some truth in this, this cannot be taken to be literally true. Agni stands for the awakening of the Soul, the light of knowledge. *Aatma chaitanya,* the soul's awakening, is the realisation that the knower, the thing known and knowledge are all the same. This is indeed the gist of the Vedas.

But, really speaking, fire worship is not the goal of the Vedas. The greatness of the Vedas lies in their not highlighting the importance of the worship of any Devata in preference to another. "The Aatma which takes the form of several Devatas should be worshipped with devotion," says the Veda (Brahadhaaranyaka 14.8). "The Aatma alone is to be seen; it alone should be heard; Aatma alone should be meditated upon *(Manana),*" thus runs Yaajnavalkya's teaching to Maitreyi and, through it, the Veda makes its goal known to us.

If a thing has to be called 'the goal' then the imagery raises the following picture: "We are in one place; from here we must necessarily go to the place at the other end."

The goal is pointed out as "something" appearing at a distance. "*Itah*" meaning "this" is the state where we are in now. From this, we have to go to that. "*Tatah*" (ततः)

But in truth is not that "goal", "here" too? Of course, it is. When the realisation comes, that everything is Brahman, both 'that' and 'this' become Brahman. There is not even a separate 'this' or 'that'. What we now say as 'this' becomes 'that' at the end, meaning the "Eternal It".

Like 'tatah' meaning 'that', the Paramaatma is also called (ततः) ("Tat") meaning "that". When we say, *'Om Tat Sat'* at the end of any karma, it means : "that which is 'tat' is alone the truth". 'Sat' (सत्) means truth.

We also add the suffix 'tvam' (त्वं) at the end of many words like "Purushatvam" (पुरुषत्वं), 'Mahatvam', etc. Here 'Tvam' means the nature or quality of the thing mentioned. The quality of 'Mahat' (big) is Mahatvam. The nature of the Purusha is Purushatvam. All right, if that were so, how is it that we call the end of the journey the 'Eternal End' as 'tatva' (i.e.) to mean the nature of 'tat'? 'Tatva Vichara', 'Tatva Upadesa' - all these mean to examine or analyse the nature of 'Tat' and to teach the nature of the same 'Tat', (तत्).

The question arises as to what use is it to us when the Veda describes the distant Supreme Being as 'tat' - that. The person who is far distant is also very near. *'Doorat dooray antikecha',* says the Veda. This means that, when not understood, it is far away; but when understood, it is near us - inside.

There is a story illustrating this. There was a girl of marriageable age and her parents had selected the groom, who in accordance with ancient customs, was first in the line of marriageable relatives. But the girl was determined only to marry a person who was the best among all. So the parents left her alone.

The girl said that the king is higher than everyone else and she will marry none other than the King. And so she kept following the King.

The king was riding in a palanquin one day and met a Sannyaasi on the way. The king got down, made his obeisance to the holy man and then continued on his way.

The girl was watching : 'What a fool I am to think that the king is the highest among men. The Sannyaasi seems to be higher than the king. I must somehow marry the holy man.' So thinking, the girl followed the Sannyaasi.

One day, when following the Sannyaasi, she saw him paying his respects to an idol of Lord Ganesh under a banyan tree. She then changed her opinion and decided to marry Lord Ganesh as she found him higher than the Sannyaasi who paid homage to Him. Instead of following the holy man, she sat close to Ganesh.

There were not many who visited the place where the idol was. It was not a temple but merely the foot of a tree. Therefore, a street dog that was passing by emptied its bladder on the idol. The girl then thought that the dog must be higher than the idol and started running after the dog.

An urchin passing by threw a stone at the dog. It howled in pain and ran faster. A young man who was watching this chastised the boy for being unkind to the dumb creature who had done him no harm. The girl ultimately thought that the one who thrashed the boy who beat the dog should be the best. So, she decided to marry that youth. It turned out, at last, that the youth was the one who had been chosen by her parents. Thus, it turned out that the person whom she thought was far away was in fact very close. Thus runs the story.

"You are wandering all over the country in search of God as though he is far away. So long as he is not known, he will certainly be at a distance. All the quest will not reveal him. He stays very close to you. Far away from the far distant but nearer than the nearest." Thus says the Sruti.

The earth and the sky seem to meet at the horizon and let us suppose that a palm tree is sighted at that point. From where we stand, it would seem that if we reached that spot we can find the earth meeting the sky. But on actually reaching that spot, the horizon would appear to have receded farther. As we travel towards it, it would also travel away from us. Can we ever reach it by keeping identification points such as a palm tree in view? Therefore where is it? It is where you are standing. The God who is referred to as 'that' implying that he exists far away, is near you - in you. 'You are that' the Veda makes you feel it. (तत्त्वमसि) *('Tat Tvam Asi)'.* "You are that" is the supreme message of the Vedas. Here (तत्त्वं) (Tatvam) does not mean the quality of being "Tat". The word (त्वं) (tvam) can be taken in two ways as a suffix or a pronoun - one indicates quality and the other means the pronoun 'you'. 'Tat Tvam Asi' means 'Tat=that', 'Tvam=you', 'Asi=are'.

The two words 'Tat' and 'Tvam' together have come to be used as 'tatvam'. In common parlance, by making use of the word which describes the nature of Paramaatma, any conclusion which has general acceptability is referred to as 'tatvam'. Thus, 'tatvam' is used to refer to any underlying principle.

The knowledge of that which you think is 'I', is realisation of God. If this light of understanding were not present, you cannot even think of a thing called God. "Knowledge springs from me, thought arises in me." This knowledge born of thought and the 'Tat' which you think is at a great distance are one and the same" is how the Veda sums it up.

What we refer to as 'it', 'tat', 'Idam', is not without an origin or root. Nothing that can be identified as 'it' can appear without an origin. There can be no tree without a seed. All the things in the world referred to as 'it', viz., mountains, sea, sky, earth, cattle, man, anger, fear, love, sense organs, power - all have an origin. Being seen, heard, smelt, thought of, felt as heat or cold - these are felt by the mind and experienced by the respective organs. All these are called 'it'. All the scientific discoveries made so far, those yet to be made, (i.e.), those that are 'known' are all 'Idam'. All these have something as their origin. If there were no origin, there can be no 'Idam'. And nothing can exist without an origin. There is always a root or seed principle behind it.

The human body comes out of a "seed". The tree owes its origin to a seed. Therefore, the phenomenal world must have an origin. And whatever power or force is immanent in the world, all that must spring from an origin.

If the seed of a tamarind tree that has just sprouted is split open, one can see a miniature tamarind tree clasped in the two halves. This has the power in itself to grow into a big tree. All seeds have such power but, in the tamarind seed, this can be seen.

In mantras, there are what are called 'Beeja Aksharas' - seed-words. Just as a huge tree is contained in a small seed, these *Aksharas* (or words) are packed with limitless power. If these *Aksharas* are repeated several hundred thousand times with single-minded concentration, we can absorb and feel the great power which it contains.

Whatever power is latent in the world, whatever intelligence or ability, all these must be present in their 'origin' or seed which is God. Without the seed, they cannot be born.

What the Vedas proclaim is that all things in creation referred to as 'it' did not appear without a root or seed or cause. The *sakti* or force which is in the cause pervades the world. Where is that cause? It is what lies within, what is referred to as 'it' but it looks outside as Aatma.

We see our reflection in a huge mirror. If four mirrors are placed around us at right angles to each other, we can see countless images. One who sees the thousand images and is their cause is just one person. Likewise, the thing that is inside the millions of created beings and which looks outside at the created thing as 'it' is none else but God.

The thing that sees is the origin or cause of the thing that is seen. The cause of all the world is 'knowledge' or *'jnana'*. Where is this knowledge? It is inside us. That which is an indivisible whole, appears as divided within us. There are many types of electric bulbs, small, big, blue, green, etc. They also come in many shapes. But the current that is inside each is the same electric current. The same electrical force which is prevalent all over is present inside the bulb and makes it glow. It also makes the fan to whirl. The cause of all these activities is the same force. That is universal electricity which is composite and indivisible but, when led through the wire, it gets separated, as it were. When lightning appears in nature, when water falls over a precipice, this force comes into being by itself.

Therefore, make the great 'Tatvam' or the truth flash though you. Beginning with *karma-anushtaana,* i.e. performance of prescribed duties, e.g., yajna and worship of deities, etc., and ending with deep meditation on the purport of the 'Mahaa Vaakya' (the great message of the Vedanta), all these practices are for this purpose alone. The social structure which the Veda lays down, rules of conduct for householders, laws of Government, art, medicine, geology and other disciplines, are the steps that lead to self-realisation *(Aatma-sakshaatkaara).* The convergence of 'tat' (that) and 'tvam' (you) will in the beginning be felt for a second like the flash of lightning. It is this stage which is referred to in Kenopanishad (4.4) that the consciousness of Brahman will be like a lightning inside a lightning, and felt only for a fraction of a second. तस्यैष आदेशो यदेतद्विद्युतोव्यद्युतदा If the practices are continued, then, like a waterfall producing electricity continuously, one can stay at that level of consciousness. This is Moksha - liberation whilst alive. After death, that consciousness mingles or merges with the Supreme Being. Even this distinction between liberation whilst living and liberation after death is felt by others but the jnaani regards both as the same.

Thus, the supreme purport of all the Vedas is to make us realise by our own experience that all is Brahman and thus lead us to a state of bliss.

We learn of what is happening in various parts of the world through the newspapers. The news is obtained through reporters in different places, news agencies, through post, telegraphic and teleprinter messages. However, there are many items which cannot be brought within the ken of modern equipments and instruments or even of ordinary human intellect. There must be another type of newspaper if we should know these items.

The news that cannot be transmitted through modern media and which pertain to a place unconnected by telegraphic or teleprinter circuits is provided through the Veda mantras. Rishis gifted with super-natural powers have communicated to us, through this agency, news beyond the grasp of our ordinary intellect.

Although the Vedas contain a lot of important items there are some items that can be skipped or ignored.

When I say ignored, I do not mean that those items are unimportant or that the Vedas contain something that can be classified as wrong.

Our elders have clarified that when the Vedas wish to make us understand an important point, many items are given to us so as to prepare us for the important item or to illustrate a point. The point has to be grasped and the other information is to be understood only to grasp the main point. Although certain subjects are relevant at the beginning or middle levels, they have to be abandoned in stages as one reaches the higher states of the awakening of the soul. The Vedas say so. Thus, what is acceptable to me at one stage is not so at another stage.

The Vedas also contain certain great truths or 'Paramataatparya', which have to be accepted in toto. The rest which can be accepted at lesser value or importance and may even be left out are called 'Artha Vaada' and 'Anu Vaada'.

The Vedas resort to the use of anecdotes and stories to edify and make us grasp a truth or law. In such cases, the truth or law has to be taken in full and the anecdotes ignored as 'Artha Vaada'. In other words Arthavaada is not to be taken literally but as illustrative.

What is Anuvaada? In order to make us understand something not known, the Vedas start off with a thing known and keep on elaborating it. Before reaching the objective which is unknown, it may resort to a repetition of the known. That is, it will resort to illustrations from things which are knowable and which are within our experience and which need not be learnt from the authority of the Vedas. What cannot be established by other authorities *(Pramaana)* and which the Vedas proclaim, that is the law *(Vidhi)*, that is the important message.

In other words, if a thing can be known through the medium

of other commonly known facts it cannot be regarded as solely subsisting on the authority of the Vedas although the Vedas may repeat it. Vedas are meant to make the unknown known. If it states what is known as also what is unknown, then it would mean that its main goal *(Taatparya)* is the unknown. It is only to make our understanding easier that it starts with what is already known to us. If this were the ultimate message, there would be no point in mentioning the unknown. On the other hand, if the Vedas went on elaborating on things unknown only, it would be a mockery to say "I take what is known and reject what is not."

Let us now examine what is this thing 'known' to us and what is that 'unknown' to us.

In the case of worldly objects, there are two views. Whether all the objects that are known to us are the same or they are different is the doubt that assails us and thus there is a broad classification of objects into two categories. Based on physical perception, we decide that the various objects are indeed different. Only if regarded as separate, can the business of this world be carried on. We have to distinguish between water and oil. If we wish to light the lamp oil has to be used; water will be of no use. If the same lamp burns high and sets fire to the house, then water has necessarily to be used to put out the fire. If oil is poured on the fire, a bigger fire will result. Thus, whatever be the job in hand, unless differentiated, knowledge is maintained and proper use is made of the same, a job cannot be done well.

This kind of differentiation is 'Duality' or 'Dvaita'. This Dvaita is at the foundation of all the karmas and Upaasanas (actions and worships) contained in the Vedas. Therefore, it is clear that in such activities Vedas are dualistic in their impact. An Advaitin (non-dualist) need not dispute this. Dualism is very much true of the phenomenal world. But let us examine if the Vedas stop at where we see dualism. If it did, then we can conclude that dualism is the goal of the Vedas. But the Vedas talk of Advaita (non-dualism) at some places in the Samhitas and extensively in the concluding part, namely the Upanishads.

In our religious texts, there are two points of view, viz., *"Poorva Paksha"* and *'Siddhaantha'.* The Poorva Paksha contains the views of those who hold a different opinion from what one holds (i.e.) an opposite point of view. After the Poorva Paksha is presented, then the refutation of those views follows. In other words the idea is to voluntarily present the opposite point of view first and then prove that to be untenable and thus establish the real doctrine.

Western scholars also admire our treatises on philosophy called *"Darsana—"* which neither glosses over nor conceals the point of view of the opposition but presents them in full and then answers every one of them.

The 'Jnaanakaanda' of the Vedas which contains the Upanishads and which mainly deal with Advaita, appears as a later or second part whilst the 'Karma Kaanda' which talks of Dvaita appears earlier and forms the first part.

Therefore, if the Vedas first postulate Dvaita which is already known to us in our daily experience and later talk of Advaita which is not known to us, it clearly shows that Advaita is the doctrine which the Vedas seek to establish. In fact, it means that it is its ultimate goal.

It may be argued that Dvaita has not been condemned as Poorva Paksha should normally have been. I will tell you why. The karma and worship performed on the basis of Dvaita are not inimical to the 'experience' which Advaita propagates. On the contrary, they are helpful as means to an end. It is not as though the opposition who is generally regarded as an enemy has been placed in the Poorva Paksha so that he can be vanquished later. The Dvaita doctrine has not been presented as an opposite viewpoint nor has it been condemned anywhere later.

Just as the flower appears first and then it drops off leaving the fruit in position, first we have to be in Dvaita and later leave it, and come over to Advaita. The flower and the fruit are certainly not enemies. Nobody condemns the flower because the fruit is the ultimate state.

Advaita philosophy would have felt no need to condemn other philosophies if the latter had confined themselves to their proper places and presented their doctrines at their appropriate level. It is only when they transgress this limit that they need to be opposed. It is in this spirit that Adi Sankara and other Advaita philosophers have viewed rival philosophies. Fortunately, scientific development has not posed any threat to metaphysical doctrines. In fact, modern science is approaching nearer and nearer to the Advaita thought which earlier it was not possible to absorb except through the authority of the Vedas. To begin with, science was of the view that all substances on earth were different from each other. Then it was postulated that there were only 72 'elements' which presented the myriad objects. The interaction of the 72 was said to cause all the differences. Then, when atomic science developed, it postulated that the origin of all these 72 elements is the same, viz., energy which we call as 'Sakti'.

Those who are advanced in philosophical enquiry and have realised the Truth, consider that Energy or Sakti is all knowledge or consciousness within whose ambit is included not only the inanimate objects but the 'Jeevaatma' or soul which stands as the symbol of cognisance.

Whether called a single energy or *Eka Chaitanya* or "Universal Consciousness", it is beyond the reach of the sense organs, whether of the physicist or the philosopher. Its manifestation as plurality of objects is known to us already as Dvaita. If Dvaita were the absolute truth, there is no need at all to consult the Vedas. There is no need for it to dwell on objects within the range of perception of the eye or the intellect. We must take the message of the Vedas as supreme only if it establishes at the end what has to be known, beginning from things already known in stages. The truth is that the individual soul (Jeevaatma) merges with the cosmic soul (Paramaatma) and becomes the Advaitic 'Brahman'.

13

THE ESSENCE OF THE MESSAGE OF UPANISHADS

What is the essence of the teachings contained in the Upanishads to reach that stage of merging?

Modern science is of the view that the phenomenal world exists as a result of the inter-play of the concepts of time and space. The Upanishad says that only when one transcends this conceptual state or gets outside it, can one realise the truth. The space-concept gets cancelled as it were in the anecdote I narrated earlier regarding horizon as the place where we stand. Likewise one should get beyond the time-concept.

Is it enough to talk theoretically of these? Is it within our capacity to perceive? To prove that it is possible to achieve this end, an illustration is available from our everyday life. In order to spend time, we read in the newspaper of an account of a war in Africa. But, if there is a war nearer, say in Pakistan or Kashmir, we become less interested in the Congo battle as compared to the battles taking place nearer. Even the editor of the newspaper takes the Africa news to a corner and presents the Pakistan war in banner headlines and bold print. Then this news appears more important to us. Then still nearer home news of some boundary dispute between two states appears, attended by acts of violence. Then even the Pakistan news is ignored and the boundary dispute draws our attention. When there is news of disturbance in the adjoining street, even the border dispute does not hold our attention. We throw the paper away and run to the next street to see what is happening. If, while there, someone reports a quarrel in our home (say between our children or say between the mother-in-law and daughter-in-law) we ignore the street fight and rush home.

In the international context, the African war may appear all important. From there, progressively the Pakistan battle, the border dispute, the street fight, the fight at home appear smaller and smaller and may reach the final stage where it loses all significance. But our interest in the above matters has been in the inverse order and increased progressively. Why? Because our interest progressively increases with diminishing distance.

Let us unfold the above symbolism and turn our vision inward. If we realise the inner conflict within us, all other conflicts including those at home, will become unimportant like the war somewhere in Africa. Now, let us try to resolve the in-fighting as the newspapers would call it and achieve peace and calmness. In that 'peace', space and time will disappear. Are we aware of space when sleeping? In sleep, there is no sense of awareness or feeling, not even of space. In the Jnaana stage, it is possible to live solely in a state of enlightenment and experience - space has no place in it.

The "Time" concept is similar. When one lost his father one wept inconsolably. Where are those tears now? Grief which found expression in choking sobs at the time of the death of somebody dear would not even last till the next day. Why is that? The joy of a promotion or the jubilation of winning a lottery also fade out in time, why? Just as proximity in space is responsible for greater involvement, so is the case with time. The nearer the incident in time, the more are we affected.

When our thoughts are projected outwards and when we are fully conscious of time and space, we find that, to a great extent, they lose their significance or impact without any effort on our part. This raises the hope that, if our thoughts are focussed inward and we try hard, it is possible to get free from the play of time and space. Although, during sleep, there is no awareness of time and space, there is no cognisance of such a state. If, as a result of jnaana (wisdom), one reaches the state where as saint Thaayumaanavar has said : "one sleeps without being asleep", it is possible to be in a state of absolute bliss, consciously free from the feeling of time and space. Then, let alone the war in Africa, even if we are stabbed, it will be a matter of little or no concern as the distant war. If a dear and near relative, say a husband, wife or child, is lost in one's very presence, it will only have a feeble impact like the loss of a father ten years ago.

Let us leave alone, for the moment, the merits and demerits of Advaita and Dvaita. What do we want most? Peace - *Shanti.*

Both good and bad affect us equally. Weeping and laughter are both a bother and one would rather not have either. Beyond a point, even laughter causes pain in the sides and, it makes us weak. We burst out in rage, 'Don't make me laugh.' Dancing may be a pleasure but the body gets tired. At some stage one says 'enough' and one longs to be quiet and to be left alone. This is what is needed by us and not Advaita nor Dvaita.

We look around to see what should be done to achieve this. If we focus attention on how to get free from bother, one thing becomes clear.

Let us go back to the war in Africa which we avidly read in the beginning but later gave up. Why? Because the more distant a thing is in space, the less is its effect on us. Similarly one's father's death ten years ago does not have any visible effect now. In other words, the more distant a thing is in time, the less is its effect. Therefore, if we are to get totally free from all bother, we should learn to treat things that happen around us as happening far away. The moment good or bad occurs, it should be treated as though it happened years ago. Happiness and grief do not last long. They are also 'relative' or dependent on some other factor. Therefore, to be totally free from any type of mental botheration, one has to catch hold of 'that' which is not relative but is full and absolute and to live eternally in that experience. This is Einstein's theory of Relativity applied to the spiritual field. He also talks of time and space.

To me, the essence of the message of the Upanishads appears to be to create a longing to be free from the play of these two concepts. To the extent we strive and struggle to get free from these, to that extent we are bound to have God's grace in our journey towards the goal.

We do not have to search for the solution in forests or mountains. Time and space are the best teachers to free us from the effects of our involvement with our feelings. All our prayers and penance should be that God may give us the power to treat happenings here and now as if they were widely separated from us by time and space.

The first of the Upanishads viz., Isaavaasya, says "That (Aatma) moves, (but) moves not; that is distant, but is near and inside us."

तदेजति तन्नेजति तद्दूरे तद्वन्तिके। तदन्तरस्य सर्वस्य तदु सर्वस्यास्य बाह्यतः (I.U. 5)

By this, it not only refers to space and time and the alternating states of the mind which are caused by their play, but it stimulates our interest to get free from both of them. In the mantras which follow the above mantra the same Upanishad asks one to see both time and space existing inside the Aatma. Once this is sighted, then there is no anger, illusion or grief, in short no agitation of the mind. Thereafter, another mantra talks of this Aatma as transcending space by being omnipresent, and then goes on to describe the stage where time is also transcended by Aatma.

Summing up, the Upanishad has the same conclusion as modern science, viz., causality is the result of the play of time and space. Science presents this as a postulate based on experiment. On the other hand, the Upanishad says that this realisation can be achieved by self experience. This is the final message of the Upanishad which is the crown jewel of the Vedas.

14

VEDA SAAKHAS

The Vedas are 'Ananta' - endless. (अनंता वै वेदाः). Vedanta means the end of the Vedas. What does it mean 'the end of the endless Vedas'?

It is called 'Vedanta' because it contains the conclusion of the various metaphysical truths, viz., the realisation of the self, which is the purport of the Vedas. In other words, it is the end of the Veda's quest. It also appears at the end (later) of the Vedas.

Everyone born as a brahmin has without asking for any reason necessarily and as a matter of duty to learn, study and practise a Veda Saakha which is one of the branches of the Vedas. A Saakha consists of first the Samhita, next the Braahmana, then the Aaranyaka, at the end of which appear the Upanishad. The conclusion of the Vedasaakha is thus the Upanishad.

What is the reason behind splitting the endless Vedas into so many Saakhas or branches? The individual has to be taught all matters so that spiritual progress is possible for him. First is the study and recitation of the Vedas, then the yajnas and other rituals which he has to study and perform and the mantras relating to these. Next comes an enquiry into the purpose of the yajnas, and, lastly, an enquiry into the *Paramaatma Tatva* and bringing it within the range of actual experience. All these are required to be given to a student of the Vedas.

What is given should be adequate to enable a person to attain self-realisation. To master the innumerable Veda Saakhas is an impossible task. A story is told about how sages like Bharadwaaja could only obtain a fistful of earth from out of the Vedic mountains even after thousands of years of study. Therefore, the optimum required to enable a person to cleanse his mind of impurities and become fit to merge with the Paramaatma has been classified and compiled from the endless Vedas and given as a Saakha.

The Saakha details the duties of a brahmin from the moment of his birth to that of his death. First, the Saakha has to be learnt and recited *(Adhyayana),* i.e. the Samhita mantras are to be learnt by rote. Then, the prescribed yajnas have to be performed with the help of these mantras as described in the Braahmanas. Then, the Aaranyaka which bridges the gap between external action and internal experience has to be cogitated upon. Then, the contents of the Upanishad, which deals only with the internal truth, has to be digested and, lastly the state of liberation (Moksha), where 'in' and 'out' lose their distinction has to be attained.

This is the plan and purpose of every Saakha.

Even one mantra is sufficient for an evolved soul to realise the truth.

But a normal common soul has to resort to a multitude of karmas, observances, chanting and meditation to reach that state. Thus, each Saakha contains that measure of mantras, karmas and philosophical instructions as would enable a common man to achieve liberation.

What about those who are not brahmins?

Is it not necessary for those other than brahmins to achieve evolution? The performance of Vedic karmas and rituals are not for them but whatever jobs they are required to do, lead them to mental upliftment and self realisation. To whatever caste a person may belong, the zealous performance of one's duties as laid down and dedicating one's fruit to God lead them to the goal. Lord Krishna makes this very clear in the Bhagavad Gita :

"Sva karmana tam abhyarchya siddhim vindanti maanavah" - 18.46

(स्वकर्मणा तमभ्यर्च्य सिध्दि विन्दन्ति मानवाः)

It is the duty of some to fight and to defend. Another is a trader. Yet another a cowherd who protects cows. Yet, another is a worker or one who supplies the labour force. Each, doing his duty in the chosen field, can attain Him.

While others perform duties and follow professions which are conducive to better living in this world, what is the duty of the Brahmin? The most important aspect of our worldly lives is to obtain the grace of God. It is the duty of the brahmins to obtain such grace for the benefit of society. It is also the duty of brahmins to obtain the goodwill of the Devatas, who are in the nature of God's officials, to men of all classes.

The mantras which he recites and the Vedic karmas which he performs are meant for the benefit of all people and not for him alone.

Since his duty is with those whose powers transcend the worldly level, he has to learn mantras and obtain mantric powers through controls and disciplines which he has to exercise in a greater measure than others. For others, these are not required to as rigorous an extent as for the brahmin. If it is understood that his duty is to pray for and work for the well-being of all, the wrong feeling that some disciplines are specially laid down for the brahmins will not be entertained.

In addition to the above, a brahmin has to master the arts and sciences and the mode of work of others, so that he can educate them on their duties. Teaching alone is his job. As regards other crafts, he must merely study them so that he could teach them but he should not practise any of those crafts not prescribed for him.

Instead of actually following occupations such as defending the life and property of others, trade, agriculture and crafts, he should endeavour to teach the methods of each occupation and the way of life most conducive to its practice and, through this, he has to mould the character, mind and intellect of others. As such, the brahmin has a very difficult responsibility. Unless a person who performs this job has purity of mind and maturity of outlook, his efforts cannot bear fruit. Only if his mind and intellect are highly evolved can he cause the upliftment of others. At the same time, he has a handicap which others have not. If he thinks that since he uses his intellect for the performance of his duties, he is superior to others, this would be a major stumbling block. For these reasons, the brahmin has to keep himself scrupulously clean in outlook. Although there is justification for his ego to swell, he has to remain humble and totally selfless. That is why forty compulsory *'samskaaraas'* (duties) are prescribed for him so that his kinks are removed and angularities smoothened out.

If mantras are to take effect, then very stringent control and discipline are to be practised. Each mantra has certain specified requirement to be met, e.g., when to practise recitation and on what day of a fortnight it should not be practised, what sacrificial offering has to be given, etc. Each mantra has a special requirement for itself. If this is not followed the potency of the mantra so far as that person is concerned becomes weak. If a mantra is recited during eclipse, for e.g., its potency is said to increase. An entire Saakha of the Vedas has been devoted for spelling out the nature and effect of mantras and for the 'Vedavit' i.e. one who is proficient in the Veda, to attain self-realisation.

The Classification of Saakhas in use

Men in ancient times were endowed with great mental and physical ability. Since they imbibed high yogic powers and possessed vast intellectual capacity, each one was able to learn and recite a good number of Veda saakhas. To many Rishis or sages in intuitive moments the Vedas flashed in their minds by themselves. Others, who were blessed with uncommon prowess, were able to learn an unbelievably large number of Saakhas from teachers. Thereafter, in many cases, the Veda mantras flashed in their minds of their own accord.

They were able to improve vastly on what they had learnt from their teachers. If the Vedas are likened to an ocean, then, it is true that no one got to know it in full. But in those ancient times, many mastered a large part of it.

As time passed, men began losing their divine yogic powers and, when Kali Yuga set in, the loss became near complete. The life, health and mental capacity, all became very small, compared to those giants of the past.

All this is the "leela", sport of God. We can think of no reason why it is so. There is no answer to the question why people who had studied the Vedas assiduously and did yajnas followed by meditation on the Self had not passed on their good effects to the generations that came after them. The only answer that suggests itself is that, instead of following a repetitive pattern, God is staging the drama of life on the stage called the world. Thus, whilst social philosophers like Darwin emphasise the progressive evolution of man and life on earth, from the point of view of spirituality, mental acumen, morality, yogic and psychic power, the trend is just opposite to the progressive evolution outlined by Darwin. There is a regression. The freezing point was reached at the start of the Kali Yuga.

The decay started in a big way with the departure of Lord Krishna from this world, when a great darkness enveloped it. The darkness was on Him too. He was born in darkness being born in a jail at mid-night. But he was the beacon of light to all the world, a lamp of mercy and compassion. With his departure, knowledge suffered and the mantle of darkness was thrown on it. *Kali Purusha* who stands for evil influences, gained the upper hand. Even this is the sport of the Paramaatma, whose ways are inscrutable.

Lord Krishna came with great glory and effulgence, but, later, created a situation where people were afraid that there might be total darkness. It is not possible for the Vedas to shine brightly during Kali. It cannot also be reconciled with the duties assigned to Kali Purusha.

But the plan was to keep Veda at least at a certain level without it going into total extinction. He fulfilled his purpose through the agency of Veda Vyasa, who is a manifestation of a part of Himself.

He was then not known as Veda Vyasa. His name was also Krishna. Since he was born in an island (Dweepa), he was called Dvaipaayana. He was known, therefore, as Krishna Dvaipaayana. He was also known as Baadaraayana.

Krishna Dvaipaayana was learned in all the 1180 Veda Saakhas that had come into this world through the Maharishis or great sages and were existing at the end of Dwapara Yuga. In those days, all Vedas were in a mixed and conglomerate state, like flood waters. Only the ancient sages had the capacity to grasp all of it. For our sake with our limited and impaired capacity to grasp, Vyasa divided the Saakhas into four major groupings each with a number of Saakhas. These four major groups are now known as the four Vedas. This was due to his yogic and superhuman powers, due to the power of his austerities *(Tapas).*

Rig Veda Saakhas are conducive to worship or prayer, the Yajus Saakhas portray the ritualistic and yajna procedures, Saama Saakhas are hymns in musical form and Atharva Saakhas stress the performance of yajnas and contain mantras designed to protect men from dangers and enemies.

The Saama Veda, the singing of the hymns of which pleases the Devatas immensely, had the largest number of Saakhas. Out of the 1180, a thousand belong to Saama Veda. Rig Veda had 21, Yajur Veda had 109 (Sukla Yajur 15, Krishna Yajur 94). Atharva Veda had 50 Saakhas.

Krishna Dwaipaayana who later came to be known as Veda Vyasa thought that, since the future generations in Kali Yuga would be men of feeble intellectual power, it would suffice if each one could study and recite one Saakha out of the total eleven hundred and odd. It was God's will that made him think so. So, the old practice under which a man was to learn as many of the Vedas and Veda Saakhas as possible was modified in favour of one Saakha. He considered that it would be adequate if a person learnt to recite one of the several Saakhas of the four Vedas and performed the karmas prescribed thereunder. He entrusted the work of propagating the four Vedas, and their Saakhas to four of his disciples. The Rig Veda Saakhas were given to Paila, the Yajus Saakhas to Vaisampaayana, the Saama Saakhas to Jaimini and the Atharva Saakhas to Sumanthu. These four were, besides being disciples of Veda Vyasa, great sages in their own right.

The word "Vyasa" means an essay or composition. Since one subject was separated from the rest and taken up for detailed study, it was in the nature of a composition - or Vyasa. To deal with a matter subject-wise and classify it suitably is Vyasa. Since the numerous Veda Saakhas in existence were thus classified and arranged subjectwise, Krishna Dwaipaayana became known as Veda Vyasa. And so great is his contribution to the work of propagating the Vedas, that he is more widely known as Veda Vyasa or codifier of the Vedas than by any other name.

Since he considered that one Saakha was sufficient for study, it should not be taken to mean that he placed a ban on learning more than one. His idea was that, as a minimum, at least one Saakha should be learnt. But, after Veda Vyasa's time, for thousands of years, one used to learn first one Saakha from a Veda, then another Saakha from another Veda and so on. Thus, we had Dwivedis, Trivedis and Chaturvedis, i.e. those learned in the sakhaas of 2, 3 and 4 Vedas respectively.

It is more than 5000 years since Vyasa classified the Vedas. To some extent, this calculation is based on historical evidence. Modern historians have not accepted possibly due to the influence of western scholars, the firm date which saastras ascribe to Vyasa. Their original calculations placed the date of Mahabharatha at 1500 B.C., as the more probable date.

Today North Indians have suffixes such as Chaturvedi, Trivedi and Dwivedi, after their names. "Dubey" and "Dave" are corrupted abridgements of Dwivedis. The Chaturvedis are descendants of those who had learnt all the four Vedas. In Bengal, they are called Chattopadhyaya or Chatterjis. Trivedis in some places are also known as 'Tiwaris'. Although, today, it is difficult to find a person versed well even in one of the Vedas, the family name suffixes bear evidence to the fact that some of the ancestors of these had learnt more than one Veda, at some earlier point of time. It will indeed be good if those who bear such surnames today really emulate their illustrious ancestors.

During the last 5000 years and more, many Veda Saakhas have gone out of use due to neglect of the study. The figure of 1180 has been steadily dwindling and today we are in the unfortunate position of being left with only seven or eight Veda Saakhas. In Rig Veda, there is only one Saakha left out of the 21 called "Saakala Saakha". Since the Aithareya Upanishad is contained in this, it is also called the "Aithareya Saakha". Out of the 15 Saakhas of Sukla Yajur Veda, only two are known now, viz., the 'Kaanva' Saakha in Maharashtra and the 'Maadhyaandina' Saakha which is more prevalent in Vidarbha and North India. Of the 94 Saakhas of Krishna Yajur Veda, the Taitreeya Saakha alone is fully available and in use. This is very much in vogue in South India. Another Saakha from Krishna Yajur Veda, by the name of 'Maitraayaneeya Saakha' just manages to survive in Maharashtra. In Sama Veda out of the 1000, we have lost 997 Saama Saakhas. In Tamil Nadu, the only one left from Sama Veda Saakhas is the Talavakaara Saakha of the Jaimini school. The 'Raanaayaneeya' Saakha is now found only in Karnataka. Gujarat and Kerala have 'Kouthuma' Saakha. We were afraid that none of the Saakhas of Atharva Veda were in existence. Persistent efforts to locate the scholars in this Veda, however, provided information regarding the existence of a person in a place called Sinor in Gujarat who has studied the Sownaka Saakha of Atharva Veda well.

Students from South were, therefore, sent by us to learn this Saakha from him so that that Veda Saakha does not lapse but can be preserved.

We have also received the Aithareya Braahmana and Kousheetaki Braahmana (also called the Sangaayana Braahmana) which belong to the Rig Veda.

The corresponding Aaranyaka portions of these which contain the Aithareya Upanishad and the Kousheetaki Upanishad are already in use.

The only Braahmana in use from the Sukla Yajur Veda is the 'Satapatha' Braahmana. This is akin (although with some differences) to the Maadhyaandina Saakha and Kaanva Saakha. This is a big book which serves as a general guide to all Vedas. The Brahadhaaranyaka, which is an Aaranyaka but is also an Upanishad, is the only one which is available to us from Sukla Yajur Veda. I mentioned earlier that the Isavaasya Upanishad appears in the Samhita portion of this Veda only.

The Braahmana, currently in use from Krishna Yajur Veda, is 'Taittareeya'. The Aaranyaka portion of this Veda also contains the Taittareeya Upanishad and Mahaa Naaraayana Upanishad. Sooktas and mantras much in use are only those from Mahaa Naaraayana Upanishad.

The Maitraayani Aaranyaka and the Upanishad bearing the same name have been found in the same Krishna Yajur Veda. Kata Saakha, (Samhita), its Braahmana and Aaranyaka are all not in use today, but the Kathopanishad, also called Kathakopanishad which appears at its end, is very much in existence and learnt.

Likewise, although the Swetasvatara Upanishad appears at the end of the Swetasvatara Samhita of the Krishna Yajur Veda, no other part of the Saakha is available.

Although 997 of the Sama Saakha Samhitas are lost, 7 or 8 of its Braahmanas have accidentally escaped oblivion. 'Dandya' Braahmana, Samhitopanishad Braahmana, Vamsa Braahmana, Shad Vimsa Braahmana, Saamavidhaana Braahmana, Chaandogya Braahmana and Jaimaniya Braahmana are all available. One of the Aaranyakas of this Veda, called Talavakaara Aaranyaka, is also known as Talavakaara Braahmana. This appears in Jaiminiya Braahmana. At its end, appears Kenopanishad. That is why Kenopanishad is also referred to as Talavakaara Upanishad. The Chaandogya Upanishad has been obtained from the Chaandogya Braahmana of Saama Veda.

Although most of the Samhitas of Atharva Veda are lost, the 'Prasna', 'Mundaka' and 'Maandookya' Upanishads as well as the

'Nrisimha Thaapini Upanishad' of this Veda are even now available and are studied. The only Braahmana from this Veda which is available is the 'Gopatha Braahmana'.

In this state of affairs what is our duty?

We have to see that the seven or eight Samhitas which alone are now available out of the 1180 Veda Saakhas do not perish and do not become unavailable to the next generation. It will be an unpardonable sin if we do not take immediate and adequate steps to preserve for posterity the few Veda Saakhas and Upanishads which are now available.

15

THE VEDANGAS

SIKSHA — The nose and the lungs of the Vedas

Of the six organs (Anga) of the Vedas, the most primary Anga is Siksha (शिक्षा). It can be called the nose of the Vedas. The function of the nose does not stop at discerning smells which is a minor role. The more important breathing is done only through this organ. Just as the nose enables us to breathe, which, in turn, sustains the life-force, Siksha is the life-breath of the Veda mantras.

Where is the life centre of the Veda mantras located? Each letter of the Veda mantra must be uttered correctly within the *parimaana*, or duration in time, as laid down. This is called *Akshara Shuddhi* - syllable purity. In addition to the time duration, there are rules as to the pitch of the sound — high, middle or low. The high, low and middle pitches are respectively called *udaattam*, (उदात्तम्), *anudaattam* (अनुदात्तम्) and *swaritam* (स्वरितम्). If these are in their proper places, then the sound is said to be *swara-shuddha* (स्वर शुद्ध) having tonal purity. Thus mantras can yield results only if the requirements of syllable and tonal purity are fully satisfied. The emphasis on proper recital of the mantras is so great that more important to the mantras are these requirements of pronunciation and accent and pitch than even their meaning.

Even if one does not know the meaning, the correct intonation guarantees the expected results. Therefore, the life of the Vedas, which are only a string of mantras, is sustained by sound alone. Let us take the mantra which cures scorpion bite. Its meaning is not to be divulged. The words it contains have all the potency. Various sounds have various effects. Why is it necessary to utter the annual death anniversary mantra *(Sraaddha mantra)* in Sanskrit and not in English or any other language? Because, their sound is different in English or Tamil and their efficacy which is all in the sound is lost. If some teeth of those who chant mantras are lost and consequently they cannot utter the sounds properly then the purity of the mantra chant would suffer and the efficacy either lost or diminished. Thus pronunciation and the tonal quality are all important for Vedas.

What is to be done to ensure its purity?

'Siksha' lays down the rules of phonetics - sounds of syllables, of pronunciation - euphony. The function of the Siksha Saastra is to fix the parameters of Vedic words.

Phonetics is fixing the method of pronunciation of a language. More than for any other language, phonetics are most important in the case of the Vedic language, because we see that change in sound leads to change in results and effect.

Hence Siksha which is Vedic Phonetics has been regarded as the most important of the six Angas (organs) of the Veda Purusha.

Upanishads which are the crown of the Vedas also make mention of Siksha. The Taittareeya Upanishad begins with the chapter called "Sikshaa Valli". The first mantra says (शिक्षां व्याख्यास्याम:) Let us explain Siksha (Seeksha). Here, as also elsewhere in Vedic texts, 'Siksha' is referred to as "Seeksha" with the vowel 'e' lengthened to 'ee'. Adi Sankara mentions in his Bhashya, "Dhairgyam chandhasam". Elongation for Vedic language, that is to say according to the poetic licence, the short "e" becomes the long "ee". We had occasion to mention earlier that the Vedic language is not called Sanskrit and that it is called "Chandas". 'Chandasam' therefore refers to the special language used in Vedas.

In the wind instruments such as the harmonium, oboe and flute, air is let out through apertures on the basis of certain calculations, to produce various musical notes. The human throat has also a similar arrangement. It is not merely the throat. From the seat of the "Mooladhaara" which is just below the navel, the breath is made to travel upwards in various patterns which results in speech or melody. The musical instrument which God has designed for man is much superior to those produced by man, e.g. the flute or the harmonium. These latter can produce only ordinary sounds. Sounds of letters such as 'A', 'Ka' 'Cha', 'Nga' cannot be produced. The human voice alone has the ability to produce these sounds. Birds and animals can lisp some of these words but can come nowhere near man who can raise thousands of such sounds.

Because man alone has been gifted with the ability to make such sounds, his importance is obvious. It would be a pity if such an important asset is frittered away in idle talk and chatter. These should be used to harness divine forces, to do good to the world at large and to elevate oneself. In order to perform these three jobs, the Rishis have caught the sounds as Veda Mantras and given them to us. Only if this fact is fully grasped, can one understand why the science of Siksha has been evolved and pronunciation given so much importance. Much to the wonderment and admiration of distinguished philologists and scientists, the Siksha lays down with elaboration down to the minutest detail, how the breath has to originate from the pit of the stomach and touch so many points and twist and roll in many different ways, before it escapes through the mouth. That is how the purity of the sounds has been ensured.

When the air travels within us in such different ways, it becomes in effect a Yoga Sastra by itself. We had occasion to mention earlier that, due to the vibrations created by the passage of breath through the pulse centres, various emotions were created and forces generated and how these vibrations had their reaction on the outside world too. That is why those who control their breath and attain yogic powers have the same stature as those who chant mantras and realise the self.

Siksha Saastra explains how the sound of each syllable should be produced, how high or low should be its pitch and how long should the sound last. The last mentioned one viz. duration is called maatra (मात्रा). Maatra deals with short and long sounds. The short sound is called *Hrasva* (ह्रस्व) meaning "short". The long sound is called *"Deergha"*. Matters such as how to pronounce compound and compounded words without splitting them into syllables and certain other guidelines necessary for those learning to chant Vedas are contained in the Siksha Saastra. The sound 'Ka' has to emanate from the region between the neck and throat. Another has to come from the nose - the nasal sounds (e.g. gya). Sounds like 'tha' have to be produced by the tongue closing over certain teeth. Some like 'Na' come out of the tongue in contact with the palate or roof of the mouth. Others like 'Ma' come through closely compressed lips. The labiodentals like 'Va' are formed by the overlap of the lower lip on the lower teeth and so on. This Saastra is built on highly scientific lines. If we closely follow and practice the methods laid down as to which parts of the body and muscles should be exercised to produce particular sounds, we would have risen from the level of the mere science of phonetics to the level of Mantra Yoga or Sabda Yoga.

The basic language is only Sanskrit

I say the sound of a word is more important than even its meaning. Whilst on the subject, another point occurs to me. 'Chandas', which is the Vedic language and Sanskrit, which has been hewn out of it, contain many words whose sounds are indicative of their meaning.

For example, take the word 'Danta' which means a tooth. For its utterance, the teeth are mostly used, with the tongue acting lightly off and on. A trial will show how difficult it is for the toothless to utter it. They cannot clearly pronounce it.

There is something of interest here to students of comparative philology who take note of even trivial points in determining the chronology of languages. Sanskrit, Greek, Latin, German etc. which belong to the Teutonic group (English also is included in this) and modern French and other languages which belong to the Celtic group are, in the opinion of philologists, derived from one parent language, which is said to belong to the Indo-European group of languages though which is that parent language has not been firmly established by scholars. They do not accept that Sanskrit (which is meant to include the Vedic language 'Chandas') is the original base or parent language. But words such as 'Danta' amply support its claim to be regarded as such.

The word 'Dental' in English means the same thing - of teeth. We can see the similarity in 'Dant' and 'Dent'. The corresponding words in French and Latin are also akin in sound to 'Dant'. This is to say the 't' sound is prominent instead of 'da' as in Sanskrit. It might then be argued: "Well - maybe there is a similarity in sounds but how does it establish that Sanskirt is the parent language?" As mentioned earlier, you need all the teeth to correctly intone the word 'Danta' (दन्त) in Sanskrit. You try and say the other words like 'Dental' in the other tongues. The teeth have not much role to play. The 'Dent' sound is created by the tongue touching the roof of the mouth. If the word itself were to indicate the meaning unmistakably, then this requirement is fully met only in the 'Danta' of Sanskrit. That is why it is the root and the word 'Dental' is obviously a derivative.

In certain other cases, a slight change of spelling results in a closely allied word. What is the chief characteristic of a lion? To torment - Himsa. "Himsa" has given place to 'Simha' the lion. Kaasyapa, the first amongst the Rishis, was the procreator of the Devatas,Asuras,and also mankind. How did he get his name? He saw the Truth - Satya. That is to say, he saw the true form of God. Wisdom or Gnaana in Sanskrit is also called *Drisyam* - sight. The Sanskrit for one who sees is *"Pasyakaa"*, which with slight change became Kasyapa. कश्यप out of पश्यक.

Laws of Pronunciation

The Siksha Saastra lays down the details of the various aspects of pronunciation, e.g. enunciation, *(uchchaarana)*, tone (swara) duration (maatra), pitch (balam), evenness (samam) compounding *(santhaanam)*. This ensures that the sound that results is as perfect as perfect can be. It further says from what parts of the human body certain syllable sounds have to originate and through what kind of effort they are to be brought forth. All this is highly practical and scientific. If it says when the lips are to be joined to a certain extent to produce a letter-sound, low, the sound is produced to perfection when the instructions are followed.

I am reminded of something else, when I say this. The lip functions only when letters such as 'Pa', 'Ma', 'Va', are uttered. Letters such as 'Ka', 'Nga', 'Cha', 'Gna', 'Ja', 'Nna', 'Tha', 'Na', etc. do not invoke the use of the lips. Someone has composed a Ramayana with words not involving the use of the lips. That is called *'Niroshta Ramayana'.* Oshta is lip, from which has come *Oushtraka,* the camel. The camel has very prominent lips. *Niroshtam* means without lips. It might be that he composed the piece to show his skill. But another reason for it strikes me. He must have been a man with an exemplary sense of bodily cleanliness. He perhaps did not want to sully God's name by mouthing the sounds.

Maharishi Paanini (the Grammarian) indicates through a beautiful stanza in his 'Paanineeya Siksha' how carefully and attentively the Vedic words are to be chanted :

Vyaaghree yathaa haret putraan
Damshtraabhyaamcha na peedayet,
Bheeta patanaadetabhyaam
Tadwat varnaan prayojayet

व्याघ्री यथा हरेत् पुत्रान्
दंष्ट्राभ्यां च न पीडयेत्।
भीत पतनादेताभ्यां
तद्वत् वर्णान् प्रयोजयेत्॥

The Vedic letters must be spoken very lucidly. The sounds should not be blurred. The sound should not slip down or fade out. On the other hand, they should not be barked out. They should neither be loosely or casually mouthed nor spat out in staccato tones. The comparison is with a mother tiger. How does the tiger carry its young? Cats and tigers carry their young by their teeth. The teeth grip the cub firmly so that the cub does not slip and fall, but, at the same time, the teeth do not cause any hurt or pain. Likewise, the words are to be pronounced delicately but firmly. So says Paanini.

The same Paanini has made an invaluable contribution to the Vedaanga, next in importance - 'Vyaakarana' (grammar). In addition to Paanini many other sages have written on Siksha. There appear to be some 30 texts on the subject. Paanini's and Yaajnavalkya's are the most important of these.

The script of various languages

The script indicates, by means of drawing, (lines, loops and dots) the sounds of various letters. That is the origin of the scripts of various languages. The alphabet of English and allied languages is said to be in the Roman script. There used to be a script called Braahmi. The edicts of Emperor Asoka are in that script. From this are derived the scripts of the present-day Sanskrit (Naagari and Grantha) and those of the South Indian languages.

From one out of the two divisions of the Braahmi script, which was called 'Pallava Grantha' and which was in use in the South various scripts of the Dravidian languages have originated.

All the modern Indian language scripts have originated from the Braahmi. But, if you look at the original Braahmi script, nothing will look familiar. That is why the expression 'Braahmi script' came to be used to denote something not known.

There is a script called "Kharoshti". "Khara-Oshtam" means donkey's lips. Just as the donkey's lips protrude out, the loops of alphabets in that language protrude out like the lips of a donkey. This is the script of the Persian language.

Just as, in Europe, the Roman script is used by many languages, one common script in India is Braahmi. This is evident from the Devnaagari script used by many northern Indian languages.

If the phonetics of a language are clearly grasped, many more things will become clear to us. In English, we may wonder why there are two letters V and W to denote the 'Va' sound. A professor of English once explained the difference. Where V is used, we must produce the sound by folding the lower lip and allowing the upper set of teeth to touch it. Whereas, when W is used, the teeth are not to be used, both lips are to be partially closed to make a round before releasing the sound. Therefore the words Sarasvati and Isvara in the Indian languages are best spelt with a V and not a W.

More than in any other language, the pronunciation in Sanskrit closely and fully follows the spelling. In English, things are confusing. Recently I read in the papers : "Legislature wound up." Absent-mindedly I read the past participle of the word 'wind' as 'wound' meaning an injury. The same spelling pronounced differently has totally different meanings. Here 'wound up' means to close down. Even the word 'wind' has to be pronounced as 'Vind' to denote air and as 'Vynd' to denote binding around. Thus there is a lot of mix-up.

In Sanskrit alone, but for two exceptions, changes in pronunciation do not occur from spelling. It is purely phonetic spelling. Which are these two? Let me explain.

One is the change that occurs when the *visarga* occurs before 'Pa'. The visarga, more or less, takes the sound of 'ha'. Rama: must be pronounced as "Ramaha". Instead of fully making it sound 'ha' it should be softened. The same visarga, when it comes before 'Pa' becomes 'fa'. If the word is pronounced solely based on the sound belonging to the alphabet, it would be wrong.

Words like (ब्रह्म) (Brahma), (Vahni), etc., have to be written like that but have to be pronounced as Bramha, and Vanhi. Except for these two, pronunciation and script are not divergent in Sanskrit.

The language that has all the sounds

From the foregoing, it is clear that, in Sanskrit, the sound 'f' does exist. There is no sound that does not find a place in it. We commonly believe that the letter 'Zha' is available only in Tamil. The parent language of Sanskrit, the Vedic language does have the 'Zha' sound. In many places in Yajur Veda and where the letter 'Ta' comes in Talavakaara Saama Veda, it has to be sounded as 'Zha'. Similarly in Rig Veda too, at some places, the 'Zha' sound has to be produced. In the first word in the first Sookta of Rig

Veda which reads as 'Agni Meelay, the 'lay' has to be thus changed to 'Zha' to read as —"Agni Meezhay" not the full 'Zha' as in the Tamil language but a sound somewhere around it.

In French too, there is a sound close to 'Zha'. But both in French and Sanskrit, there is no separate letter to indicate the 'Zha' sound. The letters J and G, in French, are used to produce the 'Zha', effect. In Sanskrit, the letter 'La' alone is indicative of 'Zha'. It is claimed that the Chinese language has also a 'Zha'. "Ramah" plus "Panditah" becomes "Ramapanditah". This 'f' sound in Sanskrit is called *"Upadaaneeyam"* which literally means to blow the fire through a pipe or tube. Then only the 'f' sound can result.

Indian and Foreign Languages and Scripts.

There is a common characteristic peculiar to Indian languages. The words are to be pronounced exactly as the letter sounds would warrant. Let us take the word 'world', in English. When pronounce ed the initial letter is neither to be sounded as 'we' or 'wo' but something in between, not clearly defined. The letter 'T' in "ofton" so also the 'L' in walk and talk has similarly to be glossed over, which gloss-over is not capable of being indicated clearly in script. There are thus many such unclear sounds in other languages. These are called *'Avyakta'* - unclear sounds. All our Indian languages contain clear sounds only.

Instead of direct rule about the letter and its sound, there is lot of confusion in other languages. For e.g. the letter 'C' can be indicative of the syllable 'Ka'. Any one of three sounds pertaining to C, K, or Q can be so. This is not so with Indian languages. In English there are three ways of spelling to indicate the sound of 'f', e.g. 'fairy' 'philosophy' and 'rough'. Although the letter 'C' is mostly indicative of the 'Sa' sound, most of the words beginning with 'C' in English are pronounced with the 'Ka' sound. Only in some instances like cell, celluloid and cinema has 'C' the sound of 'Sa'.

When you say 'fat', the 'a' sounds in one way. In 'fast' the same sounds differently. Some spellings and pronunciations have very little in common. In 'station' and 'nation' the 'tion' is pronounced as 'shun'. Since the script of English and other languages which use the Roman alphabet, have only 26 letters, it is easy to learn them. On the other hand, Indian languages are more difficult to learn as they contain many more letters. But, if for a whole year, one takes the trouble to slog at the Kindergarten class, then reading in that language becomes easy. But in the case of English, even after crossing the Master's level, one has to refer to the dictionary for correct pronunciation.

This merit, which the Indian languages have, is present more fully in the Sanskrit language. By this I do not mean to say that the foreign languages are inferior to Sanskrit. I am merely pointing out some factual details of the peculiarities in languages. My idea is to project the image of sound which is the soul of the Infinite *(Sabdabrahmaatmaka)*, as finding its clearest expression in Sanskrit.

Everyone should feel that all languages are common property. Then there will be no occasion for anyone to berate another. On the issue of language only if the fundamental fact that language is solely meant to serve as the medium of communication is understood the present frenzy of love for one's mother tongue and hatred for another's will go away. It is pathetic to hear so much talk on the need for broad-mindedness and international outlook but having such narrow and parochial views in the matter of languages.

Aksha Maala - String of beads

The word Rudra-Aksha-Maala means a beaded string of 'Rudraaksha' beads, which is believed to have come out of Rudra's eyes. 'Aksha' here means the eye. What does it mean when one says 'Aksha Maala'? It is not right to translate 'Aksha' as the eye in this case. It stands for all the letters of the alphabet beginning from 'A' (अ) and ending with 'Ksha' (क्ष). In Sanskrit alphabet, A is the first letter and 'Ksha' the last. Just as we say 'A' to 'Z' in English to indicate completeness or totality, in Sanskrit we say Akaaraadi Kshakaaraantaha. i.e. beginning with (अ) and ending with (क्ष). The total number of letters is fifty. So in an Akshamaala there will be fifty beads.

The importance of intonation

I have already mentioned that great care should be exercised in practising the chant of mantras as not only would it result in the loss of benefits if perfection in word and sound is not ensured but bad intonation may lead to malefic or contrary effects. There is a story in the Vedas unmistakably illustrating this - (Taittareeya Samhita - 2.4.12).

"Tvashta", who was not well disposed towards Indra, for some reason wanted a son capable of killing Indra so that he could settle old scores with Indra. So he performed a Homa (Fire-sacrifice) chanting a mantra: *'Indrassatrur vardhasva'.* When chanting it, the correct way was to utter 'Indra' in even tone (i.e. without raising or lowering it). In Satru, the tru should have been high, and similarly 'Vardhasva' should have been high. If said, as above, it would mean 'let Tvashta's son grow up to kill Indra'. By the efficacy of the sound alone, he should have grown up and killed Indra. But Tvashta erred in pronunciation. That is, he raised high the 'dra' in Indra, the 'Satru' was said evenly and in 'vardhasva' the 'rdha' was lowered instead of being raised. As a result, instead of 'let him grow up as the killer of Indra', the meaning got topsyturvy. Although the words and letters were not changed, due to the fault in intonation, the result was just contrary to what Tvashta wanted. His son was killed by Indra. Thus the father became responsible for the death of his son, Vrtra (वृत्र), at the hands of Indra.

A sloka draws attention to this incident mentioned in the Vedas in order to caution us to be more careful in intonation and pronunciation of Veda mantras.

Mantroheena swarato varnathovaa
Mithyaaprayukto na tamarthmaaha
Savaak vajro yajamaanam hinasti
Yathendrasatruh swaratoaparaadhaat.

मन्त्रो हीनस्स्वरतो वर्णतो वा
मिथ्याप्रयुक्तो न तमर्थमाह।
स वाग् वज्रो यजमानं हिनस्ति
यथेन्द्रशत्रुः स्वरतोऽपराधात्॥

Some small differences

So far I have said about how the Vedas should be syllable perfect. As proof of what I said, you may see that from Rameshwaram to Himalayas, in all places in India - with or without any social contacts, all the versions of the Vedas now existing in India are 99% the same, without any difference in word or letter, even though they have been preserved without the aid of printed or written books and the Vedic texts have been passed from generation to generation by word of mouth. Does this mean there is a small difference still? Yes. There is. Every Saakha in each region has a slight difference with its counterpart in another region. Can this be permitted? After saying that even a small difference would make a disastrous difference, how can even this small one per cent difference be tolerated? If there can be only one correct form, another with even a 1% difference cannot yield the expected result. Or, it should lead to a different result. There is an answer to this poser. It is true that a change in the wording of mantras would pervert the result just as a change in the prescribed medicine would affect the cure of an illness. But, this only applies to the patient; he should not by himself change the medicine. The doctors can change the prescription. There are several medicines to treat a disease. In such cases, there is nothing wrong in the doctor recommending a particular medicine and not the other. Even in the case of the same disease, the doctor may alter the ingredients of a mixture to suit differences in physique.

So also, the difference in words has been knowingly and deliberately made by the Rishis in the various Saakhas. This has been designed to suit those who may come later (in time) to chant them. The rules governing these changes are clearly spelt out in 'Praatisaakhya' (प्रातिशाख्य) texts. The word प्रातिशाख्य literally means 'provincial'. The differences in the words are very slight. The changes do not make an appreciable difference. Words with more or less similar sounds are used one for the other - words which are closely allied.

Vedic sounds as influenced by regional languages :

When the differences between the various Indian languages are examined in the light of the small differences in the word of the Vedas pertaining to the region, the startling conclusion emerges that the distinctive cultures and cultural differences have been caused by the differences in Vedic sounds. Let me state the result of my philological enquiries. The sounds 'da', 'ra', 'la', 'la', and 'zha' are close to each other. If a child is asked to say 'rail' or 'Rama' it would say 'dail' or 'dama'. This is because 'da' and 'ra' are close in sound. Since 'da' can change to 'ra', it follows that 'la' can change to 'da'. 'la' and 'lla' are really close. There is no need to stress the affinity between 'la' and 'zha'.

Let us now take those regions where each Veda is vastly popular and examine the pecularities of the language used.

These days there is a campaign going on among some that the Vedas belong to the Aryans and that Dravidianism is different from it. So let us take the three regions in the land of the Dravidians. That is, let us take Tamil, Telugu and Kannada. In Tamil, the peculiarity is 'zha', in Telugu it is 'da' and in Kannada it is 'la'. For example, there is a Sanskrit word, Pravaala. It is the same as 'Pavazham' in Tamil (coral). This is called 'Pagadaalu' in Telugu and Havalla in Kannada. Pravaala has become Pavazha in Tamil. In 'Pagadaalu' the V appearing in Pravaala has become ga. This is the characteristic of the language. Similarly when 'Pravaala' becomes the Havalla in Kannada, the first letter itself undergoes a major change. 'Pra' changing into 'Pa' in Tamil and Telugu is only a minor transformation but, in Kannada, it has become Ha. But this is the special characteristic of that language. What is 'Pa' in other languages becomes 'Ha' in Kannada. Pampa becomes Hampa, further changing into Hampi e.g.: (Hampi ruins). Although not distinguishable separately as Aryans or Dravidian, the same race is divided into those whose language is affiliated to Sanskrit and those whose language is purely Dravidian. This is the conclusion now available from research. Further research might well prove that even this language difference is not warranted but all languages have descended from a common parent langauge. It is the Rig Veda that is mostly in use in the Western India, including Maharashtra and Karnataka, that is why the 'lla' sound is in usage in Rig Veda. The Vedic 'lla' has crept into what is thought to be the Dravidian language Kannada and is in vogue.

Taking the eastern coast and the land adjoining it, viz., the Andhra region, 98% of the people belong to Yajur Veda. The rest of the 2% are Rig Vedis. It can be said that, in Andhra, there are practically no Saama Vedis. Since the most important thing is the Yajur Veda, the 'lla' which appears in the Rig Vedic chant is naturally changed to 'da'. Here, also in the regional language, Telugu, what is 'lla' in other languages has become 'da'.

In the Tamil Nadu, in later times, the Yajur Vedins became predominant but not to the extent as in Andhra. In Tamil Nadu it may be said that 80% are Yajur Vedis and of the rest 15% are Saama Vedis and the balance of 5% Rig Vedis. Although, at present, this is the position, there is evidence to show that, in times past, Saama Veda held more sway in Tamil Nadu than now. It is a fair guess that all the 1000 Saakhas of Saama Veda had their followers in Tamil Nadu.

Malayalam is the language in use in what is now called Kerala. The reason why I did not mention Malayalam in the same breath as Telugu and Kannada was that, like the Pallavas, this, belongs to a later age. Until about 1000 years ago Kerala was part of Tamil-speaking land and the language in use there was Tamil. Then Malayalam was evolved from Tamil. The Tamil 'zha' which becomes 'da' in Telugu and 'lla' in Kannada remained as 'zha' in Malayalam. Therefore, based on the differences in pronunciation of Veda Saakhas, the various regional languages have developed suitable individualistic alphabets.

What I said so far is confined to the land of the what is now called Dravidians. I am now going to look at it on an all-India and inter-national level.

It is the custom in Northern India to use 'Ja' instead of 'Ya' and 'ba' instead of 'va'. This is not only in colloquial use but is also in literary usage. 'Va' becoming 'Ba' is most noticeable in Bengal; 'ya' becoming 'ja' in Uttar Pradesh, the Punjab and further North. In Bengal, the Paaṇini sutra *'vaabayorabhedam'* ('va' and 'ba' do not preclude interchange) is followed in totality. In Bengal, all 'va' is changed to 'ba'. In fact, 'vanga' has become 'Bengal'. Vangavaasi has become 'Bangabaasi'. They themselves realise the error of this. In Bengal, an examination was held to correct this error. Its name was 'Vanga Parishad'. Their intention was to use 'V' instead of 'b' in all future publications. In so doing, they unwittingly changed 'b' into v, where such a change was not warranted. 'Bandhu' (meaning a relative) was changed to 'Vandhu'. The correct term 'Vanga Bandhu' which was orginially wrongly called 'Banga Bandhu', has now again become wrong in another way as 'Vanga Vandhu'.

In the north, to a certain extent, and in other regions too, 'ba' is used instead of 'va'. Bihar is really 'Vihar'. This was the place which abounded in Buddha Vihars. 'Rash Bihari' is none other than 'Rasa Vihari'. Why do they pronounce 'v' as 'b'? The Praathisaakya lays down that those belonging to a certain Saakha in that region should say so. That injunction which was meant for Vedic chant was followed in speech and script for ordinary purposes also. This shows that, at one time, the laws of Siksha were faithfully followed in this region.

I said earlier that the Yajur Veda was in use by the majority in the whole country. I also said that this Veda had two versions, viz. the Krishna Yajur Veda and the Sukla Yajur Veda. Of these, the most prevalent in the South is the Krishna Yajus: that in the north is mostly Sukla Yajus.

One of the many Saakhas of Sukla Yajus is Maadhyaandina Saakha. This is zealously practised in the North. Its Praatisaakhya says it is permissible for 'ja' to be used in place of 'ya'. It also says that 'ka' can be used in place of 'sha'. That is why when in the south one says *'Yath Purushena Havisha'* (यत् पुरुषेण हविषा) it is uttered by them in the North as *'Jat Purushena Havika'* (जत् पुरुषेण हविका). In course of time this change has been adopted in the case of many words in the North. The 'Yamuna' becomes the 'Jumuna'. 'Yogi' becomes 'Jogi'. 'Yuga' becomes 'juga'. 'Yatra' becomes 'Jatra' and so on. When 'sha' is changed to 'ka', 'Rishi' becomes 'Riki'. 'Ksha' and 'sha' are near relatives, aren't they? Therefore in the North 'Ksha' also becomes 'ka'. 'Kshiram' is 'Khir'. We can thus go on citing examples.

Let us now go to the inter-national level. Let us go to Palestine, the birthplace of Christianity and the Bible; to Israel and other Semetic countries. The basis of the Koran of the Muslims is the Old Testament of the Christians. Those appearing in the Old Testament also make their appearance in the Koran. But in Arabia the pronunciation changes. Joseph becomes 'Yusuf'. Jehovah becomes Yahovah. This difference is not only found between Christianity and Islam. Even amongst the Christian nations, the 'ya' sound is predominant in certain languages. In some others, the 'ja' sound takes over. If one goes towards Greece, the 'j' sound surfaces.

Research has revealed that the cause of this is the Vedas. The Devata called 'Yahvan' in the Vedas is none other than Jehovah (Yehova). Doupita is Jupiter, it is said. If a half consonant comes at the beginning of a word in Sanskit, it is dropped when it is said in another language. Thus 'dou pitar' is 'yow pitar', which is 'Jupiter'.

What does this lead to, when the original Yahvan and Doupitar as a result of the change of 'ya' to 'ja' become Jehovah and Jupiter? Does this not support the inference that when Vedic practices were universal, in the area around Greece, the Maadhyaandina Saakha of the Yajur Veda was mostly in use?

Did the Vedic pronunciation influence the regional language? Or did the regional language regulate Vedic pronunciation?

All I said above is to show that the words in use in Vedas in a particular region also figured in the spoken and written language of that region. From this, it is evident that the Vedas were in vogue in all countries.

It is indeed correct to say that the Vedic Siksha rules have come to be the principal sounds in the regional languages because the Praatisaakhya rule was not made from one region; it was made for all regions where a Saakha was in use. Whether in Kashmir or in Kamarup (modern Assam), a person chanting Jaimini Saama would say 'sha' where others would say 'da' or 'lla'. Whatever be the language spoken by a person who chants it, one who chants the Sukla Yajur Veda, whether his mother tongue is Gujarati or Marathi or whatever else, he sould use 'da' only. The Praatisaakhya which was not meant for any particular region but is a general book of rules, has thus defined the letter-sounds. In course of time, wherever a particular Saakha was much in use, the peculiarity of the letter in question infiltrated into the regional language too.

The other noteworthy points about Siksha Saastra

I say that the Vedic sounds should not be changed; the tone should not be altered. Nevertheless, I have so far explained how, based on the differences in Saakha, some small changes are permissible according to the Siksha Saastra. Likewise, in the matter of Swara (pitch), minor variations are permissible.

I said earlier that, in Vedic chant, there are the Samhita, Pada and Krama modes. Such differences in the methods of chant of the Samhita portions of Vedas have the sanction of Praatisaakhya which are a part of the Siksha Saastra.

There is no warrant for treating the matter lightly as merely one of sounds. All that there is, is in the sound. Therefore, the Siksha Saastra is the nose through which the Veda Purusha breathes.

The 50 sounds (syllables) in the Sanskrit alphabet have come from the Vedas. If the letter Gnya (ज्ञ) is taken as separate, we have 51 letters. They are called Maatruka (मातृका). There are many meanings to this. Most importantly, Maatru is 'Mata' which stands for the cosmic mother. The 51 letters are in the image of that Paraasakti (super power). If all the universe owes its creation to the Paraasakti and if creation was made through the medium of sound, it follows that Paraasakti should be the personification of the 51 letters. The Siksha Saastra says that these 51 syllables represent the various parts of Paraasakti's body and even define which syllables represents which part. In our country, the 51 seats of the sakti cult have come into being as having connection with the 51 parts of the cosmic body.

If the stature of the Siksha Saastra is enhanced by being likened to the nose of the Veda Purusha, its importance is further increased by the syllables in it being regarded as adding up to create the full image of Paraasakti, the divine Mother.

16

VEDANGAS

VYAAKARANA — Grammar

The second organ of the Veda Purusha is his mouth. Vyaakarana or grammar is this very important organ.

There are many books on grammar. The one mostly in use is the Vyaakarana of sage Paanini. Paanini's Vyaakarna is in the form of Sutras or aphorisms. His Vyaakarana Sutras have an elaborate commentary or 'Vaartika' by Vararuchi. Sage Patanjali also wrote a Bhaashya or commentary. These three together are regarded as important texts in Vyaakarana Saastra.

There is a difference between other Sastras and Vyaakarana. In the case of others, the Sutras or aphorisms are more important than the Bhaashyas or commentaries. It is not so with Vyaakarana. The Vaartika or detailed commentary is more important than the Sutra itself.

Instead of being explanatory the Sutras are only indicators. Every Saastra has a Bhaashya or commentary. Each one is called by a separate name indicative of what it is the Bhaashya of. The Vyaakarana Bhaashya alone is called Maha Bhaashya or the great Bhashya bespeaking of its importance. This Maha-Bhaashya, as already mentioned, was written by Sage Patanjali.

Vyaakarana and Lord Siva

In Siva stemples, there used to be a mandapa (hall) called the 'Vyaakarana dana mandapa'. Why does the temple of Siva have a vyaakarana dana mandapa? Why is it not there in the Vishnu temples? What is the connection between language and Siva or for that matter Siva and Grammar? Siva, as Dakshinaamurthi, is in fact silent; without any speech. I will explain. There is a sloka as under :

Nrttaavasaanay Nataraajaraajo nanaada
Dhakkaam navapancha vaaram
Uddhartukaamah Sanakaadi Siddhan
etat Vimarso Sivasootra jaalam.

नृत्तावसाने नटराजराजो ननाद ढक्कां नवपञ्चवारं
उद्धर्तुकामः सनकादि सिद्धान् एतत् विमर्शो शिवसूत्रजालम्॥

The silent Siva remains still without any movement or motion. When he at the end of the cosmic dance sounded his Dhakka, the science of language was born. This is the gist of the above sloka.

Nataraja is the name of the dancing Siva. Nataraja is one who cannot be surpassed in dancing. He is the king of the Cosmic Dance. This is the big dance. In a Nataraja image one will see something like a projection on his head adorned with a depiction of Ganga and the crescent moon. These represent the matted tresses of Siva; when Siva dances and whirls about, these tresses also whirl. At the moment of stopping, the tresses spread out on either side. This moment is what is caught by the artist in his imagination and sculpted in stone or metal.

A small drum called 'Dhakka' or 'Damaru' will be found in Nataraja's hand. It is slightly bigger than the itinerant fortune-teller's small hand-drum. When Siva dances he shakes the damaru or dhakka in tune with the rythm of the dance. This is indicated by the words *"Nanaada dhakkaam"* (ननाद ढक्कां) in the above sloka.

The important musical instruments can be classified into three groups. They are : (1) *Charma Vaadya,* (चर्म वाद्य) i.e., percussion instruments where leather or hides are used. e.g. Dhakka, Mrdanga, Chenda (of Kerala), Maddalam, etc., (2) *Tantri Vaadya* (तन्त्री वाद्य) like, Veena and Violin using strings; (3) *Vaayu Randhravaadya* (वायुरंध्रवाद्य) or wind instruments like flute and Nadaswaram, clarinet, etc. where air is forced out of spaced-out holes. The Charma vaadya or the percussion instruments can be played either by hand or using a stick. When bringing it to a close, as a finale, brisk but tuned beating called 'chopu' is resorted to. Likewise, at the time of concluding the dance, *(Nrtta-Avasaanay)*- the sound of "chopu" was heard i.e. a sort of crescendo.

When Nataraja dances the great dance, sages like Sanaka, Patanjali, Vyaaghrapaada and others stand around and joyfully watch. Being great sages and Seers they could see the dance which ordinary mortals cannot see, with their own eyes because Nataraja's dance can only be seen by divine eyes. The Gods, Sages and Yogis because of the power of their penance obtained the ability to see Natarja's dance. That ability to see the divine form is called *"Divya drshti"* or what is called *'Dhivya chakshus'* in the Bhagavad Gita.

The Sages like Sanaka and others were enjoying the sight of the Lord's dance through their own eyes. Vishnu was beating the big drum to Nataraja's dance. Brahma was keeping time or *Tala* to the movements. At the moment of the cessation of the dance the 'chopu' or the final crescendo comes out of the Dhakka as fourteen different beats in quick succession. The *'Nava Pancha Vaaram'* of the above sloka has reference to this nine plus five or fourteen (times) beats.

The number of Vidyas are fourteen on the basis of the same number of beats of the Dhakka. If fourteen Vidyas are said to be the foundation of the Hindu Dharma, the damaru or dhakka of Nataraja also gave fourteen different beats or rhythmic sounds. The stanza says that the fourteen beats helped the Sages like Sanaka and others to reach higher and to evolve further spiritually. Who are these Sanaka and others? In temples where Dakshinaamurthi is installed, we see depicted around Dakshinaamurthy four old people. They are the four great Sages: Sanaka, Sanandana, Sanatana and Sanat Kumara usually referred to as Sanaka and others. The fourteen sounds that arose became for these sages the path or medium for the realisation of Siva's form. The sounds were called the *"Siva Bhakti Sutra"* on which Nandikeswara wrote a commentary or Bhaashya.

One of those present at the dance was the Sage Paanini. The story of Paanini is mentioned in *Kathaa Sarit-Saagara.* In Pataliputra (the modern Patna), there lived two men named Varshopadhyaya and Upavarshopadhyaya. The latter was the younger of the two and his daughter was called Upakosla. Paanini and Vararuchi were both studying under Varshopadhyaya. Paanini was comparatively a dull student and did not make much progress in studies. Therefore, Varshopadhyaya sent him to the Himalayas with instructions to practise austerities. He accordingly did penance and was blessed with Siva's grace. He was blessed with the power to see the dance of Nataraja with his own eyes.

With the aid of the fourteen sounds that were produced (on the damaru) at the time of the conclusion of the cosmic dance, Lord Siva laid the foundation of the Vyaakarana Sutras. The fourteen Sutras were committed to memory by Paanini and on that basis he wrote the basic text called *'Ashtaadhyaayi'* so called because it contains eight chapters.

The fourteen Sutras are referred to as *Maheswara Sutras.* These fourteen Sutras are recited by us on Sravana Pournima at the time of Upakarma popularly known in Tamil Nadu as "Aavaniavittam".

Thus the Maheswara Sutras, which originated from Nataraja's damuru sound, became the foundation of Vyaakarana or grammar. This is the connection between Siva and grammar and why there are Vyaakarana Mandapas in Siva temples.

Books on Grammar

Lord Siva is called Chandravatamsa, Chandrasekhara, Indusekhara, etc. because He has the moon as an adornment on his head. Two of the Vyaakarana books bear the 'Indusekara' nomenclature. One is *"Sabdendu Sekharam"* (शब्देन्दु शेखरम्). The other is known as *Paribhaashendu Sekharam* (परिभाषेन्दु शेखरम्). If, in Vyaakarana, one is proficient up to the level of these books he is referred to admiringly as having studied upto 'Sekharaanta' (शेखरान्त).

Just as there are some 30 books on Siksha Saastra, there are also a number of books on Vyaakarana. But the most celebrated of these are Panini's Sutras, Patanjali's Bhaashya and Vararuchi's Vaartika, as already mentioned earlier.

Vararuchi was one of the nine 'jewels' in King Vikramaaditya's court. He has written books on Vyaakarana. Whether he also wrote the Vaaratika or not is a matter on which opinion is divided.

Bhartruhari's *"Vaakya Padyam"* is also one of the important texts on Vyaakarana. The important grammar texts are referred to as *'Navavyaakarana'* (नवव्याकरण). These nine were stated to have been mastered by Anjaneya or Hanuman the great devotee of Sri Rama, having received instruction from the Sun god Himself. One of the texts called *"Aindram"* said to be authored by Lord Indra himself is believed to be the basis of the Tamil grammar book called *Tolkaappiyam.*

Linguistic Research and Religious Text

Siksha, Vyaakarana, Chandas and Nirukta are four of the Vedangas (limbs of the Vedas) that relate to language. It might be contended by some people that religious texts should confine themselves to matters such as God, methods of worship, worship versus knowledge, words of wisdom, disciplines, laws of life and so on and not to language, grammar, phonetics etc.

Under the caption of 'Veda', such matters which were considered as purely relating to religion were mentioned. Those that are going to be dealt with, viz. *Kalpa, Meemaamsa, Nyaaya, Puraana* and *Dharma Saastra,* will surely contain such matters. But, in between, these sciences of language and phonetics, grammar, etc., which have no connection with religion, have also come up. Why? Because, according to the Vedic religion, everything is connected with God, and there can be no clear-cut distinction between matters pertaining to pure religion and those relating to other subjects. That is why medical science or Ayurveda which deals with bodily ailments and their cure and the science of Archery (Dhanur Veda) which is useful in war are also regarded as affecting the evolution of the Self and are hence grouped with the fourteen Vidyas (or disciplines). Economics and Politics which are mentioned in Artha Saastra are also part of Aatma Vidya.

These have been assigned the status of religious texts since they indicate the path to the realisation of the self which involves regulating all aspects of life.

In Siksha, Vyaakarana etc. can be found the Infinite in its most glorious manifestation, viz., sound. In order that we may be helped in our progress towards salvation by the influence of languages which is connected with sound, Siksha and Vyaakarana have been evolved.

Vyaakarana propounds the *'Sabda Brahma Vaada'* - the theory that sound and Infinite are inter-linked. One of its offshoots is the *Naada Brahma Upasana* (नाद ब्रह्म उपासना) - the cult of melody culminating in the Infinite - which is the basis of pure music. When the sounds are properly understood and used as speech, we can not only communicate our thoughts but also strive for self-purification. Towards this end, these sciences relating to language are helpful.

There was a kingdom called 'Dhar' in the old Central Provinces which under independent India has come to be known as Madhya Pradesh. This 'Dhar' was none other than 'Dhara', the capital city of King Bhoja, the celebrated patron of all arts, who was a byword for generosity and philanthropy. There is a mosque in the town of Dhara. It came to light that some Sanskrit inscriptions were visible inside a niche in the mosque. Since the place belonged to Muslims and without their consent one could not get and examine the writing, the Epigraphical Department itself could not get at it for a few years. Then some years after the attainment of Independence, men from the Epigraphical Department obtained the permission of the authorities of the mosque and investigated the writing in the inscriptions.

There was a huge wheel depicted on the wall on which were written many verses. These verses were all on Vyaakarana. The entire Vyaakarana Saastra had been written in verse and charted in the form of a wheel. What during the days of King Bhoja was the temple of Sarasvati apparently has now become a mosque.

The intention of the original sculptors and builders was obvious; that in the temple of Sarasvati, the goddess of speech and learning, the science of language should be always present through Vyaakarana which is the mouth of the Veda Purusha. It is claimed that a mere glance at the giant wheel would make the whole of Vyaakarana clear. Since Vyaakarana had the status of an object of reverence and worship, the wheel of Vyakarana was installed in a temple. Many years after the temple became a mosque we have been able to get the Chakra through the grace of the Goddess of Speech. The Department of Epigraphy has published the wheel in print. It has also been translated into English.

From this, it is evident that sciences like the Vyaakarana had not been relegated to the background as mere disciplines by Kings and Governments in those days but elevated to a level where they became objects of worship. You can realise from this how purity and refinement in language was considered very important in old times in our country.

17

THE VEDANGAS

CHANDAS — The feet of the Vedas

C*handas,* which is one of the six limbs of the Vedas, is regarded as the feet of the Veda Purusha. 'Chandas' has another meaning. It refers to the Vedas themselves. Lord Krishna refers to the Vedas as leaves of the tree of creation (छन्दांसि यस्य पर्णानि).

Here I am going to deal with 'Chandas' in a different sense meaning 'metric composition.'

Rig Veda and Saama Veda are wholly in verses. Although Yajus has mantras in prose, they come interspersed with verses. Vedas being mostly in verse-form (Chandas), also came to be known as Chandas.

If we want a coat, the tailor takes our measurements. He cuts and stitches the cloth accordingly. If measurements are not taken, the coat may not fit. Likewise, if our thoughts are to be expressed in poetry, if the thoughts are to assume the image of poetry, and clothed in verse-form, it must have proper measurements. Like a coat being so many inches long and broad, a verse has to have a specified 'metre' and number of letters in it, to obtain a good fit. Chandas lays down the rules for this. It defines the boundaries of metrical composition - into metre, rhyme, etc. The important and authoritative book on the subject is the *'Chandas Sutra'* by Pingala.

As mentioned already the organ which is regarded as the feet of the Veda Purusha is Chandas. Those who have been initiated into Mantra Japa, touch their head, when the name of the Rishi is mentioned, touch their nose when its Chandas or metre is named, and touch the heart when the name of the Devata or the presiding deity of the mantra is mentioned.

All the Veda mantras in the form of poetry are 'Chandas'. The others, i.e. those which are not part of Vedas are called 'Slokas'. Prose is called 'Gadya' and Chandas is called 'Padya' in Sanskrit. In English it is poetry. Thus, not only is Vedic poetry called 'Chandas' but 'Chandas' also refers to the metre or rhyme of any poetic expression which are all rhythmic. Of these metres, 'Anushtup' is the one which is extensively used. The slokas of the Puraanas and Valmiki Ramayana are all in this Anushtup metre. Chandas is thus synonymous with rhyme also.

There are rules as to how many paadas (पाद) or quartrets or steps are to be in each *Vrtta* or Stanza and how many letters are to be in each paadaa or line. There is a Chandas called Aarya which has also to take into account the short and long sounds. In this Chandas, the word 'Rama' is not reckoned as having two maatras only, viz., 'Ra' and 'ma'. 'Ra' is the long sound and counted as two maatras, 'ma' which is short as one, total three.

There is another method of calculation for other Vrittas where the long and short sounds are not differentiated and, in each stanza, the number of words in a paada are kept constant.

Paada or foot

I called Chandas as such being the feet (paada) of the Veda Purusha. The foot is called paada (पाद) or pada (पद) in Sanskrit. Also in English, the reckoning is in terms of 'feet' in a stanza. The metres in English also stipulate how many letters should there be in each foot. The foot, which denotes the end of the leg, also denotes the unit of division of a stanza. Thus, the foot or pada (or its equivalent) is a common expression in many languages having the same meaning. It is indeed heartening to find, in any field, an example showing a similarity common to all mankind. In a mantra or in a sloka, a paada is a quarter portion of it. In the human anatomy, the organ called 'leg' is indeed one fourth part. Half the body is upto the hip; of the remaining half below, each of the two legs is one quarter adding upto 'half'.

A Veda mantra or even a non-Vedic sloka is generally a quartet. In most cases, these are split into four, using an equal number of letters or equal number of maatras for each paada. Where one paada is not equal to another paada, it is called *'Vishama'.* Vishama is actually Vi-sama which means not equal or same.

If all the paadas are different in length, it is said to be in "Vishama Vrtta" (विषम वृत्त). Every alternate paada being dissimilar is called "Ardha Sama Vrtta" (अर्ध सम वृत्त). That is, there will be a difference in the number of letters between the first and the second paada as well as between the third and the fourth paada. The second and the fourth Paada will be of equal number of syllables.

However, in most cases the paadas will be equal in length. For example, let us take the most commonly known prayer — sloka: *"Suklaambaradharam Vishnum / Sasi Varnam Chaturbhujam / Prasanna Vadanam Dhyaayet / Sarva Vighnopasaantaye".* Let us take the four paadas in it. First, *"Suklaambaradhaam Vishnum",* second, *"Sasi Varnam Chaturbhujam",* third, *"Prasanna Vadanam Dhyaayet"* and fourth, *"Sarva Vighnopasaantaye".* If counted, each paada will have only eight syllables - not the letters in English but the syllables in Sanskrit :

शुक्लांबरधरं विष्णुं
शशिवर्णं चतुर्भुजं।
प्रसन्न वदनं ध्यायेत्
सर्वविघ्नोपशान्तये।।

For counting the aksharas or syllables only vowels and consonants with vowels imposed thereon are to be taken into account. Pure consonants should be ignored. Only then will the above add up rightly to eight.

Slokas like this, which have four paadas to a stanza with each paada having eight syllables are said to be in *Anushtup Chandas.*

The story of the birth of the poetic Chandas

Unlike in the Vedas, where the pitch of the sounds is raised or lowered to produce tonal variations or *Swara* there is no such method with *Kaavya* (Poetry) or other slokas. The Anushtup metre of the Vedas with variations in pitch was first adopted by Valmiki but without the variations. He did not do it deliberately or by design. He happened to see a hunter killing one out of a pair of birds. Then his great compassion towards the bereaved bird which saw its mate fall dead became transformed into intense anger towards the hunter. He then cursed the hunter thus :

मा निषाद प्रतिष्ठांत्वमगमश्शाश्वतीसमाः।
यत् क्रौञ्चमिथुनादेकमवधीः काममोहितम्॥

Maanishaada pratisthaam twamagamah Saaswateessa-maah
Yatkrounchamithunaadekamavadheeh Kaamamohitam

"O hunter, may you not fare well at any time; you who have killed one out of the pair of Krounchas who were happily engaged in love." Without the slightest intention, his curse, which was the result of his great anger, became so worded and got formed. The Sage Valmiki then repented for his emotional outburst and thought deeply over it. Then suddenly an idea struck him. He was a saint who was gifted with divine vision *(Gnaana Drshti).* He realised that his curse was composed in Anushtup metre with four paadas and each paada having eight syllables. Just as the emotions surfaced without his knowledge, the well-set poetic composition in the form of a curse was also not of his deliberate making. He was amazed. He realised that his curse had another meaning to it. What he said to the hunter as a curse could well sustain the meaning : "O Lord of Lakshmi, it will bring you eternal glory for having killed the male of a happy couple, who lost his head completely in lust." This stanza in verse thus fitted Sri Rama, the Avatar of Vishnu perfectly. Rama took Avatar in order to kill the lustful Ravana. Though happily married to Mandodari Ravana was a slave of lust and passions and sought other women. Valmiki saw the divine hand in this incident of the verse which spontaneously burst forth from him. He was assured by Lord Brahma, the creator

Himself, and he began to compose the Ramayana in the same Anushtup metre.

It is from here that a sloka without Vedic Swara (tonal variations) took birth. He rejoiced in the fact that he had fortuitously obtained the means of propagating high truths which people could conveniently commit to memory and remember. As the first ever poetic composition of the world the story of Rama was unfolded by him in incomparable beauty in the Anushtup metre. Ramayana is, therefore, called Adi-Kavya or the first poetic composition.

Prose is liable to be forgotten, difficult to commit to memory. Poetry is easy to remember as it is bound by metre. That is why in early days, most things were expressed in verse. When printing was invented, it became unnecessary to retain everything in one's memory, as they could well be recorded in books and so the prose form developed. But, as a vehicle of expression, poetry is more picturesque and has more vigour and beauty.

The birth of Ramayana was solely due to the divine grace in that the poetic expression (chandas) was unwittingly created. This set the pattern for the writing of other stotras (hymns in praise) puraanas, mythology, and kaavyas (poems) in the form of slokas - verse form.

Some types of metre

Indra Vajra, Upendra Vajra, Sragdhara etc. are some of the many metres used in stotras and kaavyas. Some are very complicated and can be composed only by those who are learned.

I said that 'Anushtup' was the name of the metre where a paada had eight syllables. If there are nine syllables it is called 'Brihatee' (बृहती). Where there are ten letters to a paada it is called 'Pangti' (पड्क्ती). 'Trishtup' metre contains eleven syllables to a paada. Jagati contains twelve and so on. Thus, there are metres containing as many as twenty-six syllables to a paada as in the metre called (उद्कृति) (Udkrti) in the pattern called Bhujanga Vijrmbhitam (भुजंग विजृंभितं). Any metre beyond 26 syllables to a paada is called

Dandakam (दण्डकं). There are many types here too.

The names of some metres are beautiful, appropriate and infused with poetic grace. The letters in a certain metre go leaping like a tiger at play. This is called *Sardoola Vikreedi-tam* शार्दूल विक्रीडितम्). Saardoola is tiger. Vikreedita is play. This contains nineteen letters to a paada and is a type of *Ati Dhriti* metre or fast tempo. Within each paada the syllables are split into two groups of twelve and seven. The metre which sounds like a creeping snake is called *Bhujanga Prayatam* (भुजंगप्रयतं). Bhujanga is snake. This is one of the types of 'Jagati' metre which has twelve letters to a paada. Under the rules, normally it is necessary for the twelve syllables to be equally split into six and six. For e.g. (मयूराधिरूढं महावाक्यगूढं) *(Ma-yoo-raa-dhi-roo dham. Ma ha-vaakya goo-dham)*.

The Soundarya Lahari of the Adi Sankaracharya is in the *Sikarini* (शिखरिणी) metre. Here each pada has seventeen syllables *(Adyashti* is the general name of metres with seventeen syllables to a pada). If the seventeen letters are split into six and eleven, it is called 'Sikharini'. In Sragdharaa, another metre, there is a resonant flow of sounds, as though the sounds are crammed in the mouth and rush out like flood waters. Here, the twenty-one syllables of each paada are split into three with seven letters in each group. Sankaracharya's descriptive hymns on Iswara and Vishnu called *'Keshaadi paada'* and *'Paadaadi kesa'* stotras are in this metre.

Indra Vajra which I mentioned earlier is one type of the 'Trishtup' metre with eleven syllables in a paada. Upendra Vajra also has eleven syllables to a paada but split differently. Both these, when mixed, form the *upajaati* metre in which Kalidasa begins his 'Kumara Sambhavam'.

These metres pertain to the post-Vedic poetry and hymns. The metres which appear in the Vedas are : Gaayatri, Ushnik, Anushtup, Brihati, Pankti, Trishtup, Jagati, etc.

The metre in which the King of Mantras - the Gaayatri Maha Mantra - is composed is named after the mantra itself as "Gaayatri Chandas".

Generally, a mantra is named after the Devata to whom it pertains. 'Siva Panchaakshari', 'Narayana Ashtaakshari', 'Rama Trayodasi', are the names of some mantras which combine the name of the Devata with the number of syllables in the mantra. The Devata for Gaayatri mantra is Savita. Gaayatri is only the name of the metre. But the mantra has been named after its metre as Gaayatri mantra. Just as sound and swara have divine powers, it would seem that similar is the case with the metre and its composition.

I said earlier that four quarters (feet) make one mantra or sloka and therefore, whether it is a mantra or a sloka, it must have four paadas. But, contrary to this general rule, Gaayatri has only three paadas. Gaayatri is the name of the metre with three paadas with eight syllables in each pada, making a total of twenty-four syllables or Aksharas. Since it has three paadas, it is called 'Tripaada Gaayatri'. There are other types of Gaayatri also. The first mantra of the Rig Veda starting with 'Agni Meelay' is set in the Gaayatri metre.

In some poetic hymns, the 24-syllable Gaayatri metre is split into four paadas with six letters in each.

Each paada with seven syllables — making a total of twenty-eight syllables is called 'Ushnik'.

The advantages of metres

When a mantra has taken form, Siksha ensures its correct pronunciation in the proper pitch and tone. But to ensure that the form of the mantra is correct, the 'Chandas' (metre count) is necessary. The form of the mantra cannot go wrong, because it is not composed as a result of the laboured effort of any sage but they are the result of the flash of divine grace revealed to the sages in meditation.

When we are learning a Veda Sukta or mantra, what helps us to make sure that it is in its original form, is the Chandas. If, on counting, the syllables in a mantra are not correct, then we can determine the correct version from those who know.

But, apart from mantras, which came into being by themselves, the poets who labour with poetic compositions are solely guided by the metre in translating their thoughts in words in the form of slokas. What the beat of time is to music, chandas is to slokas. Because it is brought within a framework, it gets a predetermined shape or form. It is also easy to memorise if set to metre.

Chandas alone ensures that the original form of the Vedic text is kept absolutely in tact, without adding or substracting even one syllable. It is only proper that no liberties are taken with the Vedic sounds. Even a small plus or minus is bound to disturb their spiritual content.

The feet of the Veda represent the nose of the mantra

Each mantra is dedicated to a Devata. Therefore, each mantra has a presiding deity. There is a chandas especially for it and there is a rishi who gave it to the world. The rishi who brought it to the knowledge of the world is the rishi of the mantra. When one touches his head on repeating the name of the rishi, before starting the mantra, it is symbollcally placing the feet of the sage on one's head as a mark of reverence, because the mantras were made available to us only through the sages.

When we mention the Chandas of a mantra we touch the nose with our finger. The mantra's sole guardian is the chandas. It is the nature of its life-breath. Hence we touch the nose which controls the life-breath. There can be no life without breath. Similarly for mantras, Chandas is the breath. However, if Veda as a whole is personified, Siksha is its nose and Chandas its feet.

Just as we stand on our legs, the Veda Purusha stands on chandas. We cannot stand up without legs. The body of the Vedas rests on the Chandas which are in the nature of feet.

18

THE VEDANGAS

NIRUKTAM — Veda's Ears

Nirukta is the Vedic dictionary. Dictionary is called Kosa in Sanskrit. There is a celebrated Sanskrit dictionary called *'Amara Kosa'.* Dictionary is also called *'Nighandu'.* Each word is broken syllable-wise indicating the root from which it is derived and the meaning of each syllable is indicated. This is the *Nirukta Saastra* which is called etymology in English.

Nirukta serves as the hearing organ of the Veda Purusha, i.e. the ears. This indicates the precise meaning of rare and uncommon words used in Vedas. It also explains the reason why a particular word has been used i.e., the meaning by usage.

There are many authors who have written books on this subject. But the book written by Yaska (यास्क) is regarded as most valuable.

The Vedic Nighandu explains the origin of each word in the Vedas. Let us take the word *'Hrdayam'* (हृदयं) meaning heart. Why has this word been chosen? The Vedas themselves give the answer. It means *'Hrdi Ayam'* - He lives in the heart. *'Hrid'* is the name of the human heart also. But since Isvara in the heart is also included in the word, its spiritual significance is heightened. Any Saastra must inevitably lead to Isvara. Since Parameswara resides in it, it is called 'Hridayam'. Thus, there is a reason for the formation of each word. Nirukta analyses it.

In Sanskrit, all words are derived from basic 'roots' or *Dhatus* (धातु).

Each sound has its root too. In English, only verbs have roots, not the nouns. But, in Sanskrit, all words have roots. The Sanskrit words were, with slight variations, taken into use in other languages. That is why in these languages, the root words cannot be found, as words are foreign to the language. Time is called the 'hour' in English. If the letters composing this word are analysed on the basis of pronunciation, we arrive at 'Hou' and 'or'. At some time in the distant past, it must have been pronounced as 'hora'. There is a Saastra in Sanskrit, called *'Hora Saastra'.* This word in turn has been derived from *Ahoraatra,* meaning day and night (*Aha* : day, *Ratra* : night). Hora is a measure of time equal to one hour. This 'hora' must have become in English the 'hour' and pronounced as 'our' with 'h' remaining silent. Similarly the word 'heart' has been derived from the Sanskrit 'Hrid'. There are many such words. It must have taken a very long time for them to have reached their present form in these other languages. That is why philologists are unable to find their roots in the same language.

There is not much use listening to a language being spoken when the meaning is not known. It is as good as not listening to it, or its falling on deaf ears. That is why Nirukta, which breaks up each word into its component roots and analyses its meaning, is likened to the ear of the Veda Purusha.

It is also the ear (Srotra) of 'Sruti' i.e., the Vedas which are best learnt through the ear. The sciences of Vyaakarana and Nirukta were learnt by Englishmen from the Pundits of Banaras. They learned that Nirukta traces the origin of each word and gives its meaning. They evolved the new science of language called philology as a result. Thus, the modern philology owes its birth to Vyaakarana and Nirukta of the Vedas.

Their research points to the conclusion that all languages must have been evolved from a common parent language. It is thought that the primordial man existed in the region where this language was spoken and consequently all mankind itself must have originally existed at one place. But there is difference of opinion as to in which part of the world this place was located. We need not unduly bother about it here.

19

THE VEDANGAS

JYOTISHA — Eyes of the Vedas

So far, I have dealt with four Vedangas, viz., *Siksha, Vyaakarana, Chandas* and *Nirukta.* The fifth is *Jyotisha.*

Jyotisha serves as the eye - the organ of sight of the Veda Purusha. This science or saastra has three parts or skandhas. Hence, it is called - *"Skandha Trayaatmakam"* (स्कंध त्रयात्मकम्). These are *Siddhanta Skandham,* (सिद्धान्त स्कन्धम्), *Hora Skandham* (होरा स्कन्धम्) and *Samhita Skandham* (सम्हिता स्कंधम्). The word Skandha means the main branch from the trunk of a tree.

Garga, Naarada, Paraasara and many other sages have written many treatises on Jyotisha. There is a book which cites the case of the Sun God, taking up one section of this science and teaching the same to the divine architect and builder, Maya (मय). It is called 'Soorya Siddhanta'. Thus, there are many books authored by Devas as well as sages. There are also books written by men. Varaahamihira is well known as having written many books on the subject. Aarya Bhatta, Bhaskaracharya and others have also made valuable contributions. In the very recent past, one Vedic scholar by name Sundareswara Srouti has written a book called *"Jyotisha Kaustubham".*

One without eyes is a blind man. While objects, which are near at hand, can be identified by touch, those at a distance can only be seen by the eyes. Just as the human eyes are useful in identifying objects far and near the Jyotisha Saastra is useful in seeing the disposition of planets and stars in time i.e., many years ago or hereafter in the future. The planetary position at present may be determined visually without resort to Jyotisha (astronomy). But planetary dispositions existing say 50 years hence can only be known with the help of Jyotisha. Since mere touch cannot identify colour, eyes are necessary to distinguish these. Likewise, even if a planet is sighted today, we would not know its effects based on its location and how it affects us. Jyotisha alone can throw light on the subject. That is why it is called the eye of the Veda Purusha.

There are injunctions as to the time of performing Vedic rituals with reference to planetary positions. The dates of marriage and other ceremonies are fixed when the planetary positions are considered favourable. Jyotisha is also known by the name of 'Nayana' meaning the eye. 'Naya' means to lead. A blind person has to be led by someone. For us who are fortunate in having the eyes which can see the eye performs the role of the 'leader'. Having determined the auspicious time for doing Vedic karmas, Jyotisha plays the role of the eye in leading us to their actual performance.

Astronomy and Astrology

Modern science stops at astronomy which merely indicates the planetary positions at various points of time. How does the planetary position affect the world in general? How does it affect us? What is to be done to make their influence favourable to us? The science of astrology in conjunction with and based on astronomy deals with these questions.

Jyotisha Saastra was originally designed to indicate the measure of success or lack of it when Vedic karmas are performed under the influence of a particular planet, a star or a lunar day in the dark or bright fortnight. In other words, Jyotisha was mainly intended to help in arriving at the most favourable time for performing Vedic karmas and was, therefore, made part of the Vedas - as one of the Vedaangas. Since this involved calculations regarding the transit of planets in various signs of the zodiac, mathematics became an integral part of it.

The place where a Vedic sacrifice is performed called the "Yajna Vedi" (यज्ञवेदि) and the location of the site, all these have detailed specifications.

A sacrifice performed on the basis of the injunctions in regard to the proper structure and construction of the Yajna Vedi yields favourable results. So, it became necessary to accurately calculate these requirements to conform to specifications. On this account, Mathematics or Ganita (गणित) has been developed as an auxiliary organ - *Upaanga* - of the Vedas.

Ancient Mathematical Treatises

I mentioned earlier about the three parts or Skandhas viz. Siddhaanta Skandha, Hora Skandha and Samhita Skandha. The Siddhaanta Skandha covers subjects like arithmetic, trignometry, geometry and algebra. What has taken the western world centuries to develop in higher mathematics is already found in our ancient Jyotisha.

Arithmetic is pure computation with numbers. Plain numbers are given and their resultant effect is obtained. Simple addition, subtraction, multiplication and division are the functions of arithmetic. *'Avyaktha-ganita'* deals with 'unknown' numbers, (i.e.) instead of numerals like one, two, three or four, symbols like A, etc. are used. This is called algebra. *Avyaktha* literally means what is not known definitely *'Kshestra Ganita'* is geometry. 'Gya' or Geo is earth. 'Miti' means 'metre' or measurement.' Hence, the name Geometry. The sacrificial site, the sacrificial Kunda *(yajnabhoomi* and *yajna vedi*), fixing their location, shape and dimensions of these were dealt with in this geometry. There is an arithmetic called *'Sameekarana'.* This deals with finding the unknowns through the knowns. Unknown groups of figures are separately given and they are required to be reduced to equations. This is 'Sameekarana'. It means making things equal. This is what is now called 'equation' in English.

There is a Sameekarana or equation in *Aapasthamba sutra.* It defied proof until very recently. Since it could not be solved by means of western mathematics, it was even said that it could not be proved. But, further research proved that the equation given in the Sutra was correct. This has naturally amazed the western scholars. The high degree of proficiency in mathematics which had baffled modern science for so long was already known to Indian scholars thousands of years ago. There are many more such sutras which have yet to be proved and deciphered even. These equations also will have to be proved only with the aid of Sameekarana. Our saastras mention many allied branches of mathematics, e.g., *Rekha Ganita, Guttaka, Angabhaaga,* etc. *Avyakta Ganita* (Algebra) is also called *Beeja Ganita.*

Some 800 years ago there was a celebrated mathematician by the name of Bhaskaracharya. There was an incident in his life to illustrate the point that, however much we may use our intelligence, destiny will prevail. He had a daughter by the name of Leelavati. Bhaskaracharya, being a great astrologer and astronomer realised that the girl was destined to be a widow soon after her marriage. He thought that if he could marry his daughter at a time when the planetary position was so favourable as to ensure a long conjugal life, he could alter the fate of his daughter. He accordingly fixed a time and date when the planets were in such favourable conjunction. In those days, unlike now, there were no clocks to show the time. The waterpot was then used as Ghatika or the modern *Ghatikaara* (clock). The vessel was divided into two parts the upper and the lower. Water from the top portion would drip into the lower part through a small aperture. The lower part will have calibrations marked as on a medicine bottle. The level of water will be used to calculate time. Each mark thereon will indicate time equal to 1/60 of a day. This unit of time is called Ghatika (derived from the word Ghata or pot). A Ghatika is equal to 24 minutes. Since water is subject to evaporation depending on the weather conditions and as this may lead to inaccuracies in calculation, sand which is not subject to vapourisation came to be substituted for water later on and the instrument which came to be known as the hour-glass came to be in use. As was the custom in those days, the marriage of Leelavati was fixed when she was still a child. This child came near the aforesaid "water glass' and did some mischief. In the process, a small pearl from her nose ornament got loose and fell into the aperture between the two portions of the Ghatika, which let the water drip. As a result, the size of the drip became smaller. So, when the restricted water supply reached the mark which had been made to indicate the favourable planetary position, that time had long passed and the next 'Lagna' had come which was not auspicious. Since Leelavati was married at that *Muhoorta* or time she lost her husband at a very tender age, and the prediction in her horoscope came true.

No one, including the child, had noted at that time the pearl dropping into the water glass. But when subsequently this was known, it was too late, the marriage had already taken place and it was accepted that destiny is difficult to change.

Later, Bhaskaracharya wanted to write a treatise on mathematics. He chose his daughter's name as the title of that book. He made his daughter, who had became a child widow, qualify as a high-ranking mathematician and named his book after her. This book contains various aspects of mathematics such as arithmetic, Vyaktha Ganita, Beeja Ganita, etc. To assist in the determination of the planetary positions and their movements, he also wrote a book called *"Siddhaanta Siromani"*.

There is a book entitled *"Praacheena Lekha Maala"* (प्राचीन लेखा माला) which is a compilation of all the ancient edicts. It is seen from the book that a king of Gujarat called 'Singana' had made efforts to popularise the writings of Bhaskaracharya.

Though the intermediary Chapters 7, 8, 9 and 10 from the book on modern Geometry by Euclid are stated to be missing, all the twelve books in Sanskrit are still in tact. We seem to be blissfully ignorant of even elementary mathematics. For example, multiplication is nothing but addition over and over again. Similarly division is subtraction over and over.

Long before the time of Bhaskaracharya, over 1,500 years ago, there was a mathematician by the name of Varahamihira. He is the author of many treatises like *'Brihad Samhita'* and *'Brihad Jaataka'*. Brihad Samhita is a 'digest' of all scientific disciplines. It is still a matter of great wonder that our ancient scholars were conversant with a long list of scientific subjects. The Brihad Jaataka (बृहद् जातक) deals with all matters relating to Astrology. Aarya Bhatta is the author of a book entitled *"Aaryabhatta Siddhaanta"*. He also lived over 1500 years ago. The modern arithmetic now in vogue is based on the principles propounded by Aarya Bhatta. Both Varahamihira and Aarya Bhatta are held in high esteem by modern mathematicians. All these mathematical sciences only pertain to the location and movements of the stars and the nine planets. Actually, there are only seven planets. Raahu and Kethu are shadows. Hence. they are called *"Chaayaa Graha".* They run exactly opposite to the transit of the Sun and the Moon. Hence they require no special calculations. Their particulars can be determined by reversing those of the Sun and the Moon.

What is the difference between a star and a planet? Those that orbit round our Sun are the planets. Those that belong to the solar galaxy are the stars. There is one visual means of identification. When diamond is kept moving around, there will be scintillations. Likewise the stars will be twinkling as if in movement. The planets will emit light keeping still.

The Sun and the stars are self-luminous. The stars sparkle showing various colours, something like the blue and green lights emanating from well-cut diamonds. The planets Guru (Jupiter) and Sukra (Venus) would look like big stars but they have no scintillation. The stars have scintillation. The sun is also like this. If observed closely, the surrounding halo will disappear. Then it will look like a piece of flat mirror floating in water. It will have both scintillation and movement. The moon will not be so.

Let me illustrate how the sun has both light and movement. Take the rays of sunshine coming through a small hole in the roof of a hut. The moon's rays will also come through the same hole. Whilst the sun's rays will keep shaking, the moon's rays will be still. The other planets are also like the moon. Although the stars may look small, they have both scintillation and movement.

If a star was big enough, in its sparkle, the seven colours, VIBGYOR, will appear, same as the emission of colour from a diamond. One of the names of the Sun is *'Saptasvaan'* which means that his chariot has seven *(sapta)* horses *(Asva).*

It also can be taken to mean one horse with seven colours. The word 'Asva' also means 'rays'. The reference is to the seven coloured rays which the Sun's rays emit. A single ray emits all the seven colours. VIBGYOR also refers to this. Taittareeya Aaranyaka of the Vedas says that a single ray alone is known by seven names *"Eko Asvah Vahati Saptanaama"* that is to say, the single colour, white, splits on refraction into seven colours.

The stars rise in the east and set in the west. The planets also move westward but every day they shift a little to the east. The seven planets keep moving a little eastwards. The science of astrology deals with these movements.

Planets as they affect human life

On earth, the fate of man changes in the same way as the movement of planets. Lean times, prosperous periods, misery, happiness, high position, fall therefrom - such are the changing fortunes of man. Such changes are not confined only to man. Institutions and even countries have their run of good and bad times. The great sages found out that there was a definite connection between the planetary movements and the good and bad results which were noticed on earth. In fact, they have postulated the movement of a planet with its effect on us. When a job is undertaken, it is possible to predict the outcome, on the basis of the planetary position when it was begun. This science is called the *Hora Saastra.* Keeping the time of birth as the basis, the planetary position can be fixed in the horoscope and a forecast can be made of the good and bad periods throughout one's whole life.

There are various reasons that are offered in explanation for good and bad times. It is like various causes being attributed to a disease. Doctors attribute the disease to the change in 'psyche'. The necromancer attributes it to super-natural forces. The astrologer attributes it to the change in the planetary position. Dharma Saastra would attribute the disease as due to the effect of karma (action) done in earlier births. Psychologists say that a change in feelings causes change in health. Thus many causes are attributed to the same effect. In actual fact, what is the cause?

Planets, psyche, mind forces - or something else? None of these is wrong. All have their part to play. They are the manifestations of the same. In order to help our understanding, various causes are mentioned and their combined effect results in the experience. Different people offer different explanations. If it rains, wetness results, flies swarm, frogs croak. These are consequential features after the rain. Likewise, there are many indications which point to the result of our actions in earlier births. Each explanation is an attendant proof. They are all inter-connected. The planetary disposition is determined by earlier karma. Disease appears and the mind is disturbed. Psychic forces also prevail. All these are the results of a single karma. This can be proved on the basis of each one of the causes attributed to the mishap. But the method of calculation used in planetary movements is the easiest.

Omens - "Sakuna" - "Nimitta"

I said earlier that there is a portion of the Science of Astrology called 'Samhita Skandha'. Where is underground water located? Where do rivers and streams exist underground? What are the signs seen on the ground when water is present under it? These are some of the subjects which this Skandha deals with. The method of making perfumes and cosmetics, the designing and building of houses, the Science of *Sakuna* and *Nimitta* or omens and portents are also to be found in this Skandha.

Sakuna (शकुन) is different from *Nimitta* (निमित्त) although both come under the general name of 'omens'. Sakuna means literally a bird. Omens which are caused by birds are called Sakuna. On earth, there is no subject or matter which is unrelated to another. The events that occur are also so connected. If the proper calculations are used, these can be forecast and understood easily.

All phenomena on earth are subject to the rule of one supreme force. They follow a set pattern. Hence, using one observation, the remaining can be calculated. The lines on one's palm, forecasting events on the basis of the planetary position at the time a question is asked *(Aaroodha)*, astrology are all inter-connected. All are true. One of these is Sakuna.

The Sakuna Saastra deals with such subjects as, (1) what is the effect of a bird going from our left to right? (2) What is the effect of the cry of one or the other bird, etc.?

This includes what are meant by Nimitta - portent. *"Nimittanicha pasyaami vipareetaani Kesava"* (निमित्तानि चपश्यामि विपरीतानि केशव) says Arjuna to Lord Krishna before the battle begins. It is the same as our saying that evil omens are seen. He uses the right word, Nimitta, instead of Sakuna, as only those portents which are revealed by birds are called Sakuna. If a cat crossed the path, it is Nimitta. If a vulture flew across, it is Sakuna.

Later, the Lord also talks to Arjuna about Nimitta : *"Nimitta maatram bhava Savyasaachin"* (निमित्तमात्रं भव सव्यसाचिन्) says he. "I have already decided that these will be annihilated in this war. Therefore, these can be already regarded as dead. Their slayer is none but me. You merely act as the instrument," said the Lord and in that context he said *"Nimitta maatram bhava."*

Therefore, the portent does not by itself create or alter a situation. It reveals a result which is bound to come to surface. Likewise, the portents merely announce the reaction which actions of our earlier births throw up.

Stated briefly, in the three Skandhas or parts, what is stated in the nature of general principles is mathematics and planetary movements. Separate enunciation of good and bad periods of man is called Hora or Jaataka. It is from Hora that the word horoscope has come.

Modern discoveries in ancient texts

I said earlier that Varahamihira has written a book called *Brihad Samhita*. There are many scientific discoveries which are dealt with in this book.

How do the planets hang in space without support? How is it that they do not fall down? It is the popular belief that Newton discovered the cause of this phenomenon.

The very ancient theory on the solar system begins with a sloka which says that the reason why the earth does not fall away in space is due to the force of gravity. The Upanishad Bhaashya by Adi Sankara also states that the earth has the power of attraction. If we throw a thing in the air, it falls to the earth. This is not a quality of the object. The reason why it falls is due to the attraction of the object by the earth. The power of attraction is the pull of gravity. Praana goes up, Apaana pulls it down. Therefore, the force that pulls it down is known as Apaana. Therefore, the force that pulls down is known as *Apaana Sakti*. Sankaracharya has stated that the earth has Apaana Sakti or the power of gravity. The Prasnopanishad (3.8) says : "पृथिव्यां या देवता सैषा पुरुषस्यापानमवष्टभ्यन्तरा".

That is the Devata controlling the earth which creates the Apaana Sakti in the human body. In his Bhaashya on this Upanishad the Acharya says : "तथा पृथिव्यां अभिमानिनि या देवता प्रसिद्धा सैषा पुरुषस्य अयानं अपानवृत्तिं अवष्टभ्य आकृष्य वशीकृत्याध एवापकर्षणेनानुग्रहंकुर्वती वर्तत इत्यर्थः). Just like a body, thrown up in the air, is pulled down by the earth, the praana that pulls above is pulled down by Apaana. This makes it very clear that the Upanishad talks of the law of gravitation. Our Saastras contain many other such wonderful data, of which we do not care to know but consider that every scientific discovery has come from the west.

Our astrological texts, which were written ages ago, contain all the mathematical principles which are in use in the world today. At the beginning of creation all the planets were in line. As time went by, they began changing little by little. When the next kalpa begins, they will again be in line.

Not only the pull of gravity but also the rotation of the earth is mentioned by Aarya Bhatta and Varahamihira. The western theory until the 11th Century was : "The earth alone stands firm in the centre of the Universe. The sun rotates round the earth. That is how the day and night are caused on earth." If anyone offered a theory slightly different to this, the religious heads caused the person to be burnt at stake for heresy. But we had known the truths to be otherwise from early times.

Aarya Bhatta has given a beautiful name to illustrate that the earth rotates round the sun and not the sun round the earth. It is called the *"Laaghava-Gaurava"* Nyaaya. (The theory of lightness). If a thing is done easily and lightly it is called *'Hasta laaghava',* meaning dexterity or sleight of hand. The opposite of 'laghu' is 'Guru'. What is heavy or big is Guru. Guru means a big man. He is the preceptor or Acharya. If the Acharya is Guru, then the disciple is 'laghu'. The Acharya who is the Guru is respected by the disciple. Hence he goes round the Acharya in Pradakshina. The Acharya does not go round the disciple. The biggest planet in our Solar system is the sun. Earth is laghu. Laaghava-Gaurava Nyaaya says that the smaller object goes round the bigger object. Thus, Aarya Bhatta has allegorically referred to the movement of the earth round the sun.

Today, we have joined hands with those who earlier dubbed scientists as heretics and burnt them without allowing science to progress but level the following charge against Hinduism and say that "the reason for lack of scientific progress in India is the Hindu religion which emphasises other-worldliness ignoring the things of this world." In actual fact, all the sciences were known to our ancient scholars.

The sun stays put. The earth alone rotates round it. It only seems that the sun daily rises in the east and moving slightly to the north sets in the west. But that in actual fact this is not so is a matter which finds mention in the Aitareya Braahmana of the Rig Veda. It is clearly stated therein that the sun neither rises nor sets.

It is clearly there for us to see that air does not stay put ever at any place but keeps moving. The flame does not keep steady but flickers. And water does not stagnate but moves on. When we look up at the sky, we observe as if the sun and moon are moving. The sky is also the cause of all sound. Since vibration is the origin of sound, it is clear that sound is also movement. But superficially the earth appears to be stay-put and unmoving.

The gravitational pull and rotation of the earth apart, let us look at the appearance of the earth. What do the westerners say? Earlier they thought that the earth was flat like a pan cake. They claim the credit themselves for the discovery that it is not so but is spherical in shape. All right. What do we call the science of geography? *"Bhoogola-Saastra"*. It is enough to call it Bhoo Saastra but in order to proclaim that its spherical shape is well known to us from ancient times, we call it *Bhoogola-Saastra*. *'Gola'* means sphere, *Bhoo* means earth.

Universe is the totality of all the worlds including all the galaxies which is called *"Brahmaanda"*. This means the 'Anda' created by Brahma. 'Anda' means an egg. The egg is not spherical in shape but elliptical. Modern science has proved the same - that the Universe is not spherical but oval.

Modern astronomy says that the whole universe is in a state of motion. But the very name given to the earth from early Vedic times indicates our awareness of it. 'Jagat' is the name of the Universe and it means that which keeps moving and does not stand still.

There were some in ancient India also who opposed the theory of the earth moving round the sun. Let me tell you the views of one section of these. The circumference of the earth is approximately 25,000 miles. If the earth takes 24 hours to rotate once completely, it means that it rotates at the speed of 1000 miles per hour. Therefore, in a minute it travels 16 or 17 miles. This would imply that, since the earth is always in rotation, if Madras were here (in a fixed point) now, the next minute in its place should appear land or sea which was 17 miles away.

Let us assume that a crow sitting in Madras this minute goes up straight in the air and comes down after one minute. It alights on the same tree or house from which it flew. If it were true that the earth is rotating fast, how is it possible for it to alight back at the same place? Since the earth rotates, in one minute the spot at which Madras was should have shifted out 17 miles and another place which was 17 miles away should have appeared where Madras was. So argue the opponents to the theory of the earth's rotation. I have not looked into the answer which the supporters of the theory offer. But on enquiry from modern scientists I am told that around the earth for a distance of about 200 miles is an atmospheric area comprising air. Thereafter some more regions are there like sheaths. All of them rotate along with the earth. I may not have captured what they said faithfully but there can be no doubt that not only the earth but the atmosphere around it is also in rotation.

Westerners have now discovered that the birth-place of what is called the Arabic numerals - 1,2,3,4 etc. - is India. The concept that the numeral "zero" is totally of Indian origin is now accepted by the experts. Because of this realisation, they say, that the science of Mathematics had attained its full stature in India. Further the ancient scientists did not stop at discovery of cypher. That any number divided by cypher will result in infinity is the subtle mathematical axiom which Bhaskaracharya propounded. He fused this truth with the theory of the Divine-Infinite and made this the opening sloka of his treatise on Mathematics.

The smaller the divisor the bigger will be the quotient. If sixteen is divided by eight then the divisor is eight and quotient is two. If the divisor is four, then the quotient is four. If two, then the quotient is eight. But, if the divisor is zero? Then the quotient becomes beyond reckoning i.e. infinity. Whatever be the number that is being divided, if the divisor is zero, then the quotient is infinite. Bhaskaracharya has named this as *Kaharam*. *Kam* means cypher, *Haram* means divide.

Not a blind faith, but truths which are provable

"The Hindu Saastras are full of nonsensical matter. The crest of mountain Meru is supposed to be to the North of the earth. To the Devas living there, our year reckons only as a day. That Meru is being circled by the sun. Not only is there the saline sea around the earth, but there are other seven seas whose waters are sugarcane juice, milk, etc. etc. The earth which comprises five continents is said to be composed of seven islands. All this is poppycock." This is the reaction of the west. Let us now pose some questions? Why should our sea be so saltish? Who mixed so much salt in it? If you can accept that there is a saltish sea can you not imagine seas with sweet and milky waters?

Alright. If you think the seven islands and seven seas are not correct, what does the same Saastra say about the position of the earth? It says that at the northern end of the earth lies the Meru mountain and the (Dhruva) Pole Star at the southern end.

The northern end can be assumed to be the North Pole. If we look at the South Pole, it is not exactly in the opposite direction. The 'Pole' has been named after the 'Pole star'. But now it is not directly in the same line with it. It was so in the beginning. But, due to big cosmic changes, the earth has tilted away, say modern researchers. The earth was spinning like a vertical top directly facing the Pole Star. At that time, there were seven seas which the Saastras mentioned - seven islands and seas. During the spin, the top became a little inclined from the vertical. I think, the seven seas may have got mixed together resulting in the salty taste of the waters. It is likely that, during that period, the seven islands became five continents.

If there is a place above the North Pole, that is the place where Meru is and that is Swarga - heaven. If the earth could be likened to a lemon then the top point is Meru - pinnacle. To that point or from that point, all directions point to the south only. From the point of that crest or pinnacle, we cannot go east, west or north. There is no alternative but to descend down to the south. If we placed a point at the top of the lemon this will become evident. The northern most point of all things on earth is Meru. That is what is meant by *"Sarveshaam api varshaanaam Meru uttarasthita"*.

What is the climatic position at the pole? It is day for six months at a stretch and night for the next six months. This is now being taught even in the primary classes. Just as a single day and a single night together makes a full day, in the polar region the six months of night and six months of bright day (making a year in all) reckons as one day. This is how a single day of the Devas becomes one year by our reckoning. When the earth rotates, even if all the parts constituting its sides (along the circumference) rotate the top most point and the bottom most at the South Pole cannot be said to rotate. A point is a negligibly small area, otherwise it cannot be called a point.

Depending on its position, during rotation, in relation to the Sun and the Moon, on a particular day, some regions on earth receive the sun for 18 hours and the region exactly opposite to it will only receive six hours of sun shine with 18 hours being the dark night. There are vast differences in the duration of the day and night in many parts of the world. The sun rises in the exact east only on some days, comes exactly overhead without any deviation only on some days. On other days the sunrise varies from north-east to south-east by many degrees. In the North Pole, such is not the case. There, going from six months of continuous day to six months of continuous night and again back to the beginning of six months of continuous day, if this sojourn is observed, it would appear that, instead of that place going round the sun, the sun goes round the place. This is what is referred to in the statement that the Sun goes round the Meru mountain. The six months of day-time in the North Pole is called *Uttaraayana* and when it gets dark there and the South Pole gets the day it is called *Dakshinaayana.*

The North Pole is called Sumeru and the South Pole Meru. The name of the country called Sumaria is derived from Sumeru. It is said that there the worship of the Vedic Devatas was in vogue. Just as in the north are the Devatas, in the South are the Pitrus or manes and Naraka (hell). One needs the gift of divine sight to be able to see the Devatas, the Pitrus or those in Hell. Merely because we do not have such a divine vision we cannot deny, with reason, the existence of such regions. Born in Russia, bred up in America and settled in India, Blavatsky and others who started the Theosophical Society, deal mainly with the world of spirits, of supermen or Devatas. One of the most renowned scientists of modern times, Sir Oliver Lodge, had made a special study of spirits and departed souls. His conclusion is that certainly spirits do exist and man can derive a lot of benefits through invocation to them. One need not wonder, therefore, that the Jyotisha Saastra deals with astronomy and such sciences on the one hand and then goes on to spiritualism. As though to point out that there is no conflict between these subjects, a modern scientist has gone about his business in the same way.

Our Saastras came into being in the distant past when men and Devatas (Gods) had social contacts as we now have with each other. This will be apparent from a close look at the *'samkalpa'* or introductory prayer to a ritualistic ceremony. This samkalpa determines the present in terms of time, going back to aeons, before countless Yuga-cycles, to a time reckonable after adding so many zeros after 100 millions - in short, since the world was created. At the beginning of the Yuga, the disposition of the planets as calculable through astronomy showed that they were all in line then.

Some calculations lead to different answers today. If there is a difference between physical observation and what the Saastras say, we should not rush to the conclusion that the Saastras are a bundle of lies. The Saastras prevailed at a time when the planets were ranged in a straight line, the time when the North Pole of the earth was directly facing the Pole Star. Since then, there have been cataclysmic changes to the earth over many yugas. Earth had become mountain, mountain had become sea, sea had become a desert and so on. These details are available from the geologists. In addition, astronomers say that there have been similar changes in the galaxy due to the planetary movements. That is no doubt why we find changes from what the Saastras said.

The origin of creation timed through astronomical calculations (Jyotisha) is said to be near about the same time as what is arrived at by modern research.

The Kaliyuga has 4,32,000 years. The Dwaaparayuga has twice that, viz., 8,64,000 years, Tretaayuga has thrice, viz., 12,96,000 and Kritayuga has four times viz. 17,28,000 years. All the four together, called a Mahaayuga, has 43,20,000 years. One thousand such Mahaayugas make the period of the reign of the fourteen Manus. The duration of the reign of a Manu is called 'Manvantaram' (मन्वन्तरं).

Although we may have many kings and democratic governments to govern on the earth God has kept 'Manu' in sole charge of all governments. Thus there are fourteen Manus, who will hold office from the beginning of creation to its end. Since we have sprung from the time of Manu, we are called *Manushya. (Manuja),* etc. The word 'Man' has also been derived from the word Manu. The samkalpa says that we are in such and such year during the reign of the Seventh Manu, called Vaivaswata Manu - son of Vivaswaan. Working back to the time when the first of the Manus called Swayambhuva Manu ruled, the Saastraic calculations approximate to the same time as homosapiens appeared on earth.

The root *'Man'* means to think, which is a function of the mind. Manu has been named so keeping this in view. He is the first of those sentient beings. "Man is a thinking animal" is an apt expression. The faculty of thinking which places man above animals and which originated with 'Manu' has led to the apt nomenclature, 'Man'.

As mentioned earlier, the span of time covered by the fourteen Manus constitutes a day (which does not include night) for Brahma. A similar period constitutes his night. In other words, 8640 million years constitute one full day of Brahma. 365 such days constitute one year of Brahma. On this basis his life-span is 100 such years. The duration of this Universe is the same. When Brahma ceases to be, nothing else of creation exists anywhere else. This is called the *'Maha Pralaya'.* Thereafter, for the duration of a life-time of a Brahma, there will be no creation and "Brahman", the inconceivable, the infinite, alone will subsist. Then another creation starts with the help of a new Brahma. According to our recitation in the 'Samkalpa' for religious ceremonies Brahma's life is now in the latter half.

There are seven worlds called *Bhoo, Bhuvah, Suvah, Maha, Janah, Tapah* and *Satyah.* All of creation including man and Devas live in one or the other of these worlds. Of these the Bhoo, Bhuvah and Suvah lokas belong to one group. These are often referred to as *Bhoor-Bhuvas-Suvah* in rituals. The other four are higher than these. When Brahma goes to sleep at night, these three lokas, or worlds, cease to exist. This is called the *Avaanthara Pralaya.* When his term of life ends, all the worlds including the other four also cease to exist.

Modern scientists have discovered that, imperceptibly, the heat of the sun is getting less as time passes. Life cannot be sustained without the Sun's heat. Beginning with foodstuffs, all things necessary for the sustenance of life on earth, such as rainfall, are all dependent on the sun's heat. So, it has been calculated that, after the passage of a very, very long period of time, after crores and crores of years, the world will cease to exist. The next *Avaantara Pralaya* as per our ancient beliefs and the calculations of modern scientists as to the end of the world is more or less coincidental in time.

Working back again as per these calculations, when we consider the time of creation of this universe, we more or less reach the same time as what the scientists ascribe as to the time of creation.

Since fourteen Manus complete their reign during one day-time of Brahma, a single manvatara has 71 Chatur Yugas. In our present Vaivasvata Manvantara, we are now in the 28th Chaturyuga and in the Kali Yuga thereof. Our Samkalpa describes all these. It goes on to the day and minute thereof. All this is with reference to the computation of time.

Then there is also in the Samkalpa the description of the land in which we live. It describes the whole of the Universe (called Brahmaanda) and comes down to the village where one lives. Just as we mention the place and date in our letters, we similarly mention these in our Samkalpa. All these complicated calculations are in the Jyotisha Saastra.

Empirical proof

The rays of the sun appear on the floor of a hut coming through a small hole in the roof. We do not know where the same ray would fall the next year. But calculations made as per the Jyotisha

Saastra would fix the location of that very day. In ancient times, Kings used to reward those who would hang a pearl by a thread and indicate by marking on the ground at what time the sun's rays would fall on the specified spots. With other disciplines, one had to earn his reward by verbal arguments but in Jyotisha Saastra one had to physically demonstrate his skill. There was, thus, no question of cheating. The sun and moon were witnesses to their knowledge.

20

THE VEDANGAS

KALPA —The arm of the Vedas

The sixth organ of the Veda Purusha is 'Kalpa', which is called his arm. 'Kalpa' is what induces one to Vedic action. What does one have to do after having learnt Siksha, Vyaakarana, Chandas, Nirukta and Jyotisha? One must do something to achieve results. We must do some good deeds to wash off the sins which had occurred as a result of doing what came to our mind. To do this, we must have a mantra, its correct pronunciation and meaning. To do the karma, we must have the necessary material aids. We must have a house or place to do these things. Then the result of these actions should be dedicated to God. Kalpa deals with all such matters. One has to recite the Vedas faithfully. The words therein have to be learnt faultlessly through Siksha. The grammar or Vyaakarana should be learnt. The metre and meaning should be known through Chandas and Nirukta and the proper time to perform the rituals should be determined with the help of Jyotisha. All these are only to do the jobs mentioned in Kalpa. Kalpa deals with matters such as (1) how should a particular ritual be done? (2) what functions or Karma should be performed by man of each caste or varna in which state or Aasrama? (i.e. brahmachaari, householder or sanyaasi); (3) which ritual involves which mantra, which materials, which Devata? (4) how many Ritviks (or priests) should be employed? (5) what vessels of what shape and size should be used?

The Kalpa Saastra has been compiled by a number of Sages. In regard to Krishna Yajur Veda, which is mostly prevalent in Southern India, six rishis or Sages viz., Aapasthamba, Bodhaayana, Vaikhaanasa, Satyaashaada, Bharadwaaja and Agnivesa have written Kalpa Sutras. For the Rig Veda Aaswalayana's Kalpa is the one mostly in vogue. There is also one by Saangaayana. Katyaayana has authored a Sutra for Sukla Yajur Veda. In Saama Veda, for the Kautuma Saakha, Laatyaayana and for Ranaayaneeya Saakha,

Draahyaayana and for the Talavakaara Saakha, Jaimini have done the Kalpa Sutras. In each Saakha, for the Kalpa, there are two kinds of Sutras called the Grihya Sutra and the Srouta Sutra. These two Sutras detail the forty karmas or vedic rituals to be performed from the time the embryo forms in the womb to the time the body is cremated. Cremation is also one of the Homa or sacrificial offerings. It is called the *Antiyeshti,* meaning the last rite. In this, the entire body is offered as a sacrifice in Agni.

A brahmin must perform twenty-one yajnas everyday based on Agni Hotra, viz., seven Havir Yajnas, seven Somayajnas and seven Bhaagayajnas. Of these the seven Havir Yajnas and seven Soma Yajnas will not appear in the Grihya Sutra. These fourteen come under the Srouta Sutra. These fourteen are included in the forty karmas or samskaras. (Samskara is that which purifies.)

Agni Hotra is to be done at home. Yajna is done under a canopy erected on open ground. The Srouta Sutra describes the major sacrifices. The Grihya Sutra describes the domestic rites - those done at home.

The Kalpa Sutras detail the forty samskaaras and eight Aatma gunas. Barring the fourteen Havir-Soma Yajnas, the remaining twenty-six are mentioned in the Grihya Sutra. These are in the nature of conception or Garbhadana, Pumsavana, Seemanta, Jaatakarma (rites on birth). Namakarana (naming ceremony), Annapraasana, Chowla or tonsure, Upanayana or sacred thread investiture, Vivaaha, (marriage) Anti Yesthi, etc. More of these later.

The eight Aatma gunas are : (1) *daya* (दया)or compassion, (2) *Kshama* (क्षमा) or patience (3) *Anasuya* (अनसूया) absence of asuya, anger and envy, (4) *Soucha* (शौच) or cleanliness, (5) absence of obstinacy, (6) sweet nature, (7) lack of greed and (8) absence of desire. These are called *'Saamaanya Dharma'* or injunctions applicable to all men of whatever caste.

When we do *Abhivaadana* (obeisance to elders) we declare as to which Sutra we follow. This only refers to the Srouta Sutra:

For example the Saama Vedis say they follow the Draahyaayana Sutra. Draahyaayana has authored only Srouta Sutra. Another, by the name of Gobila, has done the Grihya Sutra. But, in the past, since the Vedic rituals were performed faithfully and with gusto, the Srouta Sutra came to be called one's own sootra which practice still continues. Those who belong to the later age, do not perform any big Srouta ceremony now but only do some of the Grihya karmas like marriage. The Grihya karmas were to be taken as less important than Srouta karmas but they have now become more important.

In the olden days, even the poor performed the Srouta karmas, by seeking alms if necessary. In the past, there were some who were called *'Prati Vasanta-Soma-Yaji'* (प्रतिवसंत सोमयाजी) i.e., those who performed the Soma Yaaga every spring. If the annual earning of a person is enough to last for three years, he used to perform the Somayaaga every spring.

All this has now changed. Today, even rich men have three years' expenses lined up against one year's income. The economic climate of modern society has brought poverty and misery to all, including the traders. We should be moderate in all things. Excesses should always be avoided. All the cleverness of modern management has only led us to the point of perpetual insufficiency. Even a rich man has overwhelming expenses to meet. All these personal expenses can be moderated and resources should be diverted to the performance of good acts.

In the conduct of yajnas, there is a thing called 'Chayana' (चयन). Kalpa has a separate portion called Sulpa Sutra dealing with this. Sulpa Sutras are of two kinds. Saamaanya (सामान्य) and Visesha (विशेष). Katyaayana, Bodhaayana and Hiranya Kesa have written Sulpa Sutra. Srouta is what comes in Sruti - the Veda. These Srouta karmas are big rituals to be done elaborately. These have to be done in big open spaces under temporarily erected sheds. They cannot possibly be done inside the confines of a house. That is why the minor rituals which can be performed at home have come to be called Grihya karmas. These days, yajnas are rarely done. But some of the Grihya karmas are still being done.

All our Saastras aim at leading one to Godhead. Whatever is written or read should be dedicated to God and must be productive of spiritual well-being. Our Saastras are all so oriented. It is a matter for great regret that the Srouta Karmas (Vedic injunctions in the performance of Havir Soma Yajnas) which are the very essence of Vedas are being relegated to the background more and more nowadays.

The authors of Kalpa Sutra, viz., Aapasthamba, Bodhaayana and Aaswalaayana, with the exception of Draahyaayana and Katyaayana, have done both the Srouta Sutras and Grihya Sutras. In addition, there are certain things called Dharma Sutras. These lay down the rules of conduct for a man as an individual, as a member of a family and in society. From these have evolved the Dharma Saastras in later days.

The Atharva Veda is not much in practice now and its Kalpa Sutras are not readily available.

Kalpa teaches us every job, however small it may be. And whatever a brahmin does and however small it may be, it is connected with the Vedas. Only then every time he breathes and with every step he takes can he get us the divine forces to help out. That is why it has been laid down as an injunction, as to how he should sit, how he should eat and how he should wear his clothes. For example, the Kalpa Saastra also lays down how houses are to be built. It describes *Griha Nirmaana* (Plan of the house), *Vaastu Lakshana* (description of the materials to be used), etc. The reason why this is laid down is that the architecture of the house should help him in his job of harnessing divine forces for the benefit of the world. The Vaiswa Deva Bali has to be performed only at a certain specified portal of the house. This cannot be done in a modern flat. It is only in order to help the Anushtaana or practice of Vedic injunctions that the design of the home is mentioned in Kalpa Sutra. The Upaasana (place where the Agni is to be lit for Homa), has to have a particular design for its correct performance. Its specifications are laid down in the Saastras. If these are not according to the specified lay-out, it would be difficult to perform the ritual. Just as in a school the classroom, the benches, tables, etc., are all preplanned to help in imparting education, so are these plans laid down for the proper performance of the Vedic rituals. Even in ordinary life we see that in a school laboratory, where experiments are conducted, the lay-out and furniture are different from the rest of the school where students listen to lectures.

We should design our homes as per our Silpa Saastra. The writers of Sutras make it obligatory for a *grihastha* (householder) to build his house only in a particular design. This of course will be binding only on those who wish to follow the Vedic way of life. But if we live in a house built as per the plan of others with a different civilisation or a way of life, we find that the house plan interferes with the conduct of rituals. We start by saying that the house is not congenial to the performance of certain rituals and in course of time our resolves weaken and faith flickers. We change our way of life as it is found difficult to change the house

Siksha, Vyaakarana, Chandas, Nirukta, Jyotisha and Kalpa are the six Saastras and, together with the four Vedas, we have so far had a glimpse of ten out of the fourteen Vidyas or disciplines. Let us have a look at the remaining four.

21

THE UPAANGAS

MEEMAAMSA

After the four Vedas and six Vedaangas, the remaining four out of the 14 Vidyas are called Upaangas - subsidiary or secondary limbs. These are Meemaamsa, Nyaaya, Puraana and Dharma Saastra.

In the compound word Meemaamsa, 'Mam' is the root, 'San' is the suffix. The meaning of these two words is an enquiry or deep analysis of a subject worthy of reverence namely the Vedas. We have already seen while dealing with Vedanga that the literal meaning of Vedas has been given as in a dictionary in "Nirukta". Meemaamsa on the other hand deals with the purport and significance of the various mantras and how the correct conclusions have to be drawn regarding the significance of the Veda mantras.

I said earlier that the Vedas have two broad classifications, the Karma Kaanda and the Jnaana Kaanda. Since it appears in the first portion of a Veda Saakhā, the Karma Kaanda is called the *Poorva Bhaaga* or the earlier portion and the other which appears thereafter is called the *Uttara Bhaaga* or the latter part. In Meemaamsa also, there are two such divisions namely, Poorva Meemaamsa and Uttara Meemaamsa.

Poorva Meemaamsa stresses the importance of sacrifices and rituals mentioned in the Karma Kaanda of the Vedas while Uttara Meemaamsa emphasises the importance of self-realisation, which is the main theme of the Jnaana Kaanda of the Vedas.

I have dealt with Uttara Meemaamsa earlier when talking of the Upanishads and the Brahma Sutras. Since Uttara Meemaamsa is usually known as Vedanta, the word Meemaamsa without any prefix 'Poorva' or 'Uttara' refers only to Poorva Meemaamsa.

However, while dealing with Poorva Meemaamsa we will also be touching upon Uttara Meemaamsa or Vedanta here and there.

I had said earlier that, for every Saastra, there is a Sutra, a Vaartika and a Bhaashya. The Maharshi or sage who has written or composed the Sutra for the Poorva Meemaamsa is Jaimini. Its Bhaashya was authored by one Sabara and the Vaartika was written by Kumarila Bhatta. The *Bhatta Dipika* of Kumarila Bhatta is the most important commentary on the Poorva Meemaamsa Sutras. Kumarila Bhatta is believed to be an incarnation of Lord Subrahmanya. One Prabhaakara has also written a Bhaashya slightly differing from Kumarila. Hence the Meemaamsakas or followers of the Poorva Meemaamsa belong to two groups - those supporting Kumarila Bhatt's views and those supporting the views of Prabhaakara. We need not bother unduly with the differences involved in these two versions. Let us have a look at the general content of Poorva Meemaamsa.

The Poorva Meemaamsa sutra of Jaimini is a big book containing twelve chapters. Each chapter is further split into various padas and each paada into various Adhikaranas (अधिकरण). There are 1000 Adhikaranas in all - each Adhikarana dealing with one subject. The number of subjects dealt with in the 1000 Adhikaranas thus number one thousand. In these Adhikaranas, selected Vedic utterances are examined in detail. Vedas which are eternal and without beginning and end are the laws laid down by God. We are the subjects, He is the king. He has appointed many officials. The task of administering the entire creation has been entrusted to many Devatas such as Indra, Vaayu, Varuna, Agni, Yama, Easaana, Kubera, Nirutri, etc. They must have a code of laws to govern all the beings in the fourteen worlds. This is contained in the Vedas. On analysing the Vedas, we can determine how we should conduct ourselves and how the Devatas enforce the rules. In our work-a-day world, the resolution of mundane disputes is done by judges. The lawyers analyse the issue involved as per the law of the land and the judges give the decision. Likewise Jaimini has determined the meaning and implications of the Vedic laws which govern the actions of men. When a case comes up before a court in a particular place, one looks for precedents - what was the judgement in a similar case in, say, Allahabad or in Bombay, etc. The judge takes note of and in most cases follows precedents while giving decisions on disputed points. Similarly, in Meemaamsa the interpretation of the text at one place should be consistently carried over to other places. Thus, in the 1000 Adhikaranas a thousand types of problems are taken up and various arguments against an apparent explanation are raised before coming to a conclusion. This process of analysis is meemaamsa. First a Vedic utterance is taken up - this is *Vishaya Vaakya* or subject matter. Then the question is raised whether its meaning is such and such; this is *Samsaya* (संशय)or raising of doubts or posing the problem. The third is to argue against it which is *Poorva Paksha.* The fourth is to rebut such arguments and that is called *Uttara Paksha.* The fifth and final step is to come to a conclusion after considering the pros and cons that such and such is the real meaning. This is *Nirnaya* or decision. Each Nirnaya on a particular subject is dealt with in an Adhikarana.

Jaimini's sutras are concise. The ideas therein are elaborately spelt out in Sabara's Bhaashya. The word 'Sabara' also means a hunter-tribe. The sanyaasini, Sabari (in Ramayana) was said to belong to the hunter-tribes. According to a legend, when Lord Siva appeared as a hunter to give the divine weapon, Paasupataastra, to Arjuna, he took the form of a 'Sabara' or hunter and made this Vaartika.

Since it contains 1000 adhikaranas the Poorva Meemaamsa is also called *Sahasraadhikarani* (सहस्राधिकरणी). These Adhikaranas help to resolve the wrong interpretations that may be given to the Vedic utterances based on the literal meaning of words instead of their real meaning based on the purpose and intention.

As mentioned earlier, just as Poorva Meemaamsa determines the exact meaning of the Poorva Kaanda or Karma Kaanda, the Uttara Meemaamsa determines the meaning of the Uttara Kaanda or Jnaana Kaanda.

The Upanishads deal with the Paramaatma or the Supreme self and other connected matters and Sage Veda Vyasa was the person who propounded the meaning of the pronouncements in the Upanishad through his Brahmasutra. It is interesting to know that the person who wrote the Vaartika to Uttara Meemaamsa which pertains to the Jnaana Kaanda was Sureshwaraachaarya, the disciple of Sankaracharya who in his earlier Aashrama, i.e., before he became a Sanyaasi when he was known as Mandana Misra, was a staunch Poorva Meemaamsaka swearing by the greatness of Karma Kanda. The same person later shifted from karma to jnaana, became the disciple of Adi Sankaracharya and wrote the Vaartika on Sankara Bhaashya on the Brahmasutra.

Generally, by Uttara Meemaamsa is meant Vedanta. Why should Sankaracharya who energised the Vedic faith and put it firmly on its feet, object to Meemaamsa(Poorva Meemaamsa) which is one of the subsidiary limbs of the Vedas?

Before we answer this question, we should examine what the objective is of a discipline, be it Meemaamsa or any other Saastra. A Saastra by definition should ultimately lead one to progress in God-realisation. I said earlier that all our Saastras are so oriented. Even grammar, phonetics, etc. have the same goal. That is why they have been included in the fourteen vidyas. Now let us see what philosophy Poorva Meemaamsa propounds and what the Uttara Meemaamsa or Vedanta says about God and the God-principle and what is the difference between the two approaches.

Who is God? What are His attributes? How is He defined? The Brahmasutra of Vyasa on which Sankaracharya has written his Bhaashya or commentary talks of Isvara or God. It says *"Karta Saastraartha Tatwaat"* (कर्ता शास्त्रार्थ तत्वात्). It says that Isvara is the Karta or creator of all phenomenal existence. It may be seen that even religions that are outside the Vedic faith also refer to God as 'Karta' or Maker. Isvara is not only the creator but also the one who metes out to us the fruits of our actions, good and bad.

The Meemaamsakas, i.e. those who follow the Purva Meemaamsa school and who give credence and importance only to the ritualistic performance mentioned in the Karma Kaanda of the Vedas, are silent as to the role of Isvara or God in the creation of the world. For them this is not a matter of any real significance. According to them Isvara is NOT the *'Phala Daata',* (फल दाता) the bestower of the fruits of actions and the regulator.

Thus the two attributes of Isvara mentioned in the Vedas and Brahmasutra viz. creation of the phenomenal universe and the regulation of the results of one's karma were negated, the former by the Saankhyas and the latter by Meemaamsakas. The reason why Meemaamsakas held the view that God was not the Phala Daata was that, in their opinion, every act carried its fruit with it, that any action had a corresponding reaction irrespective of Isvara.. They believed that the proper performance of Karmas as prescribed in the Vedas are certain to yield Punya or merit and that bad deeds will certainly yield bad results. Thus, our actions would throw up the consequences automatically and the question of Isvara regulating it does not arise. Thus, among those faiths which have accepted the sanctity of the Vedas, Sankhya* has not accepted that God is the creator and Meemaamsa has rejected the assumption that He is the bestower of the just results of an action or karma.

The Meemaamsa doctrines

Let me say something about the Meemaamsa doctrines. The arguments of the Meemaamsakas go like this. "Let us not worry whether God exists or not. Let him be or let him not be. What we are to do is clearly laid down in the Vedas. The very performance of an act carries its result as action is always followed by reaction. There is thus no need for an intermediary God. Why should we pay a vegetable monger from outside to collect the vegetable from our garden for our own use? There is no need to give credit to Isvara for something which is done without his help or interference. We cultivate the land. As a result the crop is

*According to the Sankhya School, God or Isvara is not the creator or Karta of the universe. Isvara being pure consciousness and the universe being only physical matter, Isvara cannot be the creator of the universe. This argument is met by Sankaracharya pointing out that the attributeless Brahman also functions as Isvara with attributes or Saguna Brahman and appears to create the universe.

raised. Similarly, if we act as per the Vedic injunctions, the results follow without our having to know how. There is no need for a God to make the actions yield their results. To the poser that God must have made this world, the answer is why should he have made it? The world has been in existence in time, as now, without a beginning. The question of creation will arise only if the world came into being at some stage. The world has always existed as now. There was no time at which it did not so exist. Therefore, do not worry about who created it. Do your duty - the result will follow."

The Vedas which are eternal propound things beyond the reach of the intellect. According to the Vedas, action yields results or fruits.

Good actions yield good results and bad actions result in bad results. We enjoy the fruits or experience the results and keep moving around. Thus, there is no need for a manager in the form of God. We should not remain idle without activity as it is sinful and will lead us to hell. Giving up karma or activity is sin. Karmas are of three kinds — *Nitya, Naimittika and Kaamya.* The Nitya Karmas are those that have to be performed at all times, on all days as a matter of duty. What is done on any special occasion is "Naimittika". For example, taking bath and offering ablutions to dead ancesters etc. at the time of an eclipse is "Naimittika". These Nitya and Naimittika duties should be scrupulously done by all. The third karma "Kaamya" is what is done to achieve any desired objective. We wish to have rains and so we do *Varuna Japa.* One wishes to have a son and therefore, one performs the *Putra-Kaama Ishti.* For these Kaamya Karmas, there is no compulsion, and they are optional.

The Meemaamsakas have also described the characteristics of the Nityakarmas. The Nityakarmas are of two kinds, viz., "(अकरणे प्रत्यवायजनकं) *"akaranay prathyavaaya Janakam"* and *"karanay abhyudhayam".* (करणे अभ्युदयं) The former means that if not performed bad will result and the latter means good will result if performed. A good house, riches, good sons, fame, wisdom - all pertain to Abhydaya. In Vedanta, the term *Nisreyas* (निःश्रेयस्) is often used. This is the biggest attainable happiness — eternal happiness brought about by liberation or Moksha from births and deaths. But Abhyudaya refers to happiness of a relatively minor order. Meemaamsa talks only of this latter type. Meemaamsa is silent about the Nisreyas - or the happiness supreme.

Work or activity yields commensurate results. This is the Karma Maarga or the path of action. Good action when performed, leads to happiness and when not performed, leads to misery. When Nityakarma is not done, misery is bound to result.

Sandhya Vandana is a nityakarma which has to be performed daily. Many say, "we have no time and we are prepared to forgo its benefits." To this, Meemaamsa gives a fitting reply. Sandyaavandana is not an act performed for the sake of merely getting good results. It is not an optional karma. On the other hand, non-performance will lead to misery, says Meemaamsa. It is understandable that an act when performed leads to beneficial results. But where is the logic in saying that misery or evil results from the non-performance of an act? When Sandhyaavandana is not done, there are bad results though its performance will not lead to special benefits. This type of karma belongs to the category of "akaranay prathyavaaya" (अकरणे प्रत्यवाय).

When Puja is performed for a deity in a temple or when food is served to the poor, definite good results are bound to follow. These belong to the other category, viz. "karanay abhyudhaya" (करणे अभ्युदय). This looks reasonable enough.

Is "akaranay pratyavaaya" justifiable? Is there any example here in this world to illustrate it? Yes, there is. We give alms to a beggar. We give handsome donations to a charitable organisation in the faith that any help or service rendered to the needy would bring us merit or punya which will bring us happiness. Sometimes, we feel disinclined to help. Then we forgo such punya and the resultant happiness. Though one has to help the needy, one does not always think that failure to do more in the shape of charity is to be condemned.

Supposing we had taken a loan of Rs.500/- with a promise to return the amount after a specified time. When that time came, supposing we told the man: "I do not wish to deprive you of the credit or Punya of having given me Rs.500/-. And so I have no intention of returning it." The lender will certainly be not satisfied. He would say that he is not interested in earning that type of Punya, and that he is very keen on getting back his money. He would take the matter to court if necessary and not only would he try to recover his money but in addition he would request that the court should award some interest too. This incident is illustrative of 'akaranay prathyavaaya' — i.e. non-performance will yield bad results, non-performance meaning non-repayment. This analogy applies to 'Sandhyaavandana' also. The person who says he will forgo the punya which will accrue as a result of its performance is like the borrower in the above example.

It may not be enough to cite the example of a debt. Further questions arise. Let us examine the matter further. Who borrowed and when? From whom was the debt of Sandhyaavandana incurred?

In the Vedas, Taittareeya Samhita (6-3) says: "By birth Brahmins are born with three types of debts, to the Rishis or sages, to the Gods and to the ancestors. By a study and recitation of the Vedas, Adhyayana, he repays the debt to Rishis. By performance of yajnas and poojas, he repays the debt to Gods. By performing 'Tarpana' and "Shraaddha", he repays the debt to the Pitrus or the ancestors. We do not know that we had borrowed and that we owe these debts. Vedas tell us about what we do not know. We must think over the possible explanation for these debts. To those who have faith, a plausible explanation would suggest itself.

Let us say there are two brothers. One is a magistrate and the other a Purohit, i.e. a priest pursuing the Vedic profession. The former has a duty to go to the court every day and hear and decide cases. If he demurs and says, 'why should I go to the court when my brother is not going there', the answer is simple. "You applied for the job and you got appointed. You agreed to serve. Therefore, you should go to the court. That is your job. Your brother's job is different." Similarly, we had by our Karma in earlier births applied for a higher level of existence in this life. This entails the performance of certain duties in this birth. The appointing authority who gives these instructions is not visible to us but is a witness *(Saakshi)* to all our actions. This is the doctrine of the Vedantins.

The doctrine of the Meemamsakas on the other hand is that the job to which we applied gives the results automatically by itself.

Our earlier karmas have decided our caste in this birth. We should, therefore, regulate our actions in accordance therewith. If we do not do so, inconvenience, if not bad results, would follow. In whatever condition we were born, we should perform duties accordingly. The observance and practices (Vedic in origin) should be preserved and followed. It is the duty of the brahmin first to learn the Vedic injunctions himself, comfort and bring solace to others in distress and ensure that they are made aware of the duties and made to perform them as appropriate to their station in life. Likewise, everyone should do the jobs appropriate to his birth. The oil-monger should produce and purvey oil. The cobbler should make and mend shoes. The brahmin should observe great restraint in his food habits so as to be clean in body, mind and soul and thus concentrate his energies on God-realisation. He should influence others also to turn their thoughts towards God. That is why gifts of land were distributed to people of all trades and professions. This was the practice in the olden days. If the ancestral profession is abandoned, certain imbalances are bound to result. The first step would be the loss of the land gift which will go to somebody else who will be following the trade. These days even those lands are subject to land tax. Therefore, abandoning the ancestral trade would not only result in 'Paapa' or sin according to the Saastras but would cause material hardship too. In the past and until recent times, the performance of a duty which was one's birthright also carried with it a certain social recognition and regard.

Since we do not perform the duties which are required of us by birth, we find our society deteriorating day by day. Unless each one performed his appointed duties, social amenities will not be available and poverty will rule. That is the position today.

Unless the duties or nityakarma like Sandhyaavandana are performed, bad or evil results follow. If performed, they result in gain in the form of absence of evil. If a debt is repaid in time, one has the benefit of being without the burden of the debt and, in addition, earn the good name of being an honest man who repays his debt promptly. This good name is the goodwill which builds up business. Likewise, the performance of nityakarma ensures that no paapa or evil accrues to us and it adds to our well-being *(sreyas)*. Thus, there is twofold benefit.

The Vedantins accept both the "akaranay prathyavaaya" and "karanay abhyudhaya." We also naturally abide by them.

Thus, the nityakarmas must necessarily be performed. The Vedic injunctions like Agni Hotra, and the Saastraic karmas like Oupasana must be performed without fail. The Vedas say that Agni Hotra must be performed so long as life lasts. "It should be done; it is enough if it is done," say the Meemaamsakas. That is why the sanyaasa aashram finds no favour with them. In sanyaasa aashram, there is no requirement for performance of Agni Hotra and such karmas and rituals. According to the Meemaamsakas non-performance of karmas is a dereliction. Giving up karmas and becoming a sanyaasi is like abandoning one's duties. They rely on the Upanishad (Isavaasya - 2nd Mantra) which says that 'a man must live for a hundred years performing his appointed duties.' TheTaittareeyaBraahmana says that if the Agni Hotra fire is allowed to be extinguished the heinous sin called *"vira hatti dosha"* results. The Meemaamsa doctrine, therefore, says : "Just like performance of a bad deed results in sin, the non-performance of a nityakarma also results in sin." A sanyaasi is a *karma-bhrashta* (कर्म भ्रष्ट) one who is derelict in his duty. Hence, the Meemamsakas even considered that even to see a sanyasi is evil and one must atone for it. "To see a paapi, to talk to him, to touch him and to eat with him, all are paapa or evil. Likewise, we should avoid sanyaasis." Such were the views of Mandana Mishra and other exponents of Meemaamsa.

The Jnaana Kaanda of the Vedas alone talk of Sanyaasa, the Infinite, Liberation (Moksha) Jnaana (Knowledge) etc. Their authenticity is based on the Veda itself. That being so, why are they derided? Let us see what the Meemaamsakas say to this. They say :

"It is true that jnaana and Para Brahman are mentioned in the Upanishads. What is the Veda? Veda is sound, speech. Why was it created? To tell us about things we do not know. That is the *sabda-pramaana* (शब्द प्रमाण). This is to make us aware of things not grasped through the eye or even the mind by process of deduction. It was not designed to describe something which is of no use. All words have a two-fold significance. The purport of words is to communicate what is to be done and what is not to be done.'

Pravrittirva nivrittirva nityena kritakena va
Pumsaam yo nopadisyeta tat saastram abhidheeyatay

प्रवत्तिर्वा निवृत्तिर्वा नित्येन कृतकेन वा।
पुंसां यो नोपदिश्येत तत् शास्त्रं अभिधीयते।।

That is, words that describe a subject without a purpose are gossip; they merely create sounds. They are of no use. If someone says that the crow flies, what good does it do to the hearer? The statement that the crow is black has no useful purpose to serve. On the other hand, if someone says that tomorrow night there will be religious discourse here, it has an end to serve, a message to convey. It is an invitation or an inducement for people to attend it. Again, if it is said that there will be a discourse tomorrow in a distant place, it does not serve much purpose as distance precludes attendance. Therefore, words which do not serve a definite end are purposeless and, therefore, are best avoided. They may convey sometimes information but such information has no use.

The spoken word should either promote positive action or presage avoidance of action. If the five cardinal sins are described and the Veda enjoins us to refrain therefrom, this has the merit of *"nivritti prayojanam"* i.e. benefit of abstaining. The gain is avoidance of committing any sin and thereby going down in life. Words which have neither of these uses are mere gossip and are useless.

One part of the Vedas spells out what has to be done and what has to be avoided. The other part tells stories and fables etc. which though by themselves are not of much use, because they are juxtaposed with the Vedic injunctions become highly meaningful. Take the example of a health advertisement. There is a picture of a man grappling with a lion. What is the significance of this picture? No more than that you would be tempted to part with your cash and buy the tonic. The Vedic stories serve a similar but nobler purpose as they are conducive to the acceptance of the Vedic doctrines. The role of the story is known as "Artha Vaada" or result-oriented approach. Why do advertisements regarding medicines carry certificates of merit from reputed doctors? So that the medicine may have wide sales. In such purposeful campaigning, sometimes truth is stretched a little too far. Such untruth is called *"guna vaada".* There is another vaada called *"anuvaada".* This is following up the known truths repetitively. That fire will burn is already known, but to repeat it is anuvaada. *Gunarthavada* is resorting even to fiction (as distinct from fact) to illustrate and make acceptable the Vedic injunctions. "Do not drink liquor" is the Vedic injunction. If there is a story whose theme is the destruction of the drunkard, it is arthavaada. The purport is that drinking is to be avoided. "Drinking is bad. It produces intoxication" is "anuvaada". In short, all stories which can be described as arthavaada are designed to make us follow Vedic injunctions so that we may lead better lives.

To counter the objections of Jnaana Kaanda the Meemaamsakas say : "The Vedas describe a certain yajna or sacrifice. It is said that gold should be offered as dakshina and not silver. The Taittareeya Samhita also says that silver should not be offered in sacrifice but it tells a long story to press home the injunction. This story deals with the evil effects of giving silver and thus carries the message of abstaining from giving silver. This prohibition is called *"nishedha".* What has to be done is *"vidhi"* or injunction. Thus, such purposeful stories, although having no intrinsic merit in themselves, have a definite end to serve or purpose to achieve."

Using this as their theme, the Meemaamsakas counter the objections of the Jnaana Kaanda, as earlier stated. They say: "The

Upanishads talk only of the Brahma Swaroopa - the image of the ultimate. They do not attribute any function, they do not bring the subject under any type of predication. It is said that God-experience is a state where no action is involved. When and how does Veda become pramaana or authority? It has to lead to a state of positive result for it to be accepted as authority. Therefore, the Upanishad is only Arthavaada - it talks of a subject as it exists. Now, why do we have to know what is already known or do we have to be educated on what has to be done? The Vedas do not advance our understanding or contribute to our well-being by making pronouncements such as "Brahman exists; the Aatma is also Brahman." Therefore, we must perform sacrifices and other Vedic karmas and the prime object of the Vedas is to enjoin us to do them. That is why Sabda (Veda) exists. It does not require a Vedic text to know about the existence of a being which already exists. At some time or other it will come to be known. It does not even matter very much if such theoretical knowledge is not known. Therefore, that part of the Vedas which confines itself to the enunciation of phenomenal existence is mere Arthavaada. Therefore, the Upanishads do not qualify to be regarded as pramaana. Theii aim is merely to exalt the stature of the performer of sacrifices. By nature, the Jiva or the individual soul is thirsting for action and thus the individual is spurred to the performance of more and more karma. To refrain from doing karma is wrong. To become a mendicant (without any obligation to the performance of Vedic karmas) is also wrong. The identification in the Upanishads of the Jiva with the Brahman is merely to extol the individual who performs the karma and to stimulate him to greater effort and thus propagate the performance of the action by many. Just as no man, even with the help of the best tonic, can wrestle successfully with a lion, the Jiva can never reach the level of the Brahma. Thus, the Upanishads are in the nature of Arthavaada. Words such as Brahman, knowledge, Moksha and Isvara have not much use for us. Karma is all in all."

This is the doctrine of the Meemaamsakas.

Sankara's reply

What does Sankara say in reply?

It is not necessary for Sabda (Veda) to be action-oriented. The Meemaamsakas accept the sanctity of Sabda (Veda), only to the extent that it leads to a definite predication of the subject. In other words, they say that the result flowing from action is the purport of the Sabda (Veda) and the goal is not merely action in itself or for itself. But, if the goal is a state where no action prevails, then the Jnaana Kaanda which describes that state should be accepted as pramaana. In other words, if the aim of the Vedic text (Sabda) is to lead to a stage where the end result is 'no action', it fulfills the requirement of Veda (as acceptable to Meemaamsakas). Therefore, the purport of sabda should be to lead to a conclusion and not merely be action-bound. The Vedas prohibit consumption of liquor. What is the action that is required to be done as a consequence? Nothing. Does this mean that the sabda has no result-orientation? Its purpose is to prevent the ill-effects following consumption of liquor. But this kind of inaction is termed as *abhaava*, or quiescence. The purport of all restraints *(nishedha)* is *abhaava* or lack of indulgence. Even the Meemaamsakas accept the wisdom of Vedas which puts a ban on a number of actions. They also refrain from doing things which the Vedas declaim as 'nishedha'. Therefore, if some of the prohibitions which in effect are injunctions not to act are acceptable to the Meemaamsakas, how can they logically object to the state of being Brahman where no kind of activity prevails. Realisation of the self is the highest reward, whereby there is total abstinence from any kind of activity. The Vedic sabdas are therefore all meaningful. They cannot be rejected as mere arthavaada.

"Sarvam Karmaakhilam Paartha jnanay parisamaapyathay" (सर्वंकर्माखिलं पार्थज्ञाने परिसमाप्यते) says Lord Krishna in Bhagavad Gita. This means that all karmas ultimately lead to and find their rest in Jnaana or knowledge. All activity should be directed towards the supreme Lord. Total abstinence from any kind of activity is the ultimate goal. It is the supreme bliss or Brahmaananda. As a result, the birth-death cycle is stopped. This is the supreme

message and purpose of the Vedas. The whole of Karma Kaanda should lead to and merge with the Jnaana Kaanda. Only then the former becomes meaningful.

"The Vedas contain injunctions for 'Karma', (Vedic activities) in the Karma Kaanda only, because the limited purpose of purifying and disciplining the mind (Chitta Suddhi) is obtainable thereby. If abstinence from all activity could lead to a result a million times more than what karma could provide, then this would be the fullest objective of the Vedas. This is the message of the Jnaana Kaanda. But, those portions of the Vedas which deal with karma are helpful in creating mental purity and lead to the road which ultimately ends in Isvara. Because of this, they become meaningful. Mere karma in itself, therefore, has no purpose to it. The Vedas extol the 'supremacy of the sanyaasa aashrama' (life of mendicancy) as the stage which prevails on realisation of the Paramaatma and which indeed is the state of the Paramaatma. It should be our endeavour to reach this state."

Even in the Karma Kaanda itself, the Vedas reject certain karmas as leading to bad ends. But by doing such act, there does appear to be some pleasure or profit for some. It is because of this some people indulge in bad acts. One who does not perform such acts denies himself the resultant profit or pleasure. Still, the Vedas prohibit their performance. Why? Although initially, sinful acts bestow pleasure and satisfaction mostly sensual, in the long run, they preclude us from partaking of the higher bliss or happiness. That is why the Vedas exhort us to eschew sinful karmas. Though there is material prosperity in this world and, thereafter, residence in Pitru Loka and Deva Loka, where life is pleasant and sorrows are absent, are these permanent abodes? Are the pleasures endless? No. As soon as the accumulated merit resulting from good acts is exhausted, the pleasures end. After exhausting the punya, they have to fall back to earth. *"Ksheenay punyay martyalokam visanti"* (क्षीणे पुण्ये मर्त्यलोकं विशन्ति) says the Bhagavad Gita. If there is any lasting well-being or unchanging and complete happiness, it is the stage which the Jnaani reaches by merging with the Infinite and being free from any kind of activity. One must try to rise above the karmas which can bestow happiness for a limited and trifling period and try to reach up to the higher karmas. In other words, one must unflaggingly perform the Vedic karmas but then what use would they be if one cannot earn the total and continuous happiness thereby? Therefore, can one give up these karmas on this score?

Can one go direct to the stage of permanent happiness? No. One cannot. It is not easy to get to the stage of Jnaani or a wise one all at once. First, the mind should be cleansed of impurities. Karma alone is able to hold the mind in line which is for ever beset by waves after waves of thoughts. Therefore, the ritualistic karmas have to be faithfully performed. In so doing, one must turn the mind away from the benefits which such karmas can bestow, e.g., pleasures, heaven, etc. In other words after practicising to do the karma, the reward arising therefrom should be deliberately eschewed. As a result, the impurities which are natural to the mind are removed. If we consciously and sincerely pray to the Lord that we do not want the reward normally flowing from the karmas and dedicate them to the Lord Himself, He is bound to bless us with mental clarity and purity - *Chitta Suddhi.* From then on, it will be possible to begin the journey of *Jnana Vichara* - philosophical enquiry. The next stage would be to reach the state of being free from any kind of activity and be by oneself in a perpetual state of bliss.

Vedantic doctrines and Meemaamsa

To the extent that the Vedic karmas are totally favoured, the Advaitic philosophy not only supports Meemaamsa but goes along with it further in accepting for its own use the six pramaanas (authorities or articles of proof) which the Meemaamsic doctrine posits in its own support.

Shri Sankara's Advaita, Shri Ramanuja's Vishistaadvaita and Shri Madhva's Dvaita are verily Vedantic doctrines. Like the Advaita, the other two philosophies also insist on the performance of Vedic karmas. Therefore, as a general rule, upto a point, the doctrine of Meemaamsa is acceptable to all the three Vedic philosophies.

Of the six pramaanas of the Meemaamsakas, the Advaitins have accepted all, and the Visishtaadhvaitins have accepted only three of them, viz. (1) *Pratyaksha*, (2) *Anumaana* and (3) *Sabda* (Vedas). Nevertheless these three are from the six of the Meemaamsakas. I will slightly elaborate the role of pramaanas when dealing with the next Upaanga, namely Nyaaya.

Summing up, Meemaamsa is not totally discredited by or unacceptable to the three recognised Acharyas of the Vedantic faith. Using Meemaamsa as the base, one reaches the stage of bhakti (devotion) which is the instrument of faith of Visishtaadvaita and Dvaita, and then Advaita takes it up further to the stage of Jnaana or True knowledge absolute.

Since karma is regarded as the summum bonum, Meemaamsa is generally called the Karma Maarga or the path of Vedic activity, but this Karma Maarga is not the same as the one which the Vedantists have in mind when they refer to the Karma, Bhakti, Jnaana Maargas. None of the Vedantic doctrines regard karma as an end in itself or beyond which nothing is required to be done. The karma maarga or the karma yoga of the Vedantins is that karma should be done as per Vedic injunctions but without expectations of any reward, which should be dedicated to the Lord.

Lord Krishna has pointedly said this in the Bhagavad Gita. Devotion to the Lord is divorced from the duty or karma which Meemaamsa uncompromisingly postulates. These karmas not only bring prosperity and well-being to the world but also cleanses the mind of the performer (Chitta Suddhi), thereby enabling him to reach the higher stages of bhakti (devotion) and jnaana (true knowledge). In other words, what Meemaamsa regards as the end, the Vedanta regards as means to an end.

22

BUDDHISM AND OTHER SCHOOLS OF THOUGHT

Sankara and Buddhism

There are many who say that Buddhism was driven out of this country because of the condemnation of that faith by Adi Sankaracharya. This is wrong. He was more concerned with setting right the errors in Saankhya and Meemaamsa which denied the importance of Isvara though basically subscribing to the Vedic tenets. Sankara has argued that, both according to the wording and meaning of Vedic texts and the Brahmasutra, it is incorrect to ignore the very definition of the term Isvara and to say that He is not the creator or *Phala Daata*. Arguing that truth is what is stated in the Vedas, he has pointed out that the world cannot be created without Isvara . Nor can it be established that actions by themselves would recompense the doer. Isvara is the bestower as well as regulator of the results. His consciousness, His will (Sankalpa) alone created the world and established the law of Karma according to which alone the fruits of actions are enjoyed or suffered as the case may be. He has effectively countered the arguments of the followers of the Saankhya and Meemaamsa schools. Even in those places where Buddhism had come up for severe criticism he has gone no further than what was covered by the original sutra and to condemn only the denial of the existence of God by Buddhism. The Acharya's writings do not in any way show that, because of the vehemence and logic of his condemnation alone, Buddhism was deported from this land. But then, why did Buddhism disappear from this country? Someone must have been responsible for loosening its hold. The answer is the Meemaamsakas and the Taarkkas (Logicians). Those proficient in Tarka Saastra (logic) are called 'Taarkikas'. Tarka belongs to Nyaaya Saastra, which comes serially after Meemaamsa among the fourteen Vidyas. Those proficient in Nyaaya Saastra are called 'Naiyaayikas' (नैय्यायिक). Udayanacharya who was a Taarkika and

Kumarila Bhatta who was a Meemaamsaka have strongly attacked Buddhism, each for his own reason. Udayanacharya condemned Buddhism because it preached that there was no Isvara or God. The Meemaamsakas, although they said that the karmas themselves and not Isvara was the Phaladaata, they nevertheless accepted that all actions yielded results and that the Vedic rituals must be performed zealously and correctly. The Meemaamsakas, therefore, condemned Buddhism which preached that there was no need for any ritualistic karmas as prescribed in the Vedas. Kumarila Bhatta has dealt extensively with this aspect of the Buddhist faith and has condemned the same. Thus, Udayanacharya's attack on the atheistic aspect of Buddhism and Kumarila's condemnation of the negation of Vedic rituals by Buddhism were largely instrumental in preventing Buddhism in making any headway. Sankara who came later had therefore no need to deal with the negative aspects of Buddhism in great depth. He confined himself to exposing the faults which were also found in the beliefs the Buddhists propagated.

The Acharya firmly established that there is a God or Isvara who is the creator of the phenomenal universe and He alone is the one who awards the fruits of one's actions and regulates the results of one's karmas.

I have said all this only to correct the wrong information being propagated that Sankaracharya was the enemy of Buddhism.

Buddhism and Hindu Society

To me it is clear that at no time in India did people practise Buddhism in toto though they respected Gautama Buddha as a great personage. Today, there are many who have joined a movement called the 'Theosophical Movement.' Nevertheless, many of them continue to celebrate the festivals just like Hindus. Their marriages and similar other rites are performed as per Vedic injunctions. They have not given up the Hindu religion. When some great men are born, many are attracted by their great qualities like humanity, wisdom and character. Nevertheless, the missions or institutions established in their names with some modifications of or departures from the Vedic practices, are not generally followed by their votaries in their homes. They continue to stick to the old traditions. Mahatma Gandhi and Gandhism are names to conjure with. People in their enthusiasm at first placed him even above the incarnations of Rama and Krishna. Nevertheless, in their private lives they did not practise his essential teachings, viz., widow remarriage, physical contact with the Harijans, etc. To this extent, they have not practised Gandhism, although in society they passed for ardent followers of Gandhi. But since Gandhi as a person had outstanding personal qualities, such as self-sacrifice, truth, devotion to God, public service, etc., people highly respected him. This should not be taken to imply that they implicitly accepted all his preachings and sayings in toto.

Same was the case with the Buddha. His private life was highly laudable. A prince, in his youth, he even abandoned his wife and infant son, so as to dedicate himself to the task of improving the lot of the common man. These sacrifices and good qualities attracted the masses. This did not mean or result in all the Buddhist tenets from being accepted or followed in practice. Simply because Buddha condemned ritualistic practices, people did not abandon them. They still followed the caste system and the various rituals but admired Buddha for his personal qualities. Neither did people become Bikshus (mendicants) in large numbers. They married and became householders performing the duties prescribed for such life as per tradition. Although Emperor Asoka was a Buddhist and did so much for Buddhism, he did not change nor was he able to change the Vedic way of life of the society in general. The famous Asoka pillar and many of Asoka's edicts bear testimony to the fact that he safeguarded the religious freedom of his subjects. It would appear that, except for the Buddha Bikshus (mendicants), the bulk of the householders continued to follow the Vedic way of life. Although the Buddhists do not make specific mention of Isvara or God or the divinities, it may be interesting to note that even the books written by great Buddhist Bikshus have a Sarasvati Stotra in the beginning praising Sarasvati, the Goddess of Learning and Wisdom. They have worshipped many divinities like Neelaadhaara. It is from Tibet and its surroundings that we have obtained many Taantric texts specifying the method of worship of divinities. An examination of the works of Sri Harsha and Bilhana, which are written in Sanskrit, makes it clear that, even during the time when Buddhism was flourishing, the Vedic rituals and the Vedic way of life were followed assiduously.

Many reformists, who may not accept the way of life I proclaim, also come to me. Although not subscribing to my belief, they think that there is something good in me and their visit is on account of personal regard. This has been the case in our country in the past also. Not only those who slightly differed from the accepted and popular faith but even those who violently upheld and propagated their widely divergent reformism, were held in high esteem not necessarily on account of their views but on account of their personal qualities and praiseworthy way of living. Even today, the stage has not been reached when our traditional beliefs and customs have been completely thrown overboard. After all, like seasoned wood tested through the years, these are deeply embedded in the people's minds and hearts over the centuries. In short, people have been following in the footsteps of their forefathers and the traditions passed on from generation to generation. This was what happened to Buddhist religious reformism also. Therefore, when the Buddhist doctrine was brought under fire by Udayana and Kumarila Bhatta, people had no difficulty in abandoning the new faith of Buddhism and reverting to the traditional.

Sankara and the other doctrines

The ultimate stage in Adi Sankara's doctrine was the giving up of rituals and concentrating the mind on the infinite. But, unlike Buddha, he did not recommend that, even at the initial stages, the Vedic Karmas should be ignored but only after attaining mental purity, as a result of the performance thereof, should one turn to introspection and enquiry into self. First, one has to abide by the karmas, as stipulated in the Meemaamsa and go ultimately to the stage of the Buddhist cult of giving them up.

Our Acharya accepted the tenets of Buddhism, Meemaamsa, Saankhya and Nyaaya to a certain extent and upto a certain stage but was opposed to all of these at stages beyond those. These faiths can be said to have held fast one aspect of the total doctrine as their ultimate conclusion, whereas our Acharya synthesised and harmonised them all.

Saankhya

Saankhya says that the Aatma, which is not involved with anything else but is the cause of all, is the "Purusha" and that Maaya, the Sakti which activates the world is "Prakriti". It goes on to say that the world consists of 24 Tatvas (or first principles) including the Prakriti. Prakriti is the first Tatva. From this has evolved the second Tatva called *Ahankaara*, i.e. ego or the feeling that there exists something called the self. This splits itself into two. On one side it becomes the *Chaitanya* (animate life and knowledge) or the Jiva with its mind and five sense organs and five limbs or work organs. On the other side, it is the inanimate, *Jada* or matter with its five *Tanmaatras* (तन्मात्र) or elements and the five Mahabhootas (महा भूता) or big principles. The five sense organs of the Jiva (animate being) are the five organs which communicate the external objects to him. The eyes which see, the nose which smells, the mouth which tastes, the ear which hears, the skin that feels the touch are the sense organs. These that enable the Jiva to function direct or indulge directly in action are the *Karmendriyas* or working organs. The mouth also figures here. As a sense organ, it indulges in the function of speech. The hand that does all the jobs is another working organ. The functional bias of the sense organs, viz., sound (ear), touch (skin), image or sight (eye), rasa or taste (mouth), smell (nose) which are subtle, are the Tanmaatras. These principles in their Jada or inanimate existence are the five Mahabhootas as, viz., Sky (sound), Vayu (touch), Agni (form or image), Water (rasa or taste), Prithvi (earth) (smell). Thus, there are in all twenty-four tatvas comprising Prakriti, Mahat, Ahamkaara, the mind, the five sense organs, the five working organs, the five Tanmaatras and the five Mahabhootas.

These 24 are also accepted by the Advaitic doctrine of Vedanta. But Advaita says that the Being called Isvara or Saguna Brahman (Brahman with attributes) causes the union of the

Aatma (the Brahman without attributes) and Prakriti (Maya) - whereas Saankhya makes no mention of Isvara at all.

Saankhya also propounds the three Gunas viz., *Satva, Rajas* and *Tamas* which are accepted by all schools on Vedantic philosophy. Satva is the clear, peaceful, calm and exalted state. Rajoguna is all speed and movement. Tamoguna is laziness, sleep and inaction. In the Bhagavad Gita, these are elaborately dealt with in the *Guna traya-Vibhaga Yoga.* The Lord tells Arjuna to become *Nistraigunya,* meaning that one should try to remain at the level of the pure Aatma which transcends all the three gunas. Saankhya also urges that all the conflicts and dissatisfaction are the result of the clash of these gunas and their effect should be neutralised. But, unlike the Bhagavad Gita and other Vedic Saastras, it does not recommend the worship of Isvara, surrender and introspection as the means to attain such equanimity and exalted state.

"The Purusha alone has the animation of life (Jiva-Chaitanya). Prakriti is inanimate (Jada). Hence, by itself Prakriti cannot act. It, however, manifests itself as the twenty-four basic principles or Tatavas solely through the impulse of the Purusha but Purusha is totally disengaged from and uninvolved with Prakriti and is solely a matter of cognisance," so says Saankhya in apparent contradiction.

The word "Kewala" (केवलम्) means to be alone without being mixed with any other thing - by itself and by its own volition. The adjective of this is *Kaivalya.* In Saankhya, Kaivalya is the name given to Moksha. The Jiva or the self transcends the twenty-four basic principles, gets free from the inanimate or Jada and stays by itself at the level of the Purusha. This is Kaivalya.

The goal of Advaita is also to merge with the Aatma which is synonymous with Purusha, rejecting all else as Maya or illusion. but methods to achieve this objective like *karma, upaasana* (Bhakti) and later *jnaanavichaara* or introspection which are recommended by the Acharya are not to be found in Saankhya. Most of it confines itself to a dissertation of the twenty-four Tatvas.

There is another shortcoming in Saankhya. "The Purusha (Aatma) is mere knowledge without any indulgence in activity. Prakriti is mere activity but without any knowledge (jnaana) or life and animation, (Jiva Chaitanya). Such is the clear cut differentiation, without explaining how it is possible for the Jada (inanimate matter) to transform itself into the other Tatvas. The only explanation offered is that the presence of the Purusha (Jiva Chaitanya) is responsible for such mutations of the Jada. The Purusha is said to be without any activity but Prakriti is said to be active through the agency of the Purusha. How is this reconciled? Saankhya replies to this as follows : Just as the presence of the magnet activates the iron particles without any overt intention to do so, so also Prakriti is active on account of the mere presence of the Purusha. They both act in a manner which can be likened to a blind man carrying a lame man on his shoulder. The blind man cannot see and the lame man cannot walk but the blind man can travel as per the directions of the lame man. Likewise, Prakriti which has no consciousness but is active carries Purusha which is nothing but consciousness and the worldly business is thus performed. This is no doubt appealing as an apt simile, but hardly logical. Advaita on the other hand says that the action-free, attributeless "Nirguna Brahman" alone appears to exist as the active attributeful Isvara and conducts the business of the world through Maya.

There is another big difference between Saankhya and Advaita. Although it talks of the Purusha as pure consciousness, instead of all the Jivaatmas being one and the same Aatma, it says that the Jivaatmas are many and separate.

Thus, although it contains some inconsistencies, it serves as an authority for the Vedantic concept in identifying and listing the basic principles (Tatvas). The word 'Saankhya' (सांख्य) is derived from Sankhya (संख्या) which means to count in terms of numbers.

Sage Kapila has written a Sutra on the Saankhya doctrine. The important treatises on this subject are the Saankhya Kaarika by Iswara Krishna and the Bhaashya Sutra by Bigyaana Bikshu.

In the Bhagavad Gita, Lord Krishna Himself has enunciated and explained many Saankhya principles. But, when he talks of Saankhya and Saankhya Yoga as two different paths to realisation, he means the path through knowledge or jnaana.

Saankhya says that the Purusha has to be realised as separate from the Prakriti and leaves it at that. Raaja Yoga on the other hand starts from where Saankhya left off and tells us how and through what method is such a separation to be effected and what discipline or Sadhana should be undertaken. But, in Yoga, the existence of the Isvara is accepted and his worship is given as the means to control the mind. Patanjali's "Raaja Yoga" defines Yoga generally as the method or device to control the fissiparous tendencies of the mind.

Although Saankhya and Yoga do not form part of the 14 or 18 Vidyas of our Saastras, they nevertheless are two of the important disciplines and hence I have mentioned them.

It may be recalled that I made a reference to this earlier. I said that although Meemaamsa does not accept devotion to God as essential it nevertheless accepts the authority of the Vedas in the same way as Saankhya which, whilst accepting the Vedic authority, preaches Godlessness. *(Nireeshwara Vaada).* Adi Sankara has taken what is correct from the various schools of thought and rejected those that are unacceptable. He thus established the basic Vedantic faith, which is the cause of these other theories and which are also contained in Vedanta. Adi Sankara accepted the conclusion of Buddhism at the stage of pure consciousness, the unmixed jnaana of the Saankhya philosophy - in the place of the Nirguna Brahman - the Prakriti of it which corresponds to Maya, and the twenty-four basic principles which it lists, the ritualism of Meemaamsa, the Isvara of Nyaaya and the various proofs which it offers thereon. His view is that each of these doctrines stresses one aspect only and make it the goal of human existence, whereas they are to be harmonised into a single entity, acceptable to both reason and intellect.

23

THE UPAANGAS

NYAAYA — The Science of Logic and Expediency

The Nyaaya Saastra is generally known as Tarka Saastra also. This was composed by Sage Gautama. Its main object is to establish by means of disputation that Parameswara is the creator of this universe. It establishes the existence of Isvara by inference. Thus, it is a Saastra whose chief instrument of conviction is deduction.

Deduction is inescapable. Vedas talk of a particular subject. The scope and significance of the Vedic utterances are determined by Meemaamsa (Uttara).

Even though we have total faith in the Vedas, there will be a lurking doubt in the mind. Therefore, in order to dispel such doubts, many devices are used so that in conclusion the belief may become firm. When we erect a pillar, we embed it in the ground and shake it to and fro, so that it gets firmly settled in its base. Likewise, truths should be assailed on all sides by arguments so as to make them acceptable without any argument. We must welcome any kind of disputation. But these should be based on acceptable premises or authority. Argument for argument's sake, sophistry or quibbling should of course be ignored.

When Adi Sankara's last moment was nearing, his disciples who were gathered round him begged him to give them a final message. As a result, the Acharya gave them a message in five slokas known as *Upadesa Panchakam* or *Sopaana Panchakam* or *Saadhana Panchakam*. A portion of this reads as : "दुस्तर्कात्सुविरम्यतां श्रुतिमतस्तर्कोऽनुसन्धीयताम्" *Dustarkat Suviramyatam Srutimatastarkonusandheeyatam*. That is : "keep away from mere verbal arguments: adopt only those devices which respect the Vedic strain of thought and are based on a sound premise."

The devices used to establish Vedic postulates are called Nyaaya. As I said, this Sastra was authored by Gautama. Another person called 'Ganata' has also written a Nyaaya Saastra. It is called *'Vaiseshika'* (वैशेषिका).

We make a distinction between two objects because of the presence of some peculiar characteristics in them, each having some attributes not found in the other. Since this peculiarity (*Visesha* or attribute) is the main basis of examination, the system came to be called as Vaiseshika. Nyaaya Saastra, which proceeds mainly on scientific lines, joins Vaiseshika at the stage where *Adhyaatmic* (spiritual) matters such as Jiva (soul), Jagat (universe), Isvara (the Lord) and Moksha (Liberation) which, incidentally, the Vaiseshikas call *'Apavarga'* are dealt with. Both of these use Tarka (logic) and Tatva (philosophy). Philosophy is enunciated through the medium of logic.

The Nyaaya Saastra discusses the fundamental Truth through the aid of four devices. They are : (i) *Pratyaksha* (प्रत्यक्ष), (ii) *Anumaana* (अनुमान), (iii) *Upamaana* and (iv) *Sabda*.

The first named, viz., Pratyaksha Pramaana, is what is experienced by our sense organs, like sight, smell, hearing, taste etc. The next on the list called Anumaana is the most important in so far as Nyaaya is concerned.

What is Anumaana? We see smoke on a distant mountain-top. The smoke alone is visible but no fire can be sighted. The rocks in front no doubt hide the fire from our view. Thus, the smoke alone is seen rising in the sky. Even so, although not visible, we have no hesitation in coming to the conclusion that there is a fire on the mountain. This is called 'Anumaana'. Here, what helps us to conclude that fire is possible and which provides the evidence to come to such a conclusion is the smoke. This is called *saadhana, linga* or *hetu*.

Now, according to the Vedantic doctrine, which we profess, we must meditate on the *Upadesa*, after being initiated into it by a Guru. This is called *'Manana'*. This is to constantly keep in mind what the Guru has taught with the help of one's own mental devices *(Yukti).* Here Anumaaana lends a hand. It is only through Anumaaana that things that cannot be actually perceived are cognised on the basis of other proofs. The Paramaatma and Jivaatma cannot be brought within the ken of our sensory perceptions like the eyes, ears, mouth, nose and so on. The ultimate state of Moksha or liberation is also beyond their grasp. All these can be understood only through 'Anumaaana' or reasoned deduction. Knowing the unknown through the known is Anumaaana.

By performing Vedic karmas, we get mental purity. A good Guru gives certain instructions in which we have faith. At this stage, if somebody else says something different, doubts assail our mind. Therefore, before coming to a conclusion, we must run through the whole gamut of possible objections. Proofs such as Anumaaana help us so as to examine our beliefs. The Nyaaya Saastra and Vaiseshika depend mostly on Anumaaana in their disquisitions.

"Padaartha" - (पदार्थ) - Meaning of Words.

All our systems of philosophical discussions believe that, if one were to go right down to the very bottom to grasp the meaning of words, the Vedic truths will be better understood. All 'Pramaanas' (proofs or channels which lead to understanding) should be used before coming to a conclusion. The proof or channel through which understanding is made possible is Pramaana.

There are only a limited number of things that come within the ken of *Pratyaksha Pramaana* - direct perception — through eyes, nose and so on. More things are outside their reach than within. These are grasped by *Anumaaana Pramaana* - proof arising from deduction. Let us consider Anumaaana further. It helps the intellect in its effort to understand the Vedic truth. That is why Nyaaya has been classified as an Upaanga - an auxiliary to the Vedas. Meemaamsa helps through the ears, while Nyaaya helpsthrough 'Manana' - meditation or cogitation and by constant repetition.

In Nyaaya, *'Padaartha'* (पदार्थ) understanding has been divided into seven kinds, or invested with seven dimensions. Since all matters that require to be understood cannot be listed individually, they have been grouped depending on the medium through which their understanding is made possible. These seven fall under two headings. *'Bhaava',* that which exists or has presence and *'abhaava',* that which exists not or has no presence. Of these seven groupings, 'abhaava', non-existence — negation — is the seventh. 'Bhaava', or those with existence are divided into six kinds.

The question arises as to how one can conceive of a matter that does not exist. Negation is not a positive concept but the word 'negation' has a definite connotation and meaning too.

Lack of existence or presence exists in some places and does not exist in some other places. "Here there are no flowers." That is, here, there is the existence or 'lack of flowers'. "There, the flowers are present on the altar." The lack of existence (abhaava) is not there. Thus abhaava exists in some places, and does not exist in some other places. Likewise, it exists at certain times, and does not exist at certain other times. Therefore, abhaava has a definite existence, in as much as it is present at certain times or at certain places.

The seven dimensions of 'Padhaartha' are : *Dravya* (द्रव्य) or matter, (ii) *Guna* (गुण) Quality, (iii) *Karma* (कर्म) Activity, (iv) *Saamaanya* (सामान्य) species, (v) *Visesha* (विशेष) peculiarity or special attribute, (vi) *Samavaaya* (समवाय) connection between individual and species and (vii) *Abhaava* of matter and its quality or lack of presence. Dravya, Guna and Karma are termed as 'Sat' - or those which can be shown to exist. The remaining four cannot thus be pointed out. Of the three belonging to 'Sat', Dravya can be physically shown. Knowledge, desire, happiness, sorrow and such qualities cannot be separated and shown from subjects on whom they depend for their existence. Lotus is red; it is its attribute. It cannot be isolated from lotus. Thus 'Guna' is resident in an object. The thing to which it is attached is Dravya, or matter. Although happiness and sorrow cannot be isolated from a subject and shown, we can see a person who is happy or sorrowful. Thus these two emotions get to be known. When we see a red lotus, we understand what red means. Karma is work or action, movement, walking, running etc.

They also are attached to Dravya and cannot exist by themselves. The act of running cannot be separated from the one who runs. We can see him running and we can also distinguish running from sitting, sleeping etc. That is how we see and identify running. Saamaanya, the fourth of the Padaartha, refers to the *jaati* or species. There is a herd of cows. The act of being a cow is common to all of them and they can be generalised as cows. This is what we call the species which is present in every cow. Although belonging to a species, each cow has an individual quality. This is 'Vishesha'. Although belonging to the cow species, each cow can be identified as there are some special distinguishing features in each. Dravya and its quality, Dravya and its work or function, generality as in species and individuality, a whole matter and its separate limbs - the whole object and its various parts which cannot be separated - this is Samavaaya. Fire has brightness which cannot be separated from it. It is Samavaaya. If matter joins matter it is called 'Samyoga'. These can exist separately or together. Dravya and Guna are Samavaaya. Dravya and Karma are also Samavaaya. Because Guna and Karma cannot exist by themselves, they are necessarily attributes to matter.

I have already dealt with Abhaava, which comes last as the seventh. Just as all matter has been classified under seven heads, each subject has been classified under several categories. Dravya has been divided into nine types. These are Prithvi (earth) *Aap* (water) *Tejas* (fire light) *Vaayu* (air) *Aakaasa* (space) *Kaala* (time) *Dik* (direction) *Aathma* (soul) and *Manas* (mind). Of these, the first five are called *Pancha Bhootha.* Space permits the remaining four to exist in it. There is a point to wonder at regarding these Pancha Bhoothas. Corresponding to each of these, the body has five senses of perception.

The eye which sees, the ear which hears, the tongue which tastes, the sense of touch which distinguishes heat and cold, the nose that smells, these are the five instruments of perception. The sense of perception is not merely confined to the outer skin. It is spread all over the body. It is also present inside the body. For example, stomach or heartache is felt by the sense of touch located inside the body. These five sensations can be felt only through the appropriate organs. Sight is confined to the eye; one cannot see through the ears. The music which can be heard through the ear cannot be heard through the eye or nose. If something is placed on the tongue, its taste can be felt but not its smell. The sweetness of sugar connot be discerned by the nose. Thus, each of these organs can know only one of the five attributes. The guna called 'roopa' is known only to the eye. Roopa is the colour and dimensions of an object. White, yellow, black, green, red and brown are the colors. Sounds and their variations are discerned by the ear. Good and bad smell are distinguished by the nose. The six types of tastes (Rasas) are identified by the tongue. The organ of touch distingushes heat and cold. Thus the five 'Indriyas' or sense organs are able to observe or sense the five gunas. These are called *"Jnaanendriyas"*. If these organs were absent, then these gunas would have been beyond our comprehension. If we had six sense organs, we could have perhaps identified six gunas. Possibly, if we had a thousand such organs, we might have been able to discern an equal number of different qualities of matter. We do not know how many things are present in this world. If we did not have the sense of touch, we would not have known the existence of heat or cold. We owe our knowledge of thermal variations to this guna. We find the blind and the deaf being unaware of roopa (form) and sabda (sound), respectively, although there is no dearth of these in this world. Eye, tongue, nose, skin, (sense of touch) and ear - these five sense organs have their corresponding vishayas or object of discernment in Roopa (form), Rasa (savour), Gandha (smell), Sparsa (touch) and Sabda (sound).

These five gunas appropriate to these vishayas are present in the Pancha Bhootas or five elements. In earth, all these five are present. Earth has form and taste. Our body, a vegetable, sugar candy - are all of the earth only. Earth has smell too. The flower is of the earth. Hardness, heat and cold are also of the earth. Earth has sound too. A tightened string produces sound. So does a stick when it is used to beat another object. In Rasa or water, except for smell, all the other four qualities are present. When water is beaten, sound is produced. Although the earth has five qualities, it has one which none of the other four elements have viz., smell, which is the special quality of Earth. The main or special quality of water is Rasa or taste. If there is no water, there can be no perception of taste. That is why in the organ which identifies taste, viz. the tongue, water is always present. If the tongue is dry, taste is not discernible. Rasa also means water. Tejas (Fire) has neither smell nor taste, it has only Roopa (form), Sparsa (touch) and Sabda (sound). Its special quality is Roopa. There is no Roopa in Vaayu or air. It has only Sabda and Sparsa. Its special quality is Sparsa or touch. That is why when the wind blows, the body feels it. Aakaasa (space) has only sound. Modern science had earlier thought that air or the wind was responsible for producing sound. After the discovery of wireless transmission, it is slowly being realised that sound is a quality of space - wireless transmission is not dependent on the flow of winds.

The sky or space, with a single guna of sound, vayu which in addition to sound has sparsa or 'touch', Agni or Fire which in addition to sound and touch, has roopa or form visible to the eye, water having Rasa or savour and earth which has smell in addition to the four gunas — these are the Pancha Bhootas or the five elements.

There are Dravyas or matters which represent the Pancha Bhootas on whom depend the gunas for their discernment. The balance out of the nine Dravyas (excluding the above five) are *Kaala* or time, *Dik* or direction, *Aatma*, the soul and *Manas*, the mind. The hour, yesterday, tomorrow, today, year, yuga, etc., refer to time or kaala. Direction is terrritory, up, down, there, here, etc. Aatma is that which has the mind which is able to conceive all these principles. Aatma is of two types, the Jivaatma and the Paramaatma. The one who merely witnesses all that happens in this world is the Paramaatma. The one who gets involved with the world and becomes miserable is the Jivaatma. Jivaatmas are many; Paramaatma is one. Both are *Chaitanya* i.e. sentient. Vedanta says that awareness or intelligence is itself Aatma. On the other hand, Nyaaya Saastra says that one who possesses the awareness is Aatma. The one with the dulled awareness is Aatma, says Nyaaya, which is the doctrine of Dvaita (Dualism). But as per Vedanta, awareness, which is without a second, is Aatma. There is nothing else that can be known as different from it. There can thus be no question of any 'dull' Aatmas or Jivaatmas. But, according to

Nyaaya, awareness is wedded to guna. Aatma is matter; awareness is its guna or quality. Aatma is the abode of jnaana or intelligence, knowledge and the ability to know.

There is nothing that exists outside the fullness of knowledge. Hence Nyaaya calls Paramaatma as the Supreme Knowledge. The Jivaatmas or the individual souls have only a limited awareness. Hence they are called *'Kinchithajna'* meaning, with scanty knowledge. The Paramaatma is *'Sarvajna'* or all-knowledge, all-knowing. We are the abode of both full jnaana and scanty jnaana, i.e. a combination of both. On the other hand, Paramaatma is the repository of total jnaana. The Aatma is Vibhu, all-pervading. Although the Nyayasaastra also says that Paramaatma is all-pervading, the difference between Paramaatma and Jivaatma is not recognised. That is because, in the view of this Saastra, intelligence exists separately in each Jiva. The place where it resides is the mind. The mind alone causes the feeling of happiness or sorrow.

As per *Nyaaya Sastra,* gunas or qualities are divided into twenty-five types and karmas, action, into five types. The Nyaaya Sastra says that, if one has a correct *Padaartha jnaana* (true concept of matter), truth will become known when the mind will reject the rest as unimportant and thus attain the Moksha state, where there is neither happiness nor sorrow.

Although we may strive for Moksha, as per the Vedantic concept, Mananá (meditation) which is necessary for cogitating on the guru's upadesa, which is the Nyaaya method, is most useful. We come to know of the Pancha Bhootas, Jivaatma and mind. How can the Paramaatma be known? He is unknowable. Anumaana or deduction is essential to know him. To know the rest, the pramaana or the proof which the sense organs are capable of collecting is sufficient. The Sruti says that Paramaatma exists. Nyaaya avers, on the basis of deduction (Anumaana), that Paramaatma must necessarily exist.

Let us now examine a small example of Anumaana. That the chair on which I sit must have been made by some carpenter is known. Because we have not actually met the man who made it, can we say that this has not been made by the man. We have seen other chairs being made. On that basis, we know that this one must also have been made by a carpenter. We also know that it is within the capability of the carpenter to make a chair. Likewise, there must be a creator of this universe. He is all-knowledge, all-sakti, all-power. Since he protects all, he should be all-mercy too. Nyaaya Saastra establishes such matters by discussing the pros and cons and with the aid of proper deduction.

Pramaanas or Authorities

In addition to Pratyaksha and Anumaana, Nyaaya has two other pramaanas. These are Upamaana (simile or example) and Sabda (sound).

What is Upamaana? It is to know something which we have not known on the basis of similarity with the thing already known. There is an animal called 'Gavaya'. We do not know what it looks like. It is described as something resembling a cow. We happen to go near a forest. There we see some animal resembling the description. We then come to the conclusion that it must be the Gavaya we have been told about. This is Upamaana.

Sabda pramaana is Vedic text and the (oral) sayings of great men. When the Vedas and the great men (like Rishis) say something, we must accept it as authority as it can never be false. It is the tenet of Naiyaayikas (those who belong to the Nyaaya School) that the Vedas are the utterances of the Lord Himself. That is why they are their own pramaana. The sayings of great men who are without question truthful (in thought, word and deed) are also included in the *Sabda Pramaana.*

These four pramaanas form part of the Meemaamsa doctrine propounded by Kumarila Bhatta. In addition to these, he has added *"Arthapat"* and *"Anupalabdhi"*, making the number of pramaanas six. We of the Advaitic faith have accepted all these six pramaanas. 'Arthapat' has been made easily understandable by our Saastras by giving an illustration.

It takes a sentence reading as पीनो देवदत्तो दिवा न भुङ्क्ते *(Peeno devadatto diva na bhungte).* This means that "fat Devadatta does not eat during the day". He has not become thin even by not eating during the day and he still remains fat. What does this understanding lead to? That he eats well during night. It reconciles other absurd conclusions like (i) that he does not eat at all, (ii) even though he does not eat, he does not become thin. This reconciliatory approach which eschews obviously absurd conclusions and finds an acceptable way out is *Arthapat.*

Our deduction that Devadatta eats at night does not belong to the second of the pramaanas listed above, viz., Anumaana. Anumaana requires the factor of identification to be inherent in the matter that requires to be identified - like thunder from the clouds or smoke from the fire. Here there is no such *linga* - premise.

So is the case with Upamaana. It does not fall in the category of Anumaana merely because we deduce it to be 'Gavaya' on sight. Here too, our deduction is not based on identification of the animal by its form. We find the description of a 'gavaya' which is already within our knowledge coming true by similarity.

The last of the pramaanas is *'Anupalabdhi'.* This is merely to know that a thing does not exist. I said that the last and the seventh of the Padaarthas mentioned in Nyaaya is Abhaava. How do we understand Abhaava? With the help of Anupalabdhi.

'Go and see if there is an elephant in that shed' - we go and see and would know there was no elephant - if there was none. The elephant is not seen, but the fact that it is not there is known. This fact emerges from the state of there being no elephant. Thus what comes to be known in the absence of an object is Anupalabdhi. Nyaaya Saastra does not recognise these two pramaanas. These are used in Meemaamsa and Vedanta of the Advaitic School.

Common sense or sense of discrimination is only for showing God to us. When we thus go on examining with the help of these various pramaanas, where Nyaaya leaves off, Vaiseshika takes over. The founder of this method is a sage called Ganata, who concludes that all subsist on atoms. He said that Isvara arranges the atoms in various ways and creates the world.

In Nyaaya and Vaiseshika, the world and soul are deemed to exist separate from Isvara - which is actually the Dvaitic (Dualistic) Siddhaanta.

Where did the intellect of the sentient Jiva come from? Where did the insentient atom come from? Questioning on these lines, one reaches the Advaitic Siddhaanta that all these are the various appearances of Paramaatma.

To reach this Advaitic conclusion, Nyaaya is required as an intermediary step. To give due place to discrimination and logical conclusions is indeed the role of Nyaaya or Tarka (logic). It indulges actually in intellectual examination and research. It also shows that rationalism need not necessarily be atheistic or solely materialistic. The basic fact is that the world with its myraid beings and orderly conduct of life should necessarily have had a creator. Nyaaya Saastra accepts that there are limitations to intellectual understanding and therefore enjoins that, since there are areas which we cannot conceive of by any kind of proof, we must accept the verdict of the Vedas.

In short, logic should not be stretched indiscriminately to the extent of illogicity i.e. *Tarka* should not become *Dhustarka* but should serve as a means of arriving at the ultimate Truth.

It would indeed be commendable if no intellectual enquiry is indulged in and God and Saastras are fully accepted. But then such total and unquestioning faith that can take us up to the level of God-realisation is hard to come by. In such a case, one's life may well pass without sleeping and idleness. I would rather have a man using his thinking faculty and even come to the wrong conclusions that there is no God and atheism is the true religion. I would rate such an atheist who has laboured hard to reach that conclusion higher than a man of unquestioning faith who had not cared to exercise his mind at all. If that atheist continues with his enquiries, he may get mental clarity at some stage and may give up atheism. But the other lazy fellow has no hope at all.

That is why *Charvaaka* philosophy which is an atheistic doctrine was originally recognised as one kind of religious faith. *Charu* and *Vaaka* literally means what is good to the ears. "Let us not torture ourselves with fasting, austerities, mental and physical restraints. There is no need to bother with gods or demigods. Let us give free play to the mind and body and enjoy ourselves" - This, which is sweet to hear, is the essence of the Charvaaka doctrine.

But, whilst conducting one's iife on these lines, sorrow creeps in along with pleasure. In fact, there is more of the former. Only faiths other than purely materialistic offer lasting remedies for this sorrow.

All kinds of intelligence is required.

Philosophical enquiry will be helped considerably only if the mind and intellect are honed sharp with deep introspection. That is why Adi Sankaracharya, who summed up that all the phenomenal world was Maaya or illusion, has been accepted as Jagat Guru or world teacher by even those who have mastered all Saastras, arts and sciences.

Nyaaya is also known as Tarka (logic) and *Anveekshiki* (metaphysics). Our great Sankaracharya had thoroughly mastered this *anveekshiki* or *Nyaaya, Saankhya* which is also called *Kapilam,* because sage Kapila established it, the *Yoga Saastra* which is called *Patanjalam* after sage Patanjali, and *Bhatta* which is the faith advocated by Kumarila Bhatta.

Faiths that do not take note of Advaita are also contained in Advaita. This is why I, who also bear the name of Sankaracharya, am talking about all kinds of Saastras. Advaita contains in itself various other faiths such as Dvaita, Visishtaadvaita, Saivam and Vaishnavam. Although the other faiths may condemn or criticise Advaita, the latter contains within itself all the others - as part of it. Even in those situations where Advaita is critical of the other faiths it is only to the extent that they are not allowed to affirm their faith as the only true faith and that Advaita is wrong. The other faiths are never condemned by Advaita as totally unacceptable. They are given due recognition and importance at the appropriate time and place and level of development.

Treatises on Tarka Saastra

Gautama who wrote the Nyaaya Sutra is also known as Akshapaada. Since he was so constantly engaged in introspection, he was said to be wholly impervious to the world around. Even these days professors and scientists, who are deeply involved with subjects, are termed absent-minded. Their absent-mindedness is the subject of many a quip or joke. Gautama was one such. One day, his walk led him to a well into which he fell. The story goes that God rescued him and, to prevent further accidents, he placed a pair of eyes in his feet. He blessed him whereby the involuntary steps whilst walking would be guided away from obstacles by the involuntary action of the eyes. Since he acquired eyes in his feet he came to be known as *'Aksha* (eye) *Paada* (feet)'. This is another way of expressing that God guided his footsteps. Vaatśyaayana wrote a commentary on his Sutra. The Vaartika (glossorial exposition) was made by one Udyotakara. The great Advaitin, Vaachaspathi Misra, has written a commentary on this Vaartika. It is called *"Taadparya Teekaa Parisuddhi"*. Udayana has also written a book called *"Nyaaya Kusumaanjali"*. He is chief among those who were responsible for condemning Buddhism and making it scarce in our country. Jayanta has written a commentary on Nyaaya Sutra with the name of *Nyaaya Manjari*. One Annam Bhatta has written a book called *Tarka Samgraha* and has himself written a detailed deepika on it. Normally, those who set out to study Nyaaya Saastra begin with the last named two books.

Prasastapada has written a Bhaashya-like treatise on the Vaiseshika Sutra of Ganata Maharshi, called *"Padaartha Dharma Saṃgraha"*. Udayana has written a detailed commentary on this. Very recently Utthaamur Viraraghavaachariya has written a book called *"Vaiseshika Rasayana"*.

Vaiseshika goes by another name too - *"Oulukya Darsana".* (औलूक्य दर्शन). *Ulooka* is an owl. "Ulu" becomes owl in English. Oulukya is something connected with the owl. It is said that Ganata himself came to be called as Ulooka. If Gautama fell into a well because of extreme absent-mindedness and preoccupation with his deep thoughts Ganata used to be busy all through the day with his research and go out for *biksha* (collecting alms) at night. Since he was not seen during the day and was moving around only at night, he was nick-named as an owl. (When in Bhagavad Gita the Lord says that the night of the man without knowledge is the day of the man with knowledge (jnaani), he classifies jnaanis as owls.) Since it was propounded by Ganata, Vaiseshika is known as *Ganata Saastra.* It is the opinion of the learned that Vyaakarana (Grammar) and Nyaaya (logic) are most helpful in understanding all the Saastras.

The reason why this world was created

Causes are of two kinds : *Nimitta* (निमित्त) and *Upaadaana.* (उपादान). If there is an earthern pot, there must be a thing called clay to make it from. Clay is the Upaadaana - the reason for the pot. But how does the clay become the pot? It cannot make itself into one. The potter has to make the pot with clay. If clay has to be made into a pot, a potter is also required. He is the Nimitta, cause.

The Nimitta or omen mentioned in the Jyotisha Saastra or astrology is different. The view of the Nyaaya Vaiseshika doctrine is that, using the atoms as *Upaadaana,* Isvara as the *Nimitta Kaarana* has created the world.

To convert mud into a pot, it is absolutely necessary to have a potter. If he were not available, the pot can never be created. This is known as *Aarambha Vaada* or *Asat Kaarya Vaada. Sat* is what is existing. *Asat* is non-existing. In mere mud, there is no pot. The non-existent pot came into existence out of it. It is said that, likewise, Isvara with the help of atoms which do not contain the world, had created the world. This is the theory which Nyaaya posits.

According to the Saankhyas, as I said earlier, God is non-existent. According to them, nature or Prakriti threw up the world from itself. This is not to be regarded as the same as the view of modern atheists. That is because Saankhyas recognise the attributeless *(Nirguna)* Brahman or the Purusha which is total knowledge *(Jnaana Swaroopi)*. They attribute the orderly behaviour of the insentient Prakriti, in this world as due to the influence or *Saannidhya* (सान्निध्य) or proximity of the Purusha. The nearness is responsible for ensuring creation and orderliness. The Purusha as such does not indulge in any activity. Because of the rays of the sun, water evaporates, plants grow and clothes dry. These are due to exposure to the influence of the sun. The sun obviously has no plans or desire to dry the pond or make a particular plant to grow. When we keep our hand in ice-cold water, the fingers become numb. On that basis can we conclude that it was the intention of ice-cold water to benumb fingers? Likewise, although the Purusha does not at all indulge in the act of creation, Prakriti derives its power, under the influence of Purusha, to create something out of itself. Isvara does not interfere in any way as Nimitta Kaarana. Prakriti thus manifests itself as creation. This is the doctrine of the Saankhyas. This is also called Parinaama Vaada - theory of transformation.

In contrast to the *Asat Kaarya Vaada* of the Naiyaayikas, the Saankhyas project the *Sat Kaarya Vaada*. The Asat Kaarya Vaadis say that the pot, which does not exist in the *Upaadaana Kaarana*, which is the mud, is brought forth into existence by the *Nimitta Kaarana*, the potter. The Sat Kaarya Vaadis, the Saankhyas, argue thus: the pot was involved in the mud ab initio. The miller grinds the oil seed which contains oil to produce oil. Likewise, the pot which is already immanent in the mud is made to appear as pot through effort. The pot can result only by using the mud. It cannot be made from oil seeds, or conversely oil cannot be extracted from mud. The pot contains nothing but mud atoms. If their arrangement is manipulated, the pot results.

Our Acharya, Sankara Bhagavadpada, however, says: 'Neither the *Aarambha Vaada* nor the *Parinaama Vaada* is logical. Brahman, with the aid of Maaya, has assumed the garb of creation. There is no mud different from or apart from the Cosmic potter. Thus Aarmbha Vaada can have no validity. To think that the Paramaatma created the world by Parinaama - transformation - like milk into curds - is also not correct. Because, after such transformation, there can be only curd and no milk. So it would be absurd to say that the Paramaatma lost his identity after transforming himself into creation. Therefore, it is not also Parinaama. He remains himself as pure knowledge or Jnaana on one side, and presents the other side as Jiva and Jagat. All this is the appearance of the one and only Sat - manifestation - play-acting. If a man plays a role in a drama, does he really lose his original identity? So is creation. Even with all its myriad manifestations, the Sat remains unaffected by itself. This was Sankara's bold and sweeping assertion. It is called *Vivarta Vaada* (विवर्तवाद).

A rope giving the illusion of a snake is Vivarta. The rope which is the Upaadaana Kaarana has not been converted by another Nimitta Kaarana into a snake. Thus it is not Aarambha Vaada. The rope has not been transformed into a snake. The rope remains as rope. But, due to our lack of true knowledge (perception), the rope looks like a snake. Likewise, due to Avidya - lack of true knowledge - the Brahman appears to us to be the world, creation and individuals comprised therein.

To realise the truth propounded by the Acharya various devices of analytical enquiry *(Vichaara Yukti)* are detailed by Nyaaya Saastra. The true nature and significance of matter, Padaartha (पदार्थ) is to be understood by using these analytical methods. From here, one attains dispassion or *vairaagya.* From here one goes to a region called *"Apavarga"* (अपवर्ग), where there is no happiness or sorrow. Here stops the Nyaaya-Vaiseshika doctrines.

According to Dvaita or the Dualistic Siddaanta too, one can go no further. Advaita, which postulates one comprehensive 'sat' (सत्) by which we also become It leads to full and total Moksha or release from the cycle of births and deaths.

But, Nyaaya has the merit of inducing us to go to a better world called 'Apavarga' instead of being content with life as we find it in this world.

This Saastra has another claim to distinction. It has projected all conceivable types of arguments and devices (Yukti) in negating the doctrines of the Buddhists, Saankhyas, and Charvakas and proving the existence of Isvara as the creator of this world.

Some anecdotes and arguments

Gangesa Misropaadhyaaya, in his book *'Tatva Chinthamani"* has listed 64 different arguments. So far we have been taxing the brain with abstruse thoughts. Let us have a slight deviation with an anecdote about Gangesa Misra.

Gangesa to begin with was not a bright boy. He belonged to a high caste brahmin family - Kulina Brahmin of Bengal. It was the custom in Bengal to get these high class brahmins married to a number of brahmin brides, including those not so highly placed or not so kulina. A kulina brahmin thus used to take many wives even up to fifty in number. But Ganga Misra had only one wife and he lived with her parents. Obviously he did not get more offers for marriage as he was apparently a dim-witted person.

The Bengalis eat fish and in Bengal, due to heavy rains and many rivers, many places get water-logged for many months in the year. There would be no dry land to grow vegetables. During this period they consumed fish, which was in abundant supply. In East Bengal, fish was even called Jala Pushpa, the water flower, implying that it was tantamount to a vegetable. This was how the habit of fish eating developed in Bengal due to scarcity of vegetables.

It was the custom in Gangesa's father-in-law's household to cook fish for food. Gangesa used to be called 'Ganga' for short. Since he was considered dull, they used to serve him with only fish bones. The others got the meat. They then used to make fun of him. He couldn't stand the ridicule. He quietly left for Kasi (Benaras) one morning. He studied there avidly for ten years. Those at home ignored his absence as of no consequence. When he returned home after his studies, every one thought that he must have knocked around aimlessly and returned home the same dullard as before. He sat for his meal. As was the past practice, he was served fish. They were surprised to hear him remark "Naaham Ganga Kimtu Gangesa Misra" (नाहं गंगा किंतु गंगेश मिश्र).

I am no longer Ganga, I am Gangesa Misra, meaning : If I was the old dull Ganga, then it would be all right to serve me the bones, but I am now a learned man, competent to add the suffix of Misra (Pundit) after my name — he indicated all this in a short and sweet way. His in-laws then realised his worth.

The same Gangesa Misra wrote the *Tatva Chintaamani* (तत्व चिंतामणी). Many persons have written commentaries on it. One Raghunatha Siromani has written a commentary on it. It was only after the time of Raghunatha Siromani that the title of "Siromani" came to be used to indicate a senior level in Sanskrit education. One Gadaadhara (गदाधर) has written a huge tome in explanation of only ten of its slokas. But not a single sentence thereof can be regarded as superfluous. The book written by Gadhaadhara is called *Gadadhari* (गदाधरी). If one reads and understands five vaadas (वाद) or arguments from this, he can be regarded as a clever man. If he reads ten of these, he can be deemed very clever. One of the arguments or vaada is called *'Praamaanya Vaada'* (प्रामाण्य वाद). It is said that one who masters it becomes the cleverest of all. Even to this day those studying Tarka Saastra use *Gadaadhari* as a text.

The Praamaanya Vaada or discussion on Pramanas or proofs, I mentioned, would make the head reel when I try to explain it. But at the time our Acharya was living, even the parrots in the cage hung outside Mandana Misra's house are said to have been discussing Praamaanya Vaada.

Adi Sankara went to the city of Mahishmati where Mandana Misra lived. He asked from some women who were carrying water home from the river as to where Mandana Misra's house was. In that city, even ordinary women were learned. Therefore, they replied to the Acharya's query in the form of slokas or verses. One of the slokas said to have been used to direct Sankara to Mandana misra's house was as follows :

Swahapramaanam Paratahpramaanam
Keeranganaah yatracha samkirante
Dwaarastha needaantara sanniruddha
Jaaneehi tat mandana panditowkah

स्वतः प्रमाणं परतः प्रमाणं
कीराङ्नाः यत्रच संकिरन्ते
द्वारस्थ नीडान्तर सन्निरुद्धा
जानीहि तत् मण्डन पण्डितौकः

"Where the female parrots argue about swatah pramaana and paratah pramaana know that house belongs to the learned Mandana." From this, it will be seen that in ancient India not only men but women also were learned. Not only women but even female-parrots too were proficient in Vedantic enquiries. That is what the sloka indicates.

Having said so much, let us get a little nearer to this Vaada difficult though it is. There is even a humourous anecdote about it.

A South Indian went to Navadweepa in Bengal to study Tarka Saastra or the science of logic. Bengal had in those days the distinction of having many who had mastery over the subject. The one who went from the South was a gifted poet. He had earned a lot of money through his poetic works. He went to Navadeo to study Praamaaanya Vaada first-hand from the masters. He studied but could not understand much. He tried further. As a result, his flow of poetry suffered. Constant combat with logic blunted the edge of his poetical compostions. His money also got spent. He also lost the capacity to earn more through composing poems. At this double loss, his misery knew no bounds. Not having absorbed Praamaanya Vaada, he poetically wailed with what little poesy was left in him. "I bow to the Praamaanya Vaada which has robbed me of my poetry."

If an object is seen, we become aware of it. Sometimes, awareness is correct; sometimes it is not so. We may mistake alum for sugar-candy at first sight. That is faulty knowledge. Correct knowledge is called "Prama". Faulty one is Bhrama. Jnaana, (ज्ञान) or knowledge is further classified into two - namely, *Samsaya Jnaana* (doubtful knowledge) and Nischaya Jnaana (certain knowledge). That knowledge which is fraught with doubt is Samsaya. That which is known for certain without any doubt is the Nischaya Jnaana. Sometimes, when knowledge is faulty, it does appear to be correct. Then this knowledge will be taken as a Pramaana, authority or proof like alum being genuinely taken for sugar candy. Some knowledge or awareness appears doubtful even to begin with. When we see the images of trees upside down in a pool of water, we know that the trees are not standing topsy-turvey and hence we discredit the evidence or Pramaana. Thus, even at the time of initial awareness, or onset of knowledge, it gets classified as true or otherwise. The knowledge that will hold good even after the lapse of time, is *Praamaanya Griha Jnaana*. That which ab initio rings false is *Apraamaanya Grhaaskandita Jnaana*. As in "Prama" (प्रम) or true knowledge, even in Bhrama - or false knowledge, the knowledge through Pramaana or proof (identity) is present. That is why even when alum is mistaken for sugar candy, our awareness is genuine pramaana or proof.

Thus there are two types of proof, viz., one which strikes us as real initially or the one which strikes us as unreal initially. Now, the question arises whether the true - false knowledge arises subjectively from our perceptive faculties or it is objectively caused because of the quality of the object perceived. If the fault is due to us, it is *Swatahpramaana*. If the fault is due to the nature of the object, it is *Paratahpramaana*.

Which of these is correct was the subject of discussion of the female parrots outside Mandana Misra's house.

When we cognise an object, it is not subjectively possible for the cognising mind to decide whether cognisance is correct (Pramaana) or incorrect (Apramaana). The decision depends on the nature of the quality possessed by the object. Unless we test the function of the object in its impact on us, it is not possible to conclude whether its cognised identification is right or wrong. In other words, our cognisance or perception is objective — this is the view of Nyaaya Saastra. But the view of Meemaamsakas like Mandana Misra is contrary to this. They aver that it is within the domain of our wisdom to decide the true nature of the object. But when our cognisance subjectively can be proved wrong (Apramaana), it is solely due to the nature of the object. In other words, correct cognisance or Pramaana depends on us, and incorrect cognisance depends on the object. This is their contention. All these discussions are the subjects dealt with by Tarka - Logic.

The word 'Vaada' - discussion - is generally taken these days to mean arguments used to somehow uphold one's views or stand. In actual fact, it should be a balance between the views of both the parties discussing. Nay, it should throw up a conclusion based on all the arguments used, for or against. When we say that our Acharya went all over the country in vaada or wordy combat with many learned men like Mandana Misra, we mean just this, that he freely exchanged views which invariably proved him to be right. He firmly established the supremacy of Advaita, after taking into account all the arguments used by his antagonists. Therefore, vaada is exchange of thoughts, not merely justifying one's own point of view. The name for upholding with argument one's pre-determined conclusion is 'Jalpa' and not vaada. There is a third classification also. Instead of having an opinion as in Jalpa, to oppose whatever the other party says and find arguments somehow to prove all opponents to be wrong is called *'Vitanda Vaada'* (वितण्ड वाद).

Since the time Gangesa Misra came back to Bengal as a very learned man, i.e. the 12th Century, the Nyaaya Saastra had a renaissance. Having started afresh in Bengal, it grew in strength and came to be known as 'Navya Nyaaya,' 'Navya' meaning new. There is another reason why it came to be so called. 'Navadweep' is the place in Bengal where Gangesa Misra and his followers who came after him lived. Navadweep is called Nadiad also. Sri Krishna Chaitanya also hailed from this place. He was also a very learned man who had mastered all the Saastras. Later, he resorted to reciting Krishna's name as Bhajan Sankeertan and established the cult which believes that singing God's name is the way to attain liberation or Moksha.

Although Nyaaya Saastra propounds such theories as ; "The world is real and not illusory (Maaya): the individual souls are many and are different from the cosmic soul (Paramaatma)", with which Advaita does not agree, it condemns atheism *(Nireeswara Vaada)* and strongly affirms the existence of God. Since the arguments it provides for this purpose serve as the foundation to the subsequent reasonings (Yukti) which lead to Advaita, it is regarded as an important Saastra or Science.

Nyaaya is an Upaanga of Veda because it contains highly intellectual and logical discussions. However, Puraana which comes next amongst the fourteen disciplines *(Chaturdasa Vidya)* is regarded by many among the modern generation as mere superstition. Let us now examine this a little further.

24

THE UPAANGAS

PURAANAS — Veda's magnifying glass

The Puraanas can be called the 'magnifying glass' of the Vedas, as they magnify small images into big images. The Vedic injunctions which are contained in the form of pithy statements are magnified or elaborated in the form of stories or anecdotes in the Puraanas.

A brief exposition of an idea may not make a lasting or deep impression on the mind. It may, thus, leave no impact. On the other hand, if the same is presented as an interesting story or anecdote, it will stay in the mind. Let us take an example : The Vedas merely say *"Satyam Vada"* - (सत्यंवद). Speak the truth. How adherence to truth leads to undying glory is narrated elaborately through many chapters in the story of King Harischandra. *"Dharmam Chara"* (धर्मंचर) - follow the path of Dharma or righteousness. What the Vedas have stated in two words is illustrated by the story of the Paandavas in Mahabharata. *"Matru Devo Bhava", "Pitru Devo Bhava"* - Revere mother as divine. Revere father as divine. So says the Veda. This command of the Vedas seen through the magnifying glass becomes Ramayana. The Vedic injunctions such as restraint, patience, compassion, chastity and other dharmas are ably illustrated by men and women through their own lives. These are made known through Puraanas. As a result of reading or listening to their stories, we develop a deep involvement in the dharmas which they so admirably followed.

All of them, without exception, have had to undergo trials and untold sufferings. These exemplary characters have had to suffer much more than the common people who are, by nature, prone to tresspasses and transgressions. Sometimes, they are exposed to frightful sufferings. But, when reading their stories, it never enters one's mind that, since the pursuit of Dharma involves suffering, why not Dharma be forsaken. What impresses us most is the sense of duty that is uppermost and in spite of odds their unswerving faith in the righteous path which brings immeasurable mental solace to them - and to us too. On getting acquainted with their trials and tribulations our hearts melt in compassion and a feeling is created within us as though our doubts are dispelled and impurities are cleaned. Their ultimate success and fame leave a deep imprint of Dharma in our minds. This is what the Puraanic stories do.

Puraanas and History

It is generally said that there is no recorded history of events in our country. Puraanas are indeed history. But modern scholars do not accept anything as historical unless it happened after the advent of the Christian era. It is conceded half-heartedly that, on the basis of historical research, a small element of truth does exist in the Puraanas, but they attribute greater credence to those portions which support their pet theories and conclusions. Miraculous and supernatural are summarily dismissed as utter nonsense. Anything beyond the normal experience of the ordinary senses of the ordinary man is rejected as outside the realm of truth. Thus, the Puraanas which abound in 'mystery' are discredited as not being 'history'

We will be doing a great disservice to the children if we bypassed the Puraanas and, instead, made them read what has been written as history.

History contains no incidents to match the Puraanas, which not only appeal to the juvenile hearts but mould their character on ethical lines.

I do not say that history is to be avoided. Puraanas are also history and they must also be read because Puraanas are history with an ennobling purpose. One of the many reasons why history has to be read is that 'history repeats itself'. Events have a knack of happening again and again. Therefore, we can foresee the future if we learn about the past. We can learn lessons from the past too.

History shows how a particular situation, if allowed to develop, may lead to war, disruption of society or destruction of civilisation. Thus, if a similar situation were to be found now, we can be forewarned and take precautions to avert the calamity. This is stated to be one of the benefits of history.

Although Puraanas are historical in content, they present only selected events in such a way as to educate the people in right and wrong and make them tread the path of righteousness. In fact, its selectivity is confined to those kings who reaped immense benefits in this very life on account of following the path of Dharma and, conversely, those kings who came to a bad end in this very life on account of their evil ways. Otherwise, it takes us to the next birth of the respective characters and shows how they enjoyed or suffered as a consequence of their deeds in their earlier lives. There is no Puraana which does not present to us the effect of good and evil of persons in their after life. The benefits said to accrue from a study of past history are (i) past experience may guide us to face present situations, (ii) the study of the lives of good persons who did good deeds and came to a good end may serve as an example to us, and (iii) the lives of bad men, who caused misery and destruction on a large scale but who at the end themselves suffered more than the suffering they caused, may act as a deterrent to our transgressions. But none of these benefits result from a study of modern historical treatises. Puraanas alone give such results.

There is no purpose in elaborating the wars fought or the reforms introduced by a successive line of kings without at all attempting to indicate the right or wrong of their actions. There is no use of a history which has nothing to teach us to lead a better life. The object of Puraanas, however, is to benefit the mind and mould man and society to lead better life.

The Puraanas deal exhaustively with the Kings of the Surya Vamsa and Chandra Vamsa. The line of succession is elaborately laid down. But those kings of no importance and from whose lives we have nothing much to learn (either to emulate or avoid) will be merely mentioned in passing in one or two lines. Those who would serve as examples for us to follow would be dealt with at great length and in detail. For example, Uttanapaada, the father of Dhruva and Dhruva's son, who ruled after him, are referred to in Bhaagavata Puraana, but only in a sentence or two. But the life of Dhruva, which serves as an object lesson, rich in devotion, preseverence and steadfastness, is given a detailed narration.

The Englishmen who wrote Indian history dubbed the Puraanas as pure fiction. They built into it the race theory which suited their policy of 'divide and rule' as though it were the result of impartial research. If, in their view, the Puraanas contained fiction, in the modern view, (especially of independent India), Englishman's version of Indian history is also considered to be untrue in parts. Efforts are under way to rewrite it more faithfully. Here again, the writers may have their own points of view or prejudices on so many incidents. Therefore, however much one may make it appear impartial, it cannot be ensured that the whole of the truth will get recorded, especially if they are already biased by the so-called research of western writers.

It is not also right to think that history is confined to empires, wars, invasions, dynasties, etc. All things have a history. Political history has, unfortunately, been given pride of place as history by western historians. On the other hand, the Puraana keeps Dharma (ethics) as the central theme and weaves a pattern, using not only the lives and deeds of great kings but illustrious men, rishis and even commoners. A study of the Puraanas reveals not only the state of government then existing but gives an insight into the then cultural life, arts and sciences. Their main theme of course is Dharma and metaphysics.

Are Puraanas true or fabricated?

'No credence can be given to Puraanas, because it contains matters beyond the realm of known natural phenomena,' is the modern view. That the Devas freely roamed the earth and granted boons to men is dismissed as fantasy because such things do not happen today. "A woman was cursed and she turned into stone, the stone was blessed and it turned back into a woman - the sun was stopped in its diurnal orbit" - such incidents which are totally outside our capabilities lend support to the view that these incidents must indeed be fictitious and products of imagination.

That certain things do not happen today or cannot happen does not prove that such things could not have happened in the past or cannot happen in future. Every great epic of the past bears ample testimony to the powers of Veda mantras - high penance and exalted Yogic discipline which was not uncommon in the past. So long as these powers prevailed, it was possible for people of this world to easily draw on the supernatural resources. Just as where there is light, there was also darkness, the forces of evil represented by asuras and raakshasas also co-existed with the good influences. Even now, the conflict between good and bad - between devas and asuras - are in progress although not visible to the human eye. In those days, it was possible, due to powers derived from deep penance to actually see these good and evil forces. Modern scientists say that all sound or light waves cannot be detected by the human eye or ear. Some scientists, who have reached higher levels, have done research in occult (super-worldly) science and have discovered the existence of heavenly bodies, both good and bad.

Even now there are quite a few yogis and siddhas (mystics). Their bodies are unaffected by exposure to extreme cold or heat. They cause rain to fall and even stop the falling rain. Thus, men with supernatural powers do exist. Only our belief is shaky. We suspect all things. Since, in the olden days, many more persons than today possessed these powers, it appears that Puraanas contain a long list of miracles. If a miracle figures in the narrative the story cannot be rejected as not being history proper.

It does not speak well for English education if it rejects as fiction all that science cannot prove. In fact, what science could not perceive a few years ago, is being perceived by scientists now. Even today archaeologists discover human skeletons measuring ten to twelve feet and those of mammoth animals which species is extinct today but whose existence is mentioned in the Puraanas. From these, it appears that raakshasas as tall as coconut or palm trees and having bodies like a lion and trunks like an elephant might have existed in the past. In Iceland, discoveries have disclosed a human skeleton whose shin-bone alone measures sixteen feet and the back bone of an animal whose size must have been ten times that of an elephant. These are hailed with great fanfare as archaeological finds. Combining geology with archaeology, these are claimed to have existed so many hundred thousand of years ago. If mythology is superimposed on this, then the Puraanic stories will all become credible and true.

Once as tall as a palm tree, now six feet tall and in years to come hardly a thumbkin - these are the ravages which time imposes on creatures and species. These changes are also mentioned by the Puraanas.

The Puraanas are ridiculed for talking of vaanaras — man-monkies, the body of an animal with the face of a man, people with two heads or ten heads - all these are said to be going too far away from truth. Those who do not indulge in such open criticism give it their own explanation viz. that these are symbolic and the story is an allegorical representation.

It is true that moral lessons are taught through the medium of fables. But, on this score, the entire Puraanic stories cannot be dubbed as untrue or mere fables. Even now, we come across news items about the birth of a child with two heads and four hands. It is neither a man nor animal. It is a freak. When nature which, by its definition is faultless, gets a little faulty, the freak results. Such freaks might have been deliberately engineered in the past on a large scale. Since the ancient men had supernatural powers (powers over nature) much more than we have, such conditioning of nature might have been a simple matter. That is why we should not affirm that "what is knowable is known to us and that there could have been nothing different from what we know."

To label what is not known to us or what is not knowable as a lie is illogical. What had been rejected as unbelievable in the Puraanas is coming to pass now and then during modern days, such wonders as recollection of events from an earlier birth are reported in the press. I feel that, in recent times, such news items are on the increase. The Puraanas say that "Kaasyapa had a wife called Kadru. She begot serpents as children." We are inclined to dismiss this as unnatural and unlikely and hence untrue. But many of the readers might have seen from a news item (in 1958). "A Marwari girl gave birth to a serpent." When I saw it, another matter became clear to me.

Before I became a Sanyaasi, I had heard of a family in which none of the girls either born into that family or who came into that family by marriage, would use the 'Kevra' (called Taazhampoo in Tamil) flower for decoration. When asked why, they narrated a story.

"Ten or fifteen generations ago, a girl in our family gave birth to what turned out to be a snake instead of an infant. They were ashamed to disclose this and hence secretly nurtured the reptile baby. They fed milk to it like a human infant. It is said it grew up happily, playing about the house without causing any harm to anyone. But this strange child could not be taken out of the house, visiting. The mother therefore did not go out of the house unless it was absolutely unavoidable. An old Tamil proverb says "even if a stone, a husband is a husband", meaning that the relationship is unsullied by mere appearance. Likewise, the motherly love for the serpent remained in full measure. So the mother never left her home. But came a time when she had to go out to attend a near relative's marriage. There was an old woman in the house. It is not now known if she was the grandmother of the serpent child. In those days, the good custom prevailed of supporting helpless individuals even if they were distant relatives. It is only recently that, on marriage, the sons do not wish to live with their parents but like to stay separately by themselves. Formerly the normal position was that of undivided families - joint families. There was room in it for a distant widowed aunt or once or twice removed cousin of the grandfather. Thus, there was an old woman in the house about whom we are now talking. Her eye sight was very bad. The serpent child was left in the custody of this blind old lady when the mother went out of station unavoidably. What is it that the snake wants in the shape of attention? Not giving it a bath, plaiting its hair or dressing up. None of these. It had to be fed milk at regular intervals. Therefore, the mother told the old lady, "You pour boiled milk at the temperature which the finger can stand into the hole of the grinding stone which can be easily identified by touch. The child will drink it by itself when it is feeding time". With these instructions the mother left home. It would seem that the serpent has been trained to feed so. The old lady followed these instructions. And the serpent also came and took its feed as the mother said it would. Once after a few days, this routine got disturbed. The serpent which got into the hole in the grinding stone, found it empty. Perhaps the old lady had overslept. The serpent was tame by temperament and, after waiting for some time, it also curled itself into sleep inside the hole. The old lady came later to the grind-stone with fairly hot boiled milk. She did not know that the snake-child was sleeping. She poured the milk into the hole, a little careless, without checking how hot it was. The boiling milk was all over the poor snake. It died. The mother of the snake who was in another village at that time had a dream. The snake child appeared in her dream and said, 'I am dead. You go home and cremate my body in the midst of 'Kevra' bushes. In future, girls of your family whether born in it or come into it by marriage, should not wear the flower in their hair'. From that time onwards, no one in our family uses the flower."

I also used to wonder at this story - whether it could have really happened.

Then, many years later, some members of that family came to see me - not to tell me more about the story of the serpent but to give me a copperplate inscription in which they knew my great interest. It was a royal gift deed inscribed on copperplate. It belonged to the time of king Achuta Deva Raaya. It disclosed the fact that a certain brahmin gave gifts to 108 other brahmins. All this he did for the sake of the king.

Let me tell you why and what for, he did this. Since a brahmin was required to spend all his time in reciting the Vedas and performing the Vedic injunctions, he was precluded from accepting any employment for profit. But then his household had to be run.

That is why the Saastras permit him to accept gifts or donations. Kings and nobles thus rewarded and patronised them. Because they were permitted to accept gifts, it need not be construed that they accepted indiscriminately or without end. They had a lot of self-respect and accepted gifts only when required and only to the extent required. They accepted gifts only if a king was of righteous conduct and good reputation.

Nay, some went even further back. The king's ancestry should have been blameless. The kings did not have to face the unceasing demands from such brahmins. Their woe was that the brahmins did not come forward sufficiently to accept their gifts and, as a result, the punya or credit accruing from donating to worthy causes was denied to them. To overcome such situations, the kings and nobles appeared to have adopted a ruse. They would somehow coax a brahmin in more than ordinary straitened circumstances to accept their gifts. Sometimes, the gifts were as large as a whole village. But it was not meant solely for one individual's benefit. The donors hoped that their gift would reach other brahmins through the single recipient. Thus, a single individual would receive the gift in his name, but he would keep only a small part for himself and himself gift away the remainder to other brahmins. Since one brahmin receives from another, technically the transaction does not fall in the category of *Prathigraha dosha* - the odium of receiving alms. Thus the object of the kingly or royal donor would be met.

The question arises whether the intermediary who comes between the prime donors and the ultimate beneficiaries, does not get sullied. Of course, there is nothing wrong in the lords and kings resorting to this ruse with the object of patronising the learned Vedic brahmins. But what about the intermediary who was a part of this trick? Well, no blame can also be attached to him. By law, the donated gift, becomes his own property. The gift deed is made out in his name. Since he does not claim ownership rights on most of it but gives it away to others, he absolves himself of blame. No sin can be attached to giving away one's own property.

In the copperplate, I referred to earlier a brahmin had thus received a gift which in turn he distributed to 108 others. The names of these 108, together with the stage up to which they had studied a Veda and the quantum of land given, were all recorded in the plate.

Amongst the recipients is the name of one belonging to the family in which the snake-child was born. Little is known of the remaining families of recipients. The copperplate I received had been preserved through generations.

What is noteworthy is that the name which was mentioned in the copperplate was 'Naageswara'. The name of the person who brought the plate to me now is also Naageswara. On enquiry it transpired that the name Naageswara was given to a child in each generation. We were then able easily to deduce that the name is connected with the story of the snake-child. (*Naaga* in Sanskrit is snake). In addition, in support of the story, there is evidence to show that, even during the days of Achuta Deva Raaya, there was a family bearing this name.

This gave a firm reply to my earlier doubt whether such a thing could have really happened. And, when in 1958, I saw the news item that a woman delivered a snake, my doubts were further allayed and credulity took over.

It is not quite right that I should find fault with you all for lacking faith in the veracity of the Puraanas. I was myself prepared to accept the news item and the reservations in accepting the traditional story as narrated to me were removed by the news item. This is the stage to which we have come : if an item appears in the press, however improbable it may seem, we are prone to accept it as true. But the very mention of Puraana makes us disdainful. "They had plenty of leisure - palm leaves and stylograph. They turned out tomes containing fables. Some of it is unquestionably clever but the rest is poppycock" - this is the general opinion.

Although imaginative, they have a message

It is possible that the Puraanas may have resorted to a little fiction here and there. It might have come as an interpolation. But who can say which is totally fictitious, which is interpolation and which the truth? If each one discounted what in his view is an interpolation, there would be very little left as all the stories would disappear. Nothing may remain as the basic story. Therefore, although it may seem that there are some shortcomings and faults, it is our duty to preserve the Puraanas in the same state in which they are available to us.

Let there be some fictitious accounts. After all, the Puraana takes us nearer to God and brings peace of mind, is it not? We go shopping and are able to buy good sugar. Do we rejoice in having been lucky to have got good sugar or do we feel disgruntled because the goods in the shop were not well exhibited or the shopkeeper was hard of hearing? In the descriptions of geography and astronomy, description of time as in Manvantaras, let there be a fault or two. There is modern geography, astronomy and history which can correct any inexactitudes. But the Puraanas serve a purpose which geography, astronomy or history cannot provide - viz. of successfully imparting education on Paramaatma Tatva, Bhakti and Dharma.

"Rama could not have lived in Treta Yuga, so many hundreds of thousands of years ago. The culture and civlisation portrayed in the Ramayana could not have existed then" - are some of the criticisms which assail our ears. Let us assume that Rama did not live in Treta Yuga. Similarly, let us, for the sake of argument, accept that the stories said to have happened earlier in the Krita Yuga did not actually take place. Let us assume that all these happened, say, during the last last seven or eight thousand years. On this score, does the merit of Rama's story get any the less? Does it in any way minimise the lessons we learn therefrom? Just as it is said that the age factor of the Puraanas is difficult to believe, there is a counter opinion that it is wrong to question their propriety.

The Saastras say that, 5000 years ago, when Kaliyuga started Vyasa gave us the Puraanas. But there were Puraanas before his time. In Chaandogya Upanishad, where Naarada mentions a list of Vidyas learnt by him, he mentions Puraana as one of them.

Therefore, it is clear that, even at the time of the Vedas and Upanishads, the Puraanas existed. It would appear that, just as Vyasa separated the Vedas into many Saakhas because the later generations had not the capacity to get all of them by heart, he also rewrote the Puraanas succinctly.

Nevertheless, western scholars do not accept the Puraanas to be so ancient. Let it be so.

The most glaring example of modern superstition, where belief almost becomes a certainty, stems from the results of 'research'. But the results of research are all not that correct. They get outdated and disproved with the passage of time. But, even if research was infallible and Puraanas are fictitious,the Puraanas stress that the righteous are rewarded with a happy life and the unrighteous suffer - even the unrighteous receive God's pardon and grace. Since this impression is firmly established in the reader's mind, it means that they fulfil their purpose in its entirety.

The treasure that Vyasa left

The same Vyasa who rearranged the Vedas (into Veda Saakhas) so that people could understand them more easily, was responsible for giving us the eighteen Puraanas. I used to think that Vyasa was the first journalist and the foremost example for modern journalism. Fables, history, geography, philosophy, he has created treasured treatises on all these in a simple and interesting manner so that they may not only appeal to the intelligent but also to the common man. Is it not the same job that journalists do? But the latter stop with creating and producing human interest and sensationalism. But Vyasa's objective, however, was to educate the common man in the path of righteousness and he used the human interest merely as a means to it. If human interest alone were regarded as the goal of journalism, it would result in the propagation of unethical and unrighteous matters also. If Vyasa were kept as the ideal, the press would be cleaner. This will have a salutary effect on the public.

These eighteen Puranas add up to four hundred thousand

granthas. A *grantha* is a sloka with thirty-two syllables. Of these, nearly one fourth or a hundred thousand slokas are taken by Skanda Puraana (स्कान्द पुराण). I imagine it is perhaps the biggest single book in the world. The balance of the seventeen Puranas contain three hundred thousand granthas. In addition, Vyasa has produced the epic *"Mahabhaarata"* which contains a hundred thousand granthas or verses.

Each Puraana keeps a single deity as its main theme. The Puraanaas are broadly classifiable into three categories - those which are prone to the (1) Vaishnava cult, (2) the Siva cult, and the (3) Sakti cult, thus covering a large number and variety of deities.

The eighteen Puranas are : (1) Brahma Puraana, (2) Padma Puraana, (3) Vishnu Puraana, (4) Siva Puraana, (5) Srimad Bhaagavata, (6) Naarada Puraana, (7) Maarkandeya Puraana, (8) Agni Puraana, (9) Bhavishyat Puraana, (10) Brahma Vaivartha Puraana, (11) Linga Puraana, (12) Varaaha Puraana, (13) Skanda Maha Puraana, (14) Vaamana Puraana, (15) Koorma Puraana, (16) Matsya Puraana, (17) Garuda Puraana, and (18) Brahmaanda Puraana.

Of these eighteen, ten are said to be Saivite. Many of the anecdotes and fables now known to us are contained in these. History, fable, philosophy are all contained in these.

Adi Sankara has cited many examples from the Vishnu Puraana in his commentary on Vishnu Sahasranaama. This Puraana's author was Sage Paraasara, father of Vyaasa Maharshi. In Sri Ramanuja's Siddhaanta viz. *Visishtaadvaita* or qualified non-dualism Vishnu Puraana figures as the chief authority.

Before Ramanuja's time, one of the pillars of the Visishtaadvaitha doctrine was one Aalavandaar. Before Ramanuja could reach him, the former died. Aalavandaar had wished to entrust three jobs to Ramanuja. It is said that, as a result, after his death, three fingers of his hand were found bent and closed. When Ramanuja correctly guessed his master's intentions and announced them each in turn, each of the dead man's fingers are said to have straightened out.

Of the three unspoken commandments, one was to write a commentary on Brahma Sutra as per the Visishtaadvaita doctrine. The second was to cause a commentary to be written on *Thiruvoymozhi* - the Sooktis of the Alwars in Tamil. The third was to firmly establish and spread the fame of Vyaasa and Paraasara. Paraasara was given this pride of place because he was the author of Vishnu Puraana. Keeping this in mind, Ramanuja named the two sons of his chief disciple Koorathaalvaan as Paraasara Bhatta and Vyaasa Bhatta. Later Paraasara Bhatta became one of the important Vaishnavite Acharyas.

Although Sage Paraasara wrote the Vishnu Puraana, it was Vyaasa who edited and presented the eighteen Puraanas in the form in which we now find them. I had already mentioned that he also arranged and codified the Vedas and wrote the Puraanas in order that the Vedic injunctions may take firm root in men's minds.

There is another reason given as to why he wrote the Puraanas. Only certain people are authorised to study and recite the Vedas, not all. It is said he wrote the Puraanas in order that the rank and file may come to know of the Vedic philosophy and injunctions.

If Vyaasa's father Paraasara was responsible for bringing out the original text of Vishnu Purana, Vyaasa's Srimad Bhaagavata was narrated by his son Sukaacharya to King Pareekshit.

When one talks of Bhaagavata, there is some difference of opinion as to whether it refers to the text which keeps the story of Lord Krishna as the main theme but also mentions the other incarnations and stories of Vishnu, or it refers to Devi Bhaagavata which deals with the 'Lila' or the sportive activities of Goddess Amba. We, of course, like both of them. These two are indeed exalted texts. In support of their respective doctrines (Siddhaanta) Chaitanya, Nimbarka, Vallabhaachaarya and others have assigned the same status to the Vishnu Bhaagavata as to the Vedas themselves. At the same time, the Advaitins, who oppose these doctrines, also accept this (Vishnu Bhaagavata) and extol it sky high.

Siva Puraana is different from Skanda Puraana. In the Skanda, three-fourths of it is devoted to incidents and anecdotes and philosophies about Siva. Only a quarter of it is devoted to Skanda. Nevertheless, it is called Skanda Puraana, because it also contains all matters regarding Skanda.

"Durga Saptha Sati" - story of Durga appears in the Maarkandeya Puraana. *"Shaanti Homa", "Sata Chandi", "Sahasra Chandi"* - these rites are performed by using the 700 mantras in this Puraana. Here, each mantra is contained in one sloka. Hence each 'Homa' or offering is made by reciting one sloka.

Bhavishya means the future. The Bhavishyat Puraana contains many matters including an account of the mischief that we see in the present Kali Yuga. This Puraana not only mentions kings of the old Maurya dynasty but also the more recent arrival of the Europeans. Even so, present-day intelligentsia lightly dismiss the Puraana as never having been written by Vyaasa at the beginning of Kali Yuga but by someone else in recent times who had used Vyaasa's name. There might be some interpolations, but the whole thing cannot be regarded as of recent origin and discredited. Those with occult powers, can see beyond time. They can also come to know of happenings in another part of the globe. It is no easy matter for books to be written by all and sundry with any hope of making them acceptable even by ascribing their authorship to great men.

Garuda Puraana deals mostly with the world after death (Pitru Loka) and the rites to be performed for the departed soul. Hence, during "Sraddha" or death anniversary ceremonies, it is customary to read this Puraana.

"Lalitopaakhyaana" (Story of Lalita) and "Lalita Sahasranaama" are contained in the Brahmaanda Puraana. The votaries of Devi worship take pride in the fact that, at the conclusion of reading all the eighteen puraanas, the last to be read is this Puraana in which appears the coronation of Raja-Rajeshwari. The 'Ashtotharanaama', 'Sahasranaama' and 'Kavacha' which one now recites on every deity, are all taken out of the several Puraanas. Vishnu Sahasranaama and Siva Sahasranaama are, however, from the Mahaabharata.

Many stotras or hymns in use, are all taken from the Puraanas. "Aditya Hridayam" however, appears in Srimad Ramayana. The Pradosha Stotra is contained in the Skanda Purana. And so on.

Upa Puranas and small Puranas

In addition to the eighteen Puraanas, there are also eighteen 'Upa' Puraanas or auxiliary Puraanas. Vinaayaka Puraana and Kalki Puraana are among the Upa Puraanas. Although they are said to be mainly eighteen in number, in actual fact, many more exist.

Description of the glories of the months of the year, e.g., Tulaa Puraana, Naaga Puraana, Vaisaaka Puraana are all from the eighteen main and Upa Puraanas. Every holy place has what is called a 'Sthala' Puraana. These also figure in the Puraanas as stated above. There are also independent texts.

Itihasa - Puraana - Distinctions

The Ramayana and Mahaabharatha have been serving as the two eyes of both the learned and lay men from time immemorial and showing them the path of righteousness. These two are not included in the list of Puraanas, but have been honoured with a separate classification - viz. "Itihaasa".

'Pura' means in the past. Those that narrate things of the past are Puraanas. Of course they also deal with predictions as to the future.

Puraanas can be considered not only as narrating the past incidents but also to mean 'having their origin in the distant past'. In the distant past, literature was confined to poetry and drama.

Narration of stories in prose came much later. It was named as a 'novel', meaning new. As it did not have the form of poetry or drama and as it came much later, it was called 'Novel'.

By definition, a Puraana has to fulfil five requirements in the matter of what it should contain, called *'Pancha Lakshana'* or distinguishing marks. They are : (1) *Sarga* (i.e.) original creation of the world; (2) *Prathisarga* (how, after creation, the world grew with time); (3) *Vamsa* i.e. geneology, how the descendants came from one generation to the next; (4) *Manvantara* (the history of the fourteen Manus from whom all mankind descended, covering a period of one thousand 4-Yuga cycles) and (5) *Vamsaanucharita* (i.e. the history of the rulers of the country, dynastic details like Surya Vamsa and Chandra Vamsa). In addition, it should also contain a description of this world in space. Here, Puraana acts not only as history but as geography too.

Itihaasa is Iti-Ha-Asam. (इतिहासम्). 'Iti-ha-asam' means 'it happened thus'. The 'Ha' in the middle denotes truly, verily, surely. Thus Itihaasa is a record of facts without any admixture of conjectural matters. It happened at the time it was written - or it was written at the same time as it happened. Valmiki wrote the Ramayana when Rama was living. With the five Paandavas, Vyasa actually witnessed the various incidents narrated in the Mahaabharata.

Although true to the name as Puraana, he wrote about incidents long past, he must have recalled the incidents as they actually took place through his mystic powers. Nevertheless, the veracity of the incidents could not have been verified by his contemporaries, those who lived in his time. But Raamaayana and Mahaabharata do not belong to this category. Even when they were first brought out, those who then lived were acquainted with the various characters portrayed and the incidents narrated in these epics. That is why, to totally dispel our doubts as to their veracity, they are called Itihaasas, the 'ha' standing for emphasis.

The glory of Itihaasas

If the Puraanas are regarded as the Upaangas of the Vedas, the Itihaasas are deemed to be as exalted as the Vedas themselves.

Mahaabharata is called the *'Panchamo Veda',* the fifth Veda. As regards Ramayana, it is said that when the Purusha who can be known only by the Vedas took birth as Dasaratha's son, the Vedas also appeared as Valmikis' child in the form of Ramayana.

The stories of Ramayana and Mahabharata can be said to be in the blood stream of the people of our country

Every big Puraana will contain many stories - long as well as short. Each story will emphasise a particular aspect of Dharma. Itihaasa, on the other hand, is one continuous story from beginning to end. Although there may appear some interludes or other thematic presentations in the epic, they will revolve around the central theme. If the Puraanas deal with each Dharma through the medium of a separate story, the Itihaasa illustrates all the Dharmas through one main story. For example, adherence to Truth as a Dharma is illustrated in the Harischandhra Puraana as a separate story. The story of Nalaayini highlights greatness of chastity in women. The story of Ranti Deva teaches the ennobling aspect of extreme sacrifice and compassion. The Itihaasas revolving around the lives of Rama and the five Paandavas, however, show us how they followed all the various traits of Dharma under trying conditions and upheld Dharma and the rule of Dharma.

Why the difference between Gods

When I mentioned that each Puraana glorifies one particular deity, some doubts may arise. In Saiva Puraanas, it would be stated : "Siva is the Paramaatma Tatva (परमात्म तत्व)" or Supreme Being. He is the controller of creation, maintenance and annihilation. Vishnu takes orders from Him and performs his functions. Vishnu enjoys pleasures - Bhogi - who is caught in the net of illusion of Maaya. Siva alone is the ascetic - Yogi. He is the embodiment of pure knowledge - Jnaana Swaroopi. Vishnu is subordinate to Siva.

Vishnu worships Siva. There are incidents to illustrate that Vishnu defied Siva and even fought with him but ultimately he was defeated and suffered humiliation and so on. If one were to read the Vaishnava Puraanas, the version will be just the opposite and many incidents will be found in support of Siva's subservience to and defeat at the hands of Vishnu. "How can Siva who consorts with spirits and demons and resides in the cremation ground claim to be the supreme God? He is obviously the servant of the king of kings - Lord of Vaikunta" so runs the Vaishnava version.

This dispute is not confined to the greatness or superiority of Siva and Vishnu. Every Puraana will extol a particular deity. This deity will be described as the one and only highest immanent God and all other deities will be given lesser importance. It will be said that all others pay homage to that particular God (of the particular Puraana) and when they revolted, they were put down and suffered humiliation, and so on and so forth.

Looking at this, one wonders at such conflicting reports and may get confused. Which is true and which is not? Obviously all of them cannot be true. If Siva is said to worship Vishnu, the converse is absurd and just cannot be. If the Goddess Amba is superior to all three *moortis* or Trinity of Brahma-Vishnu-Siva, it would be wrong to treat her as Siva's consort, who, as a dutiful wife, subordinates herself to her husband. Therefore, all the Puraanas cannot be true or authentic. So which is correct? Or is it that all of them are false? Such are the doubts that assail us.

Although logically all these conflicts cannot be taken as true, in fact, they are so. A God gets defeated at one time, and comes out victorious at another time. One who was worshipped at one time, became the worshipper at another time.

How can this be? Why should it be so?

There is only one Paramaatma who causes creation, maintenance and destruction. The same Paramaatma manifests in many forms. Why? In order to make mundane existence interesting and worthwhile. Instead of creating all in a stereotype,

God has made men with different mental capacities and attitudes. God assumes various forms congenial to the respective mental predilections, in order that each may worship a desired deity and come to a good end. That is why the Supreme Paramaatma takes many forms as different deities.

Each one should have an unshakeable faith in his chosen deity. They should be convinced that his deity is the supreme and ultimate Godhead and nothing can be above it. That is why in each manifestation, God shows himself as superior to the rest. The others are shown as worshipping the particular one and getting defeated in a conflict.

Does this not reconcile the inconsistency of one God worshipping the others at one time and getting worshipped by all others some other time, of defeating all others at one time and getting defeated by each one of all too?

The Saiva Puraanas are merely a collection of those stories where Siva's supremacy alone is shown. The Vaishnava Puraanas would be a compilation of incidents which glorify Vishnu to the subordination of others. So also in the other Puraanas.

Thus, the intention is not to run down any particular deity. The object is to glorify the God of one's choice so that the devotee's attention may converge on that aspect or manifestation of God to the exclusion of others. This is called *"Ananya Bhakti"* (अनन्य भक्ति) - undivided devotion. The aim is to glorify a particular deity and heighten the devotion to that deity and not to vilify the others. This is termed *"Nahi Nindaa Nyaya"*.

For those who regard all creation as varying manifestations of a single Paramaatma, there is no need to have "Ananya Bhakti". The question of turning from one God to another can arise only if it is conceded that one God is different from another. If it is understood that the many forms are the manifestations of a single Entity, all the Puraanas become the sporting activities *(Leela Vinoda)* of that Entity assuming different diverting forms. If it is understood that a single entity play-acts as many, so that people with varying mental make-up could find satisfaction, then it would be possible not only to enjoy the apparent contradiction in them but also develop their devotion.

There is another reason too, i.e. setting an example to people. Chastity should thrive in the world. Therefore, the Goddess Amba must show the way by her own example. Therefore, although she is undisputedly the super Sakti, she has to accept a subordinate role in relation to her husband. Devotion should spread in the world for which the Lord should set an example. That is why in some stories Vishnu becomes the devotee and worships Siva. In some other cases, Siva worships Vishnu. Therefore, the apparent contradiction in the Puraanas, which contain stories now extolling one deity and now another should be taken as an attempt to impress on us the greatness of a particular deity so that we can whole-heartedly direct our devotion towards it. Reference to a particular God as though it were a minor deity is in fact not meant as a criticism or insult at all. It is done so that the spotlight may fall on the other one and the devotees may take a firm hold of that aspect.

One as Many

The same Paramaatma manifests as different deities. Each devotee develops a particular attachment to a particular form of God. In order to strengthen such attachment of each devotee, the Paramaatma subordinates a particular quality at some time in preference to another and emphasises a particular aspect.

In olden days, lanterns were used for street lighting (i.e.) lamps were placed inside glass cages. The lanterns were four-sided, some were three-sided also. Let us take the three-sided lantern. The light used to be dispersed from all the three sides. Sometimes decoratively the three glass windows used to be painted each in a different colour. As a result the light seen through each window would have the respective colour of the window. The same Paramaatma creates, sustains and annihilates. The root cause is the same Chaitanya (Light of knowledge). That Chaitanya is inside the three-sided lantern, as it were.

Of the three colours, one is red. That is creation. In a spectroscope, if red is separated from clear light, the remaining six colours will also get separated. This is creation where one becomes many. That is why Brahma, the creator, is said to be red in colour. Another colour in the lantern is blue. It is the colour at the end of the spectrum, violet. The beginning is red (infra-red), the end is violet (ultra-violet). When the created world is being sustained, Mahavishnu indicates through 'Knowledge' that 'this world has no existence in reality, nor is it to be confused with the total and absolute Entity. It is an illusion and the sport of Paramaatma'. In the effulgence of that understanding, the whole of the phenomenal world is reduced to cinder. This is the stage when an object is burnt out but the residue of ash and cinder still retains the original shape, giving the illusion of the existence of the original object. The appearance of existence remains and the original colour is lost. The world does exist but its peculiar property, namely, the appearance of reality is burnt out and it has become black, like the rest of the cinder. *"Sarvam Vishnu Mayam Jagat"*; - all is Vishnu who is described as dark *(Shyaamala)* or bluish in colour - *Neela-megha-shyaamala*. Blue, black, violet are all colours which are close to each other. The Paramaatma has assumed a form like the three-sided lantern in order to perform these three important functions. When the light comes out of the side painted blue, we call it 'Vishnu'.

The third side of the coloured lantern, is plain unpainted glass. When everything is burnt out in the fire of knowledge, first it becomes coal, or cinder-black in colour. If it is further exposed to fire, it is reduced to ashes and the skeleton remains. Then the skeleton also crumbles and loses its form altogether. At this stage, the original black colour becomes all white.

White is close to clear light. All the colours that originated from light i.e. all phenomenal existence which sprung from the Paramaatma, had totally lost their identity and individuality and had become Paramaatma again. Separate existence, illusory existence, are all liquidated and it is this which is Mahaa-Bhasma - the Parameswara. When everything is annihilated in the name of *Samhaara*, although it might appear to be a cruel deed, Siva does not stop at destruction but is performing the very merciful act of reuniting the world with its origin. When Vishnu through his sport brought knowledge to bear (on the phenomenal world), the *'Sarvam'* (all of) *'Jagat'* (the world) appeared like a piece of cinder to the onlooker. That is why the expression *Sarvam Vishnu Mayam Jagat* came into being. When all the sport is over and the stage of *Samhaara* or annihilation is reached, as a result of *Parama Jnaana* or Supreme knowledge, neither Sarvam nor Jagat has any existence. That is why we say 'Siva-Mayam' - Nothing but Siva.

The same lamp - 'Brahma Chaitanyam' or Cosmic Entity, when it is seen through red glass, it is called Brahma (the creator); through the blue panel it is Vishnu and, through the colourless transparent third side, the same thing is Siva.

The seers have extolled Paramaatma as "one form appearing as three forms". All great poets who were not committed to any particular philosophy of doctrine and who had an open mind and a broad outlook have been unanimous in saying that the same Entity has become the three *Moortis.*

The Englishmen also refer to Jehovah, Jove or Lord in the same spirit of compromise. Jehovah was the God of the Hebrew and semitic tribes which lived in Israel when the Bible was born. Jove was the God of the Hellenic faith, prevailing in Greece and other places around it. Lord is the general name used by all faiths to denote God. Servants of God of the Christian faith have also averred that although the names may be many they refer to the same person.

If the Puraanas are studied with humility and respect and with a view to benefit from them, no confusion will arise. Let us have the wisdom to regard them as having been solely made to bring good to us. Let us take it that even the slight deviation from the absolute truth has been made with good intentions.

Kaavya - Poetry

If a good thing has to be accomplished it can be arranged in one of three ways. One is to pass an order like Government making a law. This is called *"Prabhu Sammiti"*, the master ordering a servant. Here, whether he likes it or not, the servant has to carry out the order faithfully as otherwise he will be punished. On the other hand, instead of speaking from a position of authority and giving an order, a friend may ask us to do a job which we do promptly. Here there is no fear (of punishment). There is goodwill and affection. We do it because of our faith that as a friend he would only do us good. Thus a good-hearted friend is called 'Su-Hrit'. Therefore, to ask us to do a good thing from the position of a companion is called *Suhritsammiti*. But what will accomplish the result more easily than either of the above is the request of a loving person like the wife. If the master's order is heavy, the same thing through a friends' mouth becomes light. But, from the beloved it becomes lighter still and is called Kaantaa Sammiti - Kaantaa meaning wife.

Vedas are Prabhu Sammitam. Puraanas are Suhrit Śammitam. Kaavya (poetry) is Kaantaa Sammitam - such is the legend.

Veda merely says - "do this way and that way.' It does not say the reason why? What do the Puraanas say. "Well, if you do this way, this is the benefit. If you do it the other way, this will be the harm." It gives us the reason why a thing has to be done in the prescribed way, through recounting a story. The characteristic of the Puraanas is not merely to give reasons. Its purpose is to attract our attention by presenting the message in the form of interesting stories.

What does poetry (Kaavya) do? What does the poet do? He mixes his creative intelligence with factual stories. He creates stories out of his imagination. Some matters, he repeats again and again. This is his poetic licence. He decks the simple fact with frippery and weaves a glittering pattern for all to admire and adopt. Instead of presenting the matter in a straightforward way like a friend, the poet behaves like a good wife. In order to bring round a recalcitrant husband, she quips, cajoles, humours, entreats and does everything to gain her point with him. Poetry plays the role of the wife, Vedas the role of the master and, in between, is the role of the friend, Puraanas, all of them inculcating Dharma into our minds.

25

THE UPAANGAS

DHARMA SAASTRA

THE ROAD TO REALISE THE PURAANIC GOAL

It is seen that the characters in the Puraanas are our ideals and pace-setters. On reading their stories, we are impelled to emulate their noble qualities. Although such desire is born, it is found impracticable to stick to them under all circumstances. It is the nature of man to keep doing something or the other at all times. It is impossible to keep the mind still even for a second. In the Gita, the Lord says "Nature impels man to keep doing something without keeping still even for a second. Therefore he should learn the proper method of doing things, and by so doing, cleanse his mind, acquire good character and habits and then transcend the habits (Gunas) and become a Jnaani and merge with the Brahman."

What should be done, if we are to strictly follow the tenets of our faith, rid ourselves of sins, and having purified the soul attain Moksha - the happiness of release from worldly troubles. Our very birth has been due to sin. This should be washed off. We should not sin anew. We should elevate our minds and Gunas so that they do not indulge in sin. This is the purpose of religion. So what are we required to do as per our religion?

Generally speaking, in our present state, we are familiar with Ramayana, Bhagavata and a bit of some of the Puraanas. It is known from these as to what type of religious injunctions were practised by the characters in these at various times and places. These injunctions do not appear cogently or in a codified way; they find mention here and there. The procedure for practising these injunctions are not also mentioned in the Puraanas or Itihaasas. Therefore it is not possible for us to practise these injunctions by merely being made aware of them.

The Puraanas and the Itihaasaas have Bhakti as their central theme. But can we spend all the 24 hours doing Bhakti (Puja) meditation and singing God's praise (stotra)? No. We have to do our duty to the family. We have to eat, bathe etc. and attend to personal and bodily needs. Even to devote the balance of time to Puja is also not possible. Boredom sets in. We require therefore other directions and guidance to perform our good deeds. From where do we learn these? From only the Dharma Saastras. Of the 14 disciplines (Vidyas), what comes as the last, after Puranas, is Dharma Saastra.

The characters from the Puraanas show us the goal. The way to reach it is to begin with the actual practice of prescribed Karmas *(Karma-Anushtana)*. Thus Dharma Saastra tells us what and how we should do in our every day life. What the Vedas have said at various places as to what our duties are have been arranged systematically and elaborated by the Upaangas.

Household duties, personal work, bathing, eating have all to be done in order and as laid down, in the Saastras.

The Vedic Dharma has devised its injunctions so that all aspects of human activity are conducive to self-advancement and self-realisation. It involves all aspects of our life with religion - if one sleeps in a particular way it helps the personality; if one dresses in a prescribed way it is conducive to good living; if the plan of the house is as laid down, it would help in the proper performance of various Vedic rites. Secular life and religious life are not separated by the Dharma Saastras. Secularism is also designed to lead to religion as per the Vedic Dharma. Whatever job is done, it is Dharma-oriented and is part of the exercise for the evolution of the self. Just as secularism and religion have been unified in the duties which the individual is required to do for his own salvation, the ingredients for social welfare as also the well-being of the world, are inbuilt in the Dharma Saastra.

The Bhakti, which we have so far seen as contained in the Puraanas, is also present in the Vedas. But along with it are so many karmas or duties. Elaborate directions are prescribed for performing Puja (worship), when Bhakti is translated into action. In addition to Puja, Yajnas (ritualistic sacrifices) *Shraaddam* (death anniversary rites), *Tarpanam* (homage to ancestors) are all considered indispensable adjuncts to Vedic dharma.

The Vedas no doubt contain all these. But, they have not been codified or presented in any one place. Nor has each procedure, for doing the Karmas, been spelt out in detail.

'Vedo Akhila Dharma Moolam' says Manu, the Vedas alone are the basis or the root of Dharma of what are required to be done and how to do it.

Though Vedas have so designed it that the duties which are required to be done for individual salvation also indirectly produce commonweal, and what serves this dual purpose is Dharma, we do not find any orderly or clear-cut list or any detailed procedural instructions. Further the Vedic language is very often difficult to understand and their purport is not wholly clear to us.

From out of such Vedas, 'Kalpa', the sixth Vedaanga, has presented an orderly and consolidated list of duties or Karmas in the shape of sutras. But these are by their very nature brief nor do they offer detailed guidance. Dharma Saastras alone make these sutras understandable and explain them beyond doubt.

Dharma Sutras (of Apasthamba, Gautama and others) are, as per the rules of Sutra, brief and pithy. In fact a sutra should be so. On the other hand, the Dharma Saastras which are Smritis (of Manu, Yajnavalkya, Paraasara and others) are in the nature of slokas.

But the common authority for all these is the Vedas. What should we do and how should we do it are all clearly enunciated by the Vedas and we should follow these injunctions implicitly. The role of the Dharma Saastras is to analyse and explain in great detail the Vedic injunctions which are to some extent codified in the Kalpa. If Kalpa talks mainly of the area of the sacrificial site, house plan etc., the Dharma Saastra lays down the code of conduct for man covering all aspects of life.

"I wish to do this job. But I do not know where to look for in the Vedas to know if it is right or wrong to do the job. Vedas indeed appear endless. So I do not know where to look to see how this job should be done. I do not also find anyone who has mastered all the Vedas, what shall I do?" - these are some of the questions.

It is indeed an impossible task to pick out what we need from the vast ocean of the Vedas.

"If I knew that the Vedas had said how this job should be done, I will certainly comply. In its absence what shall I do ?"

Manu replies to these questions. "All right - let me tell you. Maharishis who have mastered the Vedas have written what are called *'Smritis'*. See what they have to say on the subject. 'Smriti' is Dharma Saastra."

'Smriti' menas an aid to memory. *'Vismriti'* means - loss of memory. Smritiş are aide memoirs for the Vedas. The Maharishis who were perfectly informed about the Vedas have compiled the injunctions (Dharma) and Karmas (procedural details as to how to do them) and have presented them in an orderly manner. These Smritis are written in a language which is easily understandable. Look at them. What you should do or should not do, how to do it, are all clearly laid down in detail - so says Manu.

Kalpa, which is the sixth 'Vedaanga', describes how to perform the Vedic injunctions. The Grihya Sutras describe domestic rites. The Srauta Sutras discuss the big sacrifices such as *Asvamedha.* The Dharma sutras are concerned with the personal and social duties of the persons according to the Varnas in which they are born and the stage of life in which they find themselves.

From the time a Jiva enters into the mother's womb, on to birth, growth, marriage, running the household and at last to cremation - the Smritis lay down all that has to be done in minute detail. It gives a chart which man should follow daily from the time he

wakes up in the morning till the time he goes to sleep at night. There are 16 main samskaaras dealing with the above aspects.

Smritis and their supporting texts

Manu, Paraasara, Yaajnavalkya, Gautama, Harita, Yama, Vishnu, Sanka, Likhita, Brihaspati, Daksha, Angiras, Prachetas, Samvarta, Asanas, Atri, Aapasthamba Satatapa - these 18 Maharishis had grasped the contents of all the Vedas through their superhuman powers and have given us their compilation in the form of Dharma Saastra. These are called Manu Smriti, Paraasara Smriti, Yaajnavalyaka Smriti, etc., after the names of the Rishis who compiled them. It is enough to study them - we can know all the Karmas *(Anushtana)* and Dharmas.

In addition to the 18 Smritis, there are 18 supplementary texts called "Upa Smritis".

It is customary for Srimad Bhagavad Gita also to be regarded as a Smriti, although its contents are not direct quotations from the Vedas. Since it is an authority in support of our faith, it enjoys the status of a Smriti.

Since there are many such Smritis, it is likely that what appears in one may not be found in another. In some cases there might be slight differences also between them. Thus some small doubt still lingers. To remove such doubts there are some texts entitled Dharma Saastra Nibandhanas.

Some Smritis stop at certain matters; they do not carry the complete instructions. Some do not contain the practice of Sandhya Vandana as though it would be superfluous or redundant to repeat what is a 'must', and has been handed down traditionally from one generation to the other. Some do not contain the instructions for *Sraaddha*, some do not have instructions on *'Soucha'* or cleanliness. "Eat thus and breathe thus" - these need not necessarily be in the form of written instructions. That is probably how the authors of Smritis regarded the omissions.

The "Nibandhana Grantha" contain all that there is to be said, without leaving out anything on the assumption that it is too familiar to be repeated. When the Smritis slightly differ, these 'Nibandhanas' effect the reconciliation or synthesis and unequivocally affirm the requirement.

These Nibandhanas have appeared as a result of the labours of great men who had studied all the Smritis, reconciled the variations and have formulated the conclusions without leaving any room for doubt.

Thus, in our land, each region follows a particular Nibandhana Grantha. The Maharashtrians follow the Nibandhana Grantha written by Kasi Natha Upadhyaya, called 'Dharma Sindhu'. The Mitakshara is a commentary on Yajnavalkya Smriti. This is accepted as an authority in law courts, when doubts on Hindu law arises. This has been recognised by courts of law as having the same status as statutes. Those in the South follow the book called *'Vaidyanatha Dikshitiyam"* written by Vaidyanatha Dikshitar. These are very important for householders. Sannyasis learn what they should do or should not from a text called *'Viswesware Samhita'.* In Tamil Nadu, Dharma Saastra is synonymous with 'Vaidyanatha Dikshitiyam'. A little proficiency in language would suffice to read and understand the Dharma Saastra. It is not like the Vedas where even after Adhyayana or learning them by rote, the meaning may not be apparent. The'Vaidyanatha Dikshitiyam has been well translated also.

It is no easy task to make everyone accept the Vedas which are the Srutis, and the explanatory Sutras that already existed in the form of Kalpa Sutra, Dharma Sutra, Srouta-Grihya Sutras and Smritis, and the many Nibandhana Granthas that later appeared. The reason why Dikshitiyam has occupied the place of an authoritative text (Pramaana Grantha) is because Dikshitar has been totally impartial and, with a broad outlook, has adopted the method mentioned in the Meemaamsas for determining the meaning of words. Having carefully collected all the earlier Saastras, he has boldly reconciled the contradictions. In places where the Smritis were at variance, he has with a liberal heart solved the impasse by saying, "let each one adopt the practice prevalent in his region, let this be done as the elders in each family had done it," i.e. according to *Sishaatachaara.*

Liberty versus Discipline

Here I must say something in general. However deep one may analyse a subject or however much in detail one may attempt elaboration, it would be impossible to cover the myriad situations which a person would face in his life-time and provide an answer to each problem. Tenets laid down in script would be irksome to follow like laws in a statute book. True that the rules should make for strict discipline and be binding and our Saastras do contain these in large numbers. But we see in practice that high-sounding words such as 'liberty' and 'democracy', in actual practice, result in action as one pleases, or the strong (majority) causing hardship to the weak (minority). Therefore the inevitable restrictions imposed by rule making should be tempered by placing a limit on such restrictions. In other words, there must be a limit to the limitations, otherwise true to human nature, severe restrictions would lead to revolt. Too much discipline would only result in rule-breaking.

That is why although our Saastras have provided guidelines on all matters, they have not assumed the compelling force of 'law'. It has been left to the individual to exercise his free-will, following the example of elders and voluntarily following suit. A little choice or liberty should be left in personal conduct based on personal example of elders, tradition, local custom, family customs, etc. so that in other matters a person may be expected to follow a strict written code of discipline. The best way to make others follow these tenets is by setting a personal example. The next best way is verbal instruction in the nature of persuasion without any compulsion. The last resort is to make laws and enforce compliance.

"Sahasram Vada Ekam Ma Likha" is an old adage. It means you may use a 1000 words to convince a person but do not commit even one to writing and compel compliance. The order of the

present day is to enact (written) laws on each and every subject. And any opinion finds ready publication.

Although the Dharma Saastras are criticised for laying down injunctions by the thousand without allowing any freedom to the individual, in actual fact it has left many things unsaid in the interests of this very freedom or liberty. It has been the considered view of the authors of Dharma Saastras that, if an individual is not to be allowed to ruin himself and society, there must be elaborate guidelines and rigid control. But if all these are written down in the form of 'law' the public would feel highly shackled. Therefore it is only part of the injunctions that has been committed to writing, the rest having been left to be followed on the basis of the regional or family custom and traditions.

The feelings of restraint created by Sastraic injunctions is not felt when the same thing is in the nature of the practice followed by great men, tradition, precept etc. Regional and family traditions are gladly accepted as they evoke a certain sense of personal loyalty.

It is not as though the last of the texts on Dharma Saastra, viz., 'Vaidyanatha Dikshitiyam', alone had accepted this large-hearted attitude. All the earlier texts held similar views. In the Aapasthamba Sutra which is accepted by the majority as authority, Maharishi Aapasthamba says at the end : 'I have not covered all dharmas in this Saastra. Many more are left. There are many which can be learnt from women and those belonging to the fourth caste. You may learn these from them.'

This will show how wrong is the charge that women were kept down by men or that the Brahmins had assigned an inferior position to non-brahmins. In the great book which is an authority on Dharma Saastra, due cognisance has been given to the wisdom of women and non-brahmins to the extent of making them authorities on Dharma.

Original Sutrakaras like Aaswalaayana have said that, during marriage celebrations, the decision of the women as to when and how the *arati* should be taken (lighted camphor is waved before the bride and groom to dispel evil influences) and the bride anointed has to be followed. Although there is a particular mantra for laying the foundation for the marriage pandal, one should take note of what the experienced workmen have to say on the subject, based on tradition.

Thus the Saastras do not hamstring a person but have given a fair amount of democratic freedom.

The Dharma Saastra also lays down the ceremonies and rituals which people of the fourth caste are required to do; that caste has not at all been ignored. In the Dikshitiya, these will be found mentioned in detail in the Varnaasrama Kaanda, Aahnika Kaanda and Shraaddha Kaanda.

Generally, Dharma Saastras are divided into two Kaandas - viz. Aacharya Kaanda, and Vyavahaara. Personal conduct is Aachara. Vyavahaara deals with law.

Chinha (चिन्ह) distinguishing mark

If we belong to a certain faith, then there are certain external symbols or *'chinhas'* to indicate it.

The scouts have a distinctive uniform. Those belonging to the army, navy, etc., have very distinctive marks of identification. In the police too, there are many sub-divisions thereunder. If they were to change their dresses or badges, their performance will not be affected in anyway. Even so, there are very definite regulations that they may not do any such thing. The sailor cannot adopt the policeman's dress. There should be discipline and orderliness in each service. Should not the same discipline and order apply to religion? That is why different marks of identification and different duties have been prescribed for persons belonging to different occupations *(Jaati-Varna)* and for those in the various Ashram - stage of life. Local custom says wear your dhotis this way; your saree this way - wear a prescribed mark on your forehead etc.

This was not merely designed as a social discipline. Each one of these has another subtle aspect to commend itself, viz., purifying the person and helping him onwards, in the spiritual pursuit.

In the offices, the peon is required to wear uniform, not the officers. We don't question why but when the Saastras prescribe various distinguishing features for each occupation and stage in life, we protest at the futility of it in the name of equality and freedom. Our special order based on the immemorial existence of Varnas, with ordained duties, has, in the interest of universal well-being, prescribed different types of personal conduct *(Aacharam)* and observances *(Anushtanam)* solely to suit their way of life.

This has been lost sight of and a non-existent gradation of high and low (caste) has been predicated which has resulted in recrimination and revolt. Ultimately today we have reached a position where no one has any religious mark of identification.

We are prepared to sport other social symbols unabashedly. But we feel abashed at the religious symbols which are designed to do good to the soul. We call it all superstition. We abandon it in the name of reform; but in order to indicate that we are reformists we wear a special cap. Or we wear shirts and towels of a particular colour. We attach more importance to these than even to God.

Smritis are not the product of independent free-will

Even those who regard the Smritis which are the Dharma Saastras with a feeling of respect,have a mistaken notion about them. That is, they think that the authors of the Smritis have independently and of their own volition laid down these tenets. The authors of Smritis are dubbed as law-givers. That is, they are regarded as having laid down the law as per their own will and pleasure, just as a coterie of jurists had assembled and evolved the (Indian) Constitution, which lays down the principles of public administration. The Smritis are regarded as voicing views of their own making.

This leads to another corollary. When a particular provision in the Constitution is found irksome to follow, we resort to amending it suitably to our liking. Likewise, the question is asked, 'why can't we amend the old laws contained in the Dharma Saastras to suit modern conditions?

Why not we trim the Saastras according to the present-day trends?' The example of Government amending the rules is cited in support.

But what is not known to many including those who have high regard for the Dharma Saastras - is that, "These smritis do not contain the personal opinion of their authors. They have merely abstracted and compiled what is already said in the Vedas. Since the Vedic injunctions are never under any circumstances changeable, there is no question of changing the rules in Dharma Saastras.

If the Smritis were merely the handiwork of Rishis, there is no compulsion for us to accept them in toto. We can reject them if we do not like them. We can do without them if they had introduced matters not to be found in the Vedas; if they had thought by their intelligence as to what is good for man and what is not. That way, there are many who had written the way their minds traversed; we can similarly legislate for ourselves.

In actual fact the Smritis closely follow the Vedic dictums and therefore we must regard them as our authority for now and always.

Then the question arises as to the basis or proof of the claim that the Smritis are written solely on the basis of the Vedas.

Veda alone is the foundation of Smritis

The biggest proof is in the verdict of the Maha Kavis - great poets. The founders of our faiths - Sankara, Ramanuja and Madhva —have affirmed that the Dharma Saastras are based on the Vedas.

But then this cannot perhaps be accepted as infallible as they had a certain overriding loyalty to their individual doctrines. They were committed to safeguarding the ancient values. Therefore they would not preach outside the limits of tradition. But the poet has no such inhibitions. He is neither dedicated nor committed to the establishment of any doctrine. He talks of truth as it appears to him without any bias towards a creed.

The most distinguished of all Maha Kavi's, Kalidasa, has thus referred to Srutis in his Raghu Vamsa : He says *"Sruterivartam smritiranvagacchat"* (श्रुतेरिवार्थं स्मृतिरन्वगच्छत्) Sudakshina followed the footsteps of the cow, even as Smriti followed the meaning of Sruti.

Here, when describing how Sudakshina followed the footsteps of the cow when Dilipa took the cow to graze, Kalidasa mentions how the Rishis compiled the Smritis. His object was not to tell us what the Rishis did or how the Smritis were made.

It is customary for the subjects of the simile *(Upamaana)* to be superior to the object with which it is compared *(Upameya)*. For example when one's face is compared to the moon or lotus, the moon or lotus will in fact be better to look at than the face. Here the subject of the simile is the very chaste Sudakshina following her husband Dilipa. It is logically implied that the Smritis follow the Srutis still more closely. Therefore the master par excellence of similes, Kalidasa, resorts to this comparison. No further proof would therefore be required to prove that the Srutis totally follow the Smritis.

Now those observances *(Anushtana)* which are not clearly spelt out in the Vedas but which are made clear in the Smritis are called *Smaarta-Karma.* Those that are clearly laid down in the Vedas are referred as *Srouta-Karma.* This should not give room for the conclusion that Smarta Karma is in any way inferior to Srouta Karma.

The Upaasana which is most important for a householder (Grihastha), the Karmas which are required to be done domestically called Grihya-Karmas, the most important of the

Vaidika-Karma, the Pitru-Sraadha, the five yajnas - are all Smaartha Karmas. Veda mantras are used in their performance. It is therefore clear that the authors of Smritis had understood the spirit of the Srutis in prescribing these obligations. Therefore, instead of thinking that Smritis are inferior to Sruti or that Puranas are inferior to Smritis, they should all be regarded in an integrated way, as a composite package.

The Puraanas narrate the Vedic dharmas in the form of stories. The Vedic dharmas and Karmas are presented not in the form of fables but advice and injunctions by the Smritis. They also indicate the procedure for doing the Karmas. The Vedas intuitively flashed into the comprehension of the Rishis. Later on, the Rishis recollected what they had seen and they became Smritis. Puraanas deal with the truth contained in the Vedas, with the recital of stories. All are authoritative.

Thus the Sruti, Smriti and Puraanas all deal with Dharma.

And our Acharya - Adi Sankaracharya — was a repository of the Dharma contained in the Srutis, Smritis and Puraanas. Hence we bow down to him with the follwing salutation:

श्रुति स्मृति पुराणानामालयं करुणालयं
नमामि भगवत्पादशंकरं लोकशंकरं

Sruti Smrti Puraanaanaam aalayam karunaalayam
Namaami Bhagavadpaada Sankaram lokasankaram